VECTOR

JUSTIN EDWARDS

SEVERED PRESS
HOBART TASMANIA

VECTOR

Dedications

For my wife, the real life Gwen Vierra.

Special Thanks, to Severed Press for giving me a chance, when others passed. To the true people behind the characters of Donovan Waterbury, Esmeralda, Doctor Hampstead, Max, and Colonel Carter. You know who you are and without you, I wouldn't have been able to give life to these characters.

Finally, I would like to say a very heart-felt thank you to all of my friends and family who believed in me and my writing ability, even when I didn't. Without your support The Vector Series would never have been written.

CHAPTER 1:
FIRST BITE

June 22nd 2008, Amazon Jungle

Apoyung sat quietly on his haunches waiting for the beast to approach. To his right, he could see his friend Gabo perched between two branches of a large tree, camouflaged by dense vegetation. His goal was to draw the beast out of its den, and force it to charge him, then Gabo would jump from the tree and strike it down with his spear. With sweat slowly sliding down his forehead, Apoyung quickly wiped a drop away before it got into his eye. The movement of his wrist caused the branches of the bush that he was hiding behind to shake slightly. In the corner of the animal's eye it noticed the movement, and slowly started walking towards the bush.

Gabo noticed the approaching monster moving in Apoyung's direction, and tilted his head back. He produced a soft clicking noise with his teeth to let his buddy know that the something was headed towards him. When Apoyung heard the sound, his body tensed, and he squinted through the branches to see if the animal was in his line of sight. From that second, the whole jungle became quiet. Apoyung could hear its soft footsteps as it approached stealthily through the brush.

When the animal was approximately fifteen yards away, Apoyung quickly rose up from under the brush, and stared directly into its eyes. It seemed like an eternity to Apoyung, and then more drops of sweat slid down his face, shocking him out of his trance. He realized that any quick movement could set it off. He glanced upward without moving, and noticed that Gabo had quietly moved directly over it. With a sly grin on his face, Gabo looked back at Apoyung and made that soft clicking noise again with his teeth, as if to say "Go ahead and run for it—I've got him!"

In a flash, Apoyung dropped his spear and began to run away. The moment the spear hit the ground, the adversary let out a guttural cry and gave chase, snorting as his hooves hit the ground.

Suddenly, he heard a large squeal that sent chills up his spine, and he stopped abruptly. He turned around, and walked slowly back to where he had last seen the beast. The heavy brush and tall grass covered the area so that Apoyung could not see it, nor his friend Gabo in the tree. An eerie silence fell upon the jungle as Apoyung crept back to where he had dropped his spear. He scanned the area over and over and could see no sign of his friend, but more importantly, he could not find the animal. His heart began to pound in his chest, and fear swept over him like a strong gust of wind. His breathing became shallower, and sweat was now beading up all over his body. Directly in front of where he stood he heard the sound of a stick being broken under pressure, and controlled breathing. His heart was beating so deeply it felt as if each beat was a large clap of thunder going off in his head. He slowly reached forward towards the branch of vegetation that was blocking his vision, and with a trembling hand he grasped the branch and began to pull it towards him slowly. As he pulled the branch towards him, a sudden flash crossed his eyes!

"YAAAAH" Gabo screamed, as he jumped up from his hiding place underneath the brush.

Apoyung screamed out and fell back onto the ground with a loud thud that caused his whole body to ache. He stared up at his friend with fierce, angry eyes swollen with hot tears. He slowly stood up, knocked the dirt off of his legs and bare chest, and began to jab at the ground in an effort to find the spear that he had dropped. The thick brush acting as a green canopy made it impossible to see the ground. The faster and harder that he jabbed at the ground and tore at the brush, the more tears came, and within seconds he was crying from fear and anger.

Realizing what he had done to his friend, Gabo searched the ground where Apoyung had been patiently waiting earlier, and retrieved his spear.

"Nychunk, toma faosa kempo syamu!" Gabo barked as he thrust the spear towards Apoyung.

Apoyung snatched the spear out of his friends hand and said nothing. He quickly wiped the tears and sweat away from his eyes, and stared at his friend for a moment before he gave a slight nod in Gabo's direction.

Seeing this gesture of thanks, Gabo pointed towards the ground, at the place that he had been hiding. Directly behind Gabo's footprints in the soft dirt was the beast they had been hunting all morning.

A large wild boar with about eleven inch tusks and dark black fur lay dead on the ground with a five-foot spear impaling it through its back. From snout to tail the boar was about four feet long and if standing would have been about two and half feet tall. The spear had gone through the boar with such force that it had embedded itself into the ground beneath the boar and had prevented it from running away. Dark crimson blood drained down the spear and had begun to pool around the dead boar's back hooves. Its eyes had rolled back, and its mouth hung open, its tongue slightly visible over its protruding teeth. The flies and insects of the jungle came alive and began to swarm around the fresh kill, sensing food.

Apoyung and Gabo swatted at the annoying insects in an effort to clear them off their trophy kill, but unfortunately this was a battle that the two boys could not win. Gabo placed both of his feet on the dead boar's body, grasped the spear with both hands, and pulled upward as hard as he could. As Gabo pulled, he realized that the spear had shattered bones in the boar's back which left jagged pieces of bone fragment embedded in the spear. Gabo took the spear and knelt down in the tall jungle grass to clean his weapon as his father had shown him to do after every kill. The blood stained the grass in long streaks and matted the vegetation together with the viscous texture of the dead beast's blood. Once the spear was cleaned, Gabo and Apoyung tied the front and back hooves of the dead boar together, and then they began to drag it down the path towards their village.

The path to their village was well worn due to the many hunting trips the tribesmen had taken. The grass was shorter, and sprinkled throughout the path, and the limbs hanging from trees had been trimmed so a tribesman could walk upright along the path. Large rotted logs lined the path in the shape of a guardrail which extended from the village far into the jungle. Beside these large logs ran a shallow ditch that snaked along the path on both sides. The large rainstorms that were frequent during the rainy season helped carve out this ditch. The larger trees on both sides of the path bore a tribal mark that was carved at eye level, and the complexity of these marks indicated the importance of ensuring that the message was understood. The marks became more and more complex the closer the trees came to the village.

As Gabo and Apoyung dragged the boar down the path, they could hear numerous species of birds and monkeys calling out to them. The distinctive sounds that each animal made would startle anyone who was not used to these sounds, but after growing up in Eastern Ecuador, the boys had grown quite accustomed to, and familiar with, the sounds.

Growing up in the Huaorani tribe, the boys were taught by their parents and the elders the meaning of the different calls all of the animals that inhabited the Amazon. Certain calls were meant as warning calls to anyone approaching while other calls were basic banter between the animals. As tribesmen, the boys were also taught the difference between certain colors on animals. The boys had learned that bright flashy colors like red, orange, and yellow usually meant that the animal was poisonous, and they should stay away, while neutral colors meant that the animal was most likely non-poisonous. Along with these teachings, every male Huaorani tribesman was taught how to use a long stick as a spear for both protection and hunting. Most Huaorani tribesmen were elite spear handlers and could hit their target from fifty yards away. Each spear was made from the wood of the Strangler Fig Trees. The wood was sturdy, and was found in abundance within the jungle. The Huaorani would fasten homemade arrowheads to the top of these spears and secure them with the fibers from green vines or leather strips from tanned hides. The lengths of the spears was determined by the skill level each tribe member demonstrated with their spear; the longer the spear, the less training a Huaorani had, while a shorter spear indicated a skillful hunter. The Huaorani lived like most tribes in the Amazon, surviving day to day, hunting to ensure that the families ate for that night.

The boys made it halfway back to the village before they needed to take a break and relax their muscles from pulling the hundred-pound beast behind them. They took turns drinking the clear water of the Napo River, while the large mass of insects caught up with their prize kill and began swarming again. As Apoyung was drinking the water, Gabo stood up abruptly and paced back and forth along the path, craning his head towards both sides of the jungle. Apoyung stood up and looked at his friend with a confused expression on his face.

"Qasi?" Apoyung said as he stood up and dusted the dirt off of his knees and hands. Gabo didn't respond, nor did he acknowledge that his friend had said anything.

In a louder and more demanding tone Apoyung called out to his friend again "QASI!" Still… there was no answer from Gabo.

Apoyung started walking over to his friend, quite perturbed at the fact that he was no more than ten feet away, and had yet to acknowledge anything that Apoyung had said.

"QASI, QASI, QASI!!!!!!" Apoyung yelled at the top lungs and flailed his arms about in Gabo's face, trying to get him to acknowledge what Apoyung had now been screaming.

Nothing.

Defeated, Apoyung turned towards the dead boar in the tall grass and began to slowly walk over to it and finish the long trek home. Gabo reached out, grabbed Apoyung on the right shoulder, and spun him around until their faces were merely inches apart. He then reached up with his right index finger, placed it perpendicular to his pursed lips, and blew, signaling Apoyung to be quiet and listen. Instead of ranting and raving, Apoyung complied with Gabo's wishes. Once he complied, he heard exactly what Gabo was hearing, and he knew exactly what it was….

Dead silence . . .

No birds chirping, no monkeys calling to each other—just an eerie silence. The boys gaped at each other in disbelief; never had they heard the jungle this quiet before in their whole lives.

The boys stared at each other in disbelief; they both felt a small tremor under their feet, as if the dirt was moving. The trees in the jungle began to sway back and forth while the ground beneath their feet violently shifted from left to right. A pair of scarlet macaws squawked and took flight, escaping the jungle canopy as the trees began to sway faster and faster. Large rocks that littered the path the boys were on dislodged from their moorings and began to roll down the path directly towards them. Gabo grabbed Apoyung by the arm and dragged him off of the path and into the brush just as the rocks careened down the path past them. A large tree to their left was shaking so furiously that it snapped from its base and came crashing down within inches of where the boys were now laying. The tree hit the ground with a thunderous smack that opened up a giant fissure in the ground. The earthquake continued for about ninety more seconds, and then as abruptly as it started, it stopped.

The dust cloud cleared, and after regaining their senses, the boys stood up and looked around to see the destruction. The original path they were on was now completely closed off due to a montage of rocks and trees that now lay littered across the old path. The large tree that fell beside them had opened up a giant fissure in the ground that was roughly fifteen feet wide and thirty feet deep. Noxious gases plumed out of the hole in the ground, and the boys were forced to cover their mouths. Both started coughing as the boys quickly turned their heads away from the cloud of gas and dust that rose up from the hole. The smell coming from the cave was so strong that both boys retched.

Apoyung was still clenching his stomach and coughing as Gabo got up and dusted himself off. He then started walking towards the hole in the ground. The cave was now beginning to be lit by the sunlight that was piercing through the jungle canopy. As he peered inside, what he saw astonished him. Large statues carved out of stone lay broken and strewn about haphazardly in a circular formation. The statues resembled Huaoranian warriors with large eyes, muscular bodies, razor sharp teeth, along with stone weapons clutched in their hands. Gabo recognized the statues not as Huaoranian warriors but as Tagaeri warriors—his ancestors.

He slowly walked around the hole and continued to study the statues. Each statue was intricately carved with multiple faces on all sides. The foreheads were slightly protruding and formed a "V" shape at the bridge of the nose. Each eye was carved at a forty-five degree angle towards the nose. Each mouth was open with fanged teeth extending outward. Nocturnal insects that were crawling all over the statues dispersed rapidly as the sunlight begin to shine directly into the cave. While Gabo was looking at these statues, the ground beneath him began to shake again as an aftershock ripped through the area. The ledge that Gabo was standing on started cracking, and before he could move the ground beneath his feet disappeared, dropping him into the hole. Gabo fell feet first, and as he hit the solid ground below, his right foot twisted awkwardly on its side. He felt a loud crack as his right ankle snapped like a twig. White-hot pain shot through his right leg and up his body; he immediately fell on his right side, clutching his fractured ankle. Gabo let out a loud scream that echoed throughout the cave, followed by a painful moan as he rocked his body back and forth.

By this time Apoyung had regained his composure, and he stood up and looked around for Gabo, who was nowhere to be found. He called his name repeatedly, but no reply. Apoyung dusted himself off and began to walk towards the large hole in the ground when he heard his friend scream in agony from within the hole. Apoyung ran to the edge of the hole and realized in an instant that this hole wasn't just a hole, but a large cave with strange statues strewn about on the floor. He saw his friend lying in the middle of the cave clutching his right foot and howling in pain. At that moment, he felt the ground beneath him start to shake, and he instinctively jumped back before the ledge fell down into the cave. Realizing that the area around the cave was still unstable, he crept cautiously back towards the ledge of the cave. As he reached the ledge again, he peered into the cave and called to his friend lying on the floor. "Gabo, chuyck tauk cayege!"

Gabo raised his right arm and waved to Apoyung to signal that he understood, and that he was ok, with the exception of the injured foot. He motioned to the surrounding statues and yelled "TAGAERI, TAGAERI, TAGAERI!"

Apoyung took in a shallow breath and held it tightly, his facial expressions telling Gabo that he understood what he meant. Apoyung knew who the Tagaeri were and understood the seriousness of the situation. The Tagaeri were an ancestral tribe of the Huaorani. The Tagaeri had mysteriously disappeared so long ago that no one could remember them. The only time they were ever mentioned was when the aged village mothers told stories with intentions of scaring whoever listened. These stories featured how the Tagaeri practiced cannibalism. Apoyung shuddered just thinking about this ancient tribe and the horrible stories that he had heard over the years. He was very glad that they had disappeared, and hoped that this cave would not lead to any current living Tagaeri tribe member.

Apoyung frantically looked around the jungle for vines, and managed to string them together to form a rope that he could throw down to Gabo. In his haste, he forgot to secure the end to a tree to give Gabo some support when he tried to climb up the vine. Apoyung realized this too late when he threw the vines down to Gabo, and all of the vines went into the hole. As he peered back over the ledge into the hole he noticed that Gabo's attention was not directly on him but on something else inside the cave.

Out of the corner of Gabo's eye he noticed something white move rapidly across the cave floor. He strained his head backwards to get a better view of this white object. The object again moved quickly out of the light and back into the darkness, as if it were hiding from the sunlight. Gabo focused his eyes towards the dark corner where the object had disappeared and quietly stiffened. The object again moved left, then right, and then ran out of the darkness and directly towards Gabo. Gabo quickly pushed himself up into a sitting position and tried to swat at the object as it came at him. As soon as the object was back in the sunlight Gabo realized that it was a scorpion spider about the size of his hand.

The spider leapt onto his chest and made a loud hissing sound as its front two legs parted, revealing two fangs with black tips poised for a strike. Frozen in fear, Gabo could do nothing but watch the spider as drove its fangs into his bare chest. The instant that the fangs penetrated his skin he let out a shrill scream and swatted the spider away from his body. The spider landed on the ground and bounced twice before regaining its focus and circling Gabo again, ready to strike again. Gabo quickly grabbed a large rock and held it up in his hand above his head, and as the spider made its second aggressive charge towards him, he brought the rock down directly on the arachnid. It was dead instantly, and Gabo gave a sigh of relief. As he lifted the rock off of the dead spider he noticed something that he had not noticed before. Instead of being dark green in color this scorpion spider was stark white. Gabo looked perplexed at the dead spider, and he wondered how the spiders were able to change colors. Then in the background of the cave he heard hissing sounds echo throughout the cave, and he was suddenly aware that he wasn't alone.

Apoyung saw the battle from the ledge, and he too heard the hissing sounds. He could see the fear in Gabo's eyes as he looked up. Apoyung stood up abruptly and signaled to his buddy that he would be back, and he bolted away from the hole through the jungle and towards the village where he could get help for his friend.

CHAPTER 2:
TROUBLE BREWING

The village where Apoyung and Gabo lived was about a mile away from the newly opened cave that the boys had found, yet for Apoyung it seemed like it was only twenty yards away. As he ran through downed trees and sprinted through the underbrush and bushes, his body began to look as though it had been drawn across a cheese grater. Broken limbs and thorns scraped and scratched his skin as he ran by, but he never stopped. He ran faster than he had ever run before, as if something or someone was chasing him. Apoyung knew that that something was fear, fear that his friend would die if he didn't get him help—and help fast.

As Apoyung blazed a trail into his village, he didn't have time to stop and help the other villagers with reparations for the damages their huts had sustained during the quake. Most of the huts were still standing due to the triple layer of mud packed around the logs forming a solid and stable foundation for the huts. The thatch roofs, though, had seen better days as the majority of them had caved inward, and others were lit ablaze due to the fires the families had going inside of the huts. The normal walk paths that would be crowded with villagers and children was in a state of chaos as the villagers worked as teams to try and put out the small brush fires that had come to life. Apoyung wanted to stop and help, but he knew that Gabo needed more help, and he continued to run even as members of the tribe called to him as he passed by.

Jonathan Steambule had been sitting under a tree in the shade near the entrance to a makeshift medical tent when the quake hit, knocking him off of his chair and onto the ground where he scrambled to a tree and hugged it until the shaking had stopped. His iPod was smashed to pieces along with his brand new pair of Oakley's. Once the quake was over he stood up and ran to the medical tent, entering in a rush as the flaps of the door fluttered in his wake.

"GWEN!!!! GWEN!!!! GWEN!!!!" Jonathan shouted as he looked over the tent, and she was nowhere to be found. The tent was in disarray as plastic filing cabinets were strewn across the dirt floor, files scattered around, and medicine bottles smashed onto the ground where chemicals were seeping into the ground. Jonathan began to frantically run towards the back of the tent where Gwen's office was. As he entered the back part, he noticed that her desk was on its side, and her chair was upside down up against the tent wall; that's when he saw a pair of legs behind the desk. Jonathan gasped as he stared in shock. He took a tentative step towards the feet when he heard, "Whew!!!! Is it over yet?" A female's voice pierced the silence as a slender woman picked herself off of the ground, dusting herself off as she turned towards Jonathan.

"Damn Gwen!!!" Jonathan spoke up rather loudly, and his voice cracked, "You scared the shit out of me! I thought you were... well, you know... I mean..." Jonathan couldn't finish as a wave a relief overtook him.

"I'm fine, just a little shook up, but I'll manage, and please stop trying to be so over protective all of the time, I'm a grown woman!" Gwen snapped harshly. She wished the moment she said it that it hadn't had come out so harsh, because his face almost crumbled in emotions. "Jonathan, I'm sorry; I don't mean to come off like a bitch, but that's just how I am. I am truly thankful that you were worried about me, but next time, think before you panic okay?" Her valiant attempt seemed to have worked as his facial expression seemed to stabilize.

Still breathing heavily and shaking, Jonathan's six feet tall, two hundred and twenty pound frame seemed fragile, but stable. His dark scraggly hair that had fallen over his wide brown eyes was drenched with sweat and matted to his forehead, while sweat continued to bead up on his five o'clock shadow. His pair of faded khaki shorts, about two sizes too big, with a dark brown belt hung low on his hips, were still dusty as he tried to dry his sweat soaked hands on them. His colorful Hawaiian shirt was now a second layer of skin as it outlined his toned physique with flowers and pictures of Caribbean drinks plastered to his chest and back.

"Thank goodness, we didn't have any patients," Gwen said as she righted her desk and chair, and began to scrape up her miscellaneous desk occupants; she looked up from the ground as Jonathan still stood there, hardly moving, and asked, "Do you mind helping me clean up the tent?"

"Huh? Uh..... No..... I mean YEA! I mean NO! Yea, yea, yea, I'll help," Jonathan managed to stutter.

The medical tent not only housed patients and the tribe hospital, it was also the living quarters for Gwen and Jonathan. All of their clothes and belongings didn't make it out of the disaster unscathed either, as Jonathan started in their living quarters which was divided by a white canvas lining, allowing both of them five by six feet of living space. Their cots had stayed upright, but Jonathan's plastic chest of drawers had toppled over, spilling his clothes along with other trinkets and memorabilia onto the floor. Gwen's space was just as messy, but he decided that it would be best if she cleaned up her own section. He finally started to calm down as he started to pick up his shirts. Most of the shirts that he had brought with him were Hawaiian style. With each new colorful shirt, the tribal people referred to him jokingly as "Rainbow Man," and even though the nickname was quite unflattering, Jonathan seemed to revel in the attention that he was given. As the screams of help had now died down, and the normal sounds of the village began to permeate the air, his stress level decreased as well. He knew that after he and Gwen had cleaned up the medical tent they would go and help the others as well; he knew Gwen would insist, and that was one of the biggest reasons why he respected her.

Jonathan had signed up for this trip at the beginning of the second semester of his sophomore year at Duke University in North Carolina. He was pre-med and decided that it would be great to go to a third world country and do some charity work for underprivileged people. He was strongly influenced by the fact that the doctor heading up the trip was an extremely attractive instructor at Duke Medical School. Jonathan had first seen her in the medical labs at the university late one summer night and decided that he could saunter over to her, and whisk her off of her feet. As soon as he finished his macho walk and sat beside her, she shot him down. The sad thing was that he didn't even get a chance to throw out a line to her; she simply turned and smiled at him and stated, "Hot shot, you never had a chance, so please don't even try." Dejected, but not defeated, he decided that he would make it his goal to go out with her before he finished his time at Duke. Even though she was cold-hearted to him that day, she was very impressed with his research, and decided to let him tag along with her on her aid trip to the Amazon. Jonathan preferred to think it was because of his irresistible charm, but even _he_ knew it was only in his mind.

As he had just finished cleaning up his side, he heard screams and the pounding of feet. Jonathan spun around in time to see Apoyung almost run right into him. Apoyung caught Jonathan off guard, startling him.

"JESUS! Apoyung, just what the hell has gotten into you?!" Jonathan shouted as he tried to grab the kid by his shoulders and get him to calm down. He was able to calm Apoyung, and he looked at the boy and saw his boy's complexion was ghostly white, his chest was heaving, and his gaze was fixed.

"What's the matter Apoyung? You look like you have seen a ghost,"

"GABO.....GABO....... Atyechi! Atyechi! Atyechi!" Apoyung kept saying over and over again as he pointed back in the direction of the cave.

"Hang on a sec, Apoyung. You have to slow down. I can't understand you," Jonathan said in a lower decibel than the boy with the hopes that he, too, would lower his voice. "English.... Apoyung, English!" Jonathan pleaded with the boy as he started to take deep breaths, hoping the boy would mimic him.

"GABO... he fall in earth! He fall in earth!" Apoyung spoke brokenly to Jonathan. "He in hole in ground with big Atyechi!" Apoyung sputtered as his breathing became more and more shallow. His pupils became dilated and his face pale. "Big Atyechi!" was the last thing he said before he fainted and fell into Jonathan's arms.

Jonathan cradled him up in both arms and ran towards where Gwen was sweeping up some broken vials off of the dirt floor.

Dr. Gwen Vierra had moved back to her desk where she was trying to reorganize everything on top of her desk. She was about five feet four inches and weighed about one hundred and twenty five pounds. Her long blond hair was tied back into a ponytail, and her light green eyes could be seen over her glasses that rested further down her small nose. She wore a light blue tank top and short khaki cargo shorts. They were covered with dirt, and her doctor's jacket was still on the floor; she was sitting in her chair, and had just put on her Boston Red Sox hat that she considered good luck charm, primarily because she had worn it during her exams when she passed her National Boards in the ninetieth percentile.

Just as she had gotten her desk back the way that she wanted she heard a loud commotion coming from the entrance of the medical tent, and she turned as Jonathan blasted through her makeshift canvas door sweating profusely and carrying a native boy into her office who had a look of fear in his eyes.

"Jonathan! What the hell is going on? What happened to this boy? What did you do to him?" She volleyed question after question at her assistant. Realizing that the constant barrage of questions was not going to help the situation, she jumped off her stool and ran over to her research table that had been cluttered with books and loose paper, but was now bare. She grabbed a sheet and flung it over the table. She ran over to Jonathan, took the boy from his arms, and gently laid him on the table. She then grabbed her stethoscope and began to do a quick examination of the boy by checking his blood pressure and his vital signs. His blood pressure was through the roof, and his pulse was racing. She jumped over to the large, uncovered barrel of sanitized water, quickly grabbing multiple towels, and drenching them into the lukewarm water, before she threw them to Jonathan, who immediately put them on Apoyoung's wrists and the back of his neck attempting to lower his body temperature so he wouldn't get sick and become dehydrated. Within five minutes she checked his vitals again, and even though he was still struggling, his blood pressure and pulse had come down from their critical levels. Feeling satisfied that he wasn't going to get sick, she then turned to Jonathan with an exasperated look of confusion.

"Easy Doc!" Jonathan gasped as he was trying to catch his breath. He continued to change out the towels on Apoyoung's body, as they were drying up, as he turned to Gwen to begin to answer her questions.

"You see, I was just finishing cleaning up in here with you and I took a quick break outside to stretch my back out, when out of nowhere

Apoyung practically runs into me frantically screaming 'Gabo' and pointing in the direction of the jungle,"

"Where is Gabo?" Gwen questioned, quickly as she looked down at Apoyoung earnestly.

"Let me finish! I tried to calm him down and get him to speak English. He was talking too fast for me to understand the dialect. He kept telling me that Gabo had fallen into a large hole in the ground, and he kept screaming 'Atyechi' at the top of his lungs. Before he could say anything else to me he fainted. Then I grabbed him and ran in here," Jonathan finished as he was finally able to catch his breath.

Almost as if to accentuate what Jonathan had just said, Apoyoung screams out "ATYECHI!!" before he passing out.

"Gwen, I ain't got a clue what 'Atyechi' means," Jonathan said as he scratched his head and looked at her with his right eyebrow cocked. "Do you know what it is?" he asked, almost in pleading tone with hope that she did, and also hoping that Atyechi didn't mean some sort of large animal. His body shuddered as he asked her what the word meant.

"Atyechi?!" Gwen said out loud as she leaned over the boy, checking him out. Pondering the word for a minute, she turned and walked over to one of the clear storage bins, pulled out one of the drawers, and removed an ammonia capsule. She placed the capsule into her lab coat pocket, walked back over to the table where Apoyung was, and turned to Jonathan.

"I know 'Atyechi', means spider to the Huaorani, but clearly a small spider couldn't have scared Apoyung this badly. I mean there are tons of spiders all over the Amazon. How could one scare him that much? Before I wake him up, please go and fetch his parents, they will need to be here to comfort him when he comes to," she instructed Jonathan as she looked down at the boy with serious concern written across her face.

"You got it. Just give me about five minutes," Jonathan barked over his shoulder as he jogged out of the tent.

****

Nateachy was busy cleaning some fruit while her husband, Ayung, was building a fire in the pit outside of their wooden house. The day had already been a hard one, and once they had finished helping their neighbors clear the debris from their plots, the two of them decided that even though the earthquake had happened, they weren't going to let it ruin their plans. Ayung had just gotten a small flame going from two rocks that he was striking together when he saw Jonathan jogging up to him with a concerned look on his face.

"Rainbow Man! What bring you to our house? We clean up tree and rock, miss you. You come for dinner?" Ayung hollered with a large grin on his face. Ayung, like most of the Huaorani tribe, cherished Gwen and Jonathan and treated them like fellow tribesmen and tribal women. He was grateful that they were helping his people. Among the Huaorani tribe it was an honor for guests to come to their house for dinner or just to talk, so both Jonathan and Gwen were treated like royalty. As Jonathan got closer, Ayung realized that Jonathan was not coming for dinner, and he immediately asked what was wrong.

"No, Ayung I am afraid I can't have dinner. I need for you and Nateachy to come with me back to the medical tent. Apoyung is there, and he is not doing too good right now," Jonathan told Ayung with a grave look on his face.

"Is he dead??" Ayung questioned in a quivering voice, while fighting back the tears.

"No!!! He is not dead, but we need your help," Jonathan quickly replied, increasing the urgency in his tone.

"Nateachy! Now come here!" Ayung yelled back into his house. Nateachy appeared in the doorway with a scowl across her face, which would show anyone that she was upset that Ayung had interrupted her dinner preparation.

"Ayung, what is hurry?" She questioned him as she stood in the doorway with her hands on her hips, like a mother getting ready to discipline an unruly child.

"Nateachy, Rainbow man, he say Apoyoung no good, bad injury, must be earthshake, we now go!" Ayung stated as he motioned for her to follow him and Jonathan towards the medical tent.

Instantly Nateachy dropped the fruit she was cleaning. Before it hit the ground she was running towards the medical tent with chaos and fear wrapping themselves around her mind. Nateachy reached the tent before both Jonathan and Ayung. She ran into the back where she saw Gwen sitting beside the table with her son laying on it. Gwen was gently caressing the boy's head with a damp cloth as Nateachy approached. Nateachy immediately burst into tears as she saw the numerous scratches and scraps all over his body. She lunged over the table, grabbed Apoyung with both hands, and pulled him close as she cried into his shoulder. Gwen gently placed her hands on the sobbing woman's back, trying to console her as Ayung and Jonathan emerged from the front of the tent, sweat pouring down their faces. Nateachy tried to regain her composure, but her sobs and short breaths wouldn't stop. Ayung reached out and pulled her away from their son and onto his chest where he calmly patted her head with one hand while the other one gently massaged her back. He began to speak in their native tongue in simple whispers trying to calm her down.

Seeing their emotional reaction, Gwen turned to both Ayung and Nateachy, "Apoyung is fine, he's just fainted," she calmly stated. Gwen could see the relief wash over the parents like a rogue wave as they realized that their son was still alive.

"We wanted you here when he woke up because we figured the two of you would have a calming influence on him," Gwen paused as she realized that her words could not penetrate the emotional field around the parents; their eyes slowly shrunk back to normal, but a sense of helplessness was still palpable within the environment. Gwen decided that it would be a good idea to give them some time. She turned to Jonathan and quickly craned her neck backwards, silently letting him now that she had something to say. At first Jonathan just stared, the residual effects of shock still ever present. Perturbed, she cleared her throat loudly, breaking his concentration; he then looked up, and she repeated her head motion. Slowly, while still watching the young boy on the table, he walked around to her, placing his left ear closely to her right shoulder.

"It seems that the family is going to need some chairs, and perhaps some calming medicine. Will you get two chairs from the back, along with a Valium for each?" Gwen asked, but the question as usual came out more like an order than a request. Jonathan obliged with a simple nod of the head as he exited the main part of the tent through the canvas flaps into the back. Gwen turned around and was startled to see two sets of fearful eyes staring right at her as the parents had now turned their attention in her direction.

"It seems that something in the jungle has spooked him. We also know that he was with Gabo there, but ...we have not found him yet. Jonathan and I heard him scream "Atyechi!" right before Apoyung fainted." I know what the word means, but do you know why?" Gwen asked both Ayung and Nateachy, with a quizzical look on her face.

"Atyechi means big spider," Ayung told Gwen as he looked curiously at his son lying on the table. Gwen nodded her head as Jonathan came from the back, two chairs in tow as well as a plastic cup in between his teeth, two pills rattling around within. She reached into her coat pocket where the ammonia tab was located.

"When he comes to he might still be hysterical. Be sure that you can hold him down so he doesn't thrash about and hurt himself," she instructed Jonathan as she pulled the ammonium capsule from her coat pocket. She broke the capsule in half, placed it directly under Apoyung's nose, and within three seconds the boy awoke with a violent shake, his eyes opened. He blinked wildly as he looked around the room in confusion until his eyes fell upon his mother beside him. Apoyung burst into tears and reached for his mother before Jonathan could grab him. Gwen quickly shot a hand up to stop Jonathan's interference.

"Mommy!" Apoyung sobbed into his mother's chest. Nateachy held him tightly and patted the back of his head, whispering to him that everything was going to be ok. After a few more minutes of deep sobs and labored breathing, Nateachy was able to calm Apoyung down enough so that he was able to speak. As he pulled away from his mother's chest his eyes were red and his nose was puffy and running, but his breathing had slowed, and he was able to talk without having to pant after every word. Jonathan reached down under the table to a small cooler and pulled out a bottle of water, opened it, and handed it to Apoyung. Apoyung downed the bottle of water in twenty seconds. He placed his hands on his knees, dropped his head beneath his shoulders, and began to breathe deeply.

"Nateachy?" Gwen asked as she began to direct her attention away from Apoyung. "I need you to ask Apoyung what he saw, and more importantly, where Gabo is."

Nateachy nodded slowly without pulling her gaze away from her son.

"Apoyung," Nateachy softly whispered to her son, who showed no response to her calling. "Apoyung!" Nateachy said this time with more force behind her statement. As she changed her tone, he slowly looked up and acknowledged with the slightest nod that he heard her.

"Apoyung, please tell Gwen where you were, and where Gabo," Nateachy asked him in a firm yet calm tone. "Apoyung, she help you, but you talk first,"

Apoyung took one last deep breath and looked directly at Gwen, who smiled at him. "Gabo... in hole in ground on hunting path," he stated as his body began to show the signs of fear boiling up again. "Earth shake bad, hole in ground. Gabo... h-h-he fa-fa-fall in h-h-hole!" he stammered as his body began to shake again.

"That's good Apoyung, really good. You're doing a great job, just take your time, and breathe after every answer," Gwen instructed as she reached out her right arm and carefully placed it on his shoulder. She softly squeezed his shoulder as she was taking slow deep breaths in an attempt help him mimic her movements. "Now, where is the hole that Gabo fell into?"

Without saying anything, Apoyung raised his hand and pointed in the direction of the hunting path.

"Good boy, Apoyung!" Gwen's soothing voice combated the young boy's anxiety. "Jonathan, you and Ayung go down the hunting path, and see if you can find Gabo and this hole that Apoyung is talking about," instructed Gwen.

"You got it, Doc! But I ain't going out there empty handed, especially if there is a giant hole in the ground," Jonathan muttered out loud as he was walking over to a large gray metal trunk in the corner of the room. He opened the box and pulled out some rope, a shotgun, and some shells. He threw the rope over to Ayung and strapped the shotgun on his back. They started walking out of the tent.

"Jonathan!" Gwen called out behind him. "Promise me you'll be careful?"

"Of course I will Gwen, you still owe me that date," Jonathan said as he turned around and winked at her. Gwen rolled her eyes at him, and then directed her attention back to Apoyung.

"Apoyung, Jonathan and your dad are going to go looking for Gabo. He is going to be all right, they will find him," she whispered in what she thought was a reassuring tone, yet his eyes relayed to her he wasn't reassured. "Now you need to tell me about the Atyechi." As soon as the words left her mouth, the young boy looked up at her with sheer terror in his eyes. His hands started to tremble. His breathing became labored again as sweat poured down his face.

"A-Atyechi in hole with Gabo! Atyechi white and big." He quivered as his eyes got even bigger. "Atyechi in hole with Gabo! ATYECHI IS IN HOLE WITH GABO! ATYECHI IS IN HOLE WITH GABO!!!" he kept screaming over and over again as he pulled his knees up to his chin. He started crying, and rocked his body back and forth. Noticing that her son was truly scared, Nateachy carefully sat down on the table beside him, and put her arms around him trying to get him to calm down. Gwen was taken aback by the boy's actions, and wondered if she had just sent Jonathan into a trap.

CHAPTER 3
THE PATH TO HELL IS PAVED WITH GOOD INTENTIONS...

The hunting path that went from the village into the jungle was hardly recognizable after the earthquake. Trees and rocks littered the path making some areas almost impossible to cross. While they were walking down the path, Jonathan and Ayung had to frequently veer off of the track and into the jungle to get around some debris that had cluttered the path.

Realizing that he didn't know the way, Jonathan let Ayung take the lead so he wouldn't get lost. Ayung stood a little over five and a half feet tall, bare-chested with broad muscular shoulders, and numerous tribal tattoos on his back and arms. He walked briskly yet confidently down the path, trying to stay as close to the original track as he could. Both Ayung and Jonathan knew the pitfalls that can occur when anyone ventures off the usual path. Jonathan admired the self-assurance that Ayung demonstrated, and wished he could be that confident in the face of danger, but the simple fact that his hands were trembling on the shotgun reminded him that he was not there yet.

As the two men rounded a corner, Ayung stopped abruptly, causing Jonathan to walk right into his back.

"Jesus, man, let me know when you are about to stop so quickly. You know, kinda like give me sign or something. I mean, I could have shot you, me, or both of us!" Jonathan voice grew louder as he continued complaining.

In a split second Ayung had tackled Jonathan down onto the base of a tree and placed his hand over Jonathan's mouth while quietly whispering "Shsssh!" in Jonathan's ear, as Jonathan flailed about.

Jonathan's eyes grew wide as saucers and his breathing sounded like the whirring of a helicopter's blades. Every inch of his body became saturated with sweat, and his mind raced trying to figure out what was going on. Carefully Ayung relinquished his grip on Jonathan's body and mouth, and then placed his right index finger against his pursed lips. Jonathan slowly regained his composure and craned his neck to look over the root of the tree in the direction of Ayung's gaze. Then he realized the urgency of Ayung's actions, because twenty yards away stood a full-grown female jaguar. Jonathan slowly ducked back down behind the root, and looked up at Ayung anxiously, wondering what to do next because his adrenaline suddenly kicked into overdrive. Jonathan had no fight complex, he was simply ready to take flight. The jaguar had not taken notice of the two men and was busy looking at something else. Jonathan and Ayung sat quietly behind the tree and stared at the jaguar in disbelief. Jonathan noticed that Ayung started to tremble, and his breathing quickened. He looked at Ayung perplexed, and finally whispered, "What's wrong?" as he noticed the blood draining from Ayung's face, making it look like Ayung had just seen a ghost, yet he was still staring at the jaguar. After a couple of deep breaths Ayung mumbled under his breath "She not know we here."

"What!?! What do you mean she doesn't know we are here? That's a good thing right?" Jonathan whispered, while silently praying that he was right.

Ayung finally broke his gaze from the jaguar and turned to face Jonathan, his eyes fixed in a piercing stare. "Jaguar, she have strong sense of smell. She should already know we are hiding behind tree. Yet she not notice us," Ayung whispered to Jonathan.

Jonathan watched as his friend tried to rationalize why the jaguar was acting differently.

"Wait a second," Jonathan whispered back, his voice gradually getting louder and more frantic. "So you're telling me that that jaguar, that big damn cat, should already know that we are here?"

Ayung nodded his head slightly and signaled for quiet before turning his attention back to the jaguar.

"Why?" Jonathan mumbled quietly, as he slowly peered over the large tree root that he and Ayung were hiding behind.

****

The jaguar was standing directly in the middle of the path staring at the leaves of a fallen tree branch. Her nose twitched as her lips slowly curled revealing razor sharp teeth. Her ears flattened alongside the back of her head, and a low guttural growl escaped her mouth. The leaves on the branch began to twitch back and forth as something moved underneath. At the top of the branch, under the last leaf, a large albino scorpion spider emerged and crawled in the direction of the jaguar. The spider was as large as a grapefruit and showed no hesitation as it continued to crawl towards the jaguar. It stopped about five feet from the jaguar's paws, raised its front two legs in the air, and gnashed its fangs together, making a soft hissing noise.

The jaguar's shoulders lowered, two paws instinctively dug into the ground as she arched her hind legs ready to spring. The two remained in this stalemate for what seemed several minutes before the spider slowly put its front legs back on the ground. Feeling dominant, the jaguar relaxed its aggressive stance and slowly started to close her mouth. Watching the jaguar relinquish her guard, the scorpion spider sprang off of its back legs and leapt into the air, landing on top of the jaguar's left shoulder. Upon landing, it jabbed its front two black tipped fangs into the soft flesh of the large cat. Registering the pain in her left shoulder, the jaguar let out a wild growl and pulled her hind leg up, knocking the spider to the ground with a mighty stroke. The spider bounced a couple of times on the ground and skidded back under the branch. Immediately the jaguar lowered her left shoulder and pulled her paw up as she walked towards the branch to ensure that her assailant was dead. The bite mark had already started oozing a bloody puss that trickled down her left front paw.

The jaguar stopped in front of the branch and began to sniff around the leaves for the spider. As her face got close, a soft hissing noise began to come from the branch where the spider was last seen. On impulse, the jaguar yanked her head away from the branch and began backpedaling. The scorpion spider crawled out from under the branch again towards the jaguar as it began to hiss. As soon as she saw the spider raise its front two legs, the jaguar turned around and ran back into the jungle, moaning as she ran away.

Once the threat of the predator was gone, the scorpion spider slowly lowered its front two legs and started crawling back down the path where the jaguar had been. A loud snap of a tree limb spooked the arachnid and caused it to turn around ready to defend itself. As soon as it turned around, it met two silver barrels in the air about five feet away, and then came blackness…

******

Jonathan re-cocked the shotgun and pulled the trigger a second time, sending the remains of the scorpion spider down the path. The thick white blood of the spider coated a tree branch nearby, giving it a frosted look.

"That should take care of that little bastard!" Jonathan said out loud as he strapped the shotgun back to his back. Once the shotgun was secure, he walked down the path to the downed tree limb with the white goo dripping from it. He knelt down beside the branch and looked closely at the white blood, and then reached his hand out towards one of the leaves. As soon as he stretched out his hand Ayung grabbed it, pulling him back violently. The force knocked Jonathan off-balance, and he fell back.

"What the hell, Ayung?" Jonathan cursed as he glared up at Ayung.

"Sorry Rainbow Man, I not mean to hurt you, but blood no good … it … it bad blood," Ayung said while he was slowly shaking his head.

"That's all right, man, but again, let me know when you are going to do something like that. You have scared the shit out of me twice now, and I don't have that many changes of underwear with me," Jonathan chuckled gruffly as he stood up. He knew he should be thankful to Ayung for what he did because he realized quickly how stupid his actions were. Of all people, Jonathan knew that only a small sample of blood can transfer diseases.

As he finished dusting himself off, he looked back down at the tree branch with a puzzled look on his face. "I have seen all grades of weird shit in my life, but I have never seen bug juice that white. I mean, it looks like milk. Have you ever seen this before?" He questioned Ayung, hoping that this was a normal occurrence in the jungle.

"No," Ayung said softly as he gazed down at the branch, slowly shaking his head back and forth.

His answer offered no reassurance for Jonathan as they both continued to stare in disbelief at the branch. Realizing that the white blood wasn't the only weird thing that had just happened, Jonathan spun around and faced Ayung with fear beginning to show in his gestures. "Wait a second. We just saw a JAGUAR run away from a spider. You got to be kidding me if you say that's normal behavior in the jungle. I mean, it was a jaguar, an APEX PREDATOR," Jonathan said in a completely awe-struck tone.

"No, Rainbow Man, you right. Jaguar not run away from anything. Jaguar mean, and strong, and chase human," Ayung told Jonathan.

"So that spider thing must have scared that jaguar. Most of the spiders that I have encountered run away immediately when they see something bigger than they are. I've never seen a spider attack a larger predator, let alone come back for seconds. That damn thing must've have had some guts or been crazy, one or the other," Jonathan said to Ayung as he tried to rationalize with himself what he had just witnessed.

"You right my friend. Something bad wrong with this," Ayung spoke softly as he patted Jonathan on his back and started walking back down the path.

"I figured that was what you were going to say," Jonathan said as he shook his head and followed Ayung. "We will need to tell Gwen about this when we get back, but we first need to focus on finding Gabo—but still, this is some crazy shit."

Ayung offered no response, but slightly nodded his head as they continued down the path.

The two men rounded the corner, and to the right of the path they saw the large hole in the ground that Apoyung had described.

"This must be what Apoyung was telling us about," Jonathan said quickly as he ran past Ayung towards the cave opening.

Ayung immediately followed and sprinted after Jonathan towards the cave. As the two men made it to the opening, they looked down into the cave. Gabo was holding his right foot with his left hand, and was furiously swinging a large branch at about seven of the albino scorpion spiders that surrounded him. As soon as he knocked one back, another one jumped onto his body and pierced his flesh with its black tipped fangs causing a shrill scream for each bite. Jonathan and Ayung watched in horror as the boy put up a valiant fight against the multiple creatures.

"GABO!" Jonathan screamed at the top of his lungs. "WE'LL BE DOWN THERE IN A MINUTE! JUST HANG ON!"

Ayung scampered back towards the path with the rope, frantically wrapped it around a large tree, and tied it off. He then ran back towards the ledge of the cave and flung the rope down into the hole. Jonathan fired the shotgun into the hole towards a large group of the spiders, causing them to disperse back into their holes. He then grabbed the rope and slid down into the cave, repelling off one of the statues and jumping the rest of the way down. He landed hard on his heels but recovered quickly. Gabo looked up at him with fear and exhaustion in his eyes. Jonathan quickly spun around with the shotgun aimed towards the ground, waiting to see if the spiders had returned. Sure enough, as soon as he looked back in the direction of Gabo he saw multiple flashes of white running towards him and the boy. Jonathan took aim and fired, sending a barrage of bullets at the spiders, lacerating them into small pieces. As soon as he reloaded he heard a soft hissing sound behind him, which caused him to spin around again and pull the trigger. He connected again, but this time some of the shrapnel ricocheted off of one of the statues and cut his right cheek. Instinctively he grabbed at his face with his left hand, but fired another shot into another cluster of spiders with his right. After the third shot rang out, the rest of the spiders retreated back into their holes for safety. Jonathan continued to spin around and around with the shotgun aimed, but nothing else came. As the adrenaline started to wear off, and his breathing became slower, he heard Ayung calling his name from above. He looked up towards Ayung who was yelling and waving frantically.

"They gone Rainbow Man, they gone!!! Hurry get Gabo out of hole. I pull both," Ayung yelled at the top of his lungs.

"That is a damn good idea!" Jonathan mumbled to himself. He turned to pick up Gabo who was hyperventilating and shivering almost like he was having a seizure. Jonathan noticed that Gabo's body was covered with bite marks from the spiders. Jonathan knew that time was of the essence; Gabo's life was in serious danger if he couldn't get him to help soon. With so many bites, the venom was probably coursing through his veins.

"Gabo!" Jonathan barked at him, while he was snapping his fingers in front of the young boys face. "Gabo! Come on kid, come on…respond! Say something," Jonathan kept pleading with semiconscious boy.

Jonathan grabbed the rope, tied it around Gabo's waist, and signaled to Ayung to pull him up as he reloaded his shotgun and started looking around in the cave. Realizing that his only way out was temporarily being used, Jonathan's pulse quickened, and every little sound caused him to spin around and fire the shotgun wildly into the cave.

Ayung had positioned himself in a seated position behind the large tree that had fallen when the cave opened so he could use it for leverage to pull both of them out of the hole. His back muscles bulged and strained as he hauled the rope up as fast as he could. After three strenuous pulls, he glanced up from his seated position to see the top of Gabo's head at the mouth of the hole. Ayung quickly tied off the rope and ran to the boy, pulling him out of the hole by his armpits. Ayung laid Gabo carefully onto the ground and undid the rope that was located around the boy's waist. Ayung's hands were sweating profusely, making it difficult to get a grip on the rope to untie it.

"What's taking so long up there?!" Jonathan shouted at the top of his lungs as he continued to spin around, looking for the spiders.

Ayung pulled out his knife and cut the rope, hoping that the remaining length of rope would be enough. He rushed back over to the ledge of the cave and threw down the rope to Jonathan. As the rope uncoiled, his fear was realized, for the rope dangled just about five feet above Jonathan's head.

"Shit!" Ayung cursed. He realized that his actions in haste might cause the death of Jonathan. He peered down into the cave and saw Jonathan looking up at the rope with despair. "Sorry, Rainbow Man, I cut rope off Gabo. Knot too tight," Ayung yelled down sheepishly.

"It's all right, Ayung, I realized that might happen," Jonathan yelled back up to Ayung, acutely aware that he needed to improvise quickly. He fired another round into the cave where he saw a cluster of spider holes, hoping the sound would keep them at bay. He quickly scanned his surroundings, and noticed that some of the statues were still standing upright. One of the faces on the upright statue had its mouth open, and the sharp teeth were partially missing from the wild shooting Jonathan had done. Where the stone teeth had been there was now a small ledge where he might get some footing. Seeing that this was the only option that he had, he decided that he would give it a try.

"Ayung!!" Jonathan yelled. "Pull the rope over to this statue," he yelled as he motioned with his free hand towards the statue with the missing teeth. "I should be able to get my feet on that ledge and jump to reach the rope."

Ayung did as he was told and dangled the rope as close to the statue as he could, but the ledge of the cave only allowed the rope to fall three feet away from the statue. Realizing that Jonathan was going to have to jump, Ayung cursed himself all over again for cutting the rope.

Jonathan slowly started walking towards the statue, when out of small hole in the ground one of the spiders appeared. Jonathan stopped in his tracks and smiled down at the spider as he raised the shotgun and took aim. CLICK!

"Oh, fucking wonderful, now I am out of shells! Hey, Ayung!" Jonathan yelled back up to the top of the cave. "We got a visitor here. When I make my move, man, you got to pull with all of your might to get me out of this damn hole."

Ayung looked down at Jonathan and nodded sternly as he tightened his grip around the rope.

"You know this only works in the movies," Jonathan muttered to himself as he quickly strapped the shotgun onto his back. "Here goes," Jonathan said, and took one last deep breath. He started running directly for the spider and the statue as fast as he could. Sensing the imminent threat, the spider raised its front two legs and started to make its hissing noises by gnashing his fangs together. Just before Jonathan got to the spider, he leapt through the air and landed his right foot into the lower mouth of the statue; he immediately pushed with his foot backwards as he spun his body around and grabbed the rope with both hands. The moment the rope went taut, Ayung pulled it up like his life depended on it, and within seconds Jonathan was able to grasp the ledge and pull himself up with Ayung's help. As Jonathan regained his footing on the ground, Ayung grabbed him in a massive bear hug and squeezed tightly.

"I so sorry, Rainbow Man, couldn't think anything else to do," Ayung stated earnestly as he looked Jonathan directly in the eyes.

"S'ok buddy. I realized that might be an issue. B…but please put me down before you b… break my ribs," Jonathan said, wheezing from exertion.

With a hearty laugh, Ayung let him go. They quickly picked up Gabo, who was barely breathing, and raced back towards the village. Neither man noticed the albino spiders slowly climbing out of the cave on the far side.

CHAPTER 4
INFECTED

Gwen paced back and forth in the medical tent with her right arm tucked around her waist, while she gnawed her left thumbnail into the quick. It had been well over two hours since Jonathan and Ayung had charged out of the tent to find Gabo. Surely they should have been able to find him in two hours. She kept telling herself this while trying to explain why they had been gone for so long. Unfortunately, she knew that the hunting path was only about a forty-five minute round trip, which left more than one hour of possible trouble for the men looking for Gabo. Thousands of thoughts filled her mind about what could be happening to Jonathan and Ayung, none of which were pleasant. With each horrific thought, her body shuddered. She tried her best to push these thoughts out of her mind, but she was not successful.

She felt as if she was responsible for Jonathan, and she was determined not to let anything happen to him. Even though ninety percent of the time Jonathan acted like a dog in heat, she liked him. He made her laugh. Gwen had always had a hard time making friends, primarily because she was so engrossed in her studies, she didn't have time for friends, let alone a love life. Jonathan knew this about her from the beginning, but he was persistent. Somehow, she admired that. Jonathan had accepted the fact that their relationship would never be more than friendship, and she respected him for this. Most guys disappeared once they realized that Gwen was not interested in them, but Jonathan stuck around. She often laughed and asked him why he kept hanging around, and he would always reply, "Hey, I guess I am just a glutton for punishment," or "maybe this is just my way of getting you to fall hopelessly and helplessly in love with me!" with a sly grin plastered across his face. Jonathan could always make her laugh, and she was able to finally know what it was like to have a friend.

"Now look what you have done. You've gone and sent your one friend into the jungle and he's not come back yet." She scowled to herself, feeling bad for her actions, and praying that Jonathan was all right. Much to her dismay, rumination set in. When she stopped pacing, the tent was slowly spinning clockwise, and her balance became shaky. She quickly pulled a chair out and sat down in it just before her stomach started to do somersaults.

****

Sensing that something wasn't right with Gwen, Nateachy squeezed Apoyung's hand and let go as she stood up and walked over to Gwen. She noticed that Gwen's face was blotched, and her breathing was quick and shallow. She reached out and placed her hand gently on Gwen's head, then quickly pulled it back. She was startled by the texture of Gwen's hair; it was completely saturated with sweat. Gwen leaned her head back, gave Nateachy a weak smile, and slowly closed her eyes in utter exhaustion.

"Gwen! You no look good, you face all red spots," Nateachy voiced her concern in a motherly tone as she gazed down at Gwen.

"Yeah, Nateachy, I am okay, just a little stressed. I am beginning to think that I put Jonathan and Ayung in danger by asking them to go and find Gabo," Gwen said with a heavy sigh as she dropped her shoulders. "I mean, don't you think that my idea to send off the men might not have been so great?"

Nateachy looked down at Gwen, and with a warm smile across her face, slightly shook her head. "Ayung and Jonathan go to jungle for Gabo no matter you ask. Both men strong, good men, they go anyway."

****

"Thanks, Nateachy," Gwen said with a deep sigh. Nateachy's words had given her a little comfort, yet she would not relax until the two men came back with the boy, safe.

As soon as Gwen had closed her eyes to try and relax herself, she heard a loud commotion coming from the front of the medical tent. Gwen jumped out of her chair and ran to the front of the tent where she saw Jonathan and Ayung standing with Gabo's limp body lying across Jonathan's arms.

"Where have you been? It's been more than two hours!" Gwen said, fighting back tears of joy at seeing her friends again, those feelings at odds with the worry of uncertainty at the boy's status.

"Trust me, you don't want to know, but I will explain after we get him some help. He needs it badly!" Jonathan said with his chest heaving from exhaustion.

Gwen ran over to Jonathan, grabbed the boy out of his arms, and ran with him into the back of the tent. Nateachy grabbed Apoyung, moved him to a cot in the front of the tent, and instructed him to stay until she came to get him, then immediately ran to the back of the tent. She grabbed another bed sheet and flung it down onto the only actual hospital gurney in the tent, and then helped Gwen lay Gabo carefully on the bed.

After putting on her latex gloves, Gwen grabbed two extra pair; she threw them to Jonathan and Nateachy as she walked to the bed to see exactly what she was dealing with. Gabo was lying on his back, and he was barely breathing as she checked his pulse, which was alarmingly faint. As Gwen reached down and pulled a blanket up to his chest to keep his body warm, she quickly ascertained that the boy was in a severe state of shock. She checked his pupils, which were slightly responding to stimulus but were extremely small, and both eyes were severely bloodshot. His lips were turning a light shade of blue, and it appeared that the blood in his face was retreating. As she looked down at the rest of his body, she noticed numerous marks that resembled insect bites all over his body and that his right ankle was swollen. Each bite was red and swollen with milky white pus oozing out. The skin around each bite had red streaks that radiated in a spider-web pattern outward from the center of the bite. Instantly she realized that Gabo had been bitten by some venomous insect and the toxin was coursing through his system at an alarming rate.

"Jonathan," Gwen spoke very calmly. "Let's get an IV in him now and get some fluids back into him because he is showing signs of dehydration. While you are doing that, please tell me exactly what happened. Take your time...and don't leave out any details." Her facial expression conveyed to Jonathan the seriousness of Gabo's situation.

"You got it, Doc" Jonathan said as walked towards one of the cabinets in the back to get the IV fluids and to prep the needle. Once he returned, he inserted the IV into Gabo's right arm and started the IV drip. "Doc, we found the hole in the ground that Apoyung was talking about, but it wasn't just a hole, it was a cave of some sort with all of these statues in it. These statues were Tagg...Jonathan faltered on the pronunciation, and looked to Ayung for help.

"Tagaeri! Bad people!" Ayung said with a shudder.

"Yea, Tagaeri statues were lined up in a circle, and Gabo was lying in the middle of the circle with a rock in his hand. He was swinging at these large spiders," Jonathan said before taking a deep breath and forcing himself to slow down and explain.

"Large spiders!?!?" Gwen asked.

"Atyechi!" Ayung said with heavy disgust in his voice as he breathed deeply through his nose and gritted his teeth. Nateachy looked at her husband and saw that he was very upset. She walked over to him and placed a warm hand on his back, hoping to sooth him.

"So Apoyung was telling the truth," Gwen stated out loud as she was grabbing a bottle of Lactodectus Mactans, the antivenom for a black widow bite.

"Yeah, he was telling the truth all right, about everything. Gwen, I am telling you, these spiders aren't like anything I have ever seen. They're about as big as a grapefruit, stark white, and extremely aggressive. It's almost like they fear nothing. You know most spiders run away at the sign of a predator, but not these guys,"

"What do you mean aggressive?"

"I mean Ayung and I saw one of these spiders go after a jaguar! You know, one of those big damn cats that hunt in the jungle," Jonathan said as his voice was quickly becoming a shout.

"I know what a jaguar is Jonathan, but you must calm down, and finish telling me what else happened," Gwen said, ever so patiently.

"Yeah, sorry about that, but you should have seen it. The jaguar stared down the spider, and instead of running away, the spider jumped on its back and bit the jaguar!"

"What did the jaguar do then?" Gwen questioned as she inserted the needle with the antivenom into Gabo's right arm. The boy's body shuddered slightly when she injected him, but then returned to its unresponsive state.

"It ran the hell away!" Jonathan said quickly, almost panting as the memory of the whole fight flooded his mind. His hands began to shake again as he continued to explain to Gwen what happened in the cave with Gabo, and how he almost didn't make it back.

Realizing that Jonathan was about to break down, she quickly walked over to him, wrapped her arms around his shoulders, and spoke softly "You're ok. Just take a deep breath, and calm down. You did everything right, and you saved Gabo from the spiders, just relax," Her soothing voice along with her body's rhythmic breathing slowly started to calm Jonathan down and bring him back to reality. Once she knew he was ok, she guided him to a chair where he slumped down, buried his face into his hands, and continued to take deep breaths. After Jonathan was taken care of, she turned her attention to Ayung.

"Have you ever seen anything like these spiders before?" she questioned, desperately hoping that he had.

"I sorry Gwen, no. Atyechi...new to me. Atyechi no attack like this," Ayung answered with a worried frown on his face.

"Unfortunately, that is what I feared," Gwen said as she rested her hands on her hips. She glanced over at the bed where Gabo was lying, and his condition wasn't getting any better. His whole body was drenched in sweat, and his breathing was becoming more labored. Nateachy continued to wipe a cloth over his body in an effort to clean the sweat away, but the boy continued to sweat as his fever continued to rise. Gwen had never seen a reaction this bad, and her concern was written all over her.

"Gwen," Ayung quietly called to her.

"Yes?" Gwen answered, never taking her attention away from Gabo

"Jonathan say Tagaeri."

"Yes," Gwen said with a confused look on her face.

"You know Tagaeri?"

"No!"

"Tagaeri mean tribe – savage ancestors, much worse than we."

"Savage?" Gwen asked. She leaned in closer to hear Ayung as his voice continued to get lower.

"Yes, savage. Tagaeri eat enemy right away. No cook," Ayung whispered while staring directly into her eyes.

"So you mean they were cannibals?" Gwen questioned as her heart began to race.

Ayung looked at her with fear pouring out of his eyes and nodded his head slowly.

"Oh my gosh! Are they still around today?" Gwen gasped as she placed her hand over her mouth.

"No see Tagaeri many day, statues Jonathan see worry me," Ayung said, trying to reassure himself more than her.

"Wait a second!" Jonathan popped his head up from his hands. "You mean to tell me that cannibals made those statues?" Jonathan asked as his eyes quickly doubled in size.

"Yes, they not around long time, finding statues in cave strange," Ayung calmly said to Jonathan.

"Cannibals or not, our main concern is with Gabo and these large spiders that you said attacked him," Gwen said as she turned her attention to Jonathan. "We need to be on the lookout for one of these spiders, and we need to let Gabo's parents know what has happened."

"Jonathan, you and Ayung go and find Gabo's parents, and bring them here while Nateachy and I try to get his fever down. You might also want to take Apoyung home, I don't want him seeing his friend in this state,"

"Great! I think I would rather go back into the jungle instead of telling Ga that his son is in trouble," Jonathan said sarcastically as he stood up and headed back out into the village.

"Me too!" Ayung muttered as he followed Jonathan out of the tent.

Gwen sighed, and returned to the bedside where Nateachy was still trying to help Gabo in any way that she could. Gwen knew that Ga would not be sober, let alone happy, but she had to let him know that his son's life was in extreme danger. She heard Apoyung ask his dad how Gabo was doing as the men left the tent. She quickly said a silent prayer, hoping that she would have the ability and equipment to save the boy's life.

***

The sun was slowly setting across the village, casting long shadows throughout. As dusk approached the air became colder, and soft cool breezes raced across the village, causing Jonathan to shiver and rub his shoulders with his hands. He couldn't tell whether or not the shiver was from the breeze or the fact that he had to go and see Ga.

Ga was Gabo's father, and the local drunk. He stood about six foot eight, and was one of the fiercest warriors in the tribe. Ga was extremely muscular, and his shaven head displayed tribal signs indicating the many different fights that he had been in and won. He had a six inch scar that started above his left ear and trailed down to his chin, a trophy from when a rival tribe warrior had tried to kill him in his sleep. Ga had awoken to see the warrior kneeling over his head with a dagger raised in both hands ready to plunge it into Ga's face. In a flash Ga had avoided the fatal blow by mere inches, and even though Ga lived, the knife deeply wounded the left side of his head leaving a nasty scar.

Once Ga had realized that he was still alive, he got up and tackled the assassin. Ga was able to wrestle the knife away from his assailant, and with one strong punch he put him on the ground, instantly knocking the breath out of him. As his assailant was trying to catch his breath Ga grabbed his machete. His assailant slowly got to his feet, only to see a flash of metal in the moon light, followed by blackness. In one vicious swing Ga had taken the warrior's head cleanly off his shoulders. As the head rolled backwards, the body slumped to the ground, and blood spewed from the neck. Exhibiting no fear, Ga took the head and marched over to the rival tribe's village with a spear in his other hand. He confidently strode to the center of the village, slammed the spear into the ground, and jammed the head on top of the spear as a warning sign. As he left the village, he noticed multiple sets of fearful eyes watching him through the shadows of the tents. As he reached the outskirts of the village, he turned around and let loose an insane howl that sent chills through the spines of the villagers.

Ga had married one of the most beautiful women of his tribe, Mayamu. Mayamu was a magnificent beauty that each man desired, but only one man could have. Ga was regarded as the alpha male of the tribe and got to choose whichever woman he wanted, even if it was against her will. Mayamu never loved Ga, but feared him. Her situation forced her to stay with him and give him everything that he demanded. Mayamu was constantly showing signs of abuse, from fresh bruises around her eyes, to multiple scratches all over her body. She could not leave him for fear of death. As the days became months, and the months turned into years, Mayamu's exquisite beauty rapidly faded, leaving only a shell of woman who barely spoke while in the company of her husband.

As Jonathan and Ayung approached Ga's home, he was sitting outside smoking from his long pipe with his legs propped up on a large boulder.

"Hey, Rainbow Man!" Ga called out with a devilish sneer plastered across his face. "You come pick flowers with my wife? Maybe she show you how make necklace to match funny shirts," Ga said as he set down his pipe chuckling to himself.

"No Ga, I haven't come to pick flowers or make any damn necklace!" Jonathan retorted.

"Oh, you big man now, no more flowers, eh?" Ga smirked as he stood up and stretched without taking his eyes off of Jonathan. After he finished stretching, he walked towards both of the men with a slight grin across the left side of his mouth. "I see you got friend with you. He no talk?" Ga said as his turned his attention towards Ayung.

"Ga know Ayung!" Ayung said as he clenched his fists so tight that his knuckles were turning white.

Ga stopped immediately, and the grin on his face became a large smile that produced a hearty laugh. "Ahh, he talk. Not like sister. She no talk, just cook, clean... an she clean me!" Ga said as he narrowed his gaze onto Ayung, baiting him.

Ayung gritted his teeth and started to charge Ga, but before he could get close, Jonathan reached out with his left arm and placed his palm on his chest, restraining his enraged friend. "Now is not the time, Ayung!" Jonathan said sternly as he turned to look at his friend, "Now is not the time."

"Rainbow man right, now not time. Never time, Ayung. Never!" Ga growled.

Jonathan turned around to face Ga and stared directly into his eyes without blinking or showing any sign of fear, "Shut your damn mouth you overgrown idiot!"

"What you say?" Ga growled with furious rage.

"I said shut your damn mouth you overgrown idiot, and listen to what we have to tell you," Jonathan said has he stood his ground against the towering man. "Gabo is in danger, and we need you and Mayamu to come to the medical tent. He fell into a large hole off of the hunting path, and he has been bitten multiple times by a large albino scorpion spider. We don't know if he will make it through the night,"

"Mayamu!! Get here now!" Ga yelled as he stared down at Jonathan, breathing heavily through his nose, and gritting his teeth. His face became a scarlet shade of red, with anger, rage, and insanity all showing through in his facial expression. No man had ever spoken to Ga like that, and he didn't know how to act. Infuriated, he whipped his head around towards the hut and screamed once more for his wife.

She came out of the doorway with her head down, walked submissively over to him, and very softly answered, "Yes."

"Something wrong with Gabo! Rainbow Man and brother need us go to tent, see what matter Gabo," he barked at her.

She tilted her head up to his, and with her chin quivering and tears welling up in her eyes, she asked him, "What happened to Gabo?"

"I not know. Lead way, Rainbow Man," Ga instructed as he grabbed Mayamu by the back of the arm and forcefully dragged her alongside of him towards the medical tent.

As Jonathan and Ayung led the couple back towards the medical tent, Jonathan quietly whispered to Ayung, "I have a funny feeling this is not going to be good,"

Ayung took a deep breath, and slowly nodded his head.

Gabo's conditioned worsened by the hour. He continued to vomit every fifteen minutes or so, and he was so violently sick that he had begun to throw up blood with the bilious vomit. His eyes seemed to sink further back into his head, and his fever was continuously rising as each hour passed. The bite wounds were looking worse than before. The red swollen areas had expanded, and were now turning to a light shade of black as they streaked in a spider-webbed pattern towards his veins. Gwen and Nateachy continued to wrap wet towels on his head and around his body in an effort to reduce his body temperature and drive his fever down. Gwen knew that Gabo's body could only withstand a high temperature for so long before his brain literally started to cook. As the two women continued to change out the wet towels, Gabo moaned in pain and thrashed about on the bed. Gwen decided to give him a heavy dose of pain medication, hoping that he would go to sleep so that his body could start to fight the infection. She ran over to her desk and grabbed a bottle of synthetic morphine, filled a syringe, and inserted it into Gabo's IV. After about five minutes the boy stopped thrashing, and his body relaxed slightly as he started to take deep breaths. Realizing that she had been able to make him more comfortable, she motioned to Nateachy to let the boy rest for a couple of minutes. Both women were drenched in sweat and decided that they, too, needed a break as they sat down in front of Gabo's bed. Utter exhaustion came over Gwen, and she closed her eyes, instantly nodding off, only to be awoken by a booming voice coming from the front of the medical tent.

Startled and still half-asleep, Gwen frantically looked around the room, trying to figure out who was now in the tent. She felt a soft hand rest on her shoulder as Nateachy whispered, "Ga is here," Gwen took a deep breath and nodded as the makeshift curtain acting as a door was yanked back, and a large native man came through the doorway.

"GABO!" Ga screamed. "Where my son? Where Gabo?"

"Ga, now you just need to calm down," Gwen answered cautiously as she raised her hands in an effort to calm him down. One look, and she could tell that he was not likely to calm down, and realized that her hands were trembling at the sight of the enraged man.

Gwen barely came up to the man's chest. After she had asked him to calm down, he leaned so that their eyes were on the same level. He pointed his finger directly in her face. "You no tell me calm down, woman! You tell me where Gabo!" Ga growled as the muscles in his shoulders and neck began to bulge outward.

Instantly realizing that this was not a battle that she could win, nor one that she even wanted to start, she stepped aside and pointed towards the bed in the back of the room where the young boy was resting. Ga moved his gaze from her to the bed in the back, and he rushed over to the bed. As he looked his son up and down, his body started shake uncontrollably. Suddenly he was screaming his son's name and violently shaking the boy in an effort to wake him up. Ga continued to shake him, but Gabo wouldn't wake up, his body becoming limper with each shake. Mayamu walked in to see her husband shaking her son, and her motherly instinct kicked in as she leapt onto his back and started scratching his face and screaming "LET GABO FREE!"

Instinctively, Ga reached his arm over his shoulder, grabbed Mayamu by the hair, and flung her off his back into a couple of chairs. He then turned around, ripped the IV out of the boy's arm, and began to pick him up. The violent jostling around caused Gabo to vomit all over Ga, and he began to moan and wail as pain rocketed through his body. Nateachy screamed, and Gwen charged the big man, trying to wrestle the boy away from his grip. She succeeded in pulling him away and quickly tossing him back onto the bed before Ga reached out and grabbed her by her hair. She shrieked in pain as he lifted her off the ground by her hair and turned her to face him. Fearing for her life, combined with the searing pain, she kicked and flailed her arms at Ga, trying to get him to set her down. He just laughed as he deflected each attack. Realizing that this wasn't working and nearly passing out from the pain, she reared back her left leg and planted it successfully into his crotch. Ga dropped her on the ground and doubled over in pain as he gasped for a breath. Gwen had about a thirty-second reprieve before the big man regained his composure and grabbed her by the throat, pinning her up against a pole with her feet off the ground. As she was struggling, she looked into his eyes and saw sheer evil staring back at her, then her vision slowly became hazy.

Hearing the commotion, both Jonathan and Ayung ran into the back of the tent to see the devastation. As Jonathan ran in he saw Gwen struggling from Ga's choke hold, and he charged the big man. Out of the corner of Ga's eye he saw Jonathan coming towards him. He turned and tossed Gwen like a rag doll into Jonathan, sending them crashing into her desk. Groggy eyed and shocked, Jonathan looked up and saw Ga standing over them with his fist clenched together as he was licking his lips. Jonathan leaned over Gwen's body, trying to protect her as best as he could, while he flexed every muscle in his back, waiting for the impending beating he was about to receive. He slammed his eyes shut, held his breath, and waited for what seemed like an eternity, but then nothing happened. He slowly open one eye, and glanced upward to see Ga still standing over him, but he wasn't moving. As Jonathan opened his other eye he peered around behind Ga and saw Ayung standing behind him with the shotgun barrel resting on the back of Ga's head.

"That enough, Ga!" Ayung calmly stated as he racked a shell into the chamber. Ayung glanced down to Jonathan and jerked his head back, silently instructing Jonathan to get Gwen and himself out of the way. Jonathan softly shook Gwen's body, trying to wake her up, but she didn't respond. He rolled her over and gently slapped her cheek a couple of times until she opened her eyes and gasped for air. He picked her up and moved her out of the way as she was trying to catch her breath, and took her over to a chair that Nateachy had pulled out for her and sat her down.

"Ayung, this not change things!" Ga said with a sneer.

"Shut up!" Ayung barked as he flipped the gun and smashed the butt of it into the back of Ga's head, instantly rendering him unconscious. The big man hit the ground with a loud thud. Ayung tied his hands and feet together, put a large strip of tape over his mouth, and then walked over to his friends to see how they were.

Jonathan was getting Gwen to drink some water while Nateachy was pressing the left side of her face with a wet towel, reducing the swelling from the backhanded hit that Ga had landed. Gwen took a few deep breaths, and shook her head back and forth, "It's ok, I am ok. Trust me, I will survive," she said as she stood wobbly on her legs.

She looked around at the destruction in the back of the tent, and quickly realized that Gabo was not on the table anymore. She looked around the room frantically until she finally saw his legs shaking on the other side of the bed. Realizing that he was having a seizure, she called out to Nateachy to help her get him back onto the bed.

Gabo's body was violently convulsing as blood and saliva began to flow from his mouth, and his eyes rolled back in his head. Gwen ran to his feet and yelled to Nateachy "Quick, get his head and shoulders. Let's get him back on the bed!" Nateachy nodded, and reached down to lift the boy up by his shoulders. As she reached down, his head thrashed back and forth and her right forearm got too close to his mouth. His reflexes took hold and he bit down on the flesh, pulling the skin away as he continued to shake. Nateachy dropped his shoulders and let out a loud cry as she grabbed her arm where she had been bitten. Ayung came to her side and caught her before she fell while Jonathan jumped across the bed and helped Gwen get Gabo back onto the bed.

"Jonathan, you must strap him down so he doesn't hurt himself or any of us!" Gwen yelled as she ran over to Nateachy to see how bad she was hurt. Nateachy's face was going pale as the blood from her wound spilled on the ground. Gwen grabbed a towel and applied pressure to the wound, trying to stop the bleeding.

"You're going to be all right! It's just a nasty bite; you'll be fine," Gwen tried to reassure Nateachy, but it was a little late. She watched Nateachy's eyes roll back in her head as she passed out.

CHAPTER 5:
SOMETIMES SECOND OPINIONS DON'T HELP

As nightfall advanced on the village, small little fires could be seen throughout the settlement as people were busy gossiping about the events that had transpired that day. Outside of the medical tent burned a fire that cast an orange glow across both Gwen and Jonathan's tired faces. Despair had a firm hold on both, and their body language indicated that they had given up the fight long ago. Earlier that morning the medical tent had had no patients, and Gwen was left alone to her research, yet as she stared up at the stars, the tent had four occupants.

One was fighting for his life. Gabo was still in the back of the tent hooked up to IVs and the few pieces of equipment available to monitor his faint vital signs. His mother and father lay unconscious on the cots in the front of the tent. Ga was still tied and gagged from before. On the other side of the tent lay Nateachy with Ayung by her bedside, softly caressing her head and shoulders. The bite that she had received from Gabo was obviously infected, and Gwen couldn't stop the infection.

Silently beating herself up, Gwen could not handle the fact that she was unable to help Gabo, and now Nateachy. She took her hat off and ran her fingers through her hair in a furious motion, not aware of the fact that she was pulling her hair out with each stroke. Jonathan noticed what she was doing out of the corner of his eye. He quickly stood up grabbed Gwen by the shoulders, and gently shook her, trying to get her out of her trance.

"I am so stupid! I am so stupid! I AM SO STUPID!" Gwen repeated over and over as her voice went from a whisper to a shout in a split second. Realizing that her movement was being restricted by Jonathan's hands, she began to thrash about trying to break his grip, but to no avail.

"Gwen. Gwen! GWEN!" Jonathan finally shouted as he grabbed her in a full bear hug and pulled her towards him, restricting her movement in a caring and compassionate way.

Unable to move but with her mind racing, she finally broke down and sobbed into his chest as he quietly patted her head and smoothed out her hair. "It's not your fault. You are doing everything in your power to help them. You have got to realize this," he softly whispered as she began to catch her breath.

"I know I have! But I feel as if I could have done more!" Gwen spoke as she choked on her tears.

"I know you think that, but you must realize that you have done all that could be expected of you. No one has ever seen an infection like this, and quite frankly, if any other doctors were here they would have already turned tail and run," Jonathan said in a reassuringly as though he understood the inner battle that his friend was experiencing.

"I don't know about that!" Gwen said with a pitiful pout.

"Gwen, you got to believe me when I tell you that I need you to be coherent. I can't function like you do in emergencies, plus I don't know what type of medicines help what types of ailments," Jonathan said quietly as she pulled away from his chest.

Gwen took a deep breath, wiped the remnants of tears away, and stared at Jonathan, giving him a confident nod that she was back in charge. "Well, here is what we know. First, we know that I don't have any medicine here that can fight this type of an infection. Secondly, we have observed that the infection seems to be transferred from person to person by a simple bite. Thirdly, we must assume that if we cannot stop the infection that ultimately the patient may die from the complications," Gwen stated out loud as she paced around the fire.

"Jonathan, I need for you to do me a favor. Do you mind?" Gwen asked earnestly.

"Just name it, doc, and I will handle it," Jonathan stated as he stood at attention and mocked the military salute.

"In Quito, there is a medical expert who has specialized in zoonotic diseases and the animals that carry these infections." Gwen said aloud.

I bet a hundred dollars that he will know what to do," Gwen stated to herself as she continued to pace around the fire.

"You not talking about that vulture, Klinefelter, are you, Gwen?" Jonathan asked, hoping that he didn't already know the answer to his question.

"Yes, I am, Jonathan. He has more experience that I do in this area, and a second opinion in any case is always helpful," Gwen said sternly. "Please use the satellite phone, and contact the American embassy in Quito to see if you can get in touch with Dr. Klinefelter."

"Klinefelter?! Are you kidding me? That guy is a prick, a know-it-all, and a royal jackass," Jonathan retorted with a whine.

"Tell me how you really feel about him," Gwen teased as she walked over to her suitcase and fumbled through it before tossing Jonathan the satellite phone.

"The US Embassy in Quito is only a couple of hours away from here, so hopefully he can be here by first light," Gwen said optimistically.

"Yeah, Yeah, Yeah. Some great doctor who thinks his shit don't stink. I can hardly wait until he gets here," Jonathan mumbled to himself as he walked back into the tent to place the call. Before he could get into the tent, Gwen stopped him by placing her delicate hand on his shoulder, causing him to turn around.

"Thanks, Jonathan. Thanks for being the rock that I can break my problems upon," she said with smile.

"Don't mention it. That's what I'm here for," Jonathan said with a quick wink before he turned to go into the tent to contact the US Embassy.

***

In Quito, a strange phone call from the jungle outpost had just ended. Silently cursing herself, Janine Cummings slammed her desk drawer back in as she leaned across her desk, resting her chin on her left hand, while nervously tapping her right fingers. "Now why couldn't you just let someone else answer the phone? I mean you are already off of the clock, but you still have to go and try to help! Now look what your helpful spirit has done gone and got you into," she said to herself as she tore off the message from the notebook that she had written it down on.

Janine was one of the assistants assigned to Dr. Scott Klinefelter while he was in Quito, Ecuador. Like most people that worked for Klinefelter, Janine truly loathed the pompous, womanizing, ass that she unfortunately had to call boss. To the media, Klinefelter was a kindhearted, respectable doctor, but once the cameras were gone his true self always returned. Klinefelter was known for making demoralizing jokes, and he was extremely critical of everyone else's work, while his was near flawless.

Janine remembered during her first couple of days at the embassy how nice he seemed to her. She didn't understand why everyone hated him until the night that he offered to further her career if she would further indulge his sexual fantasies. When she balked, his face became frozen as he told her that he would see to it that she'd never amount to anything in the medical field. From that day on, she was always respectful to his face while secretly plotting his demise behind his back.

Janine smiled to herself as she stood up from her desk and unbuttoned her blouse down to her cleavage line, partially revealing a red bra which she pushed up as if to make her breasts seem larger. Once she was done with her top, she pulled her skirt up a little higher than normal and let her long flowing brown hair down onto her shoulders. She turned around, glanced in the mirror on the back of her office door, and laughed to herself at her pole dancer style look.

"This ought to really piss him off!" She said with a smirk, reveling in the fact that she was Klinefelter unobtainable fruit. Pleased with herself, she grabbed the note and walked out of her office towards his at the end of the hall. As she approached his door she could hear soft instrumental music in the background and could smell the rich tobacco that he always used in his pipe. She knew he was either reading or sleeping, most likely the latter. She reached up and rapped on the door louder than she really should have, but she didn't care.

The loud knocking startled Klinefelter out of his slumber with a violent jolt, causing him to spill his snifter of brandy down his shirt; he dropped the glass onto the hardwood floor, instantly shattering it into hundreds of pieces.

"Son of a bitch!" he growled as he jumped up from his chair, crunching broken glass beneath his boots while quickly grabbing a towel to wipe his shirt off. Klinefelter stood about six feet tall, was grossly overweight with a receding hairline of grey and black hair, and a full unkempt beard. As he toweled off his shirt, he noticed that the thick glasses that hung around his neck had also taken a brandy bath, and he cursed again while he cleaned them. Once he was done, he sat back down into his overstuffed leather office chair, picked up his pipe, then proceeded to take a long puff from it before shouting "Whoever you are, you'd better have a damn good reason as to why you interrupted me!!"

"Dr. Klinefelter. I am sorry to interrupt you tonight, but we have had an urgent call that I think you need to be aware of," Janine said confidently as she struggled not to laugh at the commotion she had heard from the other side of the door.

"My door is open, Janine," Klinefelter said sarcastically as he leaned back into his chair and propped his feet up on his desk.

Janine opened the big door allowing the light from the hall to illuminate the dark office. As she stepped in, she had to take about thirty seconds to allow her eyes to adjust to the darkness inside the room. She saw Klinefelter relaxing in his chair with the soft glow of his laptop lighting up his face.

"Bring me the message, and explain to me why this message is so earth-shattering!" Klinefelter sneered as he stared at the rather sultry woman, as visions of her rapidly flashed through his mind, causing his body to ache for just one bout of passion with her. As she approached his desk, he quickly put his feet down and slid into the desk, not wanting her to notice his arousal.

"I received a call from Jonathan Steambule about twenty minutes ago, requesting assistance with a patient that suffered multiple spider bites," she answered as she stood in front of his desk.

"Who the hell is Jonathan Steambuck, and why does he want my help?"

"It is Steambule, and he is Gwen Vierra's assistant. They have been working in the Huaorani village," she replied sharply.

"Ohhh, so he is the shmuck that is helping the prima donna doctor with the savage tribe. Amazing isn't it, that the prodigy doctor suddenly needs my help with a little spider bite. Sounds to me like she didn't pay attention in medical school when they covered insect and spider bites. HA!!" Klinefelter said to himself as a wicked grin slowly grew across his face. "This'll be great. I will ride into this pitiful village and save them from a simple spider bite, while showing up the pretty little hot shot. I mean, I couldn't dream up a better way to get back at her for weaseling her way into that job instead of me. She probably slept with the chairman of the department to get this gig, and now it's going to bite her in the ass," he said out loud as he laughed to himself.

"According to Steambule, Gwen has never seen a bite that caused this type of an infection before in her life. They are under the impression that this infection could be something new," Janine stated cautiously, hoping that Klinefelter would finally exhibit some common sense.

"For Pete's sake Janine, it's just a spider bite; nothing to really worry about," Klinefelter snapped. "Do me a favor, and get my jeep ready. I want to leave tonight. The sooner I get there, the sooner I can teach her a lesson in life," Klinefelter ordered as he stood up to pack his things.

"I will make sure your jeep is ready," Janine yelled back over her shoulder as she walked out of his office, strutting her hips from side to side, well aware that he was watching her leave.

"You know, Janine, you could come along and help me, might be good for your career!" Klinefelter called out to her with a devilish grin on his face.

"You know, Dr. Klinefelter, I would love to go, but unfortunately I have too much work to do before the end of the week. Thanks anyway!" she hollered back as she was walking out of his office door.

"JANINE!" Klinefelter yelled. "One last thing, don't tell Russo about this. That's the last thing I need is for that cowboy to come along,"

"Don't tell Russo about what?!" Russo yelled as he popped his head into Klinefelter's office.

"Oops! Sorry, Dr. Klinefelter. I assumed you wanted Russo to join you. My mistake," Janine said with an ear-to-ear grin as she leaned back into Klinefelter's office, just in time to see his jaw hit the ground. Satisfied, she walked back out of the office and winked at Russo as she gently smacked him on the backside with a giggle.

"Easy now, hands off the merchandise, unless you want to buy," Russo whispered back at her with a grin and a wink.

Neal Russo was a former marine turned photographer with Nature Global Magazine, and he fit the stereotypical tall, dark, and handsome mold that most women found attractive. He was about six foot three with a well-defined physique, slightly dark skin complexion from Italian origins, black hair, and dark brown eyes. He usually sported a five o'clock shadow, and he never went out into the field without his lucky hat. He wore a brown fedora hat that was the duplicate of the hat that Harrison Ford wore as Indiana Jones. Russo was a huge fan of the series, and his friends kidded him all the time about it, usually referring to him as Dr. Jones. He enjoyed being seen as his childhood hero.

Realizing that he had caught Klinefelter with his foot in his mouth, he decided to give him a hard time for the gaff.

"What secret are you trying to keep from me, Doc?" he questioned as he walked into Klinefelter's office, flipping the large overhead light on, and causing Klinefelter to shield his sensitive eyes.

"Nothing that concerns you or Nature Global!" Klinefelter snapped as he squinted in Russo's direction while hastily packing his bag. The last thing that he wanted was Russo and his antics on this trip. He thought of Russo as a clown and a menace to his work, and he absolutely hated it when Russo called him "Doc". "It is just a little issue that is going on with the Huaorani Tribe, a medical issue, that is."

"The Huaorani Tribe?! That's great! They're in the heart of the Amazon jungle, which means I can get some great wildlife shots for the magazine," Russo exclaimed with enthusiasm.

"Russo, contrary to what the magazine wants, this could be a medical emergency, and this tribe is in need of a medical professional, not a cowboy with a camera and funny hat," Klinefelter snapped back at him with anger flaring in his eyes.

"Sorry Doc, but your whole trip down here is being funded by the magazine, and since I work with them, I get to go where you go. You really don't have much say-so in the matter. With that, I am going to get my stuff, have Carlos pack up my jeep with our stuff along with your medical...gadgets, and we will be outta here in about thirty minutes. Sounds good, Doc!" Russo said with a grin as his hand clapped Klinefelter on the back before he walked out of the office.

"Fine, then!" Klinefelter yelled back as Russo walked out of his office.

Thirty minutes later Russo, his assistant, Carlos Mendoza, and Klinefelter were bushwhacking through the jungle in the modified Jeep Wrangler that Russo owned. Russo had added jungle bar lights all the way around, which made it look like a moving high-powered light bulb. At night the jungle was pitch black. The lights illuminated the surrounding area so that if anyone needed to get out, they could see where they were stepping. From Quito to the location of the Huaorani village didn't seem like a long distance, but driving through thick jungle added more time. Russo drove while his assistant Carlos literally sat shotgun, a large rifle in his lap, a sports bottle with jack and coke in his left hand, and large semi-chewed cigar in the side of his mouth. Klinefelter sat in the back with his arms folded across his chest, a sour look on his face.

Carlos had been with Russo for a number of years now. The heavyset Mexican had grown quite fond of his boss and his antics. Carlos was a former mercenary who wasn't exactly sane all of the time. He was the type of soldier that everyone feared, unless he called you friend. If he looked upon you as a friend, he would do anything to keep you from harm. Russo had saved Carlos from execution in Mexico by attesting to be Carlos' alibi on the night that Carlos beat his then wife's lover to within an inch of his life. From then on, Carlos protected Russo with fierce devotion as a way of showing gratitude. Had Carlos killed the man, Russo would have not vouched for him, but the fact that the man had flaunted the affair in Carlos' face had granted him a right to retribution in Russo's mind.

"Do you mind putting that out?" Klinefelter whined from the back seat as he began to cough from the smoke emanating from Carlos' cigar.

Carlos didn't respond, and he continued to puff on the cigar as he stared out the window of the jeep.

"Sorry, Doc, but when Carlos is riding shotgun, which means he's keeping our asses safe, he gets to do what he wants. Of course, you could try and take the cigar from him if you really want to," Russo teased Klinefelter.

Klinefelter made no comment, but stared at Carlos who glared back at him in the rear view mirror with a smirk on his face.

As the jeep rounded a corner in the path, Russo slammed on the brakes, causing the jeep to slide in the mud as it skirted around a tree.

"What the hell did you do that for?" Klinefelter yelled as he grabbed the door and leaned up to see what was going on. Then he realized exactly why Russo had stopped the jeep so abruptly. In the middle of the path the halogen headlights had found a large female jaguar, growling at the jeep. Her left shoulder had a dark wound that was oozing blood. The jaguar's eyes were completely bloodshot. She opened her mouth wide, flashing white sharp teeth drenched in saliva that slowly pooled beneath her mouth. She let loose another low growl, and started to paw at the ground as though preparing to charge the jeep. Ever so slowly Russo reached down into his bag on the center console and pulled out his camera. He took aim and snapped five quick shots of the beast. The mechanical sound coming from the camera caught her attention, and the growl grew considerably louder than before.

"Kill that damn thing!" Klinefelter whispered as he stared into its eyes.

"Easy now, Doc, we ain't gonna kill it. We just want it to move out of our way. Remember, this is her territory, not ours," Russo calmly whispered over his right shoulder. After he heard Russo's comment, Carlos climbed out of the jeep window onto the windowsill and fired a shot into the sky, attempting to spook the jaguar. As the shot echoed into the jungle, the jaguar charged the jeep in animal rage.

"That didn't work buddy!!!" Russo yelled in a surprised tone. "Take him down, and let's get the hell outta here!"

Carlos bit down hard on his cigar, took aim at the approaching beast, and fired again, this time connecting with the right shoulder of the jaguar. The impact of the shot knocked the jaguar off of its feet, sending it tumbling down into the ditch beside the path. Without wasting a second, Russo reached out and grabbed Carlos's belt as he floored the accelerator and roared down the muddy path. As the jeep passed the ditch where the jaguar had fallen, she jumped out of the brush and attacked the jeep, leaving a foot and a half long scratch down the side of the door.

"Holy shit!" Russo exclaimed as he steered the jeep wildly down the path while still making sure that Carlos didn't fall out. "The damn thing is still alive?!"

The jaguar continued to pursue the jeep, and the three men heard her growl over the roar of the engine. Carlos spun around on the windowsill and took aim again, waiting for the approaching beast to move into the light. Within seconds the beast reappeared, gaining speed on the fleeing jeep. He squeezed the trigger ever so gently this time, connecting with the chest of the jaguar. Blood and fur erupted from the hole that the bullet put into its chest. The beast fell face-first into the mud and slid to a stop. Satisfied that he had killed the jaguar, Carlos slid back into the jeep and reloaded his rifle without making any comment. The muddy path took the jeep down into a canyon and out of sight of the carcass. The animal didn't move until the jeep was around a curve, then slowly it got up to shake the mud and blood off its fur before arching its head in the air and releasing a piercing scream that sent birds flying out of the jungle canopy. Then she started to quietly trot down the path, following the sound of the jeep engine as blood trickled out of her new wounds.

CHAPTER SIX:
IMPOSSIBLE BECOMES POSSIBLE

The jeep arrived in the Huaorani village as the morning sun was beginning to pierce through the jungle canopy. Russo drove the jeep right into the center of the village, directly to the white medical tent that had a flag sporting a red cross. As the jeep came to a stop, Klinefelter jumped out of the back of the jeep with his bag in hand. He walked swiftly towards the medical tent, cursing Russo and Carlos under his breath with every stomp. Russo and Carlos slowly got out of the jeep, chuckling to themselves.

The roar of the jeep's engine woke Jonathan. He jumped up from a chair that had been his bed for the last six hours. He stood up, stretched, and tried to throw the kinks out of his back before he walked over to the approaching doctor.

"Good Morning, you must be Dr. Klinefelter!" Jonathan said with a forced smile, remembering that Gwen had asked him to be nice to the man, even if it killed him.

"You must be Jonathan Steambuck, the local assistant who scared my staff half out of their minds with your frantic call last night," Klinefelter said with a sneer as he stared Jonathan down.

Jonathan narrowed his eyes and clenched his fists as his face became flushed with anger. He started to take a step towards Klinefelter, when he felt a soft hand rest on his left shoulder and gently pull him backwards. Gwen stepped out from the tent.

"That would be Steambule, Dr. Klinefelter, and yes, he is my assistant. I asked him to call you at the American Embassy in Quito," Gwen said politely.

Klinefelter's grin slowly grew wider as he realized that he had struck a nerve with Jonathan. Klinefelter took ultimate pleasure in infuriating those around him, and right now he was enjoying Jonathan's loss of composure. After a couple of seconds, he adjusted his stare towards the pretty young doctor who now stood directly in front of him.

"Okay, Ms. Prodigy, what can an old has-been doctor do to help you? Surely you can't have gotten yourself into a jam, could you now?" Klinefelter mocked sarcastically.

Swallowing her pride, she looked up at the doctor and explained to him what had happened to Gabo, and asked for his help. Gwen knew that

Klinefelter would never let her live this down, but she didn't care. All she thought about was saving Gabo. She was determined not to let him die.

"So, let me get this straight! You gave a boy an antivenom shot for a spider bite which you ASSUMED was from a black widow, yet you never actually saw the spider that supposedly bit him?!" Klinefelter interrogated.

"Yes, sir, I did. It was the only antivenom that I had, and I...I...made a judgment decision...th ...th ...that I still stand b ...by!" Gwen stammered as her confidence in herself and her work was fading.

"Do you know the ramifications of what you did?!" Klinefelter started shouting as he threw his arms up in dissatisfaction. "You could have, and probably will, kill the boy with that assumption that you made! Any type of antivenom is almost as strong as the venom itself, and is very specific as to the toxin. You should be ashamed of yourself, Dr. Vierra!"

"But Dr. Klinefelter!" she protested as he continued to rant and rave about her decision.

"But nothing! Leave me alone with the boy in the medical tent, and let me see what I can do. Hopefully, I will be able to pull your ass out of a sling!" Klinefelter screamed as he stormed dramatically into the medical tent, leaving Gwen feeling belittled in front of the crowd of natives that had gathered to see what the commotion was.

Within mere minutes Klinefelter stormed back out of the tent, his face red with anger.

"Why is the boy in the back strapped to the bed, and who are the other three individuals in the tent?"

"We strapped Gabo down because he was having such violent seizures that he began to put his own life in danger. Nateachy is the lady with the bandage on her arm where Gabo bit her during one of his seizures. The other two are Gabo's parents. You might want to leave his father alone—he is not exactly in a good mood," Gwen answered, gathering her fleeting confidence. "Dr. Klinefelter, I must explain to you that Nateachy was in great health before Gabo bit her, but ever since she was bitten, her condition has rapidly declined. It is almost like he has transferred the condition to her."

"Preposterous!" Klinefelter shouted as he walked over to his bag that he had left on the ground before he entered the medical tent. "Humans cannot contract venom from other affected humans; that is absurd!" Klinefelter reached down and yanked up his bag as he stomped back towards the medical tent with disgust written all over his face. He disappeared into the tent, and could still be heard shouting insults as he walked through the tent.

"I want a piece of his ass!" Jonathan said with his fists still clenched and his face a dark shade of red. His anger was boiling over. Trying to calm himself down, he turned to look at Gwen. Her face showed that she was fighting back tears that were beginning to well up in the corners of her eyes. Jonathan walked over, put his arms around her, and pulled her head to his shoulder as she broke down.

"It's not your fault. You did what you could do. That asshole doesn't know what he is doing. He is just trying to get you upset. Don't let him win, Gwen! You mustn't," Jonathan whispered as Gwen stomped her feet, fighting back her emotions.

"I did the very best that I could!" Gwen said aloud, mainly trying to convince herself rather than anyone else. "I might have messed up, but I don't regret my actions!" She said as she began to regain control of her emotions.

"I know you did," Jonathan said, hoping to console her.

"Of course you did!" Russo volleyed as he started walking in their direction.

Startled, both Jonathan and Gwen looked up to investigate where the voice was coming from.

"Klinefelter's a stuck-up prick who doesn't know his ass from a hole in the wall. Besides, don't take what he said personally. He is just lashing out, because Carlos and I didn't cater to his NEEDS last night as we drove his royal ass over here," Russo said with a slight chuckle. He glanced back at a grinning Carlos who had lit a brand new cigar.

*****

Taken aback by Russo's brash style, Gwen turned to face the man as he walked up. He was tall and lean. His presence exuded ruggedness, yet his eyes conveyed passion and understanding. For a second, Gwen let her guard down and gazed back into his dark eyes as he approached. Realizing that she was staring, she quickly averted her eyes and stared back at the medical tent. Then she began to let her anger creep back in, resenting the fact that Klinefelter had kicked her out of her own medical tent.

"Who is this guy?" Jonathan questioned slightly under his breath as he turned to stare at Russo.

"The name is Neal Russo, but you can call me Russo," Russo said as he extended his hand to Gwen and then Jonathan, who reluctantly took it with a gentle shake.

"I am Gwen Vierra, and this is my assistant Jonathan Steambule. We work in the medical tent that Klinefelter has now commandeered," she stammered, trying not to stare at the handsome man in front of her.

"Nice to meet you!" Russo said with a hearty grin plastered across his face as he continued admiring the young doctor. Russo had a thing for girls who could wear a hat, and he considered it icing on the cake that she was a Red Sox fan.

"Well, are you going to tell us why you're here, or are you going to just keep staring at my chest?" Gwen snapped when she realized that Russo had not stopped looking at her.

"Busted, Boss!" Carlos chuckled as he strolled up to the three of them and introduced himself with a slight nod in everyone's direction.

*****

"Shut up, Carlos!" Russo barked, realizing that he had just gotten shot down by the pretty doctor. *You stupid ass you, of all of the times you have to check out women, you go and get busted by the only good-looking woman within a two hundred mile radius! Nice going Russo. Nice!* Russo thought to himself as he continued to curse himself for making his attention that obvious.

"Well?!" Gwen questioned as she began to grow impatient.

"Basically, my company has sponsored Klinefelter's little trip down here to the Amazon on the stipulation my assistant and I get to tag along and get some quality shots to put into the magazine," Russo stammered as he could visibly see the impatience growing in Gwen's face.

"What exactly do you mean by quality shots, and what is the 'Magazine'?" Gwen continued to question.

"Quality shots are pictures that I can take and upload into our online database that will be used, hopefully, on the cover of Nature Global!" Russo quickly answered, feeling more and more like he was being put on trial.

"You're a photographer with Nature Global!" Gwen exclaimed, involuntarily letting her excitement become apparent.

"The one and only,"

"That's amazing! I've always wanted to work with Nature Global since I was a little girl; mainly because that was the only reading I was allowed," Gwen stated, her attitude towards Russo beginning to warm as he flashed his handsome smile at her excitement.

"Ok, enough with the introductions and the 'oh wow, that was my childhood dream'…" Jonathan piped up. He was visibly disgusted with the way that Gwen and Russo were beginning to get along. "We have some pressing matters at hand that we need to take care of, Gwen,"

"Well, Jonathan, there is nothing that I can do right now because I cannot go into my medical tent. What do you propose that we do?" Gwen questioned. "I hope that you have a good idea for getting me passed Klinefelter, because I'm afraid Gabo's condition is deteriorating,"

"Carlos and I are going to drive back down the hunting path. We passed some kind of a disturbance where an earthquake has uncovered what appear to be ancient artifacts. Klinefelter mentioned seeing some statues. I would love to get some shots of these statues for the magazine. You two are more than welcome to come along," Russo offered as he walked back towards his jeep.

"Jonathan, I can't leave that monster inside my medical tent; there is no telling what he might do in there," Gwen said helplessly as she could still hear him ranting inside the medical tent.

'Gwen, right now there is nothing that you can do, and you know that Klinefelter isn't going to allow you to work in peace. You need to get away from it for a minute and try to clear your head before you go back to your work. Besides, these guys shouldn't explore that cave without knowing what we do. It's dangerous, and I need to show them where the cave is and to explain what Ayung and I found inside it." Jonathan tried his best to convince her that she needed to take a break.

"But what about Gabo? He may not have that long!" Gwen protested as she began to fight an inner struggle.

"Gwen, Klinefelter might be the biggest asshole on the planet, but he is still a doctor, and is not going to put anyone's life in danger. He will try to save him—if he can," Jonathan softly spoke as he allowed Gwen to see what he was thinking. With a heavy sigh, she nodded. Frustrated and dejected, she walked over towards the jeep where Russo and Carlos were standing looking over a map of the jungle, which was spread out across the hood of the jeep. Before she got there she felt a slight tap on her right shoulder causing her to stop and turn around. Ayung stood in front of her with a determined look on his face. Perplexed, she tilted her head to the side and questioned, "Ayung?! Can I help you with something?"

"Gwen, you good doctor, you try help everyone we grateful you try hard," Ayung said as he stretched his arm out panning across the village and the villagers that were still standing around after the altercation between Gwen and Klinefelter.

"Thank you, Ayung. That means a lot to me," Gwen said as she wiped a tear from her cheek.

"If you trust he help Gabo, I OK him in room my wife. He asshole," Ayung said in a reassuring tone to Gwen.

Seeing the kindness in the man's eyes gave Gwen some of her confidence back about the decisions that she had made earlier. She smiled back at him before turning and heading for the jeep. Relieved, she decided that she, too, wanted to go see the statues that everyone was talking about.

"If you're coming with us, let's get a move on. The temperature isn't going to get any better as the day goes on, and I really hate sweating my ass off for pictures!" Russo yelled as he and Carlos climbed into the jeep. The sun was already shining fiercely through the vegetation, and the humidity was causing everyone's skin to feel clammy and sticky.

"If you're going out there you need to be prepared!" Jonathan yelled as he came trotting over to the jeep with the shotgun in his right hand and a case of shells tucked under his right shoulder. As he got to the jeep, Jonathan softly muttered to himself, "I must be nuts to go back there after what happened with Gabo

"Prepared for what? The boogey man?" Russo joked as Jonathan jumped into the back of the jeep.

"Worse than that, jackass! Ayung and I saw one of those spiders that I told Klinefelter about attack a jaguar last night as if *it* was the apex predator instead of the jaguar," Jonathan responded, ignoring the sarcastic comment.

"A jaguar?!" Russo questioned as his stomach slowly began to clench.

"Yeah, a jaguar. I didn't stutter did I?" Jonathan answered sarcastically, realizing that he now had Russo's attention.

"We were attacked last night by a jaguar on our way over to the village," Russo said quietly. "This jaguar, it had to be crazy or something. I mean, I have never heard of any animal attacking a vehicle, even a jaguar. It's like the thing was possessed or something."

"What happened to it?" Jonathan questioned as his pulse quickened.

"Carlos shot it twice and killed it on the second shot, as it was chasing the jeep."

"One tough bitch, but no more bother," Carlos said, and grinned as he flicked his cigar out of the window.

"Listen to me, Russo!" Jonathan said as he locked eyes with Russo, "Don't tell Gwen about your encounter with the jaguar, she doesn't need another thing on her mind to worry about."

"You got it kid. So what is the story with her? Are you and her... you know," Russo questioned, trying not to show obvious interest.

"No, and good luck! Because she doesn't have time to play games or deal with the bullshit. Not to mention she will cut you down to size if she thinks you are trying to play games. Trust me, I know," Jonathan said with conviction in his eyes.

"Thanks for the background kid!" Russo said as he reached back and patted Jonathan on the shoulder.

"One last thing Russo. I ain't your kid, so stop calling me that," Jonathan said as a chip began to form on his shoulder.

"You got it, kid!" Russo antagonized him.

As Jonathan was glaring at him, Gwen opened up the backseat door behind the driver, and climbed into the jeep with a small bag in tow.

After settling in, she tapped Russo on the shoulder. "All right, let's go, big shot!"

Russo gunned the engine and put it in gear as the jeep lurched forward towards the hunting path. Just as they were turning onto the path, they heard someone yell out to stop. Russo slammed on the brakes, forcing the jeep to slide to the right on the loose ground. Gwen and Jonathan looked back to see Ayung jogging up the jeep with a spear in his hand and his hunting knife in a sheath that he had strapped around his right thigh.

"I coming, too! You need me at cave!" Ayung yelled as he climbed over the back of the jeep and slid into the middle between Gwen and Jonathan.

"Glad you're coming along," Jonathan said as he winked at his friend.

"Something tells me this trip isn't going to be our regular sightseeing trip. For once I am a little nervous about what we are going to find inside this cave," Russo whispered to Carlos, who replied simply by nodding his head as he continued to stare out of the jeep window.

Through a slit in the medical tent, Klinefelter peered out into the village, watching the jeep head back in the jungle with a devilish grin appearing across his face. *You played that one very well!* Klinefelter praised himself, feeling superior. *That brought down that Dr. Vierra. She will begin second-guessing herself, and then her work here will need saving. That is when I will sweep in to save the day. Brilliant! Fucking brilliant!* Klinefelter continued to praise himself as he let the side of the flap go, closing off the tent from the outside.

As he turned to walk into the back of the tent, he looked across the room and saw the large muscular native man glaring at him with anger-filled eyes.

"Well?! Who the hell are you, and what is your problem?" Klinefelter snapped as he got close to where Ga was sitting. Ga just sat there rigid, never allowing his eyes to investigate anything but Klinefelter.

"Do you speak, or are you just a dumbass brute?" Klinefelter chided Ga as he got closer and gently started slapping the large man's face, attempting to get a reaction out of him. "No wonder your people are so easily taken over by a much smarter culture like my own," Klinefelter muttered under his breath as he walked away, gently shaking his head, not noticing the slow movement of Ga's arms behind his back.

"You no talk him, make him mad. He bad man," Nateachy said through a strained voice from her place on the cot.

"Why do you say that? He just looks like an inbred idiot!" Klinefelter chuckled as he walked over to her cot.

"You no make him mad!" Nateachy feebly tried to warn Klinefelter as he reached down, picked up her bandaged arm, and began to undo the bandage.

"Please, that hurt, please be careful. Dr. Gwen say no take bandage off. Infection."

"Oh, did Dr. Gwen say that?" Klinefelter mocked her slightly. "Well, Ma'am, I am sorry to say, but Dr. Gwen is a dumb bitch, and her mistakes have caused me to take over her hospital and everyone in it. So I guess you need to start listening to me, if you want to live to see another day," he said as he finished with the bandage and twisted her arm over violently trying to get a look at the bite wound. Ignoring her cries of pain, he was mesmerized by what he saw. Clearly this wound was more than just a bite—it *had* to be. Klinefelter had never seen a bite that looked like this. He was barely able to make out the teeth imprints because the flesh surrounding the bite had already rotted away into a dark viscous layer that slid off of her arm and dropped on the hospital floor. Dark streaks of red spider web patterns radiated outward from the center of the bite. The flesh around it appeared dark yellow with small brown spots. Klinefelter dared not touch the wound, and found himself perplexed. This wound had all the markings of a venomous bite, yet according to Gwen, the woman had been bitten by the boy, *not* a spider. He quickly grabbed some fresh gauze and re-wrapped the woman's arm as she writhed in pain. Tiring of her moans of pain, Klinefelter gave her a heavy dose of a sedative, instantly putting the woman to sleep. He needed time to think without distraction.

Puzzling over exactly what was happening to the woman, he decided that he needed to check on the kid in the back that Gwen was so worried about. He walked into the back of the hospital, and strolled to the cot where the boy was restrained. As he approached, he noticed that the boy was awake and seemed unnaturally calm, his eyes affixed on the doctor.

"Can you hear me boy?" Klinefelter questioned, looking over the boy. He reached out and touched the boy's arms and legs to see what his skin perfusion was like, and quickly yanked his hand back. Gabo's arms and legs were ice cold, yet Gabo's face was sweating. *Impossible!* Klinefelter thought to himself. These findings made no sense. Instinctively, he grabbed Gabo's wrist and searched for a pulse, but failed to find any. Yet to his horror, Gabo still stared at him.

"This is fucking impossible,! There is no damn way this kid can still be alive. He doesn't have a pulse!" Klinefelter screamed in disbelief. He dropped Gabo's arm and leaned in closer, talking to him, trying to get a reaction from the boy.

"Do you hear me kid?" he continued to question. But Gabo just stared at him with blood-shot eyes that had small black dots across the pupil. Slowly Gabo began to open and close his mouth as if he was trying to speak, yet he made no sound. Assuming that he could only whisper, Klinefelter slowly moved his head towards Gabo's in order to hear what the boy was saying.

In a flash, Gabo jerked his head upwards towards Klinefelter's face, and snapped his jaws shut just centimeters away from Klinefelter's nose as a hideous growl filled the air. With a gasp, Klinefelter stumbled as he yanked his head away from the open maw of the young boy. Sliding in the loose dirt, Klinefelter lost his footing and fell, banging his head on the side of Gabo's cot. Instantly, he jumped back up to his feet. Scrambling to get away from the crazed kid, he ran to the desk with Gwen's paperwork, and pushed his back up against the outer wall of the tent breathing loudly. He could still hear the constant smacking sound that Gabo's teeth made as they continued to feverishly bite the air, with Gabo arching his head in the direction of the doctor. Gabo's hands pulled tight against his restraints as he violently shook the cot trying to escape his shackles. Unable to see Klinefelter anymore, Gabo slowly calmed down, but continued to growl and snap his teeth in the air.

Quietly, Klinefelter slid across the back wall of the hospital tent and moved towards one of the freestanding plastic file cabinets marked "Syringes." He slid the cabinet open and pulled one of the syringes out, filling it with the sedative he still had in his pocket. He crept around to the front of Gabo's cot with the syringe in his hand and a determined look on his face as he reached out to grab Gabo's leg.

Enraged at the sight of the doctor, Gabo started thrashing about violently. The vehement battering forced the cot completely over, rendering the infuriated child motionless.

With the syringe in hand, Klinefelter stood at the foot of the cot, waiting to see what happened next. Surprisingly nothing; the cot didn't move, but from underneath black blood pooled around the sides. Slowly, Klinefelter laid the syringe down and cautiously begin to turn the cot back over. As he finished, he looked up to see Gabo's eyes still staring at him, dark blood flowing from his broken nose and smashed-in teeth. Yet he made no sound except for the low growls, and as if he felt no pain, he began to thrash around again, and he continued to snap his jaws at the doctor, straining his head upwards.

Mesmerized by these events, Klinefelter picked the syringe back up and plunged it, fully loaded, into the boy's thigh, causing his eyes to instantly roll into the back of his head, before closing. Klinefelter then pulled the syringe out of the boy's leg and tossed it aside as he sat down on one of the stools, taking some very deep labored breaths.

He buried his face in his hands and shook his head back and forth, repeating to himself, "Get a hold of yourself man, there has got to be some sort of scientific explanation for this ... gotta be!"

Klinefelter continued to repeat this over and over as he ran his fingers through his hair while he stared down at the dark blood slowly being absorbed into the dirt, unaware of Gabo's fiercely hungry eyes continually staring at him.

CHAPTER 7
WE HAVE BEEN DOWN THIS ROAD BEFORE.

The jeep engine roared down the jungle path, causing all of the wildlife to scurry off into their appropriate homes and caves. Feeling the warmth of the sun's rays and the wind on her face revitalized Gwen. With the stresses of the past night and early morning weighing heavily on her mind, the short ride to the new cave was relaxing. The reprieve was short-lived though, as her mind returned to the impossibilities she had witnessed with Gabo and Nateachy. Based on her training, she was inclined to agree with Klinefelter that it was crazy to think that a condition from a spider bite could be transferred between humans by a simple bite, but her rational mind screamed at her to trust her observations. Using that process, she rethought everything she had done. She couldn't see any flaws in her work—none! *The only way this could be possible would be if Gabo and Apoyung had accidently stumbled onto a new species in the jungle, one that contained a vector for a disease transmitted in its venom that could mutate or adapt to a new host. The ramifications of this new disease discovery would change the medical world as she knew it.* She became lost in her thoughts. Then her train of thought was cut abruptly by Jonathan yelling at Russo to watch out.

"Slow down, Russo!" Jonathan yelled from the back of the jeep as he grabbed the driver's seat and pointed at the windshield. "You're going to drive us right into the hole if you don't slow down!"

"Hold your horses, kid!" Russo snapped as he jerked the wheel hard to the left while pulling the emergency brake handle up, causing the jeep to slide perpendicular to the path they were traveling on. With a violent jolt, the jeep stopped a few feet from the edge of the opening, sending a dust cloud into the air that slowly filtered as it floated over the large hole in the ground.

Russo stood up in his seat and grasped the roll bar over the back seat, while he slowly took his glasses off and wiped the sweat from his brow with the back of his left hand. He let out a slow whistle and gently shook his head as he stared at the large hole in the ground in disbelief. The cave was about twenty feet wide and at least thirty feet deep. As he stared into it, his heart started to beat faster as his excitement grew. In all of the years he had traveled over the world, never had he seen such a site as this cave; it was as magnificent as it was mysterious. His mind raced from being photographer of the year to a Pulitzer Prize winner, causing his mouth to grow wide with a smirk of satisfaction. *This will make me famous!!* Russo thought in a moment of selfishness.

"Jesus Kid! You weren't kidding when you said it was a big hole in the ground," Russo said to Jonathan while never taking his gaze from the cave. "This cave must be at least twenty feet wide; it's almost as big as a sink hole, and I guess those must be the statues you were talking about! Amazing, absolutely amazing!" Russo exclaimed, allowing the others to see his excitement.

Ayung slightly tapped Jonathan on the shoulder, causing Jonathan to turn in his direction. Before he opened his mouth to tell Jonathan what he had noticed, he saw in Jonathan's eyes that he had realized it too. The cave had gotten bigger since they were last here.

"Russo," Jonathan whispered. "You need to move the jeep back."

"What?! Speak up kid, I can't hear you," Russo said, still gazing at the cave.

"I said, you need to move the jeep back!"

"Why?" Russo questioned, becoming agitated.

"Because the cave has gotten bigger since Ayung and I were last here!" Jonathan said emphatically as he and Ayung jumped out of the back of the jeep.

"Come on now," Russo chuckled "Really?! The cave is probably the same size it was when you guys were here earlier. Besides, we haven't felt anymore quakes or tremors which would cause it to widen,"

"That's what we thought, too, when we were here earlier ..." Jonathan's voice trailed off as he and Ayung unloaded the contents of the jeep and stacked them up further away from the cave opening.

Sensing Jonathan's anxiety, Gwen gently placed her left hand on Russo's shoulder as she softly said, "I think we need to take his advice on this one. He's been here before, and we haven't. Plus, I have never seen Jonathan act like this, like he's scared of something,"

"Aye boss. Something bad about this place," Carlos agreed while he continued to glance around the jungle with his cigar firmly squeezed between his teeth.

"All right, all right. I will pull it back down the path; besides, I need the back of the jeep to be facing the mouth of the cave so we can tie off ropes to the bumper to repel down into it. I still think we are fine though," Russo mumbled.

He whipped the jeep around and pulled it further down the path away from the mouth of the cave, and then set the emergency brake. Before he got out of the jeep he unlocked the glove box, pulled out his Glock, and an extra magazine before sliding out of the front seat. He untucked the back of his shirt and slid the gun along the waist of his jeans. He tossed the magazine to Carlos who pocketed it with a slight nod as he carried his rifle over to where Jonathan and Ayung had stacked up the coils of rope with the shotgun and ammo. As Russo slammed the door of the jeep closed, he reached into the center console, and grabbed one of his cameras. Placing the strap around his neck, he walked over to the edge of the cave.

"Jonathan, Gwen, Ayung, and I will go down into the cave. Carlos will stay topside, just in case anything happens," Russo directed as he glanced over at Carlos who was holding his rifle at ready. "Ayung, is there anything I need to know before we go jumping down into this cave, especially about these statues?"

"I sorry, Russo. I not know much 'bout Tagaeri, they eat people, even same tribe," Ayung answered Russo with a slight shrug in his shoulders.

"WON...DER...FUL! Exactly what I'd like to hear right before I go into a dark hole," Russo said jokingly, trying to relax everyone as he could see tension building in everyone's body language. Before climbing down the cave he walked over to where Carlos was standing and whispered, "Hey man, look, you're beginning to scare me. I have never seen you act like this. What's up?"

Carlos took a deep breath and turned to face Russo, making sure that he locked eyes with him before he spoke. "Do you hear that?" he questioned.

"Hear what?" Russo asked.

"Exactly. We are in the jungle, and you don't hear anything. No birds chirping, no monkeys howling, no animals running around. All we hear is silence..." Carlos whispered as his eyes slowly squinted.

Realizing that his friend was right, he shivered. He quickly looked around and realized that noise wasn't the only thing missing; there were no animals around, period.

He turned back to face Carlos, and hoping that the others would not be able to hear what he said, he whispered, "Look, all we are going to do is look around a bit, take a few pictures for the magazine, and get out of here. This place is beginning to make my skin crawl."

"Make it quick, boss," Carlos whispered back with a slight nod. Then he walked back over to the jeep and propped himself up against the spare tire.

"I think I want to take some samples of the dirt, get some scrapings off of the statues, and send those back to the lab. Maybe they can shed some light on what is going on with Gabo," Gwen voiced as she grabbed one of the ropes and tossed it over the edge of the cave.

"Agreed, but let's make this little adventure a quick one and then head back to the village," Russo spoke hastily as he grabbed the other ropes and tossed them over the edge.

Jonathan picked up his shotgun, walked over to Russo, and spoke quietly, purposely making sure that Gwen couldn't overhear them.

"You know, normally I would have picked on you for that remark, but I agree with you. We don't need to be here any longer than absolutely necessary. There is something seriously wrong with this place," Jonathan said.

"Yeah, I agree with you kid. Carlos has us covered up here, but we don't need to waste time down there. I know you and Ayung had a tough time here before, so keep your wits about you and stay focused," Russo whispered, and then slapped Jonathan on the back as he followed Gwen and Ayung down into the cave.

The air at the bottom of the cave was colder that Jonathan remembered, and this time he detected a distinct smell permeating the air. The smell was foreign to Jonathan, but the closest thing it reminded him of was that of rotting animal carcasses. The chill in the air, the smell, and his memory of his last trip into the cave caused Jonathan to rack a shell into the shotgun, instantly causing everyone to freeze and stare at him.

"Just in case," he said in a shaky voice with a nervous grin.

Russo gazed around the cave in utter bewilderment. He admired the statues in their intricacies, yet he understood the element of danger that each one conveyed. Knowing that time was of the essence, he quickly started snapping pictures of each of the statues and some of the wall markings, when he noticed movement around a mouth on one of the statues. He slowly leaned in towards the statue with his camera zoomed in and watched as a shadow began to dance around inside of the mouth. As his camera refocused closer, he saw two small hairy white legs placed over the bottom row of the statue's teeth. Not wanting to startle the creature, he tried to work silently, but the clicking sound his camera made spooked it; the legs vanished back into the mouth of the statue. As he got nearer, the shadow moved closer to the opening of the mouth, and then a white scorpion spider popped out of the opening and scurried up the front of the statue to the top, where it perched itself. Startled, Russo jumped back, tripping on a rock and crashing on the cave floor with a resounding thud.

"Are you ok?" Gwen asked, trying her best to hide her grin.

"Yeah, I think so," Russo said as he got up and dusted himself off.

"Hey kid, is that one of those spiders you were talking about?" Russo asked Jonathan as he pointed to the stop of the statue.

Jonathan walked over to where Russo was standing, and as he looked up, he immediately began shaking and pointed the shotgun towards the top of the statue.

"Everybody get ready to climb up the rope!" Jonathan yelled as sweat beaded up around his forehead.

"Take it easy kid, I am right here with you," Russo whispered as he gently placed a hand on Jonathan's shoulder which was shaking with fear. "If you shoot, you're going to alert every other one around that we are here. Let's just slowly walk away and get the hell out of this cave,"

Jonathan slowly lowered the shotgun and automatically wiped his perspiring hands on his shorts so he would have a better grip. The movement caused the spider to arch its body up, revealing its black-tipped fangs and begin the soft but recognizable hissing sound. As the hissing sound grew louder, Russo and Jonathan looked at each other and froze. In a preemptive strike, Jonathan blindly aimed the gun at the top of the statue and pulled the trigger. A staccato of shrapnel pelted the statue directly below the top, instantly causing the spider to jump off the statue, landing on the cave floor. Russo and Jonathan frantically spun around searching for the spider.

"Get out of here, now!!!" Russo yelled to both Gwen and Ayung.

"What is going on?!" Gwen yelled back.

"One of those spiders is running around down here, and we can't see it!"

"Gwen! The spider is white, but it blends in with the light grey of the statues, so be careful!" Jonathan shouted as he erratically aimed the shotgun back and forth, desperately trying to find the spider before it found him.

"EVERYONE HUSH!" Ayung yelled at the top of his lungs. "Listen for hissing!"

Terrified, yet understanding, they all froze and listened to the eerie silence, craning their heads towards the center of the cave, listening aptly for the hissing sound. Seconds turned into minutes, and still silence was all they heard.

"Maybe the blast of the shotgun scared it away," Russo said hopefully as he tried to catch his breath.

"Not hardly. It's like these things thrive on a fight. Normally more come out once they all hear the hissing," Jonathan whispered as he continued to scan the cave floor. He began to raise his line of vision up to the statues that surrounded them and then paused at one of the toppled statues lying near the middle of the cave as he noticed a flash of white. The spider streaked down the statue heading directly towards him, leapt off of the base and flew at Jonathan.

"Oh SHIIIIT!" Jonathan screamed as he fell back, dropping the gun while closing his eyes and flailing his arms wildly. As he hit the cave floor he flipped backwards and then stood up, still rapidly brushing himself off, screaming to Russo "WHERE IS IT?! WHERE IS IT?!"

"Relax, Jonathan!" Russo grabbed him by the shoulders and shook him, trying to get him to calm down. "It didn't land on you,"

"But?" Jonathan questioned him.

Russo pointed in Gwen's direction where she smiled and held out a small glass jar with a lid on it containing the scorpion spider. Inside the jar the spider arched back on its hind legs and began to rub its fangs together before springing against the side of the jar. It continued to repeat this action several times then stood still in the middle of the jar, eyes racing side to side.

"I loved catching bugs when I was a little girl, so I am an expert at catching spiders," Gwen gave a nervous laugh while she pulled the jar up to eye level to inspect her new captive.

"Thanks, Gwen, I owe you one!" Jonathan exclaimed in between deep breaths.

"Don't mention it, but I must agree with Russo that we need to get out of here, because more will be coming,"

"Yes, MUST GO NOW!" Ayung said with a panicked sense of urgency in his tone.

As the four began to climb up the ropes, a shrill growl pierced the silence of the jungle, followed by heavy footfalls as Carlos ran to the edge of the cave and shouted down to Russo, "Boss we need to go… NOW!" he growled. "Something's coming!"

"It here!" Ayung yelled as he pointed to the other side of the cave where the jaguar stood on the ledge.

The large beast growled again with its ears pinned back, ready to strike. Its bloodshot eyes were punctuated by dark black and yellow spots on its pupils. Bright crimson-red blood dripped from its fangs. A viscous black substance mixed with small bone fragments oozing from two massive holes, one in its shoulder the other in its chest, slowly dripped into the cave.

"That's fucking impossible!" Russo stated under his breath, realizing that he was looking at the same jaguar that Carlos had killed the previous night.

"Carlos!" Russo yelled.

"Already on it boss," Carlos answered calmly while taking aim at the jaguar. He fired a shot from his rifle and struck the jaguar in the chest almost in the hole that he had created earlier. The jaguar howled as the bullet struck; it never moved as it continued to growl at the five of them.

Fear gripped Gwen when she witnessed the inefficiency of the bullet, causing her to lose her grip on the rope. She screamed out as she fell to the cave floor. The impact of the fall knocked the wind out of her, and she gasped for air. After a few deep breaths, she was able to stand up, only to see the jaguar soar down into the cave where it landed five feet from her. Frozen with fear, all Gwen could do was to stare at the beast. The jaguar lowered its body, flattened its ears, and let out a low deep growl as it locked eyes with Gwen. It jumped towards her with its claws extended, never aware of any danger from above. Carlos jumped from the ledge and landed between them, and with one quick swing of a long bush knife, sliced the paw and leg completely off. The jaguar landed awkwardly and tumbled down behind one of the statues. Russo, Jonathan, and Ayung immediately let go of their ropes, fell to the cave floor, and rushed over to Gwen and Carlos.

"Th … th … thank y...you, Carlos," Gwen said with tears streaming from her eyes.

"We leave NOW!" Ayung hollered.

"Right! Carlos, thanks for… WAIT LOOK OUT!" Russo screamed as the jaguar limped back towards them, still growling, with black blood flowing from where its paw had been.

Carlos spun around and jumped back instantly as the other paw swiped his chest, leaving three large gashes that gushed red blood. He fell to the cave floor clutching his chest as the jaguar, unstable from using its only front leg to attack, tumbled down, but as before, it got right back up. It charged Carlos for another attack. Then a loud crack echoed off of the walls as the jaguar's head exploded in a cloud of black mist. Its body fell limply to the floor. Ayung, Russo, and Gwen jerked their heads around to see Jonathan lowering the shotgun. Two trails of smoke emanated from the barrels.

"Let's see you do that shit again without a head!"

CHAPTER 8
TO SAVE A LIFE MAY ENDANGER OTHERS

"AWWWAAWWA!!!" Carlos screamed at the top of his lungs, as the pain from the chest wound coursed throughout his body, causing him to flail about as Russo gunned the jeep engine, fishtailing down the path to the village.

"Quick, you two" Gwen yelled as she pointed at Ayung and Jonathan, "Grab his legs and his arms, and try to stabilize him! The more he moves the more blood he'll lose!"

Frantically, Jonathan and Ayung did their best to hold the strong man down, but with Russo's erratic driving they were unable to get a good grip on him. Russo had laid the passenger seat down and placed Carlos's legs across it with his bloody upper body resting on the middle of the back seat. Ayung finally laid himself across Carlos's lower body to restrict his legs, while Jonathan and Gwen pinned his arms down in the back. Once they had stabilized him, Gwen cut off his shirt and used it to wrap across his chest in an effort to stop the massive blood loss, but the cuts were too deep. The shirt was quickly saturated.

Gwen reached up with both of her hands, grabbed Carlos' head, and she pulled her face closer to his until they locked eyes.

"Carlos you have to stop moving... calm down ... and slow your breathing or you are going to continue to hurt yourself!" She spoke sternly yet with the compassion to be expected from a doctor who didn't want to lose her patient.

"Yes I... under...stan ... d, it just hur... ts so... ba ...d!" Carlos whispered back through clenched teeth, fighting unconsciousness.

"I know it does, but I am going to take care of you!" She said as his heaving chest began to slow. "Do you have a first aid kit in the jeep?" She yelled up front to Russo.

"YEAH, it's under my seat. It's more than your average kit. Got some stuff in there that'll give you a kick!" Russo hollered over his right shoulder. He stomped on the accelerator as the path straightened out, and the outskirts of the village began to appear.

Gwen checked underneath Russo's seat and yanked the first aid kit up from the floorboard. She ripped the top off of it and rifled through the kit until she realized what Russo meant by it having something with a kick. Inside the kit she located several small bottles of synthetic morphine and a syringe. She quickly filled the syringe with enough morphine to knock

Carlos out and plunged it into his arm. Within seconds the medicine took over. Carlos smiled at Gwen as he gripped her hand tightly in his, before his eyes rolled into back of his head and closed.

"Russo, listen to me!" She spoke in his ear as she leaned forward to the driver's seat, "If we don't get him to an actual hospital in the next couple of hours, he is going to die from the blood loss. He will need to have surgery to suture these wounds, and most likely a blood transfusion. My small hospital back at the village isn't equipped to handle this type of procedure. Do you know much about any local hospitals?" Gwen spoke calmly, trying not to scare everyone in the jeep.

"Quito is the closest city, where the American Embassy is, but I don't think they have a hospital that can handle what you're talking about," he yelled back over the roar of the engine as he was shaking his head back and forth.

"Well we have to think of something!" She yelled back defiantly.

"Listen, the magazine has provided me with a Leer jet that is located in Quito where I was staying. I can have our pilot ready for us in about two hours, and he can fly us to Miami International Airport in about four hours and we can have him medically evacuated to Miami Med Hospital. That is the best plan I can think of unless anyone else has a better idea," Russo shouted back over his shoulder. He lowered his foot on the brake, causing everyone and everything in the jeep to slide forward as the jeep came to halt inside the village.

"That idea will have to do," Gwen said, somewhat dismayed by the odds Carlos would face as a result of that kind of delay.

"I'm going too!" She exclaimed, "Besides you will need me to take care of him if he is going to survive this trip, if it's not already too late!"

"Hey!" Russo shouted "I don't want to hear you talk like that. He's gonna make it, he has to!"

"I hope you're right!" she whispered as she got out of the jeep, jogged over to the tent, and frantically gathered supplies, gloves, IV set-ups, water, bandages, and some old-fashioned sulfa powder for the wounds.

.Realizing that she didn't have much time, she grabbed and tore off the rest of Carlos' shirt. She rinsed his chest with bottled water and tied some bandages tightly across it, just praying that it would slow the blood loss. She knew with the cuts so deep that she wouldn't be able to completely stop the bleeding without stitches, but she was determined not to lose the man who had just saved her life. Then she turned to where Jonathan and Ayung had unloaded everything from the jeep.

"Jonathan," she called out, "listen. I am going too."

"I know," Jonathan cut her off before she could finish what she was going to say. "Listen Gwen, you're the best doctor that I know of, and right now Carlos needs you. You should go, and help him anyway that you can. I will take care of your work here, and trust me I won't let Klinefelter do anything to jeopardize that. Besides, with you not around, I don't have to feel guilty about slugging him one good one if he deserves it," Jonathan said with a wink as his face broke into a grin.

"Thanks Jonathan, that really means a lot to me," she said as a tear rolled down her cheek. She reached out, gave him a quick hug, and told him, "I'll keep you posted on how we do, and let you know of any changes. Keep your satellite phone on you at all times. And Jonathan....be careful out here. Something doesn't seem right," she said as she stared into his eyes with a worried look across her face.

"Don't worry about me, doc, I can take care of myself, but you need to go... NOW!" Jonathan said, just as Russo had whipped the jeep back around and had it facing the path that he had just come down the previous night.

"Hey, Gwen?!" he yelled as she was running back to the jeep. She stopped and turned back in his direction, "You be careful too!" She nodded her head as she climbed into the back of the jeep.

As soon as she got in, the back tires rooster-tailed dirt and gravel, and the jeep raced back down the path towards Quito, leaving Jonathan and Ayung in a cloud of dust. Some of the villagers came out to see what the commotion was about.

Russo watched in his rear view mirror as Gwen checked Carlos' pulse with two blood covered fingers. At least now she had gloves and a few basics. After thirty seconds she nodded her head letting Russo know that Carlos was still alive and fighting. Russo let out a long slow sigh of relief before reaching across the seat to the glove box to pull out his satellite phone to call Max.

"WHAT ARE YOU DOING?!" Gwen yelled from the back.

"I'm calling my pilot buddy, Max!" Russo yelled back, as he started punching numbers into the phone. "Max is one of the best pilots the magazine's got. There ain't an area that he can't fly into, whether by plane or helicopter. Max always makes sure that the photographers that are traveling with him get their shots. Hell, he's worked with me and Carlos on many occasions, and I not only trust him with my life, he's one damn good drinking buddy," Russo yelled back as he placed the phone to his ear.

Max, was a former marine helo pilot who spent the majority of his time in the service flying into hostile airspace to rescue fellow marines in Afghanistan. He prided himself on never being shot down nor ever leaving a man behind. Even though Max and Russo didn't serve together at the same time, the simple fact that both men had been marines in their careers gave them an attachment that could only be described as brothers.

Max always made sure that Russo got the shots, and Russo always looked after Max.

Max was around six feet tall, about two hundred and seventy-five pounds, with broad shoulders and built like a German tank. He had long straggly hair which he sometimes wore in a ponytail, and dark green eyes; he always had a cigarette tucked behind his right ear. On the surface Max reminded people of a brute thug who you didn't want to mess with, but underneath his passion for protecting his friends was second to none. No matter how big the opponent was, Max would never back down, and that's what Russo liked about him the most.

Max had his feet propped up on a desk with his ball cap tucked down over his eyes, quietly snoozing in the hanger, when his satellite phone lit up with Russo's call jolting him back into reality.

"Somebody had better be dying!" Max growled into the phone, disgusted with the fact that he was so rudely awakened.

"Max!" Russo shouted over the phone, trying to talk over the background noise of the jeep crashing through the jungle.

"Yeah! Whatcha want?" Max shouted back into the phone.

"Listen to me, man! I need you to get the plane fueled and ready! We are coming into Quito now, and we need to get stateside quick. Carlos is badly hurt and he might not make it!" Russo hollered back into the phone, as he tried to catch his breath.

"Hang on sec there, compadre?! What the hell's going on? What the hell happened to Carlos?" Max questioned as he jumped out of his chair, now fully alert.

"I will have to explain it to you when I get there, just trust me on this one, get the plane ready, we'll be there in about forty!" Russo paused. "Max, I know you never have let me down before, please don't let me down now," Russo calmly spoke back into the phone with a heavy sigh.

"Don't you worry about it, dude, I got you covered!" Max replied, sensing the urgency in Russo's tone. "You just get your asses here, and I'll get you state-side!" Max spoke back into the phone before he hung up and ran over to the hanger that housed the plane he flew for the magazine.

As Russo hung up, he took another long slow deep breath before he tossed the phone to the passenger seat. He glanced back over his shoulder to see how Carlos was doing. He noticed that Gwen was still trying to get the bleeding to stop. It seemed as if she was fighting a losing battle. Finally, she sat back and wiped the sweat off her forehead. Her gloved hands were now covered in Carlos' blood. She rested her eyes for mere minutes before the jeep jumped over another pothole in the barely recognizable road. The jolt brought her back to reality, and she checked for a pulse again. In a few seconds, which felt like minutes, she again found the faint beating of Carlos' pulse. Satisfied that he was still alive, she pulled the bandages back to see if the blood was beginning to clot and noted that thin streaks of red underneath his skin were rapidly appearing around his wounds. These streaks resembled veins in the human body, but instead of a bluish tint they were dark red, and they made a spider-web pattern across his skin. Gwen took in a sharp breath and slowly released it. She had seen this type of reaction before ... in Gabo's body. Seeing the same reaction in two different people who were attacked by two different animals sent a shiver down her spine as she realized that whatever she was dealing with was contagious. After seeing what had happened to Gabo, she realized that Carlos didn't have much time.

She leaned forward and gently squeezed Russo's right shoulder, causing him to yell over his shoulder, "Yeah? What's wrong?"

"Nothing, yet!" She yelled back over the roar of the motor. "But we need to hurry, he is beginning to show symptoms of the boy that we told you about this morning,"

"What kind of symptoms?"

"His wounds are beginning to develop a web-like streaking. I think it shows the spread of an infection," she spoke with more fear in her voice than she intended.

"All right! Look, we are almost there; I've got my buddy Max getting the plane ready for us. It'll be ready when we get there, so all we have to do is transfer him to the plane.

"Good, the less time the better. I don't know how much more he can take, but I will try to make sure he's comfortable!" Gwen shouted as she refilled a syringe with the synthetic morphine and plunged it into his arm again.

"Hey, Gwen?!" Russo shouted staring into his rear-view mirror. She looked up from Carlos and saw him staring directly at her. "Listen, thanks again for all of your help, you know you didn't have to help us. I know it meant a lot for you to leave your hospital. I just wanted you to know that I appreciate it," he said as his eyes started to glisten.

She stared into the mirror for a moment, seeing the deep feeling in his eyes and simply nodded her head.

The jeep slid back and forth down the path as Russo continued to push the engine to the max. As he came around a sharp turn to the right, the path opened up into a clearing. A small airfield had been carved out near the end of the clearing. Immediately, Russo saw the jet had been taxied from the hanger onto the airstrip. Russo jammed on the brakes, causing the jeep to veer sideways as it slid to a stop in front of the hanger. He jumped out of the jeep, and Max came running out of the hanger with his flight gear in tow, headed towards the jeep. As he ran up to the jeep he saw Russo helping a woman out of the back who was covered in blood.

"I sure-as-hell hope that ain't your blood!" Max exclaimed, taken aback at her blood soaked clothes.

"Unfortunately, I'm afraid it's not," Gwen said with much chagrin.

Taken back by her statement, Max was dumbfounded until she moved aside, and he was able to see into the jeep. Carlos' body was haphazardly positioned across the back seat which was now saturated with his blood. His shirt was wrapped around his torso. Carlos' chest was slowly rising and falling as deep gashes continued to seep bright crimson blood through the makeshift bandages. As Max approached the back of the jeep, Carlos began to convulse, shaking wildly before spewing bilious vomit into the air, causing the blood to drain out of Max's face as his dark green eyes went wide at the sight of his friend's condition.

"Shiiiit, man! What the hell happened to him? It looks like he's been filleted open!" Max shouted as he froze.

"Look, man, I'll tell you on the plane, but we gotta hurry!" Russo pleaded with Max as he slapped him on his left shoulder, bringing him back to attention.

"MAX!" Gwen yelled from behind the jeep. "Do you have a rolling table or something that we can transport him on from the jeep to the plane?"

"Yeah, we got an old hospital gurney in the back of the hanger. I'll get it, wait right here!" he yelled back over his right shoulder as he was running towards the hanger.

Within five minutes they had transferred Carlos from the jeep into the plane. Gwen had rigged up an IV holder with tape and some basic fluids she had raided from the medical tent before she left. Max had the plane rolling down the airstrip and turned around getting ready to make its run, when he glanced over at Russo rocking back and forth in the co-pilot seat, anxiety stamped on his face.

"Relax, buddy! You're doing the best you can for him," Max spoke into the microphone headset, causing Russo to stop and look directly at him.

"I sure hope so. You don't know how many times he has saved my ass from some of the stickiest situations," Russo spoke back a hint of distress apparent in his voice.

Max throttled the engine down, causing the plane to surge forward, gaining speed, and thundering down the dirt runway. Max slowly eased the stick back, lifting the plane off the ground, and climbing over the trees at the end of the runway.

Sensing the tension that was still present in the cockpit, Max decided he would try and cut it, and help his friend relax. "So what's with the girl?" he questioned.

"Yeah, what about her?" Russo answered back as he stared out the window.

"Where'd you pick her up? She doesn't seem like your type. You know she seems to have more brains than your normal type," Max ribbed him.

"Actually, she's a doctor, and she was doing some volunteer work with one of the local tribes. I met her when we transported another doctor—who is a sonofabitch, mind you—to her hospital to help with a case, a local boy who had been bitten by a spider."

"Really?! You need two doctors to help with one spider bite?" Max asked, astonished.

"You see that's just it, I don't think it's just your ordinary spider bite, it's something else," Russo trailed off.

"Like what?" Max pushed.

"I don't know, but it definitely has her worried," Russo spoke with a slight nod towards the back of the plane. "You see, Carlos and I were attacked by a jaguar the other night as we were driving to the village. But it was weird; it was almost like the jaguar didn't care that it could get hurt or killed. It's almost like it didn't sense danger. Carlos shot it in the chest directly below its head; I saw it take a face dive into the dirt. I mean it was dead, or at least I thought it was dead," Russo continued with conviction in his voice. "Then the next day that same jaguar, bullet hole in the chest and all, was still alive and had tracked us. It attacked us at the same cave opening where the boy had been bitten by the spider. Carlos was wounded fending off that same jaguar,"

"Hold on a second, you mean to tell me that a jaguar, which Carlos shot in the chest, not only lived but tracked you back down?" Max shouted into the cockpit mic in disbelief as he stared at Russo.

"I know what it sounds like, but I am telling you what I saw. That same jaguar tried to attack us again. Carlos shot it repeatedly with his rifle, yet it still kept coming. Those three gashes in his chest came from that same jaguar,"

"Impossible," Max said as he shook his head. "There is no way it was the same jaguar; you have got to be mistaken."

"Trust me friend, I would love to be telling you a lie. Hell, it would be a fantastic one, but sadly, it isn't a lie. I saw the hole in the chest where Carlos had shot it the previous night. I tell you it was still oozing blood," Russo whispered into the mic as he slowly began to rub his temples and his face, hoping to relieve some stress. "We finally were able to kill it in the cave before it could do any more harm."

"How did you do that, considering the multiple gunshots weren't affecting it?" Max questioned in disbelief.

"The doc's assistant, this kid by the name of Jonathan, took its head off with a shotgun blast," Russo answered as he took a slow deep breath and slowly rubbed his grizzled chin while closing his eyes.

"Let me ask you something, Max," Russo said with his eyes shut.

"Shoot," Max retorted.

"What happens when you are walking outside of your house, and you see a spider on the sidewalk? Does it run away or run towards you?"

"Are you kidding? They always run away, we're like giants to them. Why do you ask?"

"Her assistant, Jonathan, was describing what happened the first time that he and one of the villagers were in the cave," Russo answered with a pause.

"Yeah, and?"

"He told me that these large albino spiders in the cave were aggressive towards him, almost like they were trying to attack him. He told me that even the noise from the blast of the shotgun didn't scare them off. The way he described it was almost like they were possessed or something," Russo continued gravely.

"Man, you're beginning to sound crazy! Do you know what you're actually saying? I mean, come on man, spiders only chase and attack people in the cheap movies, not in real life."

"I know what it sounds like, but I am telling you I looked into this kid's eyes, and he wasn't lying. You and I both have seen fear before, and that was what I saw coming from him. I believe what he was telling me, I swear I do," Russo paused looking back towards the cockpit door, making sure that it was closed. "Jonathan also told me that he saw one of these spiders attack a jaguar, and bite the jaguar. I didn't believe him until I saw the jaguar that attacked Carlos and the way that it acted, as if it wasn't afraid of anything."

"You're not trying to tell me that this same jaguar that was attacked by this possessed spider is the same one that attacked Carlos, are you?" Max questioned in disbelief as he turned to look at Russo. Russo never responded to his question, his silence told Max everything he needed to know. Max turned back facing the front of the plane and looked out over the horizon at the dark green waters of the Atlantic Ocean, admiring the white caps breaking.

"Why don't you get some rest, we've got about three more hours before Miami. For right now, no giant spiders, drug crazed jaguars, or pigs with wings. Let me get you to Miami and we'll get all this straightened out, I promise you!" Max offered to Russo.

"Nah, I want see how Carlos is doing," Russo answered as he stood up and dropped the radio headset back into the copilot's seat as he walked towards the door. "Thanks, Max," he said as he walked out solemnly and closed the cockpit door behind him.

"No problem, buddy ..," Max trailed off as the door shut behind Russo.

As he walked to the back of the plane, Russo noticed that Gwen had made a makeshift bed out of a row of seats on the plane. She had attached Carlos's IV bag to a hook on the overhead compartment, letting it hang freely above as the fluid dripped through the line. In an attempt to stabilize his temperature, she had covered his body with a couple of blankets that were packed away, but he was still shivering due to the massive loss of blood. As he walked up he could hear her talking to Carlos, urging him to hang in there as she continued to apply pressure to his chest to slow the bleeding.

"How's he doing?" Russo whispered as he walked up behind her.

She jerked up, eyes wide and inhaling sharply as she was startled by his approach. Once she regrouped, she relaxed slightly, and wiped the sweat off her forehead.

"Not good, not good at all," she answered with a heavy sigh. "Listen, do you have any cuts or scraps on your hands or your face?" she asked Russo.

"Not that I know of," he answered, perplexed by her question. "Why do you ask?"

"Listen, it's just a thought, but I think that the jaguar had some type of an infection."

"What makes you say that?" Russo asked, hoping that she wasn't making the same connection that he had.

"Carlos is showing the same symptoms that Gabo showed after he was bitten by that spider. I think somehow the jaguar had the same infection, and he might have passed it on to Carlos. It seems that the infection can be transmitted by bites, or in this case, by the jaguar's claws, which would mean that it travels within the blood," Gwen explained as she checked Carlos again for a pulse.

"I think you're right," Russo answered.

Hearing this, Gwen turned and looked at him as she furrowed her brow, wondering how he had come to the same conclusion that she had.

Sensing her confusion, Russo sat down across from her. "Jonathan told me that he and Ayung witnessed one of these spiders from the cave attack a jaguar as if the spider was the apex predator, and the jaguar was its prey. His story really didn't hold much water to me until after I witnessed the jaguar attack Carlos, and then I started connecting the dots. I don't know what we are dealing with, but if what you are saying is true, then we've got one nasty infection on our hands," Russo said as he slowly shook his head.

"Then if the jaguar that attacked Carlos is the same jaguar that Jonathan saw, we do have an infection on our hands, possibly an outbreak, depending on how many other susceptible things this jaguar or the spiders have come into contact with. She said with a heavy sigh and a disconcerted expression on her face.

"Listen, if this is a new type of disease or infection, we need to alert people and see what we can do to stop it from spreading when we get to Miami. Do you have any government contacts that you have made over the years?" she questioned.

"I only know of one guy, and he is with the FBI. His office is in Miami; I will call him as soon as we land."

"He will have to do," she answered with very little confidence. "How long do we have before Miami?"

"Maybe three hours."

"Russo, I don't know if Carlos has three hours!" she said as a tear began to build up in her eye.

"He's going to make it; I know Carlos, and he is one tough bastard," Russo tried to assure her.

Russo stood up and started to head back towards the cockpit when he heard a bloodcurdling scream erupt from Carlos' mouth, followed by violent thrashing. Yanking his IV bag off of the hook as his body went into a seizure, he kicked rapidly and flailed his arms around while screaming out in pain.

"QUICK! Help me hold him down!" Gwen yelled as she jumped on his body trying to force his legs down. "Just be careful with his chest!"

Russo quickly grabbed both of his arms and forced them down to his sides while trying not to put too much pressure on his chest. His body was shaking so erratically that it was almost impossible for Russo to hold the big man down. He heard him moan and what sounded like a gargling coming from his throat, and as Russo looked up, he heard Gwen holler, "COVER YOUR EYES!" which he instinctively did just before Carlos spewed a bloody mist into the air, covering his shirt.

"I'm going to sedate him again!" Gwen yelled as she released his kicking legs reaching for her syringe. In one fluid motion she filled the syringe and plunged it into his right leg, almost instantly stopping the seizures and putting Carlos in a catatonic state. Both Russo and Gwen were completely out of breath as they collapsed in total exhaustion. She turned, looking at him with fear building in her facial expression, and then she jumped to her feet and pointed to the bathroom, "Wash!! You have infected blood on you!"

Realizing the impact of what she had said, he ran to the bathroom and vigorously washed Carlos' blood from his face and hands. . Feeling fairly confident that he had gotten all of the blood off, he walked out and instructed Gwen to do the same while he watched over Carlos. As she rushed into the bathroom, he said a silent prayer to himself, praying that neither of them had gotten infected and praying that they would get to Miami in time.

CHAPTER 9:
LIKE FATHER LIKE SON

The sun was slowly descending over the Huaoranian village. The oppressive heat from the day was diminishing as a normal breeze was starting to pick up, promising a cold front which brought with it the threat of potential strong storms. Recognizing the signs, the villagers were hurriedly gathering their belongings and the food that they planned to eat for that night into their tents. As the dust cloud from the jeep dissipated, Ayung was able to see the full village. He admired how everyone was going about their normal day. Since no one in the tribe knew what had happened in the cave, he understood their complacency. Some of the local children were running around playing as he and Johnathan started to walk towards the hospital tent. Their laughter and good-hearted shouts to each other brought a smile to Ayung's face. He felt a longing to be that young and carefree again. His reverie was abruptly cut short by a long sigh coming from Jonathan.

"Relax, my friend, it okay," Ayung said reassuringly as he lightly patted Jonathan and the back.

"I hope so," Jonathan answered back sadly, unaware of the deduction Gwen and Russo had made. "Well, in order to keep our minds off of what happened today, let's go check on Dr. Dumbass, and see how your wife is doing," Jonathan said with a sly grin on his face as he reached for the open flap of the tent.

Before he could pull the flap back, the front of tent exploded outward as Dr. Klinefelter ran out in a panic. Not looking where he was going, he was instead looking behind as if something were chasing him. He crashed into both men. All three tumbled to the ground with a large thud.

"What the hell's your problem, Doc?!" Jonathan grunted from underneath the pile. "Get the hell off me you idiot!" He continued to yell as he shoved the doctor over and slowly picked himself up while dusting his already dirty clothes. As he reached down to help Ayung up, he noticed that the doctor hadn't moved and was visibly shaking and mumbling to himself. He called his name a couple of times with no response coming from Klinefelter. Realizing that something wasn't right he reached down, pulled the hysterical man to his feet, and shook him, hoping to snap him out of whatever state he was in. As he continued to try to calm the doctor down, he noticed a strong odor. He looked down to see that the doctor had wet himself in his panicked state.

"Jesus, man! Get a hold on yourself, and stop mumbling. We can't understand you!" Jonathan yelled as he continued to shake his shoulders, now more forcefully than before. Jonathan was alarmed by the color of the skin on his face. It was ghastly white, and his eyes were the size of saucers. He quickly let him go, but Klinefelter just stood still and continued to shake with a blank expression of fear written across his face.

"The man's lost it," Jonathan said aloud. "I can tell that he is scared of something, but he won't talk to me. Nothing I am doing is getting through to him,"

Hearing the frustration in Jonathan's voice, Ayung reached up and slapped Klinefelter across the face hard enough to launch the glasses off his face. The sharp pain brought Klinefelter out of his panicked stupor, and he jerked his head back and forth trying to figure out what just happened. As he rapidly looked around, he realized that two men were standing in front of him trying to talk to him.

"Doc. Doc. DOC!!!!" one of the men yelled as he snapped his fingers in front of him.

"Yes?! Wh … wh … what do you want? What are you looking at?" Klinefelter snapped back at Jonathan as he became aware of his surroundings.

"DOC, what is going on? You were in a trance or something when you ran out of the tent and ran into us."

"YES, the tent, oh SHIT, THE TENT!" Klinefelter quickly cut Jonathan off, as he remembered why he left the tent.

"Don't go back into the tent! There is something gravely wrong in there with that sick boy. I don't know if it is contagious or not, but we need to quarantine him immediately," Klinefelter explained with conviction in his eyes.

"Wait a second, are you talking about Gabo?" Jonathan questioned.

"Yes, I am talking about Gabit or whatever that little mongrel's name is. I have sedated him for the time being. You, however, need to start telling me everything that happened to him today. I fear that what has happened is probably above your mediocre medical education, but hopefully you can try again to give me sufficient information so that I can diagnose his problem," Klinefelter snapped as he began to pace in front of Jonathan while he continued to talk to himself.

"Listen, Doc!" Jonathan answered, visibly offended by the doctor's comments. "We told you everything that happened to Gabo earlier. We're not trying to hide anything from you. We're just as much in the dark as you are right now about what happened to the boy earlier today. All we know is that he was bitten multiple times by a very aggressive type of spider that no one here has seen before today."

"I know, I know. I know all about the spider bite and the fact that your boss, Miss Idiot, used an antivenom shot for a suspected bite without even knowing what type of spider it was. I want to know what else the boy could have come into contact with," Klinefelter snapped back at Jonathan.

"Wait a damn minute! Who are you calling Miss Idiot?" Jonathan fired back, enraged at what Klinefelter had implied about Gwen.

The two men continued to bicker at each other, quickly drawing a crowd. The native villagers started to gather around, interested in the commotion. Sensing that something wasn't right inside the hospital tent, Ayung started to walk towards the entrance and began to pull back the front flap to see for himself.

Out of the corner of Klinefelter's eye he saw the native man slowly approach the front of the hospital tent and begin to pull the door flap back.

"NOOO!" Klinefelter shrieked as he pushed Jonathan aside and started to run towards Ayung.

Not knowing why, but sensing it was the right thing to do, Jonathan turned and ran towards the front of the tent, as well, where Ayung had already pulled back the flap to go inside.

As Ayung pulled back the door flap, all three men froze in their tracks and their eyes went wide at what they saw. Ga had freed himself and had freed Gabo from his restraints. He was walking out of the hospital with his child over his right shoulder. Gabo's head was gently lobbing from side to side as the sedatives still had their grip. Black blood was steadily dripping from his broken nose and smashed in teeth, cascading down the front of Ga's bare chest. Ga had a sinister grin plastered across his face as he scowled at the three men cowering in front of him.

"YOU PAY FOR MY BOY!" Ga bellowed as he stomped through them, knocking them aside and onto to the ground with his sheer girth.

Jonathan rolled over on his side and quickly jumped to his feet as he yelled at the giant man carrying Gabo away. "WAIT GA! You don't know what's wrong with him, he still might be CONTAGIOUS!"

Ga jerked around to face Jonathan with rage flaring in his dark eyes. A crowd of villagers gathered around the two men as they continued to stare each other down. Behind Jonathan Ayung was helping Klinefelter off the ground, when Klinefelter shrieked, "PUT HIM DOWN! THAT BOY IS SICK!"

Hearing the older doctor yell, Ga prepared himself for a battle. He sensed that these men weren't going to back down out of fear of his size and strength. He slowly lowered his chin down towards his chest, furrowed his brow, and maliciously squinted his eyes as the muscles in his shoulders, chest, and arms instantly bulged. He opened his mouth as if to say something, but all that came out was a guttural war cry that sent shivers up the spines of the onlookers. At the loud cry, Gabo jerked his head up, surveying his surroundings. His head snapped back as he growled an unholy sound, his eyes now flushed red with tiny yellow and black dots. His head straightened and he began to glare at his father with an open mouth as blood continued to drip down his chin.

Hearing his son's growl, Ga turned his head to face him, startled at what he saw. Gabo's blood red eyes had an eerie glow about them, causing the giant man to suddenly experience a feeling he had never felt before—fear. In a flash, Gabo latched his jaws around the side of Ga's neck and bit down hard. Blood erupted from Ga's neck as Gabo yanked back with a mouth full of his father's flesh. The ragged shreds of dangling flesh dripped bright red blood as Gabo began to chew and swallow the sinewy, leathery flesh. In an act of pure survival, Ga threw the boy off just before he fell to the ground clutching at his neck which continued to spew blood all over his hands and body. Gabo landed awkwardly on the ground, his weight crushing his small arms and forcing them outward at a wicked angle. There was a sickening crunch as the forearm bones cracked and split the skin, effectively making his arms useless.

Everyone froze in shock and sheer disbelief at what they just witnessed. Two of the villagers immediately vomited as they saw Ga gasping for life. Others quickly ushered their families and children away from the horrible scene. Still others stood and stared, unable to move, or avert their eyes. They continued to watch as both father and son struggled to live.

Miraculously, Gabo stood up on his own with his now ungainly arms hanging at his sides. He raised his head back and expelled another scream before he ran and lunged back on top of his father. Ga tried to push him off with one hand, while maintaining pressure on his bleeding neck. Gabo grabbed Ga's arm with both hands and hungrily bit down on his wrist, tearing flesh and ligaments with a violent jerk of his head. Ga screamed in pain. Just before he lost consciousness, he looked up at his son's solid red eyes and saw a curious smile appear across his blood stained teeth, and Gabo instantly snatched off his Ga's nose so that he drowned in his own blood.

Jonathan was still frozen with fear when Ayung began shaking him by the shoulders shouting, "Jonathan, come! We do something!!!" Adrenaline was now flowing throughout his body.

Jonathan came to attention and grabbed his shotgun that he had left with the other gear from the truck. He ran over to Gabo, uncertain of what he should do. As he stood over the already dead man and the maniacal son attacking him, he shouted at Gabo to stop, but the boy didn't respond. Jonathan nudged him in the shoulder with the butt of the gun, still shouting, but the boy continued to attack his father. Jonathan's instincts took over and he slammed the butt of the gun into the side of

Gabo's head, knocking him off of his father. Ayung ran over behind Jonathan in an attempt to back him up. He yelled at Gabo in their native tongue, hoping that he could get through to the boy.

Gabo slowly stood up, seemingly unaffected by his mortal wounds. He slowly looked around at the crowd and then back at Jonathan and Ayung still standing over his father's body. Then he ran directly towards them with his mouth open, his arms flailing in the air. Jonathan and Ayung quickly took two steps back as Jonathan raised the shotgun in the air and fired a warning shot, hoping to startle Gabo and to stop his charge. The loud crack of the shotgun alarmed everyone in the camp except for Gabo, who leapt over his father and lunged at the two men. Ayung tried to turn and run, but he clumsily tripped over Jonathan's feet, causing both men to fall. As Jonathan hit the ground, his right hand tightened around the trigger sending a barrage of shrapnel into the air and forcefully taking the lower half of Gabo with it in a spray of black blood that covered the ground and Ga's body.

In a flash, Jonathan was back on his feet but was breathing so deeply and so fast that he began to feel light-headed and dizzy. Ayung ran up to him, placed his hand on his back, and patted it. Softly, he spoke to him, "It OK! Gabo, " he said. "He crazy... sick... need be stopped, or we be like Ga."

"I know, I know. I just don't understand what got into him. I mean, it was almost like he was possessed," Jonathan replied with a heavy sigh as he started to walk over to Klinefelter who was now curled up in the fetal position, slowly rocking himself back and forth while mumbling. As Jonathan and Ayung walked to him, he slowly looked up at them with terror-stricken eyes and a ghost white face.

"Wh ... Wh ... What di ... di ... did you do?" He asked, not able to comprehend what just happened. "I mean, I mean, I mean what the hell was wrong with that kid?!" Klinefelter screamed.

"I don't know what was wrong, but I had to put him down before he did any more harm to anyone else in the village. He seemed possessed. I hated to do it, but I had no other choice," Jonathan answered with a guilty shrug. "Come on, Ayung, we need to try and contact Gwen and let her know what happened," Jonathan said as he started to head towards the hospital.

"He's not dead!" Klinefelter screamed as he pointed towards the *now crawling* upper half of Gabo. "Neither one of them are!"

"What the hell are you talking about now, Doc?!" Jonathan fired back in disgust. Then he turned to see the horror unfolding in front of him.

Gabo was slowly dragging his upper body across the ground with his bloody entrails and bone stumps lagging behind him. His eyes were still blood red and his mouth was still working, with his teeth continually chomping down. He growled at the men as they stared at the abomination that use to be Gabo. Behind him his father stood up on wobbly legs, his face covered with his black blood that continued to flow down his chin and onto his chest. His neck and wrist continued to spurt blood outward with each step that he took. His eyes fluttered, then slowly rolled back into his head before rolling forward to appear as bright red balls with little black specks. He lowered his head back and stopped walking before he affixed his stare on Jonathan, Ayung, and the cowering Klinefelter. He suddenly opened his bloody mouth and roared at them before charging headlong in their direction.

Hearing all of the commotion outside of the tent, Mayamu ran out of the tent and shrieked at the sight of her son desperately crawling in her direction. She quickly looked up to see her husband charging a group of men that worked at the hospital, he also was completely covered in blood. Assuming that Ga was the reason for Gabo's injuries, she flew at Ga in a flurry of slaps and screams, knocking the big man down with her momentum as she savagely clawed at his face with her hands in a blind rage.

Realizing that the interruption of Ga's charge would only end in Mayamu's death, both Jonathan and Ayung ran to try to pull her off of Ga. Her rage was so powerful that she knocked them both back and continued to pummel Ga's face. Jonathan looked back towards Klinefelter for help, but he had disappeared inside the hospital, scared shitless. Mayamu's attacks gradually slowed as she had exhausted herself. She suddenly realized that Ga wasn't exactly Ga anymore, and she noticed his blood red eyes. As she tired, he wrapped both arms around her and pulled her down towards him, sinking his teeth into her neck. Her screams of pain became garbled with blood as she tried unsuccessfully to fight him off. He threw her off of him, then he stood, towering over Jonathan and Ayung.

They feverishly crawled backwards, scrambled to their feet, and ran for the hospital tent. Ga howled into the air and chased them, fueled by hunger. Realizing that they weren't going to make it back into the tent, Jonathan, diving for his shotgun, shoved Ayung as hard as he could, sending him tumbling down a slight hill, but more importantly out of the line of sight of Ga. Grabbing it, he rolled onto his back just as Ga dove through the air landing on him, knocking all of the wind out of him instantly. He quickly jammed the gun in between Ga's bloody jaws, forcing Ga to suddenly bite down on the metal, shattering some his teeth. Jonathan was now in a deadly grapple with the larger man who continued to try to bite him with serrated teeth. The two men continued to struggle, Jonathan averting each one of Ga's attacks by keeping the gun wedged between his teeth and forcefully pushing upwards, praying that he would live through all this. He started twisting his body, and with an adrenaline filled thrust, he flipped the big man over and was now on top, continuing to apply pressure on the gun, forcing Ga's mouth further and further apart. He screamed for help, but the other villagers had all scattered back to their huts. Klinefelter was too chicken to come out and help. His arms began to tire as Ga continued to flail about with never ending strength. Suddenly he heard Ayung scream and looked up just as he was running right at him with a large ax style weapon held high above his head. In one fluid motion he swung the ax downward, separating the top of Ga's head directly above where his nose used to be. Immediately the big man's arms fell lifelessly to his sides and Jonathan rolled off, hyperventilating as he struggled to catch his breath.

"Thanks, man!" Jonathan rasped as he looked up at Ayung who had now saved his life twice in less than forty-eight hours.

"He dead?" Ayung questioned, his grip on the ax still firm.

"He'd better be, because if he ain't," Jonathan paused, catching his breath, "we don't stand a chance." He reached up with an outstretched hand which Ayung grasped and used to pull him up from the ground.

"Jonathan, you bit?" Ayung questions with growing fear in the pit of his stomach.

"No, I used the gun to pry his mouth open, and more importantly, away from me," Jonathan reassured him.

"Good!"

"What the hell is going on here, Ayung? I mean, he was dead, wasn't he?" Jonathan asked Ayung, hoping that he would agree.

"I not know … this evil!" Ayung replied as he strained his head back in the direction of Gabo to see if the boy was still crawling. Jonathan turned to look, too, only to regret it because he saw half of the poor boy still crawling towards them with those bright red eyes glaring at them.

"How?" Jonathan questioned aloud.

"Evil, friend, pure evil," Ayung answered as he walked over to Gabo. He raised the heavy ax above his head again and brought it down on Gabo's neck, severing the boy's head from his body. The upper torso stopped moving as the head rolled back up against the shoulders with the eyes now shut, and the mouth permanently left open.

"He dead now," Ayung spoke as he walked back towards Jonathan.

"I have got to let Gwen know," Jonathan said as he turned to go back into the hospital tent to locate the satellite phone. Ayung simply nodded and joined him in the search.

As the two men approached the front of the tent, they heard a bloodcurdling scream from the back of the tent followed by panicked footfalls headed towards the front of the tent.

"Now what?!" Jonathan groaned as he took a quick glance at Ayung whose neck muscles suddenly tensed at the sound of someone, or more importantly something, running towards them.

In a blur of red and white, Klinefelter burst through the front flaps of the medical tent screaming like a child, clutching his right hand close to his body. Below his right hand they noticed fresh blood cascading down the front of his shirt and his pants, effectively staining the ground where he was standing a bright red. The man was visibly shaking and was still mumbling to himself, as he ran up to Jonathan and Ayung.

"What happened now?" Jonathan questioned while staring at Klinefelter's right hand, already knowing the answer to his question before he even asked it.

"That bitch heathen in there just bit off two of my fingers!" Klinefelter stammered through short breaths. He pulled his hand away from his chest showing them the remains of his now mutilated hand. Both the ring finger and the little finger were no longer there. They had been replaced by bloody stumps with only a small white mass where the knuckle had been now visible to the naked eye. Klinefelter moaned loudly as the pain continued to rip through his body, and he quickly pulled his mangled hand back to his chest and tried to apply pressure in a feeble attempt to stop the blood flow.

"What do you mean she bit you?" Jonathan questioned in disbelief.

"Exactly what the fuck you think I mean!" Klinefelter grumbled back, "You know these heathens have always been cannibals, it's a wonder they haven't attacked us before now!"

"Clearly, Doc, you must have done something to set her off. Nateachy is a very peaceful woman. I mean, she wouldn't hurt a fly, let alone harm a human being," Jonathan retorted, mostly trying to convince himself by his speech instead of Klinefelter.

"Well, wise ass, if you don't believe me then go in there, and have a look for yourself! Klinefelter screamed at both of them before falling to his knees from utter exhaustion and pain.

"All right, all right, we'll take a look!" Jonathan answered as he tightened the grip on his shotgun and walked to the front of the hospital tent where he slowly pulled the front flaps back and entered with Ayung trailing.

As they entered the tent the men paused to allow their eyes to adjust as the late afternoon had cast a darker shade into the tent. Jonathan nudged Ayung slightly and nodded in the direction of one of the portable electric lanterns that was hanging from one of the central posts that supported the tent. Ayung nodded back quietly in agreement, reached up, and flipped the switch, instantly illuminating the inside of the tent. The front part of the hospital tent looked like a tornado had gone through it. All of the infirmary cots had either been flipped over or were lying on their sides. Each desk where the volunteers helped to complete paperwork had been shoved aside, and the papers covered the ground around them. The small plastic file cabinets that housed some of the medicines had been tipped over, shattering the glass vials within, leaking valuable medicines and vaccinations. Jagged slits in the canvas tent decorated the sides of the tent, allowing for flies and all other sorts of insects to invade. Jonathan and Ayung slowly scanned the interior of the front of the tent, shocked by the destruction, but more importantly, they looked for what had not been located—Nateachy. Jonathan took a step forward, and by not looking where he was going, his boot made a crunching sound as he stepped on broken glass. The sound echoed throughout the tent, causing both men to flinch, knowing that the element of surprise had been lost. After a few seconds, which seemed like hours had passed, they heard nothing; then a sound coming from the back caused both men to hold their breath. A faint crunching sound was coming from the back of the tent where Gwen's desk and all of the emergency medicine was located.

Ayung quickly wiped the perspiration off his forehead with his forearm before he stuttered his wife's name out loud. No response, just the continued soft crunching noise. Again he tried, but this time with more force behind it; the crunching sound promptly stopped, followed by the sound of shuffling feet. The back flaps separating the front and the back of the tent slowly rose upward as Nateachy exited the back of the tent and stopped at the sight of the two men. The bandage on her arm was saturated with black blood, and her skin surrounding the wound was almost pitch-black. Radiating out from the wound, her skin color was almost a gray hue over nearly her whole body. Her head was pointed towards the ground as her jaws continued to slowly rotate in a chewing motion.

Ayung was fear stricken as he looked upon his wife who was now hardly recognizable. Tears began to well up at the corners of his eyes as he slowly put a fist up to his mouth to stifle his cries. He took a hesitant step towards her, only to be pulled back by Jonathan who whispered, "Ayung, I ... I ... don't think that you should go near her,"

Ayung didn't reply, he simply nodded, unable to tear his eyes away from her.

"Nateachy!" Jonathan called out after swallowing the lump that was building in his throat. Nateachy made no reply to her name, but simply stared at the floor while still chewing.

"Nateachy! Can you hear me?" Jonathan called out louder this time.

She suddenly stopped the chewing motion and slowly raised her head and stared at both men through blood red eyes. She opened her mouth, where the remains of Klinefelter's two fingers dribbled down her chin and fell to the floor. She made a low growl at both men before extending her arms and running straight at Ayung in a feral rage.

"Shit! She's one of them!" Jonathan screamed as he stepped back and racked a round into the shotgun before aiming it at Nateachy. Ayung quickly reached out with his arm and forced Jonathan to lower the barrel.

"But ... " Jonathan barely protested, knowing already that he wouldn't have been able to pull the trigger anyway.

"No," Ayung solemnly said as he raised his ax high above his head, "I so sorry, Nateachy," he said sobbingly as tears streamed down his face.

Jonathan jammed his eyes shut and lowered his head as the sickening sound of metal on bone instantly stopped the screaming woman dead in her tracks. He heard a loud thud as her body slumped to the ground. As he opened his eyes he could see the handle of the ax in Ayung's hand. His eyes slowly followed the handle upwards until they stopped on the blade that was deeply lodged into her skull. Her eyes were now shut as a steady trickle of a black blood slowly glided down the bridge of her nose. Ayung turned to Jonathan, eyes red and swollen, chest heaving, as he fell into Jonathan's grasp and let out sorrowful moan followed by heavy deep breaths.

"It's okay. buddy, she wasn't herself. The Nateachy that you knew unfortunately died long before now. She's in a better place, I promise you," Jonathan tried to console his friend.

"I know, brother," Ayung answered through sobs. "You think me see her again?" he questioned as he released his grip and straightened himself up wiping the tears away.

"It's called the "other" side, and I am positive that she will be waiting for you when you get there," Jonathan answered reassuringly with a smile.

Appreciating Jonathan's reassuring answer, Ayung nodded his head and began to walk to the front of the tent. "We need find Apoyung," he spoke over his shoulder.

"Agreed, but I need to get some supplies from the back, and unfortunately bandage up Doc Dumbass; even though I would like to see him just bleed, I can't in my right mind allow that to happen," Jonathan said as he stepped over the still body and rushed into the back of the tent. He quickly turned on another electric lantern and filled a bag with syringes, pill bottles (filled with various painkillers), glass bottles for syringe use, and the satellite phone that Gwen kept at her desk. He stopped for a moment, contemplating trying to contact Gwen to tell her what was going on, but he squashed that idea because right now, he really couldn't believe what he had seen, so how would she believe him? He decided that he needed to get to the bottom of this before he alerted her. Before he walked out he grabbed a pack of water bottles that Gwen had behind her desk, and said to himself, *"They won't do anyone any good here. Gwen will understand why I took them,"*

As he finished packing the bag and reached down to zip it up, he began to feel a tremor under his shoes as the ground started to shake. He grabbed the bag and ran out to the front part of the tent where Ayung was standing holding his ax in his hand, looking down at his wife, slowly shaking his head.

"Ayung?!" Jonathan called out to him, snapping him out of his trance. "Did you feel that?"

Ayung quickly jerked his head around the tent, noticing the sensation that Jonathan was talking about. "Ground moving!" he answered.

"Yeah, the ground is moving, but it doesn't feel like another earthquake, this is just a small continuous tremor. Maybe this is an aftershock from the original quake that occurred the other day, although I don't recall reading about aftershocks occurring days after a quake," Jonathan said aloud, trying to understand what was going on.

Suddenly the nighttime air was filled with the shrieking and growling of what seemed like animals.

This can't be a stampede; there are no herding animals in the Amazon. Something is seriously wrong, Jonathan thought to himself before he and Ayung rushed out of the hospital tent. Villagers were exiting their tents looking around and talking to each other as everyone was trying to determine where the noise was coming from and why the earth was shaking.

Suddenly, the jungle erupted as hundreds of native tribesmen and women poured out of the jungle, screaming and shrieking at the tops of their lungs. They savagely attacked the villagers and pulled them to the ground, four and five to one. Jonathan and Ayung, frozen with fear, could only watch as the crazy tribesmen began to tear the villagers apart. They were separating them literally limb from limb as they devoured them in a bloody mass. Some villagers tried to fight back and defend themselves with spears and hand-made axes like the one that Ayung carried with him. With brute force, one of the villagers hacked off an arm from one of the enraged tribesman, only to see that the mortal wound had no effect on him. Stunned, knowing that he could not win, the villager simply dropped the ax where he stood and succumbed to his fate. Two more tribesmen clamped onto his back and took enormous bites out of his shoulder and neck, spewing blood and flesh all over their bodies.

Women and children screamed as their attackers, seemingly fueled by rage, cut them down in a fury. The screams of the children were so loud and shrill they pierced Jonathan and Ayung's heart as all they could do was simply watch in horror. In an attempt to fight off an assailant, one of the villagers grabbed a torch and drove it into the assailant, but it had no effect. The assailant continued to charge after him, and in the process set a few of the tents on fire. Black billowy smoke and terror-filled screams filled the air as the battle raged on.

As the slaughter continued right in front of Jonathan's eyes, he started to notice a horrifying fact about the attackers. Some of them already looked like they had survived a previous attack. One of the attackers was missing the whole right side of his cheek, which seemed to still be oozing black blood, while another one's left arm was barely connected to her body by a few strands of muscular tissue, yet she exhibited no concern or care for this wound. All of the attackers had blood and flesh, splattered across their mouths, and they continued to bite, chew, and pull their victims apart.

Seeing this caused Jonathan to double over and vomit profusely while he was still holding his shotgun and the medical bag. As he looked up, he noticed that all of the attacker's eyes were completely blood red, just like those of Ga, Gabo, and Nateachy right before they tried to attack them.

Ayung was practically speechless as he watched his friends and neighbors slaughtered like livestock. He heard Jonathan scream at him "Who are these people, and why are they trying to destroy your village?"

"Know some!" he answered hesitantly, "but most tribes here peaceful?!." Perplexed by his notion, he realized that the stories he had told Jonathan earlier, concerning the statues in the cave might be true after all. Evil had come to his village, and there was nothing that he could do to stop it!.

"Ayung!" Jonathan exclaimed as he pulled himself up, "Look at their eyes. Gabo and Ga's eyes were the same color before they attempted to attack us,"

"I see this evil... pure evil,"

"I don't know what it is, but we need to get the hell out of here, and I mean like yesterday," Jonathan said hastily, pulling on Ayung's arm in the direction of hospital tent.

"No can leave now. Apoyung still here, need help," Ayung protested stubbornly.

"Fine, let's look quickly and get 'em him the hell outta here. We need to get to Quito, they have an American Embassy there, and I know we'll be safe," Jonathan shouted over the wet sound of flesh being pulled apart.

Ayung yelled for Apoyung at the top of his lungs, and instantly realizes that that was not the best course of action to take. Suddenly a group of crazed tribesmen turned their attention to the two men outside of the medical tent and charged at them with their arms outstretched and hunger stamped in their eyes. Immediately sensing the danger, Ayung took a defensive stance with the ax in his hands while Jonathan was reloading the shotgun. Jonathan aimed the shotgun into the crowd that was running directly towards them, and he unloaded three slugs into the group, separating their upper torsos from their lower torsos. With the attackers neutralized, Ayung frantically scanned the gruesome scenery looking for any sign of his son, but he couldn't find one. He began to yell his son's name at the top of his lungs, again bringing unwanted attention to their way.

Behind both men, they heard what sounded like a dog whining, and as they turned around they realized that Klinefelter was directly behind them, curled up in the fetal position, still clutching his right hand to his chest.

"Listen to me, Doc!" Jonathan said as he purposely kicked the doctor in the shins, hoping that would get him up. "We need you to help us fight these odds and get to Ayung's son," Jonathan ordered.

"You mean to tell me that we are going to sacrifice our own lives for some kid who's probably already dead, instead of getting the smartest doctor in the world to safety? You're insane, Steambuck." Klinefelter sniffled but joined reluctantly.

"APOYUNG!! APOYUNG!" Ayung continued to call at the top of his lungs as the three of them trekked around the tents on the outskirts of the jungle, avoiding the center which was quickly becoming a death zone.

As they circled around the back of the village, an enraged tribesman jumped out of the jungle brush, knocking Jonathan and Klinefelter to the ground. Klinefelter quickly latched onto Jonathan like a child who hasn't seen his mother in a couple of days. This cowardly act hampered Jonathan from using the shotgun as he continued to struggle with the doctor, unable to free his hands.

Ayung and the tribesman started to pace slowly around in a circle sizing up how the other was going to attack. Ayung spun the ax handle around in his hands, helping him to feel loose and ready to handle this problem. His attacker lunged at him, catching him off-guard, forcing him to drop his ax as the two collided and fell to the ground. Ayung pushed the tribesman's chin upward with all of his might as he continued to hear the slamming of his attacker's teeth which were only about two feet away from his face. He screamed for help, but all Jonathan could do was struggle and watch as Klinefelter's grip was still making it hard for him to get back up. Sensing that this was the end and longing to see Nateachy, Ayung began to give up the fight, allowing his attacker's teeth to get closer and closer to his flesh. Just as he was ready to give up completely, he heard a young battle cry and his face was suddenly covered with his attacker's black blood. He quickly threw the body off and he looked up to see his son, Apoyung, standing over him taking deep breaths with a bloody machete in his right hand.

Seeing his son reminded Ayung that he still had something to live for. He reached up and hugged his son tightly. Apoyung started sobbing, telling him that he had seen his friends and their neighbors being eaten by these crazy people.

"Pa-pa, I scared, never see you again!" Apoyung said through tears as his emotions from the previous two days were tapped out.

"I here. I not let anything happen. I promise!" Ayung reassured his son.

"Get the hell off me, you yellow bellied coward," Jonathan shouted harshly to Klinefelter, as he was finally able to get out of the man's death grip. "Is everyone okay?" Heads nodded from Apoyung, Ayung, and Klinefelter, even though his head was nodding reluctantly.

"Well we need to get to Quito some way," Jonathan continued as everyone listened to him. "Ayung, I don't know the way, can you give me good directions on how to get there from here?" Jonathan asked, not realizing that two attackers had honed in on their location.

Ayung quickly pointed to a small clearing behind the hospital tent, and the four of them ran as fast as they could, unaware of the two tracking tribesmen following them.

Following Ayung's point, Jonathan knew they would have to bushwhack through the Jungle to get to Quito. Even though Jonathan loathed bushwhacking, right now he would take a fierce jungle over these attackers. They ran single-file behind the tents, effectively putting them under the radar of the attackers. When the group got to the clearing, Jonathan and Ayung found an old walking path and decided that they would try their luck. As Jonathan and Ayung viciously began cutting through the overgrown path, Jonathan couldn't help but wonder how Gwen was doing. He made himself a promise to call her as soon as he had gotten to safety.

CHAPTER 10
I'M NOT CRAZY...

"This is NAT GEO 501, Alpha Zulu Niner, do you copy Miami air traffic control?" Max questioned into his radio, hailing the controllers from the Miami-Dade County International Airport. Clouds littered the skies above the tip of Florida making it impossible to see the nighttime lights that light up the popular tourist attractions. Knowing that Carlos was on borrowed time, Max had pushed the small jet to the maximum, shaving off about thirty minutes of their flying time from Quito to Miami. His gamble had worked in his favor, but he also needed to make sure that they would have a runway to land on, and that they were not in another plane's flight path.

"NAT GEO 501, we copy. Please state your name and purpose of your flight over," an operator replied in such a robotic way that Max confused them with an automated response line. Realizing that he was crazy for even thinking this, he quickly replied,

"My name is Max Rogers. I'm an employee with National Geographic and I am transporting two employees stateside from Ecuador to the United States. One of them is critically injured and will need immediate medevac to any hospital nearby for injuries sustained from an animal attack. Do you copy?" Max replied into his radio, hoping that they understood the importance of this grave situation that he was in with Russo and Gwen.

"Copy that Roger!" The Controller spoke softly into the transmitter. "You are cleared for landing on runway C-12, that is Charlie One Two. Do you copy?"

"Copy that!" Max replied, expelling a long slow deep breath relieved that they would be able to accommodate a runway for him. He knew that Carlos was now on borrowed time, and even if they got him on the ground and to the hospital, that he may still not have enough time.

The operator replied back with the coordinates for Max, and as he finished programing them into the flight computer, the back of the cockpit exploded open as Russo came running in with perspiration flowing down his colorless face.

"Jesus! Man what happened to you?" Max exclaimed as he looked into his friends eyes.

"Do you have any open wounds on your body?" Russo yelled.

"What are you talking about... open wounds?"

"Do you dammit?!" Russo yelled again.

"No man! For Pete's sake, what the hell is wrong with you?" Max answered, more perturbed than concerned.

"Good!" Russo retorted as he exhaled, while he wiped the sweat from his face. "Sorry for the scare, Max. Gwen and I have feel that whatever Carlos was infected with when the jaguar hit him is contagious and transferred through body fluids, most importantly blood," Russo finished explaining while he was continuing to catch his breath.

"You mean that he is still contagious?" Max questioned as his fear began to build.

"Yes... Well, maybe? I don't know—possibly. But only transferred through body fluids even though it might be a good idea to alert the airport that we have a potential infection on our hands," Russo said, reassuring his friend that he was safe, at least for right now.

"Good idea!" Max said as he hailed the operator again to explain the situation and request additional support.

"Miami-Dade, this is Nat Geo 501 again, with an update on our current situation. Do you copy?"

"We copy Nat Geo, please advise of your update," the robotic operator responded.

"Our critically injured party is potentially contagious. Recommend clean suits for medevac team. Origins of contagion unknown, they will need to proceed with caution. Do you copy that?" Max replied into his radio head set hoping that the operator wouldn't notice the fear in his voice.

"Copy that Nat Geo 501, message has been sent to the team. Proceed with your landing, Operator out."

"Whew, they didn't ask any questions, I guess that's a good thing," Max said aloud to himself, realizing that he, too, was sweating as the situation seemed to go from bad to worse. As he came through the thick clouds he was able to see the lights of the airfield directly ahead, and he thought back to the first time he flew into Miami at night and how the millions of lights made the tip of Florida look like one giant Christmas tree. Knowing that his reverie about Christmas would calm him down, he indulged in these thoughts for a couple of minutes, effectively lowering his stress level. Feeling satisfied that he was in more control of his thoughts and actions he turned on the overhead speakers to alert the others of the impending landing.

"Hey, guys! We're going to be touching down in about seven minutes,

and I have alerted the authorities to Carlos' condition. They will have a medevac team

ready and waiting with clean suits. Buckle up for the leading. It's gonna be hard and

fast; the team will meet us on the runway,"

Russo looked over in the direction of Gwen and Carlos, noticing that Gwen had fallen asleep due to sheer exhaustion. As he got up to wake her, he looked at Carlos whose eyes were open, yet almost fully blood-shot. Wondering if his friend could hear him or at least communicate with him, he gently leaned down closer to Carlos to speak to him.

"Hang in there, buddy! We're gonna get you taken care of, I promise," Russo whispered.

Carlos made no response, he just continued to stare at Russo unblinkingly with his mouth slowly opening and closing as if he was trying to say something, but no audible noise was made. He suddenly jerked forward towards Russo with his mouth wide, only to be pulled back down, the restraints they had used to secure him made it hard for him to move, let alone hurt himself. Startled by the reaction, Russo fell back up against the back of the row in front of him. He continued to watch his friend in shock as Carlos struggled mightily against his bonds, yet never taking his eyes away from Russo. Russo 's stare continued until Carlos unexpectedly allowed his eyes to roll into the back of his head as he slowly shut them. Confused, Russo looked around and behind him, where he noticed Gwen pulling the syringe out of Carlos' make shift IV and placing it back in her bag. She looked groggy and overexerted, yet she continued to try to keep his friend alive and in as little pain as possible. Her clothes and skin were stained with dried blood and a dirt sweat mixture that which made a grime color, and yet with all of the filth that covered her body, it still couldn't hide the fact that she was a very attractive woman, one whom Russo couldn't stop staring at.

She sat down on the floor of the plane, took her Red Sox hat off, and tried her best to straighten out her greasy hair. After fiddling with it for a few seconds and accepting defeat, she pulled her auburn hair back into a ponytail and put her hat back on with a heavy sigh and a look of disgust written across her face.

"You know I always thought that if a girl looked good with a baseball hat on, then she would look good in anything," Russo said with a sly grin on his face as he attempted to make her smile with his cheesy line.

"Thanks," Gwen replied with a half-hearted laugh, feeling somewhat better and slightly flattered by the line. "You know I never fancied myself as the good looking type. I mean I knew I wasn't ugly, but I never thought that guys would consider me attractive, mainly because I knew I was always smarter than them, and most guys find that intimidating," she continued as she picked herself off of the floor and sat in a chair, adjusting the seatbelt preparation for the landing.

"Hah!" Russo said with a smirk, "I never considered myself smart, so I have nothing to be intimidated by nor jealous of."

"Well, I guess, I will need to figure out a new category to put you in ... Hmmm, how about arrogance?" She picked at him with a quick wink.

"I can handle that!" Russo picked back, feeling confident. "Seriously, I really want to thank you for all of your help today with Carlos. You know a lot of people wouldn't have tried to help, especially if they felt that there was a risk of infection. Most people would have run away. It means a lot to me that you stayed and tried to help my friend. I appreciate it, and I know deep down inside he does as well. I owe you one," Russo said as he stared at his friend who seemed to be still fighting for his life.

"No problem, that's why I got into medicine in the first place," she replied with a gracious smile.

"Hey, guys. We will be on the ground in about four minutes, get yourselves secure, and be ready for a quick departure. I can already see the ambulance lights ahead of us on the runway. Russo, as soon as we land and come to a complete stop I want you to open the emergency exit door and pull the cord in the door shaft to inflate the air slide. That will be the quickest way to get Carlos off the plane. I have alerted the ambulance to our intentions, and they will meet you and Carlos at the bottom. Good Luck!" Max's voice boomed over the speakers as Russo and Gwen felt their stomachs rise into their throats as Max brought the plane down towards the runway.

Max landed the plane with very little complications, and as it came to a complete stop Russo yanked off the emergency exit door and pulled the cord, inflating the air slide as the two EMT's jumped out of the ambulance and ran to assist at the bottom of the slide.

"I'll go first, and I will help them catch him as he comes down the slide!" Gwen hollered to Russo over the sound of the jet engines cooling down. Russo acknowledged with a quick shake of the head as he turned to pick his buddy up off of the chairs that he was haphazardly laying across. He disconnected the make shift IV bag, leaving the IV, so the EMT's wouldn't have to waste time setting up a new one. He ensured that Carlos' arms and legs were still strapped, and he couldn't flail about as he went down the slide. All of the moving woke Carlos up out of his drug-induced sleep, and he began to violently thrash about. His mouth continued to snap as his body convulsed in seizures; Russo finally picked him up and carried him to the exit door.

As Gwen exited down the evacuation slide, the two EMT's met her at the bottom and helped her to her feet. Both men were in their early thirties, and they had on the generic EMT pants with white short-sleeved button down shirts with the words "Dade County: Fire and Rescue" embroidered over their left chest pocket. They both sported the traditional military haircut, were clean-shaven, and wore heavy-duty boots and protective gloves. The taller one reached down to give Gwen a hand and help her off of the slide.

"Name's Tim, ma'am!" Tim shouted over the sound of the jet engine. "This here's Ivan!" Tim shouted as he pointed to the other EMT who gave a quick nod in Gwen's direction before looking up towards the emergency exit of the plane where he saw Russo gently place Carlos on the top of the slide.

"We're here to help you get your injured party to the hospital. Can you give me a quick rundown of what happened to him? I need to know what I am dealing with," Tim continued as Ivan motioned for Russo to let Carlos go.

"I thought you guys would be in your clean suits!" she shouted back to Tim.

"We don't need 'em! We both are up to date with our shots; besides those things are too damn hot this time of the year," Tim replied back as he joined Ivan at the bottom of the slide to catch Carlos.

"I understand Tim, but you don't know what you are dealing with here. I can't confirm whether or not he is still contagious," Gwen pleaded desperately with Tim.

"Trust me, ma'am, we got this under control," Tim replied back, abruptly ending the conversation as he yelled up to Russo, "Let him go! We got him!"

Hearing the confirmation that he needed, Russo gently let go of Carlos' shoulders, and the big man quickly zipped down the ramp into the arms of the two EMT's. Within mere minutes, Tim and Ivan had Carlos strapped down on a gurney and loaded into the back of the ambulance. Once Carlos was secured, Ivan jumped into the back and began to check the vitals and administer medicine and fluids through the IV.

"So you're telling me that he was attacked by a Jaguar? And that this jaguar was sick with something and you think that this sickness was transferred to this man. Have I got this correct?" Tim asked both Russo and Gwen in disbelief.

"Yes, Tim, I know it sounds crazy, but I have practiced medicine for a couple of years now, and I have never seen an animal bite have this type of effect on a person, but I am telling you that something is drastically wrong with this situation. A boy in the Huaorani tribe was bitten by a spider, and he exhibited the same symptoms before we had to leave the tribe. Whatever bit him must have somehow attacked a Jaguar and transferred this infection to the jaguar, and I fear that the jaguar has infected this man with the same virus," Gwen explained to Tim as she was subconsciously trying to convince herself that she wasn't going crazy.

Tim stood at the back of the ambulance and just stared in disbelief to what he was hearing from Gwen. Never in his life had he even heard of what she was talking about, but the conviction in her voice perplexed him so much that he began to believe what she was saying was true. As he continued to stare into her deep blue eyes, something told him that she was telling the truth so he tentatively chose to believe her, at least until she could be proven wrong.

"Alright, ma'am, that's ... what ... I'll tell them; they'll probably throw me in the loony bin, but I will be sure to explain everything you told me," Tim tried to reassure Gwen as he turned and slammed the back doors shut. "Listen, we are heading to Miami Med. It's a private hospital close to the airport. We have already alerted them to our situation, and they are ready to take him in at the emergency room. I figured you guys will want to follow us, so if you got transportation get ready, be sure to stay close with your hazards on," Tim instructed as he walked to the front of the ambulance and climbed in to the cab.

"One other thing." Tim said before he shut the door, "We're going to take care of him, he's going to be alright."

"Thanks, Tim!" Russo said as he shook Tim's outstretched hand.

"Thank you for believing me Tim," Gwen replied with a heavy sigh.

"Yep yep," Tim said before he shut the door and hit the sirens.

"Russo, do you have any transportation here at the airport? I know that I don't, so we might have to get a taxi or see about renting a car," Gwen said as she began to feel more energized with the hope that they might have gotten Carlos to a hospital in time.

"Nope, I don't have anything here, but I can call the Magazine and see if they can get me a rental ASAP; that is about the best that I can ..," Russo replied before being cut off by the sound of a car horn blaring loudly behind him. Alarmed by the noise, he and Gwen turned around to see Max jumping out of a Silver Dodge Dakota crew cab with a grill guard with four extra halogen lights lighting up the road for a good two miles. They shielded their eyes as they walked to the driver side where Max is standing with a crafty grin plastered across his face.

"Bambi, here is my pride and joy!" Max said as he tossed the keys to Russo. "She'll tell me if you get a scratch on her, or if you don't treat her respectfully. You know she gets very emotional when people don't talk nice to her,"

"Max, I don't know what to say," Russo said as he laughed and shook his head. "I'll be sure to take care of her and give her a good bath once this is all over with. I owe you yet another one good buddy. You coming to the hospital?" Russo asked as he and Gwen hop into the truck.

"Not yet, Rus! I'm gonna check in with HQ and advise them of what is going on. I am pretty sure they will want to be kept informed as the night goes on. Once I have debriefed them on what happened, I'll head over," Max answered as he shut the driver's side door.

"Hey, Max?" Gwen called out.

"Yea?"

"Can you be sure to get our stuff from the plane and bring it with you when you come? I have my notes and research in there, and I want to make sure that the doctor's that are working on Carlos have all of the information in front of them," she said.

"Not necessary! I already packed your gear in the back of the cab behind your seats," he answered with a quick wink.

"Thanks, Max!" she replied.

"We'll see you there, buddy!" Russo said as he dropped "Bambi" into gear and sped off behind the ambulance.

Tim steered the ambulance out of the airport, onto the interstate, and throttled the gas, forcing the diesel engine to roar as they blazed a trail down the road. He checked his rear-view mirror, and he saw Russo and Gwen behind him in a Silver truck with their hazards on, weaving in and out of traffic only about fifty feet behind him. As the adrenaline began to pump through Tim's body he remembered how this part of the job was always his favorite. Everyone on the road got out to the way, and he was able to go as fast as he wanted with no fear of getting in trouble. He secretly wished that his personal car had a siren and lights, that way he would never be late for anything and everyone would get out of his way. He knew it was selfish to wish for this, but the thrill of having the highway all to himself always was stronger than the selfishness he seldom felt.

He reached down, detached his radio from its holder in the truck, and radioed ahead to the hospital that they were in route, and the estimated ETA was about fifteen minutes. Once he received confirmation he switched on his closed circuit radio and checked on Ivan in the back with the patient.

"Hey, Ivan. How's he doing back there?"

"Bad man, real bad. I've never seen an attack like this one before," Ivan responded.

"Talk to me man, tell me what you see," Tim advised, his curiosity getting the better of him.

"Well, for starters his eyes are fully red. I can't even make out a distinctive pupil; it's almost like he doesn't have one. Also his eyes have these small black spots all over them. I have opened his shirt, and I can see where the animal attacked him, but it's really weird looking,"

"Ivan, please be more descriptive—weird looking doesn't help me. What does his chest look like?" Tim replied back, slightly agitated in the vagueness of Ivan's description.

"Alright, he has three parallel gashes across his chest originating from directly below his left shoulder and ending above his right hip. These gashes have been crudely stitched up to stop the blood flow. It's almost as if the blood doesn't contain any oxygen, because it is very dark and viscous. Another thing that I notice is the fact that his blood isn't clotting. Do we know if he is a hemophiliac?" Ivan asked in the middle of his description.

"I don't know if he is or isn't, they didn't mention anything about it when we took him in. Please continue with your description, Ivan, and this time do it without any more interruptions. Time is of the essence," Tim answered with a hint of impatience in his voice.

Sensing that his boss was getting impatient, Ivan quickly got back to his description of Carlos' body, "Dark blood is continuing to seep out of these wounds, but its consistency is very thick, unlike the normal watery consistency of blood. Surrounding all of the gashes in his chest are weblike trails under his skin. The tips of these strands are bright red, but they shade into a darker red color the closer that they get to the original gash. His wounds are also oozing a white pus. His forehead shows signs of perspiration, yet when you touch his body, his skin is ice cold. He is definitely suffering from some type of an infection, but I ain't ever seen anything like this before. Have you boss?" Ivan asked as he concluded his brief examination.

"No, Ivan, I can't say that I have," Tim answered, completely astonished by Ivan's examination of the body. "I am going to alert the ER to what we are bringing in. Hopefully, they will know what we are dealing with. Do me a favor, I want you to check his blood pressure and his pulse, and make sure you mark it down legibly on his file sheet, I don't want another call from an ER nurse telling me that they can't read your damn handwriting," Tim chuckled to himself as he remembered his first time in the back with a critical patient and how his hands were trembling as he was trying to complete the patients file. The first report any EMT makes is usually the hardest, it's almost like a rite of passage, only for Ivan, his handwriting hadn't gotten any better.

"You got it, boss!" Ivan replied back. He reached into one of the overhead compartments, pulled out a sphygmomanometer, and attached it to Carlos' arm. He hit the button on top of the device, and the cuff slowly inflated on his arm. As the device was constricting the arm, Ivan thought back to all the times he was a kid in the pharmacy store with his mother and begging to put his arm in the free BPM game, and the crazy noise that it made. The device beeped twice, letting him know that the measurements had been obtained. He leaned over the arm and tilted it slightly upward so he could read the digital screen. The readings came back as zero over zero. Perplexed, Ivan hit the button again for it to redo the test, and had convinced himself that the device had to be malfunctioning because the patient was clearly not dead; his eyes were open and he was watching him intently. The machine had to just be malfunctioning, had to be. The machine beeped twice again, and he looked down to see that the readings hadn't changed at all. Ivan leaned back, utterly confused at what he was witnessing, but still chalked it up to the fact that the device was most likely broken. He searched the back of the ambulance, but that was the only sphygmomanometer they had with them.

"Oh, well, I will have to note that on my report so the ER staff will be sure to get it once we get him there," Ivan said aloud as he reached for his stethoscope and began to listen to the patient's breathing. He placed the scope on the chest to right of the large gash marks and listened intently. Tiny droplets of sweat began to appear on his forehead as he could feel his shirt start to cling to his back. Before he realized it, his whole body was sweating, and he knew why he was beginning to panic. He couldn't hear the patient breathe. He sat back and stared at the patient's chest and suddenly he became alarmed at the fact that it wasn't rising and falling like a normal living patients would. He watched the patient's chest for about three minutes and never saw it move. His eyes slowly crept upwards towards the head, where he stared in disbelief at two fully red eyes staring right back at him. The patient's mouth slowly opened and closed repeatedly, yet he couldn't hear him talk.

"This is fucking impossible. There is no way this guy can be alive, yet not be breathing nor have any blood pressure," Ivan shouted as he erratically checked the arm for a pulse on the patient's arm. He checked both arms, but was unable to find any semblance of a pulse. He yanked his arm back from the body and sat dumbfounded in the back of the ambulance with a forlorn look etched into his face.

There is no way that this man cannot be breathing, have no blood pressure, nor a fucking pulse yet his eyes are still open and his mouth is still moving. There is absolutely no way in hell. Get a grip on yourself, Ivan; don't go crazy, Ivan said over and over to himself attempting to calm his nerves. He suddenly jumped in shock as Tim's voice boomed in his ear across the radio.

"Ivan, did you get his vital statistics yet?" Tim questioned.

"Ahh, yeah, I guess," Ivan stuttered.

"What do you mean you guess?? You either did or you didn't, now which one is it!"

"Listen to me boss, I checked everything, but there is just one problem,"

"And that is?"

"He's got no blood pressure, no pulse, and he's not breathing at all,"

"Ivan, is he dead?" Tim asked calmly, realizing that his partner was beginning to lose it under pressure.

"I don't know boss, I don't think so, but I can't really tell," Ivan whispered into the radio as his voice was still quivering with what he had just told Tim.

"Ivan, it's very simple. If he doesn't have a pulse, then the man is dead. Plain and simple. You should know that."

"Yeah, your right, I should, but when a man doesn't have a pulse and he isn't breathing but his DAMN EYES ARE OPEN AND HIS MOUTH IS MOVING WHILE HE IS STARING AT ME, IT'S KINDA HARD TO DETERMINE IF HE'S DEAD OR NOT!" Ivan screamed back into the radio as he began to take long slow breaths quelling his anger for being talked to like he was a child.

"What do mean his eyes are open, and his mouth is still moving? I thought you said he had no pulse," Tim questioned with a slight shrill tone in his voice.

"Exactly what I said Tim!" Ivan retorted.

"Alright, alright, alright, let's both calm down, there has got to be some reasonable explanation, and when we get to the ER they will help us out. Let's not lose our heads over this. I apologize for being condescending towards you," Tim sheepishly replied.

"That's fine," Ivan replied back as he continued to stare at the dead— yet alive— man in the back of the ambulance. Ivan noticed that as his mouth was slowly opening that the space between his lower jaw and his lower lip was swollen, as if something was in between. Ivan leaned in closer for a better look, but he was unable to determine what the object was.

"Hey, Tim?" Ivan radioed.

"Yea, what's up?"

"Listen there seems to be some type of foreign object in between his lower lip and his lower jaw. I am going to check it out."

"Alright, Ivan but be careful, the two that dropped him off feared that he was contagious," Tim cautioned.

"I will," Ivan replied back as he steadied his hands. He grabbed a hold of the lower jaw of the man, who moaned in pain at his touch.

"Sorry fellow, I need to see what that is," Ivan answered the moan. With a firm grip on the lower jaw he prevented the man from closing his mouth again with the voluntary action that he had been exhibiting during the ride to the hospital. With his other hand Ivan slowly reached into the man's mouth with his thumb and index finger in a pinching motion to dislodge the object. The moment that his fingers touch the lower jaw the man's teeth snapped forward with unexpected force tearing a hole in Ivan's glove and separating a piece of flesh from his index finger.

"Son of a bitch!" Ivan screamed out in pain as blood squirted all over the man's man and on Ivan's uniform. He yanked his finger back, quickly covered it with his other hand, and immediately applied pressure, trying to stop the blood flow. He instinctively reached behind him for a can of disinfectant and some gauze. He sprayed his hand and gritted his teeth through the searing pain in the open wound. After he finished spraying his finger, he wrapped it in gauze, and taped the gauze tightly to his finger. Feeling satisfied that he properly bandaged his finger, he grabbed a set of tweezers from his back and gripped the man's mouth again with more force than before. He angled his jaw outward and used the tweezers to pull the object out. The object came freely out of the man's mouth and Ivan stared at it in disbelief. The object was lightly colored pink and was caked in the slimy dark blood that was all over the man's body. As he continued to stare at the object, his radio beeped with Tim asking what he had found.

"It's part of his tongue!" Ivan answered.

"Did you just say part of his tongue?" Tim questioned.

"Yep, the bastard had bitten off a piece of his own tongue," Ivan said stoically.

"Holy Shit!" Tim exclaimed. "Why were you screaming back there a minute ago?"

"The bastard bit me."

"You okay?"

"Yeah, I'm fine I got it under control, just a small flesh wound; no need to worry about it,"

"I still think you need to get that checked out, I mean you don't want to become infected with whatever he has," Tim urged.

"Nah, I am up to date on my shots; if it gets worse in the morning I will stop by an urgent care on my way out of town," Ivan answered.

"Oh, yeah, that's right, you're going where again?" Tim asked, trying to lighten the mood.

"I got two weeks of vacation coming to me, and I hope to be in Greece sampling their fine cuisine of topless beaches!" Ivan replied back with a large grin plastered across his face. "Let's just drop this headcase off at the ER, give 'em our reports, and get the hell away from this guy. He's beginning to give me the creeps."

"I agree, something is seriously wrong with him, and I really don't want to sit around and find out what," Tim spoke back into the radio as he exited off of the interstate heading towards the gigantic hospital, Miami Med. It's high level, all glass penthouse suites could be seen miles away from the hospital. An eyesore to the locals, but a symbol of money to those who have it.

CHAPTER 11
THIS JUNGLE HAS EYES

The electric lanterns casts auras around Jonathan and Ayung as they continued to hack away at the dense jungle foliage that had grown over and all around the long abandoned walking path. The thick overhead jungle canopy made it virtually pitch black in the jungle as the moonlight was unable to pierce its way through. It had been well over two hours since the group had escaped the ravaging horde of crazed tribesmen, yet they had made very little headway into the jungle as bushwhacking at night proved to be more dangerous and time consuming than they had originally planned. Insects constantly tormented the group with their constant buzzing sound and continuous needling of the flesh with their stingers and teeth. With every new branch that Jonathan's and Ayung cut down, a flood of indigenous wildlife scampered away as giant beetles, small birds, hordes of insects, and extremely long snakes dispersed. With each new species that Jonathan encountered a small shiver ran down his spine as he realized that he was never cut out for "roughing it." He longed for his own bed in his air-conditioned house with his sports channels and an ice-cold beer, but he had to quickly come to the realization that he was a long way from home, and there weren't any ruby slippers that could instantly bring him home.

The night air was hot and humid, and it whisked away their energy faster than an ice cube melting in the Sahara Desert. The group came upon a large tree with a base twice the size a midsize SUV and decided that it would be a good place to rest for a few minutes to allow everyone a chance to catch their breath. Jonathan took out two water bottles, kept one for himself and Klinefelter, and tossed the other one to Ayung and Apoyung.

"Thank you, brother!" Ayung replied as he twisted the top off and gave it to his son for him to drink first. "Apoyung don't drink too much or fast, it make you feel bad and your stomach will ache," he instructed his son who nodded slowly and took short quick sips from the bottle before he returned it to his father.

Jonathan uncapped his bottle and held it in the direction of the ailing doctor who greedily yanked it out of his hands and purposefully drank half of the bottle.

"Easy Doc!" Jonathan's voice rang out. He was visibly upset with the way that Klinefelter was not properly rationing the water. There was only six bottles in the pack, and they had to last them to Quito which Jonathan knew was a good two-day hike through an easy path; there was no telling how long it would take them if they had to bushwhack the whole way.

"Easy my ass!" Klinefelter snapped as he began coughing violently. He was able to regain his composure after his coughing fit, and he glared at Jonathan with blood-shot eyes, and snapped, "Do you know who I am? I am a world-renowned doctor of medicine, and quite frankly my life means more to the world then all three of yours. I am destined to save people's lives!"

"By killing others," Jonathan smirked.

"If that means that I can live, then so be it!" Klinefelter snapped back in a jealous rage.

"It's okay, Jonathan, Apoyung and I will share with you," Ayung said as he sent a piercing gaze towards Klinefelter. He handed over the bottle, and Jonathan took two large gulps before capping it and putting it back in his bag. He knew in the back of his mind that everyone's water usage would have to lessen each time if they were going to make it.

"Alright asshole, take one more swig, and hand it over. I'll keep it in my bag," Jonathan said as he gestured with his hand towards Klinefelter. Naturally Klinefelter pulled the bottle away from Jonathan's outstretched hand and snarled at them. "Oh hell no, I know how this goes. You're going to keep it for yourselves, and the old doctor, isn't going to get any more, because only the young and the strong survive. I'll prove you all wrong. I've survived worse than this," Klinefelter put the bottle up to his mouth and began to drink more of the refreshing liquid.

"Listen to yourself!" Jonathan yelled. "Just what in the hell are you talking about, only the young and strong survive. What kind of bullshit is that anyway? You're a doctor for fuck's sake! You should start acting like one, you self-righteous bastard!" The words spewed out of Jonathan's mouth like venom as he began to feel his adrenaline pumping again, ready for a fight this time.

Realizing that he had riled the young man, Klinefelter quietly put the cap back on the bottle as he smirked at Jonathan, "Looks like our fearless leader can't control himself, let alone our little band of misfits,"

Playing into Klinefelter's childish game Jonathan pitched forward grabbing for the doctor, only to be intercepted by Ayung who calmly yet sternly whispered into his ear that he wasn't worth it. Jonathan struggled for a bit, still enticed by the accusations the doctor had made, but eventually he succumbed to his senses, realizing the game that Klinefelter was playing. After a moment Ayung let him go, and Jonathan gently patted Ayung on the back and said perhaps louder than he should have, "You're right my friend, he ain't worth it!"

Klinefelter snorted at the comment and shook his head while he continued to nurse his bottle of water.

"Hey, Doc?" Jonathan yelled out.

"What!" Klinefelter sniveled as some of his precious water dribbled down his chin.

"What exactly did you mean by you have been through worse? I mean, I don't know about you, but seeing human's attack and EAT other humans is some pretty bad stuff. I can't think of anything else that would be worse than that," Jonathan stated, interested in his response and hoping that the man might be able to shed some light on the situation; perhaps he had witnessed this before in the medical world, and they had a scientific name for it or something. Unfortunately, in the back of Jonathan's mind he already knew the doctor's answer, but he had to try.

"Heathens... They're just plan heathens. Hell, most of these tribes practice cannibalism anyway!" Klinefelter retorted.

"That not true. My people are peaceful. We not want to hurt anyone," Ayung spoke up in defense.

"Whatever, heathen man. I bet you're just waiting for the right moment for you and your mangy little kid to pounce on us and have us for dinner. Heathen!" Klinefelter rasped as he glared at both Ayung and Apoyung with vengeance.

"The Tagaeri no longer exist!" Ayung spoke solemnly as he stared back at Klinefelter.

"Probably 'cause you ate them!" Klinefelter mumbled under his breath as he lifted the bottle to his lips again for another drink of the water. Suddenly he started choking and fell down to his knees where he continued to have cough violently which quickly turned to gargled dry heaves, before he vomited blood onto the ground below him. The normally bright red substance was darker than before, yet in the glow of the electric lantern it looked like black ink. After a few moments Klinefelter stopped the coughing and wheezing, he wiped his mouth with the back of his forearm, and as he pulled his forearm away, he froze at the color of the liquid on his forearm.

Very carefully as if not to startle, Jonathan leaned down close to Klinefelter and gently whispered, "Doc, can I see your hand where Nateachy bit you,"

Startled, Klinefelter shot up off of the ground and backed away from the group, "WHY?!" he yelled out.

"Because you're beginning to show the same signs that Gabo showed after he had been bitten by that spider," Jonathan's answered calmly with his palms up in the air, trying to show Klinefelter that he meant no harm by his reply.

"I am fucking fine; I am not sick like that heathen child was," Klinefelter retorted quickly and abrasively.

Not moving, and with his palms still raised, Jonathan calmly replied, "Alright, if you are, then I just want to take a look at that hand and bandage it up properly. We can't have you getting it infected."

"I'm fine! Besides, who has more medical experience, me or you? That's right I do," Klinefelter snapped. "Let's just keep moving fearless leader, we need to get to Quito. They will need my knowledge there."

"I agree, Jonathan, we need to keep moving. I keep feeling like I should look behind us with every step. I fear that we are still in danger," Ayung said without looking at Jonathan as he kept his eyes affixed on the way that they had already come.

"Agreed. Let's keep going; I think the path leads this way," Jonathan said as he pointed northwest with his machete. The group continued to bushwhack their way through the jungle, the lanterns giving off an eerie glow in the jungle darkness.

Unbeknown to the group, this eerie glow was quickly becoming a beacon for their pursuers to follow as the two crazed tribesmen continued to stalk their prey through the jungle, their dark gray colored flesh, dark dried blood covering their mouths, and hands acting as a camouflage in the dark jungle atmosphere. As the group's arguments continued and the louder they got, the two tribesmen quickened their pace, and once the group was in sight, they broke out in a sprint towards them, howling a bloodcurdling scream into the night air.

Hearing the scream, Jonathan and Ayung spun on their heels; they knew what was coming next.

"They must've followed us from the village," Jonathan whispered as his hands tightened around the stock of his shotgun. Ayung made no audible reply, he just slightly shook his head as his knuckles began to turn white under the pressure that he was putting on his ax.

The leaves and branches from where they had traveled began to rustle violently as the heard another howl from one of the beasts. Jonathan raised the shotgun up and aimed it down the path from where the noise was coming, slid his finger down, and rested it on the trigger. He took a long slow breath as he squinted one eye and took aim in the direction of the noise, then suddenly everything stopped moving, and no noise could be heard except the beating of his own heart. Perplexed, he and Ayung looked around as everything in the jungle seemed to freeze. The creatures had stopped making any sound, making it impossible to pinpoint their location. He lowered his shotgun and tried squinting his eyes in an attempt to see through the night, but he was unable to make out any shapes.

In a flash the brush beside him exploded as one of the tribesmen leaped into the path, effectively knocking Jonathan into Ayung and putting them both on the ground. The blood-crazed tribesmen glared at both men with black eyes, his mouth filled with dark blood and sinewy flesh still clinging to some of his teeth. He growled at both men before diving on the ground after them. Jonathan was able to scramble back to his feet, but before Ayung could get off of the ground, the tribesman had him by the ankles and was furiously pulling his ankles to his gaping maw as his teeth continued to slam against each other in anticipation of the impending meal. Ayung screamed as he kicked his feet madly at the tribesman trying to throw his grip off, but the tribesmen maintained his hold and continued to pull Ayung across the ground with unearthly strength.

"SHOOT IT!" Ayung screamed at the top of his lungs as he felt the hands move higher up towards his shins.

Jonathan frantically pulled the shotgun up and took aim at the tribesman's head where he noticed a small patch of his skull was missing, and he could see the crazed man's brain. Realizing that if he shot the man this close, he would injure Ayung as well, with the buck shot, he quickly looked around on the ground for anything he could still see in the light glow. He saw Ayung's ax lying beside him, and he instinctively yanked it off of the ground, and with a violent thrust he slammed it into the hole in the skull, instantly making a larger hole. The sickening crunch and syrupy slosh of crushed brain matter ended the crazed man's rage, and his head fell in between Ayung's shins.

With his feet free, Ayung kicked the corpse repeatedly while sliding himself back away from the puddle of dark red blood that was forming below the man's mouth. With his chest still heaving, he reached up for Jonathan's outstretched hand and jumped to his feet. Jonathan handed him his ax, and he quickly rubbed the bloody end of it off in the dirt.

"Thank you, Jonathan, you have returned the favor of saving my life," Ayung said through broken breaths as he tried to regain his composure.

"Don't mention it. Something is seriously wrong, though. I mean, that man was missing part of his skull before I killed him. He should've already been dead. No one can take that type of damage to the skull and live," Jonathan replied as he looked down at the corpse that was giving off a horrible rotting smell.

"And that smell, that is not the smell of a living person, I can tell you that," Jonathan continued as he rolled the corpse over with his shotgun. He leaned down to inspect its wounds closer. As he and Ayung continued to stare at the corpse, they abruptly heard another growl come from where Klinefelter and Apoyung had retreated to during the first encounter.

Another crazed tribesman was slowly walking towards the child and the doctor with the same rage colored eyes and open mouth. This guy looked worse than the other. His right arm had been severed below the shoulder, and his left eye was missing. His body was covered in dark red blood, yet it seemed like these injuries were superficial to him.

"Oh, no you don't, you damn heathen!" Klinefelter hollered at the tribesman. He reached down, grabbed Apoyung by the shoulders, and pulled him in front of him almost like a human shield. "You'll get this boy before you get me, I can promise you that," Klinefelter continued to holler at the beast as Apoyung struggled under the doctor's vice like grip.

The tribesman lowered his head and hunkered his shoulders before growling at them both. His knees slowly bent as he prepared to leap at them from his stance. Fear took Klinefelter over as he cowardly pushed the boy forward to intercept the attack as he ran behind the trees to hide. Apoyung slid to the ground on his knees and pulled his arms up in an attempt to defend himself from his attacker. The last thing he saw was the tribesman's feet leave the ground before he slammed his eyes tightly shut and screamed for help. He suddenly heard a loud thud as something big hit the ground beside him. Very carefully he slowly opened one of his eyes, and as his vision cleared, he noticed the tribesman was on the ground and not moving. He quickly opened the other eye and got up to run before he noticed his dad's ax handle standing erect from the middle of the man's skull. The blade had sunk into his skull a good three inches. He turned around to see his father still in his release position with his left foot staggered forward and his right arm still pointing in the direction of the now dead tribesman.

"Pa-Pa!" he yelled as he ran to his father's open embrace and hugged him so hard that he felt his father strain from the pressure.

"You saved my life, and I will continue to save yours as long as I live!" Ayung quietly whispered as he tilted his head down and kissed his son on the head.

"Good work Ayung, I never knew you could throw and ax like that, but trust me, I am glad I know it now," Jonathan chided him as he looked in the direction of where the cowardly doctor had run.

"Hey, chicken shit, you can come out now, the bad people are gone," Jonathan yelled. He wanted the doctor to think that everything would be okay and let his guard down, that way he could slug him one for using a poor defenseless child as a shield to save his sorry ass.

"I... I... ah ... didn't mean to do it th ... that way. I was trying to pull the kid along with me, but he wouldn't budge. I... I ... I ... tried," Klinefelter stammered as he came from around the back of the tree, still cradling his injured hand. He walked carefully around the trunk of the tree, staring at the ground to ensure that he didn't trip over any of the roots or branches laying around, completely unaware of the small coral snake that was hanging off of the tree waiting for its next dinner.

Jonathan saw the snake before Klinefelter did, and he began to try to tell Klinefelter to stop where he was, but Klinefelter wouldn't hear it.

"But Doc, you need to...!" Jonathan's tried again to no avail.

"I need to do what, to apologize to the kid? Well, I am sorry, but that just ain't going to happen," Klinefelter replied defiantly as he continued on his path. As he walked underneath the snake, it fell from the branch and landed on the back of his neck where it quickly tried to slither away. Klinefelter reached up quickly and tried to grab it before it bit him. As he grabbed the middle of its body, it jerked back and sunk its fangs into the top of his good hand.

"OWWW! Sonofabitch!" Klinefelter yelled as he tossed the snake to the ground, where it rapidly slithered away.

"Holy shit that hurt. What the hell type of snake was that?" Klinefelter questioned out loud.

"Doc ..," Jonathan hesitated "that was a coral snake. I could tell from the orange and black stripes with the small white bands."

"Coral ..." Klinefelter let the word roll of his tongue as it sunk in, "Holy shit, that is one the most poisonous snakes in the world. You fucking bastard snake!" he shouted at the top of his lungs.

"Listen, doc, just sit down; let me see if I can find something from Gwen's medical supplies that will help," Jonathan said as he yanked off his pack and began to rummage through it, trying to find something that would help.

"There is no time, you dumbass!" Klinefelter snapped at Jonathan as his right arm went numb. His whole body started to convulse as he went into seizures that were so violent that he accidentally bit off the top of his own tongue. He fell to the ground and continued to shake for about a minute before he screamed in pain; he threw his head back as his heart suddenly stopped working.

Jonathan walked over to him and knelt down to close his eyes. As he leaned over the doctor, he heard Ayung's voice in the background.

"Hey man, don't forget that he has been bitten as well, and we know what happens to people when they have been bitten."

"That's right, he is still possibly infected," Jonathan said as he quickly stood up from the body. He pulled his shotgun out and aimed it at the dead doctor's head, waiting to see if he would come back to life. Nothing happened at first, but just as soon as Jonathan was getting ready to lower his weapon, Klinefelter's eyes popped open. They were completely red with little black dots all over, just like Gabo's. Klinefelter's corpse turned his head to face Jonathan and opened its mouth as if it were trying to say something before its head was replaced by a buckshot. Jonathan pulled the smoking barrel back away from the twice-dead corpse and walked over to join Ayung and Apoyung.

"I know that you're both tired and you want some sleep, but I really feel that we need to keep going, because I fear that encounters like we just had are going to be more frequent," Jonathan said as he rejoined Ayung and Apoyung.

"I agree!" Ayung answered as he followed Jonathan down the North Westwardly path."

"Me too," Apoyung piped up as he joined his father and Jonathan as they continued to blaze a trail through the thick jungle.

CHAPTER 12
WELCOME TO MIAMI, POPULATION SOON TO BE EATEN

Miami Med was a state of the art hospital with all of the expensive trimmings; nothing was spared in constructing this monumental giant healthcare facility. Like most modern day hospitals, the first floor consisted of the administrative offices, patient check -in, cafeteria, and an emergency room capable of handling over fifty patients at once. The next five floors consisted of over-sized plush patient rooms which sported queen size hospital beds, 40" plasma screens, colossal leather sleeper sofas, and an ornate business desk with matching credenza. In the back corner of each room was a separate bathroom with a Jacuzzi tub and walk-in shower accompanying a granite countered vanity with a mammoth mirror. The next two floors consisted of the doctor's offices with a central lounge and multiple leather chairs and sofas surrounded by a plethora of flat screen monitors. Each doctor's office was on the outer side of the floor with at least one wall of floor to ceiling windows. Elevators with access to the first eight floors were located in the middle of these floors allowing doctor's access to all of the patient's floors. The two floors that were dedicated to the doctor's offices required an electronic badge verification in each elevator. On the backside of the doctor's lounge was another set of elevator doors that went up to the senior management and the board of director's offices, as well as the luxury suites and the penthouse. In order to access this elevator shaft, a separate electronic badge was required. Directly across from the VIP elevator shaft was a stairwell which also required the same electronic badge to gain access.

Miami Med was privately owned and functioned as the hospital for the rich, wealthy, and famous. If your pockets weren't deep, then the administrative staff had no problems turning patients away, no matter how badly they needed medical attention. The hardly ever full capacity hospital entertained regulars from politicians to movie stars and sports celebrities, basically anyone who had money was allowed to be sick at Miami Med.

Tim killed the sirens on the ambulance as he turned into the complex lighting up the night sky with the flashing lights that created dancing shadows on the edifice of the building. As he pulled up to the emergency room docking station he was flagged down by a heavyset security officer. With his flash light the security officer stepped up on the running boards of the vehicle and rapped on the driver's side window. Tim obliged by quickly rolling down the window.

"State your name and your patient's affiliation to proceed!" ordered the security officer in a gruff tone.

"Ah, yea... We picked this patient up from the airport after he was flown in from Ecuador. He has sustained significant damages due to a wild animal attack and he needs immediate medical help," Tim replied, trying to help the security officer understand the urgency of this situation.

"Sir, I don't give a damn if he came in from the moon! I need your name and the patient's affiliation or you won't being getting in!" the security officer snapped back into Tim's face.

"Alright, alright. My name is Tim Vangus, and I am an employee of Dade County and my patient, WHO IS CRITICALLY INJURED, is an employee of National Geographic," Tim snapped back at the security officer.

"Thank you, sir" the officer replied, emotionless as he picked up his radio and radioed inside to check to see if the affiliation was accepted. After a few seconds, Tim overheard a reply on the radio. "Affiliation accepted as a level two, please have the driver advance to the emergency bay, we have medical staff standing by,"

Hearing the acknowledgment, the security officer clipped his radio back to his utility belt and pointed Tim towards the emergency bay, "Straight ahead of you, docking station zero two is clear,"

"Thanks!" Tim replied sarcastically, and added "the truck behind me is with the patient, and they are both employees of the same AFFILIATION,"

Begrudgingly the security officer gently nodded his head as he motioned for Russo to follow the ambulance towards the docking station.

As explained, a medical team with a fresh gurney were patiently waiting at the docking station. Tim backed the ambulance into the docking station while Ivan prepped Carlos for transport. As the diesel engine shut off, Ivan kicked open the back doors and pushed Carlos' gurney onto the pavement at the docking station. Tim jumped out of the cab and jogged around to the back to help Ivan transport Carlos onto the fresh gurney. Once he was transported the orderlies rushed him into the ICU leaving Tim and Ivan to debrief the intake nurse with their reports. Ivan handed over his reports as he gave a brief description of what Carlos' symptoms were. The nurse quietly jotted down some notes on her file, but never acknowledged Ivan's report. After he was done, she simply grabbed the report and thanked the gentlemen before turning to go back into the hospital.

Russo and Gwen caught up to the nurse right before she entered the hospital, "Ma'am, where are they taking him?" Russo questioned.

"Are you friends or family of the patient?" she asked with a stoic face.

"Umm, I'm his best friend, he has no family that I know of here," Russo stuttered, taken back by her directness.

"Sorry, only family are allowed in the ICU, you will have to go around front, and check in at our after-hours admin desk," she replied curtly before turning to enter the building.

"Ma'am, please wait!" Gwen shouted.

"Yes dear," the nurse replied shortly.

"Ma'am, I'm a Dr. Gwen Vierra, and I was running a small missionary hospital in the Amazon, where this man was injured, and I feel that he might still be contagious with a very deadly virus. It is imperative that you let me speak with your head of medicine so the proper precautions can be taken to ensure that no one else gets infected," Gwen explained.

After hearing Gwen's explanation, the nurse's blank expression slowly changed into a smile as she spoke to her. "I understand honey, I really do. I know you fancy yourself as some hotshot doctor who's going to save everyone, but here at Miami Med with have protocols and procedures that we have to follow every time. I am sure that our well-trained staff of doctor's will be able to handle this situation without your ... how do you say ... expertise, efficiently. Now if you would like to see your friend later on, you are more than welcome to go to the admin desk and register. Until you have done that you will not be allowed access to any part of this hospital. Toodles," the nurse replied sneeringly as she entered the building, passing by two armed security officers with dull expressions plastered across their faces.

"What a bitch!" Gwen replied, frustrated with the situation.

"Tell me about it," Russo commented. "Come on, let's get to this admin desk and see what we can do to help," he said as he gently put his arm around Gwen and started walking in the direction the nurse had pointed them too.

"Hey, guys, thanks for the help," Russo spoke to the two EMT's as they finished loading all of their gear into the back of the ambulance.

"No problem, we hope your friend is okay," Tim replied as Ivan simply nodded his head.

"We do too," Russo answered back as he and Gwen hurried around the side of the building searching for another entrance to the hospital.

"Man, I don't know about you but I don't think that guy is going to make it. I mean, I think he's already gone," Ivan whispered, not wanting Russo and Gwen to hear.

"Unfortunately I think you're right. His complexion was almost fully gray by the time we got him on the new gurney. Although, I've never seen a dead body, or an almost dead body, turn gray and lose all of that color so fast. I mean, it's really weird, plus you combine everything you told me about his vitals ... it doesn't make any sense," Tim whispered back as he shut the back doors to the ambulance.

"Listen, I know you've been an EMT longer than me, but I can't ever remember treating a person who was still alive physically, yet had no pulse or blood pressure. That type of stuff only happens in the movie," Ivan said as he wiped the perspiration off of his forehead.

Tim noticed that his partner was sweating more than usual in the cool night air. Perplexed, he continued to stare at him while Ivan continued to load up the gear. As Ivan was getting ready to walk around to the front of the ambulance, he noticed the attention that Tim was giving him and answered the stare with a perturbed, "WHAT?!

"You alright man?" Tim questioned with genuine concern.

"Yea, I'm fine! Why you ask?" Ivan answered.

"You just look rough ... I mean you're sweating more than usual, and you seem to be out of breath. I was just wondering if you were okay."

"I'm just tired, tonight has been kinda rough, especially with the last one that we had. Other than where that joker bit my finger, I'm good, just tired and ready for my shift to end and get started on my vacation," Ivan replied as pulled a towel out of the front cab and wiped his whole face down.

"Speaking of your finger, you better let me take a look at it. Besides, I got to complete a report on it for the boss," Tim said as he looked down at Ivan's hand, and noticing the blood seeping through the gauze.

"Look, Tim, I'm good. I'll go home, clean it up myself, and re-bandage it. No problems! As for the report, I sign off on it when I get back, the boss will understand. Besides, I don't need to go wait at some doctor's office tomorrow morning and be late for my flight in the afternoon. Didn't you hear what I told you about the topless beaches?!" Ivan said with a relaxed smile.

"Yea, I heard you alright. I'm just concerned. Something about this whole night doesn't make sense. I just got a bad feeling," Tim said disconcertingly.

"Oh, no, here we go again, Tim with a bad feeling. Do you know how many of your bad feelings turn out to be nothing at all? All of them," Ivan responded in a sarcastic tone, beginning to become more annoyed with Tim's fatherly protection emotions. "Let's just get the hell outta here. What'ya say?" he continued as he climbed into the cab, slamming the door with more force than necessary. Tim simply climbed in, started up the diesel engine, put the ambulance in gear, and left the docking station without making any comment, his mind still racing with unease.

The nighttime air of Miami would still be unnerving to most, especially during the beginning of the summer, but compared to the nighttime air of the Amazon, the subtle change was somewhat refreshing for Russo and Gwen as they briskly walked around to the front of the mammoth hospital towards the main entrance. Exhaustion and frustration continued to weigh them down, yet the fear of the unknown was a stronger force which propelled them on, even though their bodies screamed rest. The unknown of Carlos' condition and the unknown of what he was infected with silently told their rational minds that they couldn't rest until they had at least alerted the authorities.

The front entrance to the hospital was decorated with enormous marble statues behind electronic sliding glass double doors. One statue was of the Greek God Zeus, and the other the Greek Goddess Athena. The statues were over eight feet tall and sported bronzed plaques at their base indicating their philanthropic sponsors. The front lobby consisted of an over-sized dark cherry walnut workstation with multiple monitors built in at angles. The back wall behind the desk supported four substantial flat screen monitors that were tuned to three of the major news networks, while the fourth one presented a magnified radar image of the city of Miami, showing variable clouds with the current time of three-thirty a.m. To the left of the check-in desk was a custom-built aquarium running the length of the wall. The five hundred gallon saltwater aquarium exhibited a complex system of coral rock with vibrant colored fish swimming in and out of the crevices in the coral foundation. The floor of the aquarium was finely colored white Bermuda sand, home to numerous small crabs and crustaceans. The visual impact of the aquarium was stunning and often a talking point for the families that came to the hospital to visit their loved ones. Various leather chairs and sofas decorated the rest of the lobby with two oblong glass coffee tables on both sides of the lobby.

"Holy Shit! Who pays for all of this stuff?" Russo mumbled under his breath as he walked through the lobby awe-struck by the decorations.

"Remember, this is a private hospital. It's probably got a river of money running through it. I really hate these types of hospitals because the patient normally comes last after the check clears," Gwen responded as she quickly approached the front desk.

Sitting behind the desk was a young girl in her mid-twenties with white hospital scrubs on, her head buried in what seemed to be a rather large textbook. She had short blonde hair that was pulled back and dark rimmed glasses. Her petite figure contrasted drastically with the massive desk as she had to step on a stool to see over the top of the counter to speak with guests. A cup of coffee with steam still pirouetting off the top accompanied a freshly opened can of diet soda to her left with a small bag full of grapes that she absentmindedly ate as she continued reading her book.

"Excuse me," Gwen said as she slightly tapped her knuckles on the top of the counter.

"OH, MY GOSH!" the startled woman exclaimed as she jerked her head up from her book, and would have fallen over had she not caught herself. "You scared me to death!" She said while she quickly regained her composure.

"I am sorry, I didn't mean to scare you," Gwen replied.

"Oh no it's not your fault, it's mine. I shouldn't be studying here, it's against the rules, but I have so much to read before tomorrow's class, and I know I will not get it done unless I try and study here. Please don't tell anyone, I beg you," she pleaded with genuine concern in her eyes.

"Oh, please dear, we won't tell; it looks like your reading a book about medicine," Gwen stated.

"It is, I am a second year med student, and I had no idea how hard this would be,"

"Trust me, it'll get better. I remember nights like this, you'll be fine," Gwen reassured the still visibly shaken girl. Something Gwen saw in this girl's eyes told her that she was a good person. Her kind eyes reminded Gwen that some people in this world still cared about others.

"Thanks! What can I help you two with?" the girl replied as she bookmarked her page and closed her book. "Oh, dear God!" she exclaimed as she suddenly realized that Gwen and Russo looked like they had just been attacked in the swamp by a gator or something. Her eyes widen with the amount of blood and dirt that was present on their clothes, and she found herself unable to pull her stare away.

"Relax, it's not our blood," Russo piped up, hoping to catch her before she lost it again. "Our friend has just been admitted to your ER, and we wanted to see how everything is going, plus she needs to speak to your Director of Medicine," Russo explained as he tilted his head in Gwen's direction.

"Yes, it's really important that I get a chance to talk with the Director. I think that our friend may have a potentially fatal virus, and I don't know if he is still contagious or not," Gwen explained as the young girl listened intently while gently nodding her head. Understanding the urgency in their tone, she quickly hit an electronic button on her desk that sent an emergency message to the head doctor on staff.

"I know this is a very serious situation, and I want you to know that I just alerted the head doctor on staff; she should be here shortly, but in the meantime I do have some questions that I need to ask. Everything will be okay," she tried reassuring them. "And by the way, my name is Carol; please don't call me ma'am."

"Thanks Carol. I'm Gwen Vierra, and this is Neal Russo. I was a mission doctor in the Amazon Jungle, and he is a photographer for National Geographic," Gwen hurriedly explained.

"Great, thanks for the information I take it that your friend is Carlos?" Carol asked.

"Yes, how did you know that?" Gwen asked perplexed by her knowledge of the situation.

"The EMT's report was scanned to my inbox, I have already reviewed it somewhat," Carol replied.

"Then you understand the sense of urgency we have with him," Russo said.

"Yes, Dr. Hampstead was already called to the ER the moment we got him, and she is with him right now, I assure you. Dr. Hampstead is one of our most talented doctors, and trust me, your friend is in good hands," Carol spoke calmly trying to calm the two of them down as well.

"Alright! Thank you, but we really need to see Dr. Hampstead soon. I need to talk with her, it's very important," Gwen said.

"That is why I already paged her on the emergency line," Carol said. Feeling satisfied, Gwen simply nodded her head and stepped back away from the desk. She leaned over towards Russo and whispered something to him; he nodded in reply as she walked over to one of the chairs and sat down with her hands resting on her knees as she slightly rocked her body.

Russo turned and flashed his brilliant smile, and said quietly, "You're a hell of a lot nicer than that other bitch that we dealt with earlier tonight,"

"One of our staff?" Carol questioned.

"Yea, the head nurse, you know nurse Super Bitch," Russo answered with a smirk.

"Oh, you must mean Nurse Johnson. We all call her Nurse Ratchet behind her back. Don't worry, she comes off like that to everyone, it's not just you guys. She was one of the first one's hired here, and she takes the senior management motto to heart," Carol explained.

"And that is?" Russo inquired.

"We want to help everyone, but everyone can't help us, so we only help those that can," Carol replied as she held her hand up and rubbed her thumb against her index and middle finger. Understanding what she meant, Russo mumbled profanities under his breath as he gritted his teeth. Russo had always hated the way that senior management's run businesses, and after hearing what Carol had just explained to him it reaffirmed his hatred. Russo knew he would never succeed in life as a business manager, he didn't like lying to people, and he preferred not having to deal with them at all. Photographing in the wild always seemed to relax him. He never really had a boss in the wild, except for nature itself, and he had been through enough sticky situations in the corps to where he knew what he was getting into long before it became a problem. Russo had never quite understood business and politics; more importantly, he never understood the quote, unquote science behind either. Sure he could manage himself and a company, but having his job held over his head by the torturous bottom line never made sense to him. Russo always believed that if you were good at something, then do it for an honest price, not do it for way less and then expect your customers to grovel at your feet. To Russo, the tightwads in three-piece business suits who monitored the stock market religiously, and whose cell phones were permanent appendages to their body, would ultimately be the fall of mankind, no more wars just simple greed.

Russo was stirred out of his torment as he heard an elevator in the back chime, signaling that it had reached its destination. The consistent beat of high heeled pumps echoed down the grand halls behind Carol's desk as an older woman in a doctor's coat rounded the desk, instantly causing Carol to jump out of her seat and stand almost at attention.

"Good Evening, Dr. Hampstead ... er ... Good morning! I was just reviewing my case book, all of my tasks are up to date, and I don't make security rounds for another forty-five minutes," Carol offered nervously.

"Relax Carol, how many times to I have to tell you that I respect that fact that you are trying to work through Med-School; I am completely fine with the fact that you are studying up here. Besides you're trying to better yourself, unlike some of your co-workers who incessantly check and update their Myspace pages," Dr. Hampstead replied with a kind-hearted smile that had the desired effect on Carol as she noticed the young girl's shoulders relax.

"Thanks, Dr. Hampstead," Carol replied sheepishly, as she was grateful for the guidance.

"Don't mention it,"

Dr. Hampstead was a slender woman who clearly looked younger than her fifty years. She stood roughly five-foot seven, with long brown hair accompanied by faint silver strands. Her long hair surrounded the aged face of a mother to whom the world could call mom, with dark brown eyes. Her facial features rarely required the use of make-up; besides, she never saw the importance of such, as she felt beautiful within, which was all that mattered to her. Her neckline proudly displayed a heart shaped pendant with one prominent peridot and two smaller emeralds representing her husband and two children who meant the world to her. A dainty digital watch called home to her left wrist, as a charm bracelet with various sports pendants occupied the other. She personified intelligence and confidence, with a simplistic understanding of human nature.

"Okay, on to business, what was the urgent message about?" Dr. Hampstead questioned Carol.

"These two individuals are with the man who was brought here just a little while ago. His name is Carlos, I believe," Carol answered as she opened her hand and gestured in the direction of Russo and Gwen.

"Good morning, Doc!" Russo said as he held out his hand.

"Good morning to you," Dr. Hampstead replied, accepting his handshake. "I'm Dr. Hampstead, Head Doctor here at Miami Med. I understand your friend is being treated here. How can I help you?" Dr. Hampstead replied.

"Yes, my friend Carlos is being treated here for severe wounds inflicted by an animal, and we feel that this animal possibly infected him with some sort of virus," Russo explained.

"Okay," Dr. Hampstead said as she nodded her head in understanding.

"This unfortunately is where I get in way over my head. Gwen, excuse me, Dr. Gwen Vierra, can explain better than I can," Russo said with slight grin.

"Vierra, of the Ecuador mission, am I correct?" Dr. Hampstead asked.

"Why yes, that is me; I am truly surprised that you have even heard of me," Gwen replied, slightly blushing at the accolades.

"Of course, I have. You are somewhat of a pilgrim young lady. Most mission trips are headed up by male doctors with female assistant doctors, but never a female head doctor," Dr. Hampstead replied with a genuine laugh. "I bet you really pissed off some of the so called "Fathers of Missionary Medicine!"

"Yea, they kinda don't like change," Gwen answered, satisfied with Dr. Hampstead's respect.

"Enough with the pleasantries, though; you two look like you've been through hell and back," Dr. Hampstead stated as she suddenly realized that these two looked like they just got out of a bar fight.

"Well, Doc, you could say that," Russo replied grimly as he ran his fingers through his dirty sweat saturated hair while he gently shook his head.

"You see, Dr. Hampstead, Carlos, our friend, was attacked by a jaguar that was either rabid or infected with some kind of virus. It was almost like a mind-altering virus or something. I know that sounds crazy, but you have to believe me," Gwen explained.

"I believe you, don't worry about that, but can you explain mind-altering?" Dr. Hampstead questioned with a growing concern.

"As best as I can, it was really quite remarkable, which is a crappy word choice, but the only one I could think of. Basically, this jaguar that attacked us was already hurt, and hurt bad, with what looked like a mortal wound in its chest. This was the same jaguar that had attacked Russo and Carlos the night before; Carlos had shot it and thought it was dead, but it wasn't,"

"Shot it with what?" Dr. Hampstead questioned.

"Rifle shot ... twice," Russo answered.

"And you're sure this was the same jaguar?" Dr. Hampstead continued.

"Yes, one hundred percent," both Gwen and Russo answered quickly.

"The jaguar had a gaping hole in its chest where the bullet penetrated its body the night before," Gwen continued "Yet it wasn't dead, and it didn't even seem to be fazed by it. It came after us in a rabid rage. Carlos shot it again, but to no avail. The hole that he shot into it didn't bleed like a normal animal either. The blood was very dark, almost black colored, and it was extremely gelatinous in texture. As it attacked, Carlos sliced off its paw, yet it continued to attack. It ripped open Carlos' chest before one of our friends was able to kill it."

"How did your friend kill it?" Dr. Hampstead asked, amazed at the story she had just heard.

"He took its head off with a shotgun," Russo answered with a heavy sigh.

"Did it die then?" Dr. Hampstead continued.

"God, I hope so," Russo replied.

"Alright, so let me make sure I got all of this. Your friend was attacked by a possibly rabid jaguar, and you think that the rabies virus transferred itself into your friend, Carlos, from the scratch of the jaguar. Also you believe that Carlos might be able to infect others. Does this about sum it all up?" Dr. Hampstead asked.

"Yes, I know that sounds crazy but, I swear to you, I'm telling the truth. Trust me, I am not one to believe in outlandish stories, therefore, I would never tell one," Gwen said as she tried to catch her breath. Her emotions were wreaking havoc on her already distraught body, and she was slowly losing the fight of self-control.

"Oh, I believe you Dr. Vierra," Dr. Hampstead said in a palpable tone. "I have learned to believe in what people say, especially if their emotions complement their statements. But believing and understanding are two completely different concepts,"

"There is more," Gwen continued. "This is not the first animal attack that we have encountered."

"Oh, boy, please continue," Dr. Hampstead said.

"A boy in the Huaoranian village was attacked and bitten numerous times by a spider that is native to that area, yet extremely rare," Gwen continued as she explained the circumstances revolving around Gabo's encounter with the spiders. She explained to Dr. Hampstead in great detail the nature of the bites, the symptoms that he exhibited, and the failed treatments that she attempted. As she was talking, she noticed that Dr. Hampstead's facial expression changed from that of shock to understanding. Russo began to notice the slow change as well. After she finished Dr. Hampstead took a long slow deep breath and the two could tell that she was beginning to comprehend all that had been explained to her, yet this information was clearly not alien to her.

After a long silence between both parties, Russo broke the silence. "Doc, something tells me that you have seen these symptoms before ... haven't you?" Russo asked, already knowing the answer to his question.

"I'll tell you what I know," Dr. Hampstead started, "You're very astute in your observations for a photographer, and yes you're correct, I have seen these symptoms before and, unfortunately, I have seen them rapidly deteriorate as well,"

"Carlos," Gwen replied in almost a whisper, reading the doctor's facial expression.

Dr. Hampstead slowly nodded her head as she explained what she had witnessed, "You're friend came here and was basically pronounced dead on the scene when the EMT's dropped him off, yet it was weird, because his body was still functioning as if he were alive and in considerable pain. His eyes, though severely blood-shot, were still open, and he continued to open and close his mouth with no audible noise exiting beside moans from the amount of pain he was under. He had no pulse or blood pressure, and he didn't seem to be breathing at all, yet he was still alive. The emergency room doctors paged me immediately once they determined that this man was all but dead. After my examination of him, it was determined that he should be dead, yet he wasn't."

"So what exactly does this mean Doc? Is he dead or alive?" Russo questioned in a defeated tone.

"That's a good question, Mr. Russo, and to be quite honest with you," she paused, "I really don't know. Nothing like this has ever happened in the medical world, at least nothing to the best of my knowledge. I ordered him to be quarantined immediately, and they had to restrain him after he attacked two of the nurses that were trying to take his blood. He bit one of them on the hand and knocked the other down with an impressive amount of strength for a man in his condition. He is currently in our quarantine area and being monitored by a team of doctors and nurses. Based on what you have told me, I will make sure that the nurse that he bit is kept under close observation. I will alert Nurse Johnson to this as soon as I finish talking with you two,"

"Doc, this doesn't make any sense," Russo said with frustration building. "I mean how can anybody still be alive without a heartbeat? I don't understand, we've got to be missing some crucial element. I mean is there any kind of virus that would slow person's heart rate down so much that it would be almost impossible to obtain a pulse?"

"There are any number of complex viruses in this world, and there are probably some that would give a host these symptoms, although I haven't run across a virus like this yet," Dr. Hampstead answered Russo the most reassuring way that she could.

"Alright, Dr. Hampstead, where do we go from here?" Gwen questioned.

"For now, it is very late or extremely early depending on your preference, I don't think there is really anything we can do other than observe Carlos to see if he changes. I will make sure that we have around the clock observations on him, and I will personally monitor any changes to his conditions. In the meantime, the two of you need rest," Dr. Hampstead said as her motherly instincts kicked in.

"I agree; I for one am beat," Russo admitted.

"Me too," Gwen chimed in. "Are there any hotels in the area?" She questioned.

"Hotels, are you kidding me?" Dr. Hampstead replied with a hearty laugh. "Do you know what hospital you're in? We are one of the most state of the art hospitals in the country and in the world. You can stay in one of our executive suites upstairs. I will have Carol arrange it for you. You'll find closets full of appropriate clothing so you can change out of those filthy clothes that you have on. The room's on the house, although I'll only be able to get you cafeteria food, as I won't be able to explain luxury dining to the upper ups," Dr. Hampstead said with a quick wink.

Shocked by her kindness and generosity Russo and Gwen stood shell-shocked at the offer. They both expected the super hospital to be stingy at the least with regards to their luxury suites.

"You two looked like you've seen a ghost," Dr. Hampstead said with as she reveled in her caring nature.

"I would've never expected this, especially from a private hospital," Russo said with a dumbfounded look plastered across his face.

"Yea, and senior management will most likely frown on the appropriations of funds, but anytime they get their panties in a wad is a good day in my book," Dr. Hampstead replied as an inner sense of gratifications riveted throughout her body.

"Thank you so much! Your kindheartedness will not go unappreciated, I assure you," Gwen said as she began to give in to her body's need for rest.

"Carol, please set them up in the Gator Suite," Dr. Hampstead instructed Carol.

"You got it, Dr. Hampstead," Carol answered with enthusiasm. Of all the doctors that worked at Miami Med, Carol respected Dr. Hampstead the most. Dr. Hampstead had taken Carol under her wing and given her the opportunity to shine, through her guidance.

"You have to excuse the names of our suites, our trustee board is full of avid sports fans; therefore, each one of our suites is named after a popular sports team. For instance the presidential suite isn't called the presidential suite it's called the Bowden Suite," Dr. Hampstead explained as she rolled her eyes, visibly disgusted.

"Thank you again, so much for your kindness, Dr. Hampstead. I don't know what to say, other than thank you again!" Gwen said graciously.

"You don't have to say thank you, you already have by showing me that a woman as young as yourself has the capabilities and the confidence to be in charge of her own mission trip. I wish I had your confidence when I was your age. You've done us all a great favor in the medical world, and for that I say thank you," Dr. Hampstead replied with a quick wink.

Russo thanked the doctor once more and happily shook her hand before walking back up to the front desk to obtain the electronic key cards for the suite. Gwen embraced Dr. Hampstead with a meaningful hug before joining Russo at the front desk.

Carol quickly programmed the two electronic keys for the appropriate suite and then explained the elevator system with the layout of the hospital floors to both Gwen and Russo. She advised them that on the eighth floor they will need to exit the elevator and get on a new and different set on that floor to access the suite rooms. She informed them that each suite room was denoted by the beginning letter of the suite in the elevator, not a particular number. After she finished her explanation she inquired as to what time she needed to set up the wake-up call.

"Russo and Gwen, it's about three am now, how about a meeting around nine? We still need to discuss what is going on, and if there are any changes to Carlos condition. I also will update you with the reports that I get from my staff who'll be checking in on him. If this is what you say it is and it is contagious, I want to get the CDC here also for their input. The longer we wait the more chance we have of an outbreak. I'm sorry you can't get more rest," Dr. Hampstead explained.

"No, Dr. Hampstead, I totally agree with you the sooner the better, and if anything changes throughout the night please be sure to let us know," Gwen replied.

"I will," Dr. Hampstead said.

"Hey Doc? Can I leave a card on file for some long distance phone calls I got to make? I need to let the Magazine know what's going on, plus I have a few other phone calls to make," Russo questioned before pushing the upward elevator button.

"On the house Russo, the mini-bar however is not," Dr. Hampstead answered with a smile.

Russo and Gwen entered the elevator and made their way to the Gator suite, feeling slightly relieved that they had found an ally, yet troubled at the news that Dr. Hampstead had given them concerning Carlos' condition.

Dr. Hampstead and Carol watched the LED lights above the elevator as it indicated that Russo and Gwen had made it to the appropriate floor that contained the Gator Suite.

"You know Materson's going to be royally pissed tomorrow morning when he gets in. Especially with the use of a quarantine room and a luxury suite. I can just see him right now, yelling at everybody and wanting to know who's gonna pay for it, and why he even has a staff," Carol commented.

"Why Carol, you seem nervous about Matty boy's reaction tomorrow, are you beginning to go soft for our beloved boss?" Dr. Hampstead teased.

"Oh no, I just wish I could be a fly on the wall to see his facial expression when he comes in and gets his morning reports. You know, he really does look like a weasel when he gets pissed. I mean his lips pucker up, his face turns all different shades of red, and that horrible comb over begins to stand on end. It's almost like it has a mind of its own," Carol teased back as she continued with the humiliations in her head, choosing not to sound like a broken record. "But in all seriousness, what do I say if he does question me?"

"You tell him that I authorized it," Dr. Hampstead said as she began to walking towards the emergency room.

"Yes Ma'am!" Carol said with a grin covering her face. She eagerly dove back into her studies seeing who she wanted to model herself after, after hearing of the achievements Dr. Vierra had already achieved. The fire inside of her burned furiously with ambition as she realized that she had found her calling.

The elevator chimed as the doors opened up to an expansive hallway with premiere decoration just as they had seen present in the lobby. In each crevice of the hallway stood more marbled statues of Greek Gods and Goddesses; at the end of the hallway was a five-tiered pyramid shaped granite waterfall with silently cascading water. As Russo and Gwen unlocked and opened their suite door, the entryway lights automatically came on, illuminating the gigantic suite. The carpet was the same style of plush rug as present downstairs, but softer with a higher fiber thread than the lobby. A walk-in closet was located on the left of the entranceway that was as large as an average sized child's room, complete with a free-standing mirror in the corner. As they continued in they noticed the dining room area with a six-person table complemented by six ornately designed chairs with intricate designs as chair backs. The dining room led into an expansive kitchen with high caliber stainless steel appliances and an island in the middle with a gourmet style cutting board. The French door refrigerator housed all grades of restaurant style pre-made meals that were stocked daily, along with all grades of drinks from sparkling mineral water to three hundred dollar bottles of champagne. The kitchen bar opened up to the main living room where a leather wrap around couch sat with two leather recliners on each side. The extravagant furniture centered around a glass coffee table with an acrylic stand. The coffee table faced a sixty inch plasma screen with wall mounted speakers and magnificent paintings on both sides. In the back of the main room was a balcony that oversaw the hospital grounds. The balcony consisted of two Adirondack chairs and a small stone topped table with two delicate rocks glasses on top of a box of imported cigars. The master bedroom was just as lavish as the rest of the suite with a California king-sized bed with eight hundred count Egyptian cotton sheets and a mini chandelier hanging over the bed. The master bedroom was a mirror image of the patient bathrooms with a free-standing shower and a Jacuzzi tub. The only difference in the two was the "Jack and Jill" sinks present in the suite's master bathroom. The suite resembled more of a Vegas style honeymoon suite instead of a hospital hotel room.

"Just who in the hell stays here anyway? I mean, this room is decorated for the royal family, not patient's loved ones," Russo exclaimed as he stood in awe of the luxurious room.

"I'm guessing this is where Miami and the world's elite stay when they have a loved one who is being treated at this hospital," Gwen answered, as she too was taken aback by the overly lush setting.

"Who pays for all of this?" Russo continued his questions.

"You remember what Carol said was senior management's motto," Gwen replied with a smirk.

Replaying the conversation in his head only made him sick to his stomach at the evil bureaucratic morons who had more money than they had sense. Hospitals were created to take care of people, not cater only to the rich and those who could afford medical care.

"This is absolutely disgusting," Russo said with clear frustration.

"I agree, but right now isn't the time or the place to debate the expenditures of the rich. We need to get some rest, because I fear that tomorrow is going to be a long day," Gwen said, feeling her body slowly winding down.

"Sounds good. Look I'll take the couch, and you can have the master bedroom, just toss me a pillow and a blanket," Russo said chivalrously and quickly, avoiding an awkward conversation.

Gwen smiled and thanked Russo for his sincerity before she quickly hugged him and then shut the master bedroom door, her mind still trying to race about the complications of what she had discovered over the past forty-eight hours. She made a mental note to contact Jonathan in the morning to see how everything was going and advise him of what she and Russo had discovered concerning Carlos' predicament. Her thoughts drifted back to Carlos as her eyes began to well up. Carlos wouldn't be where he was had he not saved her life. A part of her felt that it should be her in the quarantine room and not him. Feeling somewhat responsible for Carlos' condition she vowed to herself that she would get to the bottom of the situation, and if it was a virus, she would find a way to stop it. Her eyelids became too heavy for her eyes to sustain and slowly she succumbed to their conquest. As she drifted off to sleep, Russo stretched out on the couch and gently placed his hat over his face covering his sight in total darkness. His mind too was racing, as he continued to replay the previous day's events over in his head trying to figure out exactly what happened. As he continued to study his thoughts, he was unable to pull his thoughts away from Gwen. Her passion and ambition amplified her feminine qualities. Before he knew it, he was fast asleep, deep down inside impatiently waiting for what tomorrow brings.

Eight floors below them in the quarantine room Carlos' eyes now fully red with dark black dots scattered across, madly darted around the room as his ankles and wrists strained against the restraints that held him in place. An electronic hum serenaded the room, but Carlos was unaware of the noise, as the only feeling he had now was... hunger.

CHAPTER 13
RUSSO'S FEARS COME TRUE

Robert Materson stared silently at his cell phone as he sat behind the wheel of his sports car. His cell phone represented his lifeline to his work, and any day that he was without it, he had the strange sense people got in their dreams when they dreamt that they were naked or missing a vital part of their wardrobe. Materson's days consisted of morning conference calls and meetings, followed by indulgent lunches with board members or potential patients, followed by afternoons filled with daily and weekly debriefings combined with his usual ass-chewing of his staff; the latter he enjoyed more than any other. Materson was in his late fifties, severely overweight for his relative short stature, balding with a horrible comb over originating near his left ear and ended in a gigantic curl above his right. Being the director of the hospital and having numerous doctors and staff reporting to him, he never felt the need to impress his staff with his wardrobe selection unless a board member was coming to the hospital. His normal attire consisted of stone washed jeans with numerous tears and holes throughout, and a sweaty pair of flip-flops that announced his arrival with their odor long before he arrived, and double layered shirts from his favorite bars and other various places he spent a major part of his day at. He was rarely clean-shaven; usually a five-o'clock shadow was present when he arrived at the job. As usual he wore his mold covered NY Jets hat with faded signatures from players long past.

His eyes slowly rose from the phone awaiting a call from his personal assistant to inform and snitch on what his staff did while he wasn't there. He stared at the sign that he parked in front of; it read: "Reserved for the Director of the Hospital. All others will be towed at owner's expense." He had had the sign put up to correct the problem of patients and their families parking in his parking spot nearly twenty feet away from the entry to the hospital. He understood why they parked there, especially when they had to drop a sick loved one off, but they weren't in charge of making multi-million dollar deals for this hospital, and he was; therefore, he deserved the best parking spot. As he sat in his car waiting, he smiled as he thought of the empire that he had created. Miami Med had only been around for about ten years, and he had been there from the start. He had gotten the support from the various board members, he had hired the most competent doctors and staff administrators, he had contracted with agencies to decorate the hospital with the most elaborate and lavish decorations; all of it was done by him, and he expected dedication and an overwhelming sense of gratitude from everyone for what he had created. In Materson's mind, he felt that he deserved the same recognition as likes of Gates, Jobs, Rockefeller, and even Kennedy, although he truly believed that when he was finished he would be more powerful and revered than even them.

The small screen on his phone lit up, jarring him from his delusion as his assistant was finally contacting him. The screen read "Sara Calling," A little later than I expected, but she does such good work that I will let it slide, he thought to himself as he pressed the talk button.

"A little late this morning, aren't we?" Materson answered somewhat coldly.

"Yea. Yea. Yea. So it's after nine a.m., sue me why don't you," Sara replied.

"Hmph."

"Anyway, asshole! I was just finishing the numbers for your predicted budget, and it seems that once again we will be in the positive. It looks like we'll be twenty-seven percent over our forecasted predictions!" She paused waiting for acknowledgment, but he offered none. "This is amazing; I don't know how you did it, but you did it once again. You're amazing, babe!" Sara finished knowing the expected gratitude would elicit a response.

"How many times do I have to tell you, don't call me babe over the PHONE!" Materson yelled, becoming exceedingly frustrated with Sara's short-term memory problem.

"Relax would you, I'm in my office and the doors are shut with my music playing; no one even knows that I'm on the phone. Besides you had all of the cameras in my office shut off anyway. What's got you so pissy this morning? I would've thought my good news would have had you singing this morning, not to mention what I did for you last night," Sara replied, slightly pouting at his harsh comment.

"Alright fine, I'm sorry I shouted at you. Better now?" Materson calmly replied as he began to regain his composure. "I am excited about the numbers, but I already knew that we would come in higher than expected. For Pete's sake, I'm the one who told you what to forecast," he said before pausing to reach down to massage his crotch as his mind was saturated with thoughts of last night.

"You know I really did like you dressed as a female plumber, coming to help me with some clogged pipes," he whispered as his breath quickened, while gentle shockwaves traveled through his body, originating from his crotch.

"Oh, Robert, you were amazing last night, and I really think I'm falling in love with you," she admitted as her face became flush, while the butterflies in her stomach fluttered around in a rapid pace.

"Me too, me too. I promise we'll be together soon. My wife will be served with divorce papers today, and I will leave that wench homeless with three mouths to feed. Then she will have to agree to my terms if she wants those precious children to survive," he said with an evil sneer.

"But if she can't afford to take care of your children, then they will have to come and stay with us, and let me tell you something," she paused as she collected her thoughts "I will not play second fiddle to those three snobbish brats in my house. You know they will need to be sent off to school so we can have our time together,"

"Don't worry about it, I got it all taken care of. Now on to business… anything I need to know about last night? Did anything out of the ordinary happen? You know I need the inside information before the staff meeting at nine thirty," he questioned impatiently.

"Nothing major happened last night although the charts show that we received an intake early in the morning with severe blood loss from an animal wound," she answered.

"Who's the patient, and what is their affiliation?"

"His name is Carlos and the only affiliation that I show is with National Geographic. I didn't know they were on our list of acceptable companies," she answered as she continued to read over Carlos' report.

"We don't but that asshole board member, Braddock's brother works for them, and he has insisted that we accept any employees of them on a temporary basis. It's alright, they should have just stitched him up and sent him off, no need to waste money on this character. What time did they discharge him?"

"That's just it, they haven't yet, and get this, he's currently in our quarantine room as we speak," she continued, knowing an emotional explosion was about to occur.

"WHAT DID YOU SAY? YOU MEAN TO TELL ME THAT SOME HAIRY WETBACK IS IN MY QUARATINE ROOM, AND HE DOESN'T EVEN HAVE AN AFFILIATION? JUST HOW IN THE HELL ARE WE GOING TO EXPLAIN THAT? YOU KNOW THAT IT COST $10,000 DOLLARS PER TWELVE HOURS IN THAT ROOM, AND THAT ROOM IS ONLY AN OPTION FOR OUR MAJOR CONTRIBUTORS. YOU KNOW, THOSE WHO HAVE CONTRIBUTED MORE THAN TWO MILLION TO MIAMI MED!" He continued on his rant for a good five minutes before he finally stopped.

Not wanting her ears to continue to ring she jerked the phone away from her ear and waiting until she couldn't hear him yelling before she put it back.

"Are you still there?" He hollered into the phone, not as loud as his previous rant.

"Yes babe, I'm here, please don't yell at me, I didn't approve it," she replied timidly.

"I know that. Who approved it?" He snapped.

"I'll give you two guesses, but you'll only need one," she answered as she tried to stifle a giggle. She absolutely loved it when Dr. Hampstead got in trouble.

"Fuck me running! That woman is going to put me in an early grave. Every time I come down on her she goes running to her daddy, and then I have to have a long chat with him. If only he wasn't the board president, I'da fired her old ass years ago," he said with venomous disgust.

"It gets better," she continued with a snicker.

"Do you think this funny? Are you actually laughing?"

"No, I promise. Anyway, the Gator Suite is in use by the friends of this Carlos, and she approved that as well."

"That fucking bitch! She's through after this, I don't give a damn who her father is. Besides, he is out of the country right now anyway, and he'll agree with me in the end, I know how much he enjoys his own private yacht. She'll be gone by sunset tonight, I promise you," he quietly said, seething as he hung up.

"Well, good-bye to you as well," she remarked as she tossed her phone onto her desk before walking over to her widespread view of the hospital grounds from her corner office on the tenth floor.

Sara Maysworth was the type of girl that didn't care how she moved up in her life, she just had an insatiable desire to be at the top, and to her being at the top meant having more money than everyone else. She had gone to an all girl's college in West Virginia, and just like in all of her previous schools, she never really got along with her classmates. She always considered them to be snobby and cheats and she felt the need to express that to others, especially teachers, who the traitors were. She never considered herself to be a snitch, she just didn't care whose life she ruined on her way to the top. What little friends she had would cease to exist the moment they found out what she was truly like. She chalked her constant aloneness up to the simple fact that no one would ever hold her back. In the final semester of her senior year, she found herself in strange waters as she was failing her final class, business ethics. One night, determined that she wasn't going to allow herself to fail, she seduced her teacher and recorded their intimate night. The next day she walked into his office and demanded an A, or she would ruin his marriage and his job. The blackmail worked, and she was granted her A. After her graduation she mailed a copy of the tape to his wife and a copy to the dean of students simply out of spite, and the fact that she felt that he was trying to stop her from her goals. Two months later that same professor put a snub nose 38 to his temple and blew his brains out. When asked about it, she would simply say with a smile, "He got what was coming to him,"

After college Sara learned that the world was cruel and wouldn't cater to her every need like a princess that she believed that she was. She bounced around from meaningless job to meaningless job, never achieving more than an assistant's role. Combined with a weak constitution, Sara slipped into a depression that further debilitated her life physically and mentally. She came to the realization that the only way she was ever going to reach her goal was to use her "A" getting talent. One night in a lousy bar with sawdust on the floor and cheap beer drafts, she ran into herself, only this version was of the opposite sex. Robert Materson promised her the moon and made good on that promise, all Sara had to sacrifice was her dignity, and seeing that she never cared about it in the first place, it became a win-win for both parties.

Six years ago, almost to the date, Sara walked into Miami Med as Materson's personal assistant, her dreams finally obtained, and all she had to do was what she knew best. As she stared out the window, her mind replayed the last six years of her life—a reminder to her that Miami Med wouldn't be what it was today without her ingenuity. She stood roughly five feet five inches tall, with long black hair and cold dark brown eyes. Her hair gently flowed over her pudgy figure which she always tried to hide with expensive business suits and double tucks. With all of the money she could ever imagine, and all the advice from doctors and her parents, Sara had a weak constitution, therefore, she would never be able to fully police herself back to good health.

She heard a knock to her office door, the door quickly opened, and Dr. Hampstead walked in to drop some updates off for her to give to Materson.

"Dr. Hampstead?" Sara called out.

"Yes?" Dr. Hampstead answered with her back turned as she rolled her eyes in frustration.

"Home many times do I have to tell you that you need to gain permission to come into my office before you barge in here?" Sara replied coldly.

"You know, Maysworth, it just must've slipped my mind. I will have to try and remember next time," Hampstead retorted.

"That's what you said last time, and the time before that. I don't think it's sinking in, Dr. Hampstead."

"WOW! What makes you think that?" Hampstead replied sarcastically before exiting the office covering up a grin with a patient's folder.

"You know all I ever tried to do was help you Hampstead," Sara yelled as the doctor walked out of her office.

Unable to let Sara get the last word in, she turned around, marched back into her office, and proceeded to get right in her face, sensing the trepidation that she had caused the younger girl.

"Alright Hotshot! Name the last time you actually tried to help me," Hampstead snapped as she narrowed her eyes with her hands planted firmly on her hips.

"Umm… Well there was that time when… um… you know I did that thing… that um… helped you… and you were very grateful… and you told me that I… I… was the be… be… best you've ever de… de… dealt with," Sara replied as she struggled to show that she still had the upper hand.

"Ahh… yes I remember that time, it was just the other… hmmm… was it the other day?" Hampstead replied goading her.

"Why, yes it was, I remember exactly helping you handle that situation," Sara replied, taking the bait.

"And just what situation was that?" Hampstead inquired with a smile.

"I can't remember! Besides, I shouldn't have to help you out, you're the famous doctor right?" Sara replied with a pout.

"Figures!" Hampstead said under her breath as she turned to leave her office.

"Oh yea, Dr. Hampstead!" Sara called out wanting to keep her attention "I just got off the phone with Mr. Materson, and he told me to tell you that you have some explaining to do,"

"Let me guess… He wants to know why the quarantine room is being used and why I have authorized the Gator Suite to be occupied. It just astonishes me how he already knows what has happened last night, and he hasn't even got to his office," Hampstead said with great disgust.

"Well, I told him, and that's why he already knows," Sara continued feeling proud of the fact that she was a complete snitch.

"Shocking statement of the year!" Hampstead replied before she exited her office. "Tell him he'll know where to find me,"

Sara never really understood why Dr. Hampstead paid her no respect, she just assumed it was because the doctor was envious of the fact that Sara had accomplished so much in her young life. Sara's blind vanity never allowed her to see what the real world saw when they looked upon the accomplishments she had achieved in her life; to her the real world was jealous.

The mechanical hum of the entrance doors signaled Materson's arrival as he briskly walked through with his cell phone attached to his ear. As he walked past the front desk, Carol stood up and politely greeted him, which received no acknowledgment as he headed for the elevator doors. Materson made his way up to the tenth floor where his office was located. The tenth floor consisted of Materson's office, Sara's office, and the executive cafeteria that only catered to the board of directors, senior management, and the luxury suite occupants. Deep down, Materson hated the fact that he had to share a floor with a cafeteria, he believed that his office should be at the top of HIS premiere hospital, but for the time being he would accept his mediocre office that covered the entire east wing of the tenth floor.

As he entered his office, his automatic lights came on, along with a seductive female robotic voice that greeted him. "Good Morning Director Materson!" Materson's office was the size of five corporate boardrooms put together. The north end of his office was decorated with floor to ceiling dark mahogany bookshelves housing numerous books, almost all of which he had never read. The bookshelves came together in the middle forming an inlaid cabinet which entertained a forty-inch plasma computer monitor with Bose speakers adorning the top corners, and a pull out docking station at the bottom right. This monstrosity faced a large mahogany desk that supported various stacks of paper combined with sophisticated awards and accommodations along with a V9000 desk phone. To the left of his desk was a refrigerator that was built in to the wall with an electronic password pad that only he knew the code to. In front of his desk sat four leather chairs in a tight semi-circle followed by a sixteen-person conference table with wireless computer and phone adapters staggered quarterly. The south wall of his office supported three massive flat panel televisions that were constantly on, tuned in to the weather, sports, and the world news. Large Corinthian leather couches garnished the spacious floor in front of these massive screens. His walls were muddled with an assortment of pictures, predominately of the New York Jets, integrated with awards, and plaques he has obtained over the years since Miami Med first opened.

After he sat his briefcase and cell phone down on his desk he walked over to his wall of windows and peered aimlessly out at the ample grounds the hospital was located on. His eyes stared down near the entrance to the hospital and casually followed a westerly path until he saw the highway and the abomination that had been erected across the highway. A large shopping center with top line stores, restaurants, and hotels graced the grounds across from the hospital. To the hospital employees it was an ideal place for them to get away, go shopping, or grab lunch, but to Materson it represented the second bane of his existence. He had opposed the construction of this mammoth shopping center since its inception, but he was overruled by the city management's office which explained that every major airport should have an area like Cypress Mill close by so tourists and travelers had a place to go once they got off the plane. Two colossal parking decks acted as bookends for Cypress Mill, but to Materson they were just another place that the local gangs and hoodlums could park, do their drugs, and party. Materson often thought that he would do the world a favor if he brought one of his high powered rifles to work and decided to stay late into the night of a Friday night, but he realized that the ensuing court trial would hurt his reputation, not to mention the money he would have to spend on money grubbing lawyers.

Materson finished his cigarette and flicked it off of the building before walking back into his office. As he sat down in his executive's chair he tapped the speakerphone button and quickly dialed Dr. Hampstead's cell phone. He needed to rid him of her presence once and for all.

"Hello, this is Dr. Hampstead, how can I help you?" Dr. Hampstead answered, after the second ring.

"Dr. Hampstead, can you report to my office ASAP and bring along our two guests, I have some questions for all of you," Materson's voice echoed in her ear as if he was in a tin can. To Materson all calls were on speakerphone, he never cared who heard his conversations, more importantly he liked the fact that others could hear him talk and give direction, that way it was never misconstrued who was in charge.

"Why, good morning to you, too, Mr. Materson!" Dr. Hampstead replied with a fabricated cheerful salutation. "What seems to be the problem? You know our guests arrived here late last night and they are probably still tired; they need their rest. Can this wait until later?" she questioned, knowing that she was already getting underneath his skin.

"No, Dr. Hampstead, it can't wait. Wake them up if you have to, but be in my office in fifteen minutes!" Materson yelled before he hit the speaker button, effectively ending the conversation.

"Hmph," Dr. Hampstead said aloud as she inwardly smiled to herself and the fact that she was able to always get under his skin. She looked down at her rounds chart and decided that Materson could wait a little longer as she still had four patients to check in on before she went for her morning meeting.

***

Special Agent Bruce Jenkins glanced over his report that he was reading and noticed that his phone line was lighting up, indicating a private call was coming into his office. Tired of reading the reports, and hoping to have an update on the situation that he had been briefed on earlier in the morning, he anxiously answered his line.

"This is Jenkins," he replied in a gruff voice before he cleared his throat.

"Bruce! It's Russo, how the hell are you?!" Russo answered back, excited that he had gotten in touch with his friend.

"Russo, man, it's great to hear your voice. Especially after the reports that I got this morning. Are you still in South America?" Jenkins asked as he straightened his body in his chair.

"No, man, I'm in Miami right now, but I need a favor from you. Sorry to call and be so direct, but it's kinda important," Russo replied with a sense of urgency.

"I'll see what I can do, can't make any promises. This morning the shit hit the fan, and now everyone is in crazy fuck mode. Whatcha need?"

"I need to know if you know anyone in the CDC, I need a good contact. Don't ask any questions right now, but I will definitely keep you informed. This is pretty urgent ol' buddy, I really need this favor. Also, I was wondering if you could come down to Miami Med and see me for a little bit; I need to show you something, along with your contact," Russo explained.

"No can do on the trip, buddy. Everyone around here has been put on high alert due to a potential terrorist attack in South America last night. The reports are still coming in, so nothing is concrete yet, but this one seems fucking hardcore. According to some of our contacts down there the body count is already piling up. Of course, you don't know anything about this," Jenkins cautioned. "But I can give you the name of a guy here in Miami that works at the CDC. I normally go to lunch with him once a month. He's a good guy, I trust him, and when you talk to him, tell him you know me,"

"Thanks, man, I owe you one. So what are they saying about Ecuador?" Russo questioned with a strange feeling in the pit of his stomach.

"Nobody is saying much right now, and none of the major networks have even claimed this one; that's what's got everyone in a stir. Listen man, I hate to be short, but I got to go; here is the number to Jerry Constance," Jenkins explained quickly as he gave Russo Jerry's number before quickly hanging up as his agent's cell phone exploded again with ten different emails and an incoming call.

"Thanks..." Russo said into the already dead line. His face etched with concern about what was going on in Ecuador, and hoping that what was happening to Carlos was connected. As he started to let his mind wonder and create mountains in the sky, he noticed movement out of the corner of his eye. Gwen had just walked out of the master bedroom suite. She had cleaned up and showered, and she looked totally different than last night. She had on a pair of black nurse scrubs that fit her body well. Her hair was still pulled back in a ponytail, an aspect that made her almost irresistible. For a moment Russo became lost in his stare, almost forgetting everything that had happened over the past couple of days, until she turned and acknowledged him as she sat down on the couch.

"Sleep much?" he questioned as he walked over to the couch with Jerry's number in his hand.

"Somewhat, more of a restless sleep, but rest nonetheless. I feel better than I did earlier this morning. It was nice to take a shower and get out of those clothes, although I think this suite is set up for Hollywood couples, not average people," she offered.

"What makes you say that?" Russo asked.

"Well, for one thing, the wardrobe is almost like something out of a gangster movie. There aren't any normal clothes, just all grades of expensive suits for men and flashy sequenced micro mini-skirts and halter tops that don't leave much to the imagination."

"Now come on, you could've worn that, you'd have looked great," Russo teased while paying her a compliment.

"Alright hot shot, I appreciated the flattering compliment, but I wouldn't look good in that, I would look like a tramp," Gwen replied, disgusted with the waste of money.

"Well, in my many dealings with women, clothes don't make the tramp, the woman makes the tramp," Russo said.

"Thanks," Gwen said with a heavy sigh and a wink.

"I just got off the phone with my buddy in the FBI here in Miami, and he gave me the name of a contact in the CDC. I say we talk with Dr. Hampstead, and then give this guy a call," Russo explained.

"I agree, the longer we wait on this, the worse it'll get, I fear," she replied. "I tried to call Jonathan this morning, but the SAT phone keeps giving me a busy signal. I hope everything's alright."

"I'm sure it is. Look, you did a phenomenal job in that village and Jonathan will be able to pick up right where you left off and steer the ship until you get back there. You wouldn't have left it unless deep down inside you knew what I was saying was true," Russo said, trying to quell her fears.

"I hope so," Gwen replied softly as she let her guard down and gently rested her head on his shoulder as the two sat and stared at the massive blank screen.

Gwen slowly closed her eyes as she felt herself falling back asleep until a soft knock came from the door leading out. Startling them both, they jumped up at the sound. Russo answered the door, and Dr. Hampstead greeted them cheerfully while quickly apologizing for interrupting their sleep. Russo quickly explained that they were up and they had been up for a while, as he invited her into the suite.

"Well, I'm glad you two finally got some rest; I wish I had good news, but unfortunately I don't. Your friend's current condition hasn't changed throughout the night. It's very eerie, though, that he still doesn't have a pulse, yet he is still alive and moving. I've never seen anything like this before in all of my years. He hasn't been able to make any recognizable statements to any of the doctors or nurses, he just seems to grunt and moan as they try to talk to him," Dr. Hampstead explained.

"Dr. Hampstead, he seems to be showing the same signs that the little boy in the village was showing after he had been bitten by the spiders," Gwen said as she slowly shook her head, feeling defeated once again.

"Well, if it's viral, then he's definitely got it, but I thought you told me that he never came into contact with the boy, that he was attacked by a jaguar," Dr. Hampstead questioned.

"You're right, he never did have any contact with the boy," Gwen answered.

"Then how in the devil, did he get the same infection? Unless the jaguar was infected as well, but that's a stretch," Dr. Hampstead continued.

"Well, that jaguar certainly wasn't acting the normal way a jaguar should act, that is if there is a normal way," Russo chimed in.

"This doesn't make any sense to me, but right now is not the time that we need to be asking these questions. The Director of the hospital wants us to meet with him as soon as you two are ready. Now let me caution you, he's a pompous ass, and I have zero respect for the man. Please don't be offended by anything that he says or does, he knows nothing, and he thinks that the world was created for him … and only him," Dr. Hampstead explained.

"Well, I've dealt with my fair share of assholes in the past twenty four hours, so I think I'll be okay," Gwen offered as she started walking towards the door. "Hey Russo!"

"Yea?" He answered.

"Try not to agitate this one like you did to Klinefelter," Gwen gently teased him with a smile.

"Hey! That wasn't my fault, he had it coming, and it was just too easy for me, you know, kinda like stealing candy from a baby," Russo said with a half-hearted laugh.

"I would love to hear the story, but we're already late," Dr. Hampstead replied as she ushered the two out of their suite and down the hallway to the elevators.

As they entered Materson's office, they noticed that he sat with his chair back to them.

"You're late Dr. Hampstead. Are you ever on time?" Materson spoke coldly while he slowly rotated his chair to face them.

"I had rounds to get to," Dr. Hampstead tried to explain.

"I don't give a damn if the Pope was here, and he called you to his bedside. If I give you a directive, dammit, you follow it," Materson snapped as his face quickly shaded red.

"Easy now," Russo piped up before he sat down, as he glared at Materson.

"You! Are a guest in my hospital, you're not my boss, and you will have some manners while you are staying FREE in my hospital," Materson said as he as he aggressively pointed at Russo.

Accepting the challenge Russo's biceps slowly tightened as his knuckles became white with pressure. He set his jaw, and as he opened his mouth to reply, he felt a soft delicate hand on his right arm lightly squeeze as Gwen intervened.

"We thank you very much for your hospitality, Mr. Materson, it was truly thoughtful of you to set us up with a room, free of charge," Gwen commented, trying to diffuse the testosterone-filled situation.

"Well, I'm so glad you enjoyed yourself!" Materson replied sarcastically as he continued to stare at Russo, a sly grin creasing his face.

"Enough with the pleasantries! Can one of you explain to me why I have a non-affiliated man in my quarantine room, which costs me and astronomical amount of money to run, and while you're at it, maybe you can explain to me who's going to foot that bill," Materson said as his voice decibel level started to escalate.

"I can Materson," Dr. Hampstead replied calmly.

"I'm waiting, and it's Mr. Materson to you," he answered back as he squinted his eyes in her direction.

"Okay Materson," Dr. Hampstead said, failing to acknowledge his directive as she quickly rolled her eyes. She quickly explained the whole situation to the Director on a third grade level so he could follow along. After she was done, she then explained her theories and reasoning as to why she put Carlos in the quarantine room, and why he should stay there until they knew exactly what they were dealing with. Erring on the side of caution had always been Dr. Hampstead's approach, although it was often frowned on because of its economics, especially at a private hospital. After she was done, Materson was silent as he continued with his cold stare at the three of them. He gently leaned back in his chair and started to rock it very slowly.

"So let me get this right. We have a guy who was attacked by a jaguar and now he's dead, and you want to keep him in a room that costs more money than he is worth because you think something could be wrong with him. Is that about the gist of things?" Materson said in a sarcastic tone, as he continued to stare at the ceiling.

"Well, kinda... sorta... The reason I want to keep him in the quarantine room is because I fear he's still contagious," Dr. Hampstead explained, slightly agitated at his lack of eye contact.

"Well, good doctor, let me ask you one question … Is he dead or alive?" Materson snapped as he tilted his head downwards and locked eyes with her.

"That's just it, we don't know. As I told you before, he doesn't have a pulse but … she tried to explain before he cut her off.

"I know what you said, you don't have to sound like a broken damn record. I'm not deaf you know," Materson snapped again, as his face became flush. At this comment Russo stirred in his chair as his hands quickly turned to fists. "Young man, you make another aggressive move towards me, and I'll have your ass thrown out of here so fast your damn head will spin off," Materson quietly said without looking in Russo's direction.

Gwen reached out with her hand and gently squeezed Russo's knee in an attempt to calm him down. Russo yielded to her expertise in this type of situation, plus he didn't want to let his anger get the best of him. Although deep down inside he knew that before he left this hospital he was going to tell this Director exactly what he thought of him, and he didn't care if it hurt his feelings.

"Well, Materson, if you already know what I said, then you should trust in my instincts on this one," Dr. Hampstead added coolly trying to play mediator.

"Your instincts, eh?" Materson grunted. "What do your instincts tell you when one of your beloved patients doesn't have a pulse? Are they dead or alive?"

"In this situation," Dr. Hampstead started.

"Just answer the question, Doc!" Materson growled.

"They would be dead," she replied almost in a whisper.

"WOW! Can you believe it? A person who doesn't have a pulse is dead… HOLY SHIT! GET THE HELL OUT! REALLY … ACTUALLY DEAD!" Materson mocked as his eyes grew wide with each childish comment.

"Alright then, it's settled, he's dead and he needs to be taken out of the quarantine room and sent to the morgue," Materson said satisfied that he was going to get his way.

"But you can't, he's still showing signs that he is alive, and he might still BE CONTAGIOUS!" Dr. Hampstead cried out in disbelief.

"I don't care if the man stands up and sings me Happy Fucking Birthday. If he doesn't have a pulse, he's fucking dead and that's that," Materson yelled as he picked up his desk phone.

"Sir, you're making a huge mistake," Gwen pleaded with him.

"Awww, touching!" Materson answered while pretending to whip a fake tear away from his eye. "You know, honey, with your good looks you would fit in great here at MY hospital. I could put you on TOP of the world you know," Materson said with a perverted grin etched across his face.

"That's it, I'm going break you in two!" Russo hollered as he jumped up and began walking briskly to the back of Materson's desk.

"Easy now Rambo, one more step, and all I have to do is hit that little red button on my phone, and ten armed security officers are going to make you wish that your mother never met your father," Materson quickly said as his finger rested on the red button.

"Neal!" Gwen called out, "He's not worth it! Come on, let's get downstairs and try to get Carlos to another hospital,"

Russo stopped his progress, but continued to stare Materson down. His piercing stare conveyed to Materson his conviction, and he realized that had the pretty young doctor not said what she said, that man might have tried to kill him. In the end, though, he still won, and that feeling caused him to smile while he subconsciously patted his own back. Feeling satisfied, Materson pressed the button to call the head of security.

Joe Malone was sitting in his office reviewing the security reports from the previous night when his cell phone vibrated off the edge of his desk. As he picked it up he swore aloud as he recognized who it was that was calling. Against his own objection, he answered the phone. "Security, this is Joe,"

"Joe, it's Materson. Listen, the wet back that was brought in last night, you know the one that's in the quarantine room. He's dead and his corpse needs to be removed IMMEDIATELY!" Materson squawked in his ear.

"Yes, sir, Director Materson, I know the one that you're talking about, but Dr. Hampstead has given us strict orders to not go near him."

"Let me ask you something Joe? Who pays your ridiculously high salary?"

"Umm, you do, sir. I'll have two of my men grab some orderlies and get him out of the quarantine room, tag him, and bag him for the morgue," Malone stammered.

"Whatever, I don't care if you throw him out with the garbage, just get him out of my hospital … NOW!" Materson screamed into the phone before he slammed the receiver down.

"Asshole!" Malone mumbled under his breath as he paged his two roving guys.

"Now that wasn't so bad, was it Dr. Hampstead?" Materson continued as she sat dumbfounded in front of his desk.

"You're making a huge mistake," Gwen said as she stood up and started to head for the door.

"Yea, that's what all my ex's say… as I kick them out. Oh, yea, one more thing Dr. Hampstead. Have your office cleaned out by five today, because your fired!" Materson said as he took a big sigh of relief.

"You son of a bitch, we'll see what my father has to say about that," Dr. Hampstead said as she got up and abruptly walked to the door of his office.

"I know what he'll say. He'll agree with me, plain and simple," Materson said with a shit-eating grin. "Now all of you get the fuck out of my office and my hospital and never come back."

Before the trio left his office Russo turned around and looked at Materson with his own sly grin … "I'll see you soon."

A shiver crept up Materson's back as his smile disappeared. Agitated that another man had seen fear in his eyes, he jammed the button on his phone to his assistant.

"Yes," Sara answered.

"Get in here, I'm stressed out," he yelled into the speaker before jamming the button again, effectively ending the conversation.

CHAPTER 14
THERE GOES THE NEIGHBORHOOD

Dee Thompson and Craig Jefferson quickly exited Joe Malone's office before they could be hit with flying objects as Malone was having one of his angry fits ... again. This time Malone had just gotten off of the phone with Materson, and evidently the call didn't go like Malone had planned. Most conversations with Materson never went as planned, but normally Malone would wait until his subordinates were out of earshot before he threw his tantrums; however, this time was not the case. After he hung up the phone Dee and Craig watched their boss's face turn a dark shade of red as a string of curse words escaped his lips. The two decided that it would be best if they left right after Malone gave them their assignment, primarily because they knew that shit always rolled downhill.

As Craig delicately shut Malone's door so as to not disturb his plaques and pictures on the wall, he heard a shrill crash against the back of the door as something glass shattered upon impact.

"Whew!" Craig whispered as his wiped the sweat from his brow, "I've seen him pissed before, but never anything like that. It's a good thing "Mad Dog" Materson wasn't here to deliver the news in person, I think Malone would have taken his head off."

"Yea, I don't think I've ever seen him that mad before, but then again I've only been here for about four months. Every time I see him, he's nice to me. Always asking me if I feel comfortable with this job, and telling me that if I ever need anything to come to him," Dee spoke as he acknowledged his partner's disgust in the situation.

"Well you're right, he's always nice to us, the staff, and the patients, but I don't think he would lend a hand to the seniors if they were hanging off a cliff," Craig continued, still amazed at Malone's break in self-control.

All of the security staff, and a good majority of the hospital staff, referenced the senior management and board of trustees as seniors. They were given this nickname due to the fact that they always introduced themselves as "Senior Management" then their job title. The security staff being the most underpaid department had come up with the name, and it stuck.

Craig, a heavyset experienced security officer with old Navy tattoos on his forearms, a withered scar above his left eye, and a prominent chin, walked slightly ahead of his younger colleague. Out of respect for the man and all that he had taught him in such a very little time, young Dee admired the wily vet, and considered him a quasi-father figure.

Dee stood roughly five-feet seven inches was lean, clean shaven, and always wore a smile, which earned him the nickname Smiley from his fellow co-workers. Dee was fresh out of college and ready to change the world before he even knew that it spun on its own axis. He looked up to Craig and utilized his partner's experience. Like most college kids during their first year out, Dee wanted to change the world, and change it overnight. Seeing the potential in the young man, Craig took him under his wing and taught him everything he knows about life, love, and the world of Miami Med Security. The two kindred spirits requested to be partners on the same shift, and understanding how Craig could benefit Dee's career goals, Malone saw no problem with scheduling the two together. Malone liked it when his officers went on to better themselves, and he never stood in their way. Craig could remember countless times when Malone himself would call an employee into his office and demand that they apply for a better job, and fifty percent of the time these employees obtained the better job. Like Malone, Craig believed that to help oneself, one must help others succeed.

"Man, I can't tell you how NOT excited I am to go in and cut the zombie lose. I got a real bad feeling about this one," Dee said as the two rounded the corner and headed straight for the quarantine room.

"Why'd you call him the zombie?" Craig inquired.

"That's what everyone is calling him. I mean he has no pulse, heart rate, or blood pressure, yet his eyes are open, and he's still able to open and close his mouth," Dee answered as a chill crept down his back, causing him to shiver. "Don't you watch horror movies, old-timer?" Dee asked jokingly.

"Yes, you young brat, I watch horror movies, but only the good ones, and I know what a zombie is, but I was just concerned why you called a patient that," Craig replied.

"Besides... who is everyone?"

"You know, everyone. The nurses, staff, our co-workers, and even some doctors, although I hear them mumble it under their breath," Dee answered defensively.

"Alright, alright. Listen, just because they do it doesn't mean that it's right. How would you feel if you came to a hospital to see your friend or loved one and heard people calling them a derogatory name?" Craig questioned, hoping that Dee would understand the implications of what he said out loud.

"Yea, I know what you're try to explain to me, but this guy's weird, man." Dee tried again to stand his ground.

"I understand that the situation is weird, but come on, let's be respectful," Craig continued. "You like Malone, don't you?"

"Yea. Malone is the best boss I've ever had," Dee answered immediately.

"Alright, then think how he would feel if he had to explain you using these types of names for patients to Materson?" Craig asked.

"Yea, yea, yea. I see your point, but you got to admit, it's still pretty weird that this guy is still alive, yet he has all the signs of being dead," Dee agreed.

"I will admit that it does seem weird," Craig admitted as they continued towards the quarantine room. Craig would never let Dee know how he felt about the whole situation, but it was quite unnerving what this patient was exhibiting. In the back of Craig's mind he knew there had to be a simple explanation, but he couldn't figure it out. The whole situation was troubling to Craig, but ultimately he decided that he would go along with it, cautiously though.

The quarantine room was a completely air sealed room with a built in hospital bed surrounded by numerous machines that checked various vitals for the patients. The tiled floor was solid white, matching the ceiling and the walls. White because any spills or discharges from the patient could be found easily. The back wall was composed of multiple computer monitors. They monitored the patient's vitals and the equilibrium of the room. If a patient had a contagious virus, and the virus mutated and became present in the air, the bottom monitor would flash red, indicating a change in the air quality of the room while effectively sealing off all of the air ducts to contain the virus. A decompression chamber attached to the entryway was the only way in or out of the quarantine room. In case of an outbreak, the decompression chamber would seal itself off from the rest of the hospital with re-enforced glass, effectively quarantining the virus and anyone infected in the room. The wall opposite the monitor screens was decorated with seven small angle view-rotating cameras that feed a viewing room for doctors and nurses to track a patient's progression or regression. Each camera was set to oscillate, but could be overridden through manual controls. Due to the sophistication of the electronics in the room, it had to be cleaned regularly on a four times a day schedule. If the room wasn't properly cleaned the sensors would alert the operators immediately. Anyone who entered the room had to don on the traditional clean suit.

As the two approached the quarantine room, the registration counter window was pulled back slowly as another security officer placed a clipboard on the window track allowing a pen to slide down before it rested at the bottom.

"Morning fellas," the old security officer said from behind the counter window.

"Morning Carl, how's it going?" Craig replied cordially.

"Same ol' shit, new day. You know how it goes," Carl answered.

"Do we ever," Dee said with a sigh of disgust.

Carl had been around since the beginning of Miami Med. He was an old timer who just didn't want to stay home and retire; he needed something to keep him going. He often laughed and told people that if he didn't get out of the house his old lady was going to put him six feet under and enjoy his retirement by herself. Carl was a retired beat cop from Ft. Lauderdale where he worked for forty years before retiring. He was a simple man who didn't care too much for the ultra-rich clientele that the hospital catered to, but he did enjoy the money.

"Malone called me about five minutes ago and said that Butch Cassidy and The Sundance Kid were headin' my way," Carl said with his slow southern drawl.

"Well, we gotta let that guy go that came in earlier this morning. According to Materson, he's gotta go now!" Craig said, smiling at Carl's nickname for him and Dee.

"Hmph," Carl replied. "Seems we oughta leave that fella right where he is, something ain't right with him."

"See, that's what I've been telling you," Dee piped up as he finished completing the sign-out form.

"Orders gentlemen, we've got orders," Craig said as he and Dee accepted their clean suits from Carl.

"Well, when you fellas get done with him, I've got his personal effects in a box back here. I'll sign them out for you. Gimme a sec and I'll unlock the security doors. Your two know the drill, you gotta wait until the green light goes off in the decomp room before the doors will open for the Q-room," Carl explained as he had done so many times before.

"We got it, Carl," Craig said before zipping up his clean suit. Dee was already in his giving Carl his traditional thumbs up and smile as he joined Craig in the decompression room. The doors closed behind them with a hiss as all of the air was sucked completely out of the room. The fans above them turned on automatically commencing the decompression process. Carl watched them patiently from his stool, and once the green light in the room shone, he turned on the microphone for the room. The metallic ping signaling the open frequency exited the speakers in the corners of the room before they heard the Carl's voice telling them the coast was clear. The two men exited the decompression room timidly as they stepped into the immaculate quarantine room.

The room was eerily quiet sans the electronic hum of all the machines connected to the patient. They slowly circled the patient gazing down at him as they continued to walk around him. Carlos' hospital gown was covered in dried dark blood, almost black, yet all of the blood was old, there were no new fresh stains. His eyes were completely blood red with small black dots scattered across the pupil. His chest no longer rose, and the color of his skin had turned to a gray hue. His fingers continued an almost mindless grasping motion while his eyes persistently flashed around the room, as if symbolizing a fear of some sort. As the two men approached, his eyes suddenly stopped moving and directed their attention to the two men while his fingers subsided and rested palms down on the bed.

"Man, this is freaky. How can his eyes still be open yet all of the monitors show him flat-lined?" Dee questioned through his headset radio.

"Honestly, I don't know, and I really don't want to know. Let's just get him up and out of here like the boss said," Craig returned as he reached down to the patient's wrist and began to unclasp the wrist restraint.

"Good morning gentlemen!" Nurse Johnson's voice boomed in their ears, frightening the two men as they both jumped in shock.

"HOLY SHIT! You could've given me a damn heart attack. How 'bout a little warning next time," Dee complained into his radio.

"Easy Dee," Craig replied calmly, as his heart rate began to slow to its original pace. "Nurse Johnson, perhaps you can give us a little more warning next time before you greet us in a somewhat stressful situation," Craig continued as he turned around to face the wall of cameras.

"Warning ... Aren't you gentlemen in security?" Nurse Johnson mocked.

"Yes, we are, but we don't have a camera on you to know when you are going to say something to us," Craig answered, fighting back his anger.

"Gentlemen, if you can't handle this, then I will gladly let Director Materson know that you two aren't fit for duty, and he will simply replace you," Nurse Johnson continued, demanding respect.

"Listen we can handle anything, just give us a head's up next time. Sheesh!" Dee said, frustratingly shaking his head.

"Enough with the comebacks gentlemen. Director Materson and Ms. Maysworth informed me that Mr. Carlos is leaving this morning. Please undo his restraints and disconnect him from the monitors, then escort him off the premises," Nurse Johnson said emotionless.

"Yes, Nurse Ratchet!" Dee mumbled.

"WHAT WAS THAT?!" Nurse Johnson demanded as her face burned red with rage. She knew that people called her that behind her back, and it infuriated her, the lack of respect that she was given.

"He said yes, Ma'am," Craig calmly answered as he silenced Dee with a stare. "We've got it from here. Please put a technician on to direct us in the disconnection of these," Craig continued as his stretched his arm out and pointed to the numerous wires and tubes inserted into Carlos' body.

"Very well," Nurse Johnson replied. As she turned the microphone over to the lab tech, Craig looked at Dee and put his hand up to his neck and slid it across quickly, signaling to Dee to cut out his antics. Defeated and shamed, Dee dropped his head and slowly nodded it forward.

Over the next couple of minutes the lab tech directed Craig and Dee to appropriately remove all of the wires and tubes from Carlos' body and restore the machines to their appropriate places in the room. After they were done, all that was left were the wrist and ankle restraints. During the whole ordeal Carlos never made a sound, his dark red eyes just simply followed the men around the room.

"Can you hear us, sir?" Craig spoke loudly as he looked down at Carlos whose eyes were affixed on him. He tried again, but Carlos gave no acknowledgment that he understood or even heard Craig's voice. Slowly they unbuckled his wrists and held his arms in place to ensure that he didn't try and move them. Gingerly they released their grip on his arms and to their surprise, he didn't move his arms at all, he just continued to stare at them. His eyes cautiously darted back and forth between Craig and Dee, yet he still made no sound. Dee motioned for Craig to undo the restraint on his ankle while he kept a watchful eye on Carlos. After Craig was done, the two switched duties as Dee undid his other ankle restraint. Once they were finished Carlos was free from his restraints. The men gently placed one arm on Carlos' wrist, while they dug their hands underneath his back and slowly rose him to a seated position. All the while Craig continued to talk to him and ask him questions, but no response was offered. They mildly turned his body ever so carefully as to not cause him any undue harm or stress, until his feet hung off of the bed, and he faced the door. Craig looked in horror at his back where his skin was colored dark purple, almost as if he was bruised from his neck to his buttocks. He motioned for Dee to come around and look.

"Why is the rest of him grey and his back, almost black ... did he get burned or something?" Dee questioned.

"It's called blood levity," Craig answered while he continued to stare. "It happens when a person dies, and all of the blood stops circulating and gravity takes effect. The dark coloration is the fact that the blood isn't oxygenated anymore. This doesn't make any sense."

"Well, can dead people sit up?" Dee questioned as his tone revealed his anxiety.

"No, let's just get this over with. I've seen and heard enough today to last me a lifetime," Craig said as Dee walked back around to face Carlos. "Put his slippers on him."

"Yea, let's hurry this shit up," Dee said.

Dee reached down, grabbed Carlos' left ankle, and began to slide the hospital slipper onto his foot. Almost instantaneously Carlos snapped out of his trance and yanked the top off of Dee's clean suit in an unheralded rage. He threw the top of the clean suit to the side absentmindedly as his other hand latched onto the top of Dee's head. The massive man jerked Dee's head up, pulled it backwards exposing his neck where he sunk his teeth in. Dee screamed in terror as he tried unsuccessfully to break Carlos' grip. Bright red blood spewed from his neck as Carlos pulled his teeth back with sinewy flesh and muscle hanging haphazardly off of his chin. He took two bite, before he dove back into Dee's neck and began to chew the flesh directly off of his neck. Dee screamed again this time more gargled as blood ejected out of his mouth and onto the floor. His struggling became lest persistent as the massive blood loss and pain forced his body into an unconscious state.

"DEE!" Craig screamed in horror as he watched his friend being devoured by this man. Craig couldn't move as his body was in a state of shock, as the blood drained out of his face. Suddenly with all of his will power, he forced his legs to move as he tried to run around the edge of the bed to aide his helpless friend. As he cornered the bed he lost his footing on the slippery blood stained floor. He fell to the ground, banging his head against the side of the bed as he went down. Trying to fight off the stars that he saw, he screamed for help into the microphone, but no one heard him as the lab tech had stepped out for a quick break. He struggled to push himself off of the slippery floor, but with the clean suit he was unable to get a grip on the now blood soaked floor. He continued to flail around on the floor before flipping himself over onto his back just in time to see Carlos fling Dee's dead body up against the wall and reach down for him. Craig wailed in panic and feverishly fought with Carlos, inadvertently pulling Carlos directly on top of him. His clean suit protected him from Carlos' vicious bites as his teeth were unable to penetrate the texture of the suit. The two men continued to wrestle on the ground until Craig as able to temporarily subdue Carlos' hands while he wrapped his legs around his chest and pulled downward, buying him a few vital seconds to regroup and try to figure out what to do next.

Suddenly a shadow appeared over him, causing him to look up, where he recognized the outline of Dee's body. He had to squint because the bright ceiling lights temporarily blinded him. As the shadow lowered itself closer to his head, it effectively blocked out the blinding light, and Craig stared up into the eyes of his worst nightmare. Dee's eyes were completely red, just like Carlos', while his gaping neck wound still oozed blood down the right side of his body and his clean suit. With his mouth open and a malicious rage in his eyes Dee wrenched the top of Craig's suit off. Craig let go of Carlos' arms and quickly brought them up in defense, but it was too late. Dee latched his teeth on the right side of Craig's face and pulled the flesh back, exposing the muscle lines and his teeth. Pain seared through his body as he tried to cover his face with his hands, when he felt the rest of his suit being torn apart as Carlos' free hands began ripping into his warm flesh. Craig screamed in agony once more before he conceded the fight, and his eyes shut. The two men continued to pull chunks of his flesh off and stuff it into their gaping maws. The floor became coated in fresh blood and body fluids that were violently sloshed around as the men feasted.

On the outside of the back wall of the quarantine room the lab tech leaned with headphones on and a cigarette in his hand. He bobbed his head up and down to the rhythm of his music while he took another drag on his cigarette. After he was done with his cigarette he flicked it into the woods, took off his earphones, and shoved them into his pocket before he pulled out his electronic access card and re-entered the building. As he walked back into his lab his computer monitor was flashing red, indicating contamination in the quarantine room. He quickly checked the monitoring link which yielded the level of contamination as massive. He refreshed the screen thinking that the system had an error, but in the seconds that it took to refresh the screen the contamination yielded outbreak, which was a step above massive.

"That can't be," he said as he turned to the security monitors and froze in shock as he saw the three men facing the camera wall standing in at least an inch of blood. The two security officers had their clean suits in tatters and sported fatal wounds on their neck and face. Their blood which was no longer bright red, but dark crimson continued to ooze out on their suits. Their eyes were completely blood red with small black dots, and their mouths were open with stringy material hanging from their teeth. The third, the actual patient, had no new injuries, but his face was covered in blood and his jaws moved in a chew motion.

Sweat began to bead up on the lab tech's head as he carefully reached for the microphone. As he pushed the transmit button, he could only squeak into the headset, "Craig?? Dee?? What's going on?"

The instant that his voice filled the room the three broke into a frenzied rage as they ran around the room turning the bed over on its side, ripping equipment off of the counters, knocking rolling monitors to the ground, frantically looking around the room. They looked as if they were searching for something. Suddenly the bottom right camera screen went snowy as the lab tech noticed one of the men knock it off of the wall with a computer monitor. He watched in awe as they knocked each and every one off, until they were at the last one. Craig leaned in real close to the camera, almost putting his eye on the lens while the lab tech unconsciously leaned in closer to the monitor staring at Craig's blood filled eye; then all he saw was snow as the camera was jerked out of the wall. Fear set in as the lab tech grabbed the radio and called for Carl. Carl answered and the lab tech explained to him that something was going on in the quarantine room, and that he better get in there to see what was happening. He explained that everyone was acting weird and violent, and there was a lot of blood. He instructed Carl to proceed with caution. After he got done he switched the monitors to the decomp room to see if he could see anything.

Carl came around from behind his security counter and walked slowly to the air lock doors of the decomp room. As he peered inside he couldn't see past the decomp room because the lights were flickering off and on in the quarantine room. He entered his access code into the electronic pad and waited until the doors slid open to enter. Once he entered the decomp room he un-holstered his automatic Glock and flipped the safety switch off. As the doors behind him slid back together he listened to the whistle of the air being sucked out of the room as he continued to gaze into the darkness of the quarantine room. The lights flickered like strobes, and he stood closer to the glass doors trying to see what was going on, but the flickering was too fast. For a moment he thought he saw Craig's face, not protected by the clean suit, but he couldn't be sure. The hum of the exhaust fans drowned out any noise he could possibly hear from the room. Suddenly a wet smack jarred the door causing him to physically jump back up. A chill ran down his spine as the lights flickered once again and he saw the bloody handprint on the glass door.

"Cra… Cra… Craig? Da… Da… Dee?" Carl called out sheepishly, as his whole body suddenly became saturated with sweat. Neither Craig nor Dee answered as the exhaust fans turned off, and the humming noised slackened. The lights above the door went from red to green indicating that the room was not pressurized, and that he could enter the quarantine room.

The lab tech watched unblinkingly from his console as he continued to lean closer and closer to the monitor until he could see that his breath was fogging up the bottom of the screen. "Carl, you need to go in there and see what's going on," he said into the microphone, projecting his voice into the decomp room.

"I know that!" Carl shouted at the camera. "Didn't you just see what happened, why don't you get your skinny li'l ass down here and do it? Hunh? Exactly, let me take my damn time, you little mongrel." The last part was mumbled under his breath and went undetected by the lab tech.

"Hey guys, I'm coming in," Carl said, louder this time with more force behind his voice. He slowly languidly reached his hand up and gently grasped the silver door handle leading to the quarantine room. He pulled the door back cautiously and quietly as he propped it open with his right foot. Gingerly, he took a small step forward, and as he placed his foot down he heard a small splash and looked down. To his horror he saw that he was splashing dark blood onto boots. Carl started shaking uncontrollably at the horrific site before he vomited all over himself. As he tried to regain his composure he heard multiple footsteps displacing and splashing the blood as they seemed to be headed in his direction.

"Guys, if you're in there, you better make a sound before I unload this clip. I ain't fucking around, either," Carl called again into the room, but received no feedback. What he did notice was that the steps toward him stopped, and the room fell deathly silent, as the only sound he could hear was his own heart beating in his chest. Then unexpectedly a voracious roar erupted from the room, followed by the sound of multiple footsteps rapidly approaching the doorway. Carl screamed in panic as he was able to fire off five rounds before the three men tackled him down to the ground in the decomp room. The force of the three men shattered the other glass door and covered all of them in a sea of glass shards that pierced their skin. Carl screamed in anguish as fiery pangs of pain stabbed all over his body from the rain of glass from the door and the teeth of his attackers as the ripped at his flesh, pulling chunks away three at a time. He madly swung his fist and the butt of the gun at his attackers and was able to knock them back as he flipped onto his stomach and tried to crawl away. As he started to stretch out his arms to pull himself away, he felt hands on both of his legs as they were pulled upward off of the ground as his attackers started to pull him into the quarantine room. He fought their attack for a mere second before screaming as they savagely yanked him back into the quarantine room. As he was viciously dragged back into the room his reflexes took over, and he uncontrollably fired the gun in the direction of the glass doors leading into the decomp room. The reinforced glass was strong, but the multiple shots weakened it considerably causing the glass to splinter and spider web before chunks of glass fell into the hallway leading to the decomp room. The sounds of Carl's cries only lasted a minute before the only sound that could be heard was the grotesque sound of animals in the wild feasting on a fresh kill.

The lab tech watched in horror as he picked up the phone and dialed Nurse Johnson's emergency number while simultaneously breaking the glass case that contained the emergency alarm button. The button was only to be toggled in the event of an outbreak. He jammed his finger down on the button, instantly causing all of the hospital alarms to blare loudly with the robotic phrase, "This is a Code Red Alert!" repeatedly, as the strobe lights throughout the hospital instantly turned on.

CHAPTER 15
A PALE RIDER... AND HELL FOLLOWED AFTER HIM

The blaring sound of the alarm startled Dr. Hampstead as she was seated in her office talking to Russo and Gwen about their options. The jarring sound forced all three out of their chairs while quickly covering their ears.

"What the hell does that mean?" Russo shouted over the clamor as he and Gwen looked around like deer in the headlights, an expected reaction to the massive alarm system.

"It means that we have a potential outbreak!" Dr. Hampstead shouted back.

"Outbreak, you mean like a disease ..." Russo's shout quieted off as he realized what the women were thinking ... Carlos.

"I don't know what it means; the sirens will cease after five minutes, but the strobe lights will continue until they are shut off. Our system is connected to both the fire department and the police department, so they'll be here soon. I need to get in touch with Carol and figure out what is going on. You two stay here," Dr. Hampstead shouted as she picked up her office desk phone and dialed the front desk. Russo and Gwen nodded their heads as they held their hands up to their ears. They exchanged a look that told the other that they almost expected this. Gwen then turned her head away and stared out the window, lost in her thoughts. Thousands of thoughts ran through her mind as she began replaying everything that had happened since Jonathan brought Gabo into her hospital tent with the spider bites. She remembered how he looked, how sick he was, and how nothing she did worked. She thought back to the jaguar and how it attacked them with a blind rage as if it felt no pain. She strained her mind as she forced herself to try to find a connection; she knew there had to be one, but she just couldn't see yet. As she continued her strenuous researching, she never even noticed the sirens stopping and Russo talking to her until she felt his rough hand gently shake her shoulder, bringing her back to reality.

"Gwen, Gwen ... hey ... you okay?" Russo spoke calmly, not wanting to scare her.

"Yea, I'm fine. I'm just going back through everything in my head to ..." she started before he cut her off.

"Gwen, it's not your fault," Russo interjected, thinking that she was doubting herself again.

"No, let me finish," she snapped coldly. "What I was trying to say was that I was trying to find a connection between all of this. There has to be, I just haven't figured it out yet, but I will," she said confidently.

"Sorry, I assumed wrong," Russo said sheepishly as he realized that he had insulted her.

"No, I'm sorry, I didn't mean to snap, but trust me I'll let you know when I'm having one of my breakdown moments, and I'm pretty sure you'll be around with your broad shoulder for me to lean on," Gwen said with a smile and a quick wink.

"Anytime!" Russo replied as his body slightly tingled all over with a small amount of excitement. Gwen intrigued Russo for two reasons: first of all she was intelligent, and secondly, she could take care of herself. These two traits were never common in the normal caliber of women that interested Russo, but the change was intoxicating, and he decided to go with the change.

"I just got off the phone with Carol," Dr. Hampstead said as she hung up her desk phone and pulled her doctor's robe on while picking up her keys with her ID badges and access cards.

"And?" Gwen questioned eagerly.

"There's been an incident in the quarantine room. She didn't know exactly what happened, but Malone has closed off the hallway and ordered all of his men there," she explained as she headed for the door.

"Where are you going?" Russo questioned.

"Well, to the quarantine room of course. You two coming?" she asked while opening her door. Without answering, both Russo and Gwen jogged over to the door to catch up. The three proceeded down the hall and headed down the elevator to the first floor.

"What about Materson? Should you even go down there?" Gwen questioned in the elevator.

"What about him?" Dr. Hampstead laughed. "That chicken shit wouldn't be anywhere near that room with all of the sirens and alarms going off, are you kidding me? Besides, the protocol for something like this requires all senior management to stay in their offices behind a locked down, just in case an outbreak occurs. You know they're the most important people in the hospital, so they HAVE to stay alive," Dr. Hampstead joked in a sarcastic tone.

"Figures," Russo muttered. "That man would throw his mother to the wolves if it meant saving his sorry hide."

"Exactly," Dr. Hampstead agreed as the elevator chimed and the doors opened. Carol met them as they exited the elevator, she was clearly shaken and concerned about everyone's well-being.

"Dr. Hampstead, I've never seen Malone like that. He ran by my desk barking orders into his radio and screaming at his men as he ran down the hall. Normally he's cool, calm, and collected. It was truly frightening," Carol explained as her hands shook uncontrollably.

"It's okay, Carol! Everything's going to be alright, but we need to get back there and help if we can, and the authorities will need to know where to go when they get here, so I need for you to go back to your desk," Dr. Hampstead said in a soothing tone as she gently massaged Carol's back.

"Ok, Dr. Hampstead," Carol reluctantly agreed. "One other thing, some of the patients and their families are asking what is going on. What do I tell them?"

"Contact the nurse's stations on all floors, and have them along with the orderlies go door to door and calm the patients and their families down and reassure them that everything is under control," Dr. Hampstead instructed, knowing that giving Carol something to do would take her mind off of the situation.

"Understood… Be careful Dr. Hampstead," Carol said as she turned and went back to her desk.

"We will be, I hope," Dr. Hampstead said, while only whispering the last part so only she could hear.

The three rounded the corner and walked up to the electronic access port beside the closed double doors that led to the quarantine room. The doors wouldn't budge, even after she hit the handicap button on the wall. She inserted her card in, the electronic lock clicked green, and the doors swung open.

As the heavy wooden doors mechanically swung outward all ten of Malone's security staff swiveled on their feet, pointing their automatics at Dr. Hampstead, Russo, and Gwen as they walked into the hallway.

Frozen with fear the three of them stopped in their tracks and instantly raised their hands above their heads.

"Stand down men!" Bellowed Malone as he stepped out from the lab tech's office. "Jesus Christ, men! The problem is in the quarantine room, not out of it. Each one of you holster you weapons … NOW!"

Nervously the security staff holstered their weapons before turning back and carefully watching the already spider-webbed door leading into the decomp room. Normally when all of the security staff was together it was more of a boys locker room atmosphere as they joked around with each other and played practical jokes, but now in the presence of danger the atmosphere surrounding them was deathly somber. None of the men spoke, they just restlessly fidgeted around while keeping a constant eye in the direction of the quarantine room.

Malone motioned for the three to join him in the lab tech's office. Introductions were quickly given as Malone offered the women a chair, which they promptly declined.

"Just what in the hell are you doing here, Doc?" Malone questioned gruffly.

"I want to know what is going on, and I have the background on the patient," Dr. Hampstead answered assertively.

"Which one?" Malone asked with a heavy sigh.

"The one in the quarantine room Malone, the one that caused the alarms to sound."

"Again Doc, which one?" Malone asked again as he stared at the ground. This time the stress that he was under came through in his answer. Based on this, and the fact that Malone couldn't look her in the eyes, she realized that they had a bigger problem than she had first thought.

"Well, my friend Carlos is in the quarantine room; he is the one that we are concerned about," Russo tried to explain, unable to pick up on what Malone was trying to convey.

"How many are in the quarantine room, Mr. Malone?" Gwen asked, sensing that others had now come into contact with Carlos and that he was possibly still contagious.

"I got three of my men in there as well, and right now nobody's going in until we can figure out just what in the hell we're dealing with," Malone explained.

"So he's still contagious. Is that what you're trying to say?" Dr. Hampstead questioned.

"I guess you could say that, but I ain't never heard of any infection causing you to act this way," Malone said.

"Act what way?" Russo questioned with a perplexed look on his face.

"According to Marcus," Malone said as he stretched his hand out in the lab tech's direction, "your friend, Carlos, viciously attacked two of my security officers, Dee Thompson and Craig Jefferson, with some kind of brute force. According to Marcus, he ripped the helmet top off of one of Dee's clean suit and bit him on the neck, before throwing him against the wall," Malone stopped to take a sip of water from a bottle that he was carrying. After he put the top back on and sat the bottle down, he noticed the horrified look in the three as they were silently listening.

"Your faces are exactly what mine was when Marcus explained the same story to me; unfortunately… it gets worse," Malone continued. "He then wrestled with Craig and was eventually subdued before Dee, the one with the gaping hole in his neck, reach down and tore his partner's clean suit away from his body, before he preceded to bite his nose clean off of his body. With Craig trying to stop him, your friend was freed. Then the two of them attacked Craig, holding him down while ripping parts of his flesh off with their teeth," Malone explained as his body suddenly shivered.

"You mean they were trying to eat him? That's impossible!" Russo shouted, as he was completely astounded by Malone's story.

"See for yourself," Malone said quietly as he nodded in Marcus' direction. "Let them see what happened," Malone instructed Marcus. Marcus obliged and typed a few keystrokes and clicked the mouse, instantly bringing up the video on the main monitor in the room. He clicked the play icon, and the previous events from the quarantine room began to unfold. As they watched, both Gwen and Dr. Hampstead covered their mouths with their hands as they were completely appalled at the savagery they were witnessing on the video. They continued to watch, shocked at what they saw, as hope to save Carlos' life disappeared in the wind. As the video ended, Malone turned to the three and just stared at them, recognizing the look that he had when Marcus first showed him the video. He waited to say anything until the horrible truth had sunk in.

"Holy shit!" Russo exclaimed quietly as his eyes were still affixed on the main monitor. In all of his years he had never seen something so horrible before. In all of the missions that he had done for the corps, all of the death and destruction he had witnessed when he was in, didn't even amount to a drop in the bucket to what he had just observed on the screen.

"My words exactly!" Malone commented, "The next part gets even worse; unfortunately we don't have video because these people knocked out the lights and the security cameras,"

"Intentionally?" Dr. Hampstead questioned.

"Not from what I can tell, they just seem to be acting in a blind rage. They destroyed the whole room," Malone explained as his stress level became more visible on his face.

"Please continue with your story," Dr. Hampstead instructed as she stared off into space, trying to figure out what happened.

"Marcus informed Carl, the other security officer I have on staff here, to cautiously check out what was going on. Now we don't have a camera in the decomp room, but based on what I could see by looking in on it, they came through the electronic doors and attacked Carl. He evidently tried to fight them off, judging from the way the blood splatter is patterned, but he didn't win, and he must have somehow discharged his weapon at the decomp doors, causing them to crack and almost shatter," Malone continued.

"This might be a stupid question, but do we know if he survived or if they killed him?" Gwen asked concerned.

"Right now, we don't, but based on what I saw on that video, it'll shock me if he's alive," Malone answered sadly.

"I don't have any expertise in infectious diseases or any of that stuff, but based on what I saw, this looks to me like rabies. Am I right Doc?" Russo asked Dr. Hampstead.

"Yes and no," she began. "The behaviors that all three men have exhibited are consistent with the manic state that a person can be in if they have been infected with rabies, although this manic state is a rarity because most individuals become too sick to move once they have been infected, but these men ..." She trailed off as she realized the magnitude of what she was thinking.

"Should have been dead," Gwen finished her explanation, with a slight nod towards Dr. Hampstead.

"Dead?" Russo and Malone questioned simultaneously.

"Yes, a wound like that to someone's neck is almost fatal any time, not to mention the sheer volume of blood that was spilled in that room. All three men should be dead, but more importantly, Dee should have never been able to stand back up after an attack like that. It's impossible to say the least," Gwen explained as Dr. Hampstead silently nodded her head.

"Okay, so why aren't they?" Russo questioned in disbelief.

"I don't know, I really don't know," Gwen said as her eyes drifted back to the monitor, reminding her of what she had just seen.

"Well, one thing's for sure, we're not going to know any more until we can get into that room," Malone said as he pulled his sidearm out and checked the clip.

"Correct, but we also don't know what type of virus we are dealing with. Is it airborne, is it only transferred through the exchange of bodily fluids, or what? I don't think rushing into that room is going to do us any good, and it might just get you killed," Dr. Hampstead said with compassion in her eyes as she looked at Malone.

"What do you suppose we do then Doc, because I can promise you that I ain't letting anybody get near that door until the threat is eliminated," Malone said.

"I think we need to contact the CDC," Gwen said.

"I agree," Dr. Hampstead said quietly.

Suddenly there was a loud commotion in the hall causing all of their hearts to suddenly leap into their throats as the door to the monitoring room swung open with force. Nurse Johnson marched in scolding everyone with her gaze as she peered over her glasses.

"Marcus, can you explain to me why you pushed the alarm and why the quarantine room has been sectioned off by the brutes?" Nurse Johnson questioned coldly.

"Well, the reason being ..."Marcus started before she cut him off.

"Never mind that, we'll discuss later. I want you to unlock the doors to the decomp room, the quarantine room, and get that non-affiliated heathen out of our hospital. Evidently the security staff is having a problem following orders!" she continued as she shot a dagger like glance at Malone, who simply stared back. "Also, why are the security cameras down? Just what the hell is going on in here?"

"Well, Nurse Johnson, Marcus was trying to explain to you what happened before you cut him off so rudely. I will give you the short version. Basically, three of my staff have been attacked by this person, they have been infected with whatever he had, and they have now turned your precious quarantine room into a dump. Now we don't know if the virus can be transferred other than through bodily fluids, but I'll be damned if I let anyone go in there without knowing. This person's attacks should have been fatal, but they weren't, and now we fear that he may have infected my staff with this virus," Malone explained quickly as he continued to stare at Nurse Johnson.

"So we have three employees in the room, they have been attacked by this heathen, and they could be dying, yet you're not allowing anyone to go in to help them. Is that about right, Malone?" she asked sarcastically.

"Basically, yes but we still don't know what we are dealing with Nurse Johnson," Dr. Hampstead spoke up as she quickly stepped in between Malone and Nurse Johnson, trying to politically handle this delicate situation.

"Last I heard from Director Materson is that you've been fired, therefore you have no authority in this matter, and since Malone doesn't seem to value the lives of his men, I guess I have no choice but to assume control and help the injured, hopefully before it's too late," Nurse Johnson said as she abruptly walked to the exit of the monitoring room.

"You fucking bitch!" Malone shouted as he followed after her, followed quickly by Russo, Gwen, Dr. Hampstead, and Marcus. Nurse Johnson elbowed her way through the throng of security officers as she traipsed her way to the electronic security pad of the decomp room.

"Nurse Johnson, you open that door, and you might doom us all," Russo hollered over the heads of the security officers. As his words sunk in to everybody, the consequences of his statement lingered in everyone's mind as they all tensed up as Nurse Johnson began to enter her code into the electronic pad.

"You'd love to think that, wouldn't you? Then you can save the day to impress your pretty little doctor there," Nurse Johnson said as she entered the last number for her code into the pad. An electronic chirp sounded with an artificial voice stating "Welcome Nurse Johnson!" as the glass decomp room doors slid open with a mechanical hiss. As she walked in she noticed the blood stained streaks leading into the already opened quarantine room. She turned back to look at the group with a perplexed look on her face, but was forced to look back into the quarantine room as she heard what seemed like a quiet growl emanating from the back of the quarantine room. The room was completely dark except for the occasionally flutter of the ceiling lights. Each time the room was lit up for a split second she could see fast blurry movement, but before her eyes could adjust the room became dark again. Hesitantly, she took a small step forward, straining her eyes to see, and craning her head to listen.

"Get ready men!" Malone instructed. Hearing this the security officers took up their positions and un-holstered their side arms. They formed two rows, the front row kneeling with their left arms rising at a forty-five degree angle from their planted left foot, and their right arm parallel with the floor above the knee on the floor. Their sidearm was sandwiched between both hands directly level with their chin. The second row was standing feet shoulder width apart with their left elbows tucked in closer to their body and their right elbows roughly pointed outward with their sidearm in the same position as the kneeling group. Sweat immediately began to bead up on their foreheads as each of their hands became sweaty as nervousness danced throughout their bodies. Each man continued to tell himself that he was ready for anything, but believing this was a harder accomplishment.

"Here, I suppose you still remember how to fire one these?" Malone questioned as he pulled his second sidearm out and handed it to Russo.

"Just like riding a bike. Thanks, Malone!" Russo said as Malone acknowledged his appreciation with a simple nod.

"You two need to stay behind us, just in case the shit hits the fan," Malone instructed Dr. Hampstead and Gwen. They agreed quickly, stood behind the two men, and leaned around their inner shoulders to watch what was happening.

A low yet loud moan escaped the quarantine room and filled the hallway as a pungent stench invaded everyone's nostrils. The smell was a distinct odor that reminded all of them of a rotten dead animal. The lights continued their dysfunctional flicker as a sloshing sound permeated the air. Nurse Johnson continued to squint her eyes to see if she could locate the origin of the noise, but each time the lights came on a blurred vision was all she could see. Wanting to see more of what was going on, she took another hesitant step forward, this time as her heel rested on the floor a loud crack sounded under her heel as she realized she had just stepped on broken glass. The instant the crack was heard everything in the quarantine room suddenly stopped moving, and the only sound that could be heard was the static burning of the flickering lights. The sudden silence sent her heartbeat into seventh gear as she tried to muster up the courage to call out to those in the quarantine room. Her first attempt was a complete failure as she was unable to make any sound, and she realized that she was more scared than she thought. She steadied her nerves and opened her mouth.

"This is Nurse Johnson, please show yourself. You're in a restricted area, and you must leave immediately," Nurse Johnson said quietly, with no confidence. She waited for a reply and received none. She was about to try again when she heard a defining growl coming from inside of the room. The growl was so horrific and alien to her that she froze in fear as her world suddenly stopped. The sound of metal clicking immediately followed the growl as each of the officers switched their safeties off as their breathing quickened.

"H ... Hello?!?!" was all Nurse Johnson could squeak this time as her whole body began to convulse with fear. Suddenly the quarantine room erupted with howls, moans, and growls, followed by the sound of liquid being splashed about as somebody was running through it. In an instant four blood soaked shadowy figures emerged from the quarantine room and tackled Nurse Johnson to the ground where they began to attack her flesh with their hands and mouths in a primitive way. Her screams filled the hall, followed shortly by Malone's signal to fire. The hallway became a warzone as bullets whistled down the hallway, imbedding themselves into the walls, floor, and the rotten flesh of the attackers. Each officer emptied his clip into the barbaric scrum at the end of the hallway. After the last bullet found its mark, the hallway was filled with a light colored smoke and the smell of cordite.

"Cease fire men!" Malone ordered behind his officers.

As the smoke cleared, the distinguishable sound of flesh being ripped from the bone still lingered as the officers looked on in horror as the four attackers continued to feast on what was left of the oversized nurse. Their flesh light grey was littered with bullets and hung off of them in a stringy, sinewy mess, but they seemed unfazed, and more importantly, their heads were completely unscathed of bullets.

"That's impossible!" Russo exclaimed, "You can't tell me that four men can take one hundred and sixty bullets and still be alive. That shit ain't right."

"Reload men!" Malone ordered as each officer pulled a fresh clip from their duty belt and jammed it into their sidearms. As each officer finished reloading they again took their aim at the loathsome four, but unlike the first time, the four had suddenly become five, as the body of Nurse Johnson slowly stood up and began to wobble towards them. The flesh on her cheeks had been ripped off, exposing her sides of her jaws. Parts of her scalp were missing as bright red blood oozed down her face and continued down the front of her body where it was smeared over her exposed bra. Her nurse's outfit was in bloody tatters with chunks of flesh still clinging to it. Her left arm was harshly severed below the elbow and parts of the bones in her legs gleamed through the jagged tears in her skin. As she continued towards the officers, her mouth continued its mindless chomping while her eyes had rolled into the back of her head. She stopped abruptly as her head continued to drunkenly lob back and forth before steadying itself. As her head stopped moving her eyes began to roll back, but this time they weren't their normal color, as that color had been replaced by full colored red with black dots scattered about. As she steadied herself, she jerked her head back and let out a shrieking growl that was accompanied by her attackers, as all four bum rushed the ghost white security officers who stood and stared in disbelief.

The four undead attackers relentlessly attacked the security officers with savage brute force that they were unable to repel. Shots were fired off as the officers attempted to defend themselves against the raging horde, but these shots seemed to go unfazed by the attackers as they continued forward. The attackers crashed into the security group like bowling balls, instantly knocking some of the officers onto the ground while slamming others against the wall. The officers tried to fight them off with punches, kicks, and swings with their sidearms, but nothing seemed to affect their attackers. They ripped into their flesh with their teeth and hands as blood spewed outward. The officers cried out in blood-filled gargles as they were quickly decimated. Bits of flesh were atrociously strewn about the hallway as the attackers continued to feed upon the dying security officers. As their last breaths of agony escaped their mouths, the officer's eyes slammed shut, only to reopen mere minutes later completely covered bright red with small black dots scattered across the pupils. Soon after they reopened their eyes, they got to their feet and cocked their heads upward letting a horrid growl loose as they began to look around for food. Security officers who had just died suddenly stood back up and began to walk around again, as if they couldn't feel their missing body parts, or the massive amounts of blood loss, it was as if they had no feeling at all.

In just under ten minutes the attacking force of five infected people quickly became fifteen. As they all stood up and looked around, they began to amble towards Russo, Gwen, Dr. Hampstead, and Malone who stood at the end of the hall completely awe-struck. The four of them backed up slowly as to not bring more attention to themselves. As they continued to take small steps backwards, suddenly their backs were up against the closed doors leading into the hallway.

"Russo, we've hit a wall," Gwen whispered into his ear as she stood up on her toes to speak directly into his ear in an effort to stay completely quiet.

"I know," he whispered back.

"I've never seen anything …"Malone started before he cut himself off at the small gesture of Russo's hand, followed by a simple nod. The crowd of undead simply stared at them, with their totally blood shot eyes, as their mouths continued to chew the rest of the flesh that was still there.

"Malone, very slowly reach out with your access card and scan it on the door to open it. Do not make any fast movements; we don't want to piss them off," Russo whispered out the side of his mouth so he didn't have to move his head.

"Got it," Malone whispered back. He very slowly reached into his pocket and pulled out his access badge. Very carefully and slowly he gently swiped his card across the reader as a green light shown above it, indicating that the reader had accepted his card. A mechanical chime sounded before the doors began to open, forcing all four of them to quickly hold their breath at the sound. The chime shocked the undead attackers out of their gaze as each one turned to face the group and slightly tilted their heads in their direction. The doors opened outward and the group of four began their slow movement backwards into the hall, as the undead attackers continued to watch from a stationary position.

As the group got completely out of the hallway and behind the doors, Marcus suddenly appeared in the monitor room doorway. His face was deathly white, and he had been crying as the tear streaks were apparent down the sides of his face. Russo shot him a glance with wide eyes, trying to convey the serious of the situation, but Marcus didn't pick up on the subtle hint. He cried out "Don't leave me!" before he ran from the doorway in their direction. Marcus made it about three steps before two of the undead latched on to his back. He screamed out in fear before they lowered their powerful jaws onto his shoulders and neck. Fresh red blood spewed from these wounds, instantly covering his face as the two undead pulled giant chunks of flesh from his upper body. He could no longer support their weight and fell face first into the already blood covered floor. The force of his fall smashed his nose up into his brain and he was dead before the horde of undead fell to the floor to feast on his flesh.

"Oh, my God!" Dr. Hampstead gasped as she watched the horror unfold.

"Quick, close those doors!" Russo whispered loudly to Malone.

Malone grabbed his access badge, placed it in the card reader, and input his code once again. The green light shone as the heavy wooden doors began to mechanically close again. As they slowly approached the gears retracting them they let loose a shrill squeak, alerting the undead attackers. The shrill sound forced the foursome to hold their breath as they stared at the massacre taking place, praying the doors would close faster. As the shrill squeak echoed down the hall, one of the undead attackers lifted its head up from Marcus' body and stared in their direction. The attacker cocked its head to the side as if it was studying them before it opened its blood covered mouth and let loose a terrifying scream that forced the others to stop mid chew. With lightning speed they were on their feet and running towards the closing door, as a chorus of screams and growls resonated down the hall.

"We don't have enough time!" Malone yelled as he began pulling Dr. Hampstead back.

"Russo, we can't take them all on at once, we need to find shelter and fast!" Malone hollered.

"Yea, but where?" Russo yelled back as he and Gwen started backpedaling from the advancing crowd.

The undead hit the closing doors with a sudden force that unhinged both of them, effectively sending them crashing to the floor with a loud thud. They ran after the survivors in a mad rage.

Russo and the group rounded the corner of the hallway and they began to see patients and family members coming out of rooms with confused looks on their faces. They had heard the noises and the screams and wanted to know what was going on.

"Get back into your rooms!!" Malone shouted at the top of his lungs as he waved his hands at them trying to get their attention. Various questions and ramblings came from the disoriented crowd as they were trying to figure out what had happened. Realizing that these people weren't listening to him he did the only thing he could think of, he raised his gun high into the air and fired a shot. The report of the weapon's large discharge reverberated down the hall, instantly sending the questioning bystanders scurrying back into their rooms or down the hallway towards the exit. Malone's crude method had gotten the point across to most of the people in the hallway, unfortunately it also alerted the undead again to their location, which they charged towards with a renewed vengeance.

The undead rounded the same corner and with their prize within sight the blood covered mass of rotten skin gave chase once again. Russo turned back and saw the mass of bloodied security and staff charging for him, and he raised his gun to fire.

"That ain't gonna work man!" Malone shouted, but Russo never acknowledged as he pulled the trigger back. The Glock jumped in his hand as the spent cartridge flew out of the top of the shaft. The bullet careened down the hall and found its target directly above the nose of one of the former security officers. The bullet penetrated the front skull, and liquefied the brain as it exited out the back of the skull, blowing bone fragments into the faces of the attacking force. The security officer ran two more steps before diving head first onto the hard floor, skidding to a stop. The others watched in awe as this time he didn't get back up.

"It works if you put one in their heads," Russo said as he took aim again at another undead attacker that was sprinting towards them. He was about to pull the trigger again when he felt a firm grasp on his lower back, as Gwen pulled him back.

"You can't stop them all before they overtake us," she shouted as she tried again to pull him in the direction of Malone and Dr. Hampstead who had quickly opened one of the unoccupied rooms.

"Yea, but ..." Russo started as he struggled to reset himself.

"Come on, you'll end up just like the others; you can't win this battle!" Gwen screamed as she pulled on his shirt.

She's right you know, you can't kill 'em all! Russo said to himself as he pulled down his weapon and chased after her into the room. They dove into the room and Malone slammed the door shut on two of the undead who had covered the distance between them in record timing.

Malone quickly locked the door, but soon realized that a simple deadbolt won't hold these things.

"Quick, help me barricade this door!" Malone yelled to Russo as he put his back to the door and tried to use all of his weight to stop the force on the other side. The undead pounded on the door with their fists and arms as they continued to moan and growl with malice. The force of their blows on the door started to jar the hinges, and Malone noticed flakes of plaster and paint flying off with each slam. He knew that they didn't have much time left.

"HURRY! I can't hold them back for long," he yelled as Russo was finally able to free up one of the free standing closets and slide it over towards the door. Malone jumped off of the door, and the two men exerted what little energy they had and slid the closet to block the doorway. They jammed the closet into place as they began to hear the splintering of the wooden door as the undead continued their assault on the door relentlessly.

"We're going to need more than just a closet!" Russo exclaimed in between gasps for air.

"I agree, but what else can stop them?" Malone said as he bent over resting his hands on his knees as he took in some long breaths.

"Over here, guys," shouted Dr. Hampton, as she finished pulling all of the wires away from the wall that connected the oversized king hospital bed. Blue sparks erupted from the outlets as she yanked out the last plug and dropped it on the ground.

"Good idea Doc!" Russo yelled. The four of them rolled the bed towards the entrance and once they got it into the hallway leading to the door they flipped it onto its side and wedged it into the hallway flush up against the closet. Satisfied with the barricade, the four of the collapsed onto the floor with utter exhaustion while the pounding began to lessen as they heard the groans began to echo down the hall intermixed with terrified screams from patients as they opened their doors to a gruesome discovery.

"All of those people! What are they going to do?" Gwen started, "Is there anything we can do to alert them?"

"Maybe. I'll have Carol hit the alarm again; maybe people will stay in their rooms," Dr. Hampstead said as she stood up and ran to the table where the phone was. She picked it up and dialed the four-digit extension to the front desk. The phone rang five times before the receiver picked up.

"H ... He...Hello?" Carol's voice a mere whisper on the other hand.

"Carol, it's Dr. Hampstead, are you okay?" Dr. Hampstead questioned urgently.

"W... W... What's going on Dr. Hampstead? Everyone is screaming and people are running out of the entrance. I keep hearing this horrible moaning sound. I'm scared Dr. Hampstead," Carol answered quietly.

"Carol, you've got to listen to me. The infected people from the quarantine room have escaped and they are infecting others as we speak. They're in a manic rage state, so don't try to approach them or even draw attention to yourself. Hit the alarm button again, and then stay down. If any patients ask you what's going on, direct them back to their rooms quickly, and tell them to lock the door," Dr. Hampstead instructed. She heard Carol fumble around on the front desk, and then she heard the piercing blare of the alarm as Carol had pushed the button. She was about to hang up when Russo gestured for the phone.

"Carol, I am going to put Mr. Russo on the phone, he has some advice for you. Please stay safe," Dr. Hampstead continued to instruct Carol before handing the phone over to Russo and quickly wiping a tear from her eye.

"Carol?" Russo spoke into the phone.

"Y...Y...Y...Yes," Carol answered almost hysterically.

"If anyone has anything that looks like a bite, scratch, or another wound on their body that is fresh, avoid them at all costs. That's how this virus seems to be transferred, so stay away from them," Russo explained as his pulse quickened at the screaming he could hear in the background.

"O...O...Okay," Carol replied uneasily.

"One more thing, if any of them try to attack you swing whatever you can for their head, that is where they are the weakest," Russo finished before telling her to hang in there and that they would come get her when they could. He hung the phone up, turned around, and met Gwen's eyes. Neither said anything to the other, yet they were able to read each other's thoughts as they realized they had already seen this type of behavior once before.

Outside of their room a war raged on as patients, family members, and hospital staff were brutally attacked by the undead. Arms were chewed off completely, ankle bones were shattered by brute force while the flesh around the head was ruthlessly ripped into shreds as the horde began to feast on their unaware victims. Minutes after each attack was over, the victims eyes rolled back into place completely blood shot with black dots sprinkled throughout the pupil. They then gathered themselves, stood up—or attempted to—before joining in on the fight, this time on the other side. In the span of twenty minutes the undead horde that originally consisted of Carlos, Nurse Johnson, Marcus, and the complete security team, sixteen in total, had grown to over one hundred strong.

Waves of undead attackers filled the stairwells and moved upward rapidly, occupying the higher floors where patients and staff were inevitably trapped, and couldn't get away. Multiple undead teamed up against the victims, ruthlessly pulling and ripping at their flesh, oblivious to the searing pain they were causing this innocent people. When one victim had taken his or hers last breath they would immediately stop what they were doing and look for a fresh victim; they never continued once the heart had stopped beating.

Seeing the horror became too much for some of the hospital's staff as they chose not to be eaten alive. Desks and chairs were thrown through windows, followed shortly by hospital staff, knowing they were falling to their deaths.

One group of orderlies locked themselves into a patient's room where they tried the phone to call for help, but no one picked up the other line. Feeling somewhat safe they tried to relax before thunderous strikes assaulted the door, effectively ripping the hinges off as more of the undead crashed into the room. The orderlies never had a chance as their blood marred the walls of the room.

Some of the doctors were able to use their access badges and make it up to the doctor's lounge where they quickly called the authorities to alert them of what was going on. Knowing that the elevators were the only way into this lounge, two of the doctors stood guard in front of the elevator doors. They used makeshift spears made from broom handles and scalpels fastened together with tape. The elevator lights suddenly lit up forcing the two standing guard to take defensive stances with their spears. The doors opened and they charged in, only to stop as they realized one of their counterparts was in the elevator and none of the infected.

"Help me!" Their counterpart screamed as he stepped aside, and they could see one of the nurses was lying on the floor. Her outfit was stained bright red as blood continued to flow from her jugular vein that had been uncovered from a bite. She was barely conscious as the other doctors quickly ran into the elevator to help get her out. They laid her down on one of the tables and furiously went to work, trying to stop the bleeding and save her life. As they were working her pulse expired, and her eyes rolled into the back of her head.

"She didn't make it!" One of the doctor's said as he lowered his head. The other ones stopped what they were doing and slowly turned away from the body in defeat. Her eyes slowly rolled back, fully red with black dots.

The screams coming from the doctor's lounge rang throughout the upper floors of the hospital. Sarah jerked her head up from Materson's desk as she snorted deeply the white powdery substance that was in a line across his desk.

"Just what in the hell is going on down there!" she shouted at Materson while wiping the cocaine off from the bottom of her nose.

"I don't fucking know. How the hell do you think that I'd know what's going on, I've been up here with you, don't you remember?" Materson snapped as he looked out of his window at the hospital grounds.

"Watch the fucking attitude! Show some respect, especially after what I just did for you!" She snapped back as she pulled her skirt back up and adjusted her blouse, while walking over to one of his mirrors to check.

"Don't act like I'm the only one that got something out of that. You got two vials of blow from me, don't you remember?" Materson scolded.

"Yea, I do. Where's the second one?" She continued, pouting.

"Here!" Materson said as he tossed in the air to her. "You know what else you could use as a hard surface to take a line off of. Eh?" Materson said in a perverted tone with a devilish grin.

"Yea, off that fellow, Russo's chest!" Sara teased back, "He is one sexy piece of meat," she continued as she began to imagine Russo without his shirt on.

"He's a fucking asshole, and we never should have let that type of slime get in this hospital. What a fucking waste of resources and MY MONEY," Materson angrily barked as his face flushed.

"Why the hell is no one picking up their damn phone? I've tried the front desk, Nurse Ratchet, and Malone. None of them are answering, and what is going on with these alarms today? And what the hell is all of the screaming for?" Materson shouted as he threw his phone across his office, shattering it into a dozen pieces. After he was done with his screaming and stomping, the screams from the doctor's lounge ceased.

"Finally!" Materson said with great disgust, "It's about time the fucking authorities got here. I sure am glad nobody was dying here or something," Materson continued angrily as he pointed at the fire trucks and police cruisers that were entering the complex.

"Who the hell are they?" Sara asked as she pointed to a group of people that were running towards the authorities.

"I don't know, but they look like patients, see the gowns?" Materson instructed as he and Sara squinted at the group of people who were running headlong towards the first police cruiser.

"What have they got all over them? It … it … it looks like … blood," Sara said with a puzzled look.

"Impossible. I don't know who they are, but Malone's gonna pay for this one. Do you know how many hospital violations that we're gonna be hit with because we have patients running on the complex grounds without supervision? I mean that's his job," Materson grumbled as he continued to watch the interaction.

Two police officers appeared to get out of the first cruiser and put their hands up as if they were trying to stop the group that was running towards them. The group didn't stop, forcing the officers to pull their guns. The threat of the guns seemed to go unfazed by the group who came within ten feet of the officers. They opened fire on the group, showering the ground with dark red blood and bone fragments; still the group kept advancing.

"Holy shit, why are they shooting at them?" Sara asked as she watched in horror.

"More importantly, why didn't they go down?" Materson asked quietly as the blood in his face began to drain out.

The officers were soon overtaken and forced to the ground by the angry mob where they were savagely attacked. The officers screamed in agony for help which arrived, but it was too late as they died choking on their own blood. Dozens of firefighters and police officers came to their rescue only to be shocked at what they saw. Hospital patients with mortal wounds attacking, and more importantly, cannibalizing their fellow officers, with no concept or understanding of pain. They fought aggressively with the undead attackers and were able to knock them back until they looked up and saw the swarm of undead flowing out of the front doors of the hospital heading in their direction.

"What's going on? Look at them, they're attacking the police. What are they doing to them?" Sara said as she was in hysterics.

"It looks like … they're … eating them," Materson said in disbelief. He closed his eyes and quickly shook his head, hoping that what he thought he saw wasn't true. When he opened his eyes, his face was bleached white in shock as he saw the wave of patients exiting the hospital running towards the authorities, who began to flee towards the shopping center across the highway. Hundreds of undead continued to pour out of the front of the hospital, running erratically across the hospital grounds heading for Cedar Mill. To his amazement, he looked back at the two dead police officers who were first to be attacked, yet they weren't dead. They had gotten up and began to follow the crowd. The ground where they once laid was soiled with their blood, but they were still alive. One of the officers had a sheet of flesh that was hanging off of his chest about three inches wide, exposing his rib cage.

Materson turned to Sara and grabbed her by the shoulders, shaking her violently as he screamed, "Go and shut down all of the elevators to this floor. No one gets up here! Do you hear me?"

"Ye ... Yes, b... but w... why? Don't they need help?" She replied as she started to cry.

"Don't fucking question me, just do what I say. I'm saving your life dammit!" Materson yelled as he continued to shake her shoulders. She broke free from his grasp, ran to the elevator access panel, and put in the emergency lock code. As she ran off, Materson was trying to figure out just what had happened, and before she came back his thoughts suddenly rested on the guy that was e-vacted from Ecuador.

"That fucking asshole!" Materson screamed as he stomped his foot.

CHAPTER 16
IT'S A JUNGLE OUT THERE...

Quito was one of the most magnificent cities in Ecuador. It resembled the modern world with a slight rustic charm. Fashionable, sturdy built homes with modern day attributes combined with an unsophisticated blend of nature that is ever present on each home and throughout the streets. This picturesque city never completely destroyed the jungle that it was erected in, it merely embraced it in a symbian circle. Neither allowed the other to overtake, and when one fails, then the other is destined to fail. The streets would normally be lined with older cars parked and people walking up and down the streets shopping at the festivals and food markets, with routine customers and routine market owners catching up on local gossip combined with shoptalk. Children constantly nagged their parents to let them go play or asked when they are going home, while older kids zigzagged around the market stands chasing each other. The sounds of their laughter dispersing into the atmosphere combine with the normal buzz of a busy town on the rise, with businessmen in suits counting money and looking to make the next big deal. The smell of warm fresh baked pastries and bread would permeate the market, intoxicating everyone into a better mood. This was a normal day in Quito, and society has always proven that normal and routine are better than change and most certainly better than an abrupt change, but as the old saying goes, either you roll with the punches, or you get knocked out. This mental picture of Quito will only remain in the memories of those who have survived, as Quito has quickly become a cesspool of death and destruction. The once vibrant streets are now littered with death as dead bodies, body parts, and extensive amounts of spilled blood are scattered about. In the distance large billowy clouds of black smoke arise from the numerous auto accidents that people have had. Behind these clouds of thick black smoke, structural, and vehicular fires rage on completely uncontained, almost unobserved by the mass of people who continue to walk up and down the streets. Their collective moans can be heard blocks over as this raging horde of undead stalks the streets in search of survivors. Buildings which once had customer lines out the door with sales now have broken windows up and down their storefront, and the merchandise has been completely ravaged. Screams from survivors still echo throughout the city, but those in hiding dare not come out to help, for surely that would be suicide. The once beautiful town of Quito is no more; all that is left is a dead husk of a city that once was.

"It quiet here, not many crazy people," Ayung whispered to Jonathan, as he, Jonathan, and Ayung's son, Apoyung, crouched in a back alley. The trio had bushwhacked for more than two days straight with very little rest. Their ultimate goal was the American Embassy at Quito, but from the looks of it the Embassy is just as bad off. Their bodies ache, and their stomachs continue to turn from the lack of sustenance over the past two days, but a small sense of relief has filled their hearts in the realization that they have made it this far.

"Alright, Ayung, you've gotten us this far, and without a map, which is pretty damn good. Now just get us to the embassy, and we'll hopefully be doing better," Jonathan whispered as he fought inwardly with himself about despair as he looked at the demolished city. *How could this city be completely over run by those things?* Jonathan thought to himself. He knew there was no way possible the city could have been taken as fast as it had by the small number of tribesmen that he had witnessed attack the Huaorani village. The numbers to take over a complete city had to be more than a couple hundred. None of what was going on was making sense to Jonathan, and the simple fact that he couldn't figure out what was happening pissed him off even more.

"Embassy is three block down from us," Ayung whispered, breaking Jonathan's concentration.

"Papa, I tired. Can rest now?" Apoyung pleaded quietly as his body was losing the battle with total exhaustion.

"No, not yet. Soon, Apoyung, but now you strong like me," Ayung whispered in a stern voice, hating himself inside for forcing his boy to stay alert, but he knew if he didn't, he wouldn't have made it this far.

"Alright, let's hang here for a couple of minutes, and make sure we don't run into any stragglers along the way. I have a few more shells in the shotgun, but I would prefer not to use them as the noise will attract others," Jonathan explained in a quiet voice. He thought about turning on the lanterns that they had with them, but the light could attract attention, something they didn't need. The three of them had waited on the outskirts of the town for nightfall so they would have some cover with the cloak of night.

The American Embassy was a large fortified building with multiple tiers that extended to the east and west of the central entrance. The normally solid beige colored sides of stone had become dingy with dirt, grime, and a mixture of other substances that couldn't be ascertained from Jonathan's distance. The first floor windows were shattered, and thin streams of black smoke slowly rose out of them. The second, third, and fourth floors seemed to be more intact, only sporting a couple of shattered windows. Various lights cast shadows within the higher floors while the first floor harbored a pitch-black atmosphere. The normal country flags that decorated the front were now tattered and ripped into multiple strands, and hanging on barely to the fastening hooks connected to the awning of the front lobby. The Embassy resided on about two acres of land with fresh cut grass surrounding it. Four concrete paths lead into the Embassy, one leading to the front and back, and two others leading to secondary side entrances. The four corners of the massive building contained attached cages of stadium lights, three rows of six-megawatt lights that were shining brightly through the dark night. The lights arched in one hundred and eighty degree angles around the corners of the building providing light for the grounds. The Embassy was encircled by an eight-foot cast iron fence. The tops of the fence posts were adorned by gothic spearheads made of cast iron which were separated twelve inches from each other. The rear entrance to the Embassy supported lower entry points which lead to a basement garage that housed employee's cars and any foreign dignitaries who were visiting. The top of the Embassy housed four military grade watchtowers and a helipad, along with a shelter containing four emergency back-up generators. Two of the four watchtowers were occupied by military personnel armed with sniper rifles and spotlights. The mechanical hum of the generators running drowned out the loud moans and growls of the undead hordes below which consistently attacked the iron gates.

Jonathan peered around the corner of the alley they were hiding and squinted his eyes trying to see if he could see any of the signs designating which building was the American Embassy. He remembered how Gwen had explained to him that in any time of potential war or just plain turmoil within the country, the Embassy would lock its gates and have the army stationed there on full watch. Hoping that that directive was still in place, he knew if he could just get to the embassy they might have some shelter.

"Ayung, is it the one with the fencing around it?" Jonathan asked.

"Yes, Embassy has iron fence around to protect Americans," Ayung answered as he looked around the corner as well.

"Alright, then that's our target. Judging by the fact that the street from here to there looks somewhat clean, I say we make a run for it. What do you think?" Jonathan asked Ayung who was still squinting and trying to see if any commotion was going on in front of the entrance gate.

"I not agree, movement at the front gate ... Not good movement," Ayung whispered hesitantly.

"Shit, you're right," Jonathan said as he took a deep sigh. His eyes had finally adjusted, and he could see the crowd that Ayung was talking about. About fifteen of the undead were crowding around the front gates, and they seemed highly agitated because they were growling and banging their fists and heads at the gate while others were reaching through trying to grab at something.

"Ayung do you see the little wall surrounding the front and side that the fence stands on?" Jonathan asked.

Ayung squinted his eyes again, and took a few steps closer before he stepped back and nodded his head in agreement.

"I think we can make it to the side wall. Then we can hide below the wall, perhaps get someone's attention, and they can let us in a back way. That's all I got; I know it seems risky, but standing out in the open is not a good idea," Jonathan explained.

"Unfortunately, I agree with you, it not a good idea to have no shelter," Ayung said as his shook his head. He walked back over to where Apoyung was crouched down, he explained the plan to him a couple of times, and in the end Apoyung understood what they were going to do. He could see in his child's eyes fear beginning to build and they only thing he could think of was to tell him that his mother was looking down on him right now, and she would send him courage to help. With this a little tear slid down Apoyung's face only to be caught by a smile as he began to gain more confidence from what his dad had told him. Ayung hugged Apoyung tightly and then trotted back over to where Jonathan was standing.

"Is he ready?" Jonathan questioned as he gestured towards Apoyung.

"Yes, he ready," Ayung answered with confidence.

"You ready kid?" Jonathan whispered with a wink and smile as Apoyung jogged up to where they were standing. Seeing Jonathan's smiling face and what Apoyung had always liked, Jonathan's wink, the confidence in the kid was beginning to soar. He replied with an energized thumb up.

"Alright you two, let's go, stay low to the ground, and by all means stay as quiet as you can," Jonathan instructed before he took off in a crouched run. The three of them traversed the three blocks stealthily and completely undetected by any undead in the area. They made it to the side wall of the embassy's grounds and crouched low behind the wall. No one moved for about three minutes as they all quickly caught their breath. Jonathan was in charge of any trouble in front of them, Ayung carefully watched the way that they had come, and Apoyung attentively eyed the dark alley leading to the back of the Embassy. As the three sat in silence they could hear the angry growls and moans coming from the undead mob that was attacking the front gate. Their putrid rotting smell polluted their nostrils, and each man had to breathe through his mouth so the noxious smells wouldn't force them to vomit. The incessant clanging of the front gate was deafening and continuous; it became hard for any of them to think clearly. Jonathan slowly crept forward trying to see what they were attempting to get to, but fear of being seen forced him back down into his crouch.

"Get back you SONS OF BITCHES!" Suddenly exploded into the air from a feminine voice.

"Did you hear that?" Jonathan questioned Ayung.

"Yes, somebody is fighting, no?" Ayung offered.

"Yea, somebody is fighting, and that means that we have run into some survivors. I hope they're on the inside of this fence and not on the outside," Jonathan whispered. "I'm going to try and see who it is and see if there is any way we can make contact with them."

Jonathan again slowly rose from his crouch, placed his head above the wall, and looked in the direction the voice came from. It didn't take him long to find the origin of the voice. A women in a black skirt, light colored blouse, and long brown hair was standing in front of the gate with a long pole like spear vigorously stabbing at the undead while yelling at them. Jonathan ducked back down below the wall, and he turned and faced Ayung and Apoyung.

"It's a woman, and she is on the inside of the fence; she seems to be trying to fight them off. Maybe if we can get her attention she can help us get inside. At least it sounds like a good idea," Jonathan explained.

"Attention how?" Ayung questioned, as he didn't feel comfortable with them standing up and calling out to her for help, for that would alert the undead to their location.

"I am going to send a shrill whistle in her direction, and when she looks my way I am going to quickly light the lantern a couple of times to alert her to our location. If this works, then hopefully we're in; if it doesn't, we're screwed. If we attract the attention of those crazies, I want you and Apoyung to stay here; I will lead them away. Understood?" Jonathan explained quickly.

"Yes, but you not out run all," Ayung stated with concern in his facial expression.

"Let's just hope it doesn't come to that," Jonathan said before pulling the lantern out of his bag. "Here we go!" Jonathan said as he raised his head up again above the wall. He waited until there was a small lull in the moans and growls, and then he let out a baseball style whistle that pierced the air around the Embassy. The undead seemed unfazed by the sound, but the woman with the spear stopped trying to stab at them and looked in Jonathan's direction. He hit the light switch a couple of times, flashing their location. She watched for a couple of minutes before turning back to stabbing at the undead. Perplexed, Jonathan just stared at her for a moment, not understanding why she wasn't trying to help them. Maybe she didn't care, or maybe she thought there was no hope for them; either way it was hard to understand, but then suddenly he heard her yell again.

"Major Powers! Nine o'clock!" She yelled without stopping her actions against the undead mob.

Jonathan was completely confused by her actions, and he was beginning to get angry with the fact that she wasn't helping them until he heard three quick pops from a suppressed rifle and ducked down. The bullets landing ten feet in front of them on the grounds of the embassy, showering dirt and grass overhead.

"Why the hell are they shooting at us?" Jonathan shrieked as he was beginning to feel like he was stuck in between a rock and a hard place.

"Papa, this hit head," Apoyung said as he handed an object to his father who handed it to Jonathan. The moment Jonathan felt it, he realized that it was a beanbag bullet and they hadn't fired real ammunition at them. He then questioned to himself, why they would be using beanbag bullets instead of real ammunition. The answer to his own question hit him like a brick wall when he realized that they were trying to communicate with them. That was why they didn't actually try to shoot any of them. He quickly slid back up to the wall and looked in the direction of where the bullets came. As his eyes rose higher he noticed a soldier with a light that was flashing in their direction. He raised his hand up to signal to the operator that he understood what was going on, and then he watched as the operator moved the light down the iron fence to the back where the operator flashed it again three times.

"They want us to go to the back of the Embassy," Jonathan said as he quickly nodded his head.

"How you know?" Ayung questioned.

"Somebody just flashed a light in that direction, and I think they want me to follow it. The way I see it is that we don't have any other choice right now, so let's see if what they are trying to communicate to us is correct," Jonathan explained as he grabbed his gear and swiftly crouch walked down the wall line headed for the back. Ayung and Apoyung were shortly behind him.

The American Embassy took up the whole block, and the path from the front side to the back side was a good fifty yards. Jonathan's back ached as he neared the end corner, and upon turning the corner he saw an army soldier dressed in green fatigues anxiously standing on the outside of a gate with his weapon at the ready. Jonathan quickly flashed his lantern to the soldier alerting him of their presence as he continued to head in his direction. Seeing the light, the soldier quickly motioned them to hurry, and get inside the fence. Jonathan ran through the gate opening followed shortly by Ayung; Apoyung was trailing slightly behind as exhaustion had taken over forcing him to slow down. Jonathan and Ayung had turned and quietly told Apoyung to hurry when they saw the soldier harness his rifle and aim it in the boy's direction. Fear shot through both men as they frantically called out to the soldier that the boy was with them. The soldier ignored their pleas and focused his sights on the boy who had slowed, realizing that he was now the target. Apoyung froze when he heard the discharge of the weapon, and for a moment he couldn't feel any part of his body. The moment passed and he frantically felt all over his body for the wound, but he couldn't find it. Confused, he looked back to see Jonathan and his father running directly at him with panic-stricken faces; suddenly he heard a wet smack across the pavement behind him. He quickly turned around to see the headless body of an undead attacker lying nearly two feet from where he stood. Dark blood oozed from the stump of the shoulders as the already mangled body lay lifeless on the sidewalk. Apoyung quickly regained his breath as he realized that the soldier wasn't aiming at him, he was aiming at an undead. As he jerked back around, his father picked him up in a fluid motion before turning and running back towards the gate. Jonathan quickly picked up the gear that Apoyung had been carrying before running back to the gate as well.

The three survivors and the soldier quickly entered the gate, and the soldier slammed the door shut before grabbing thick steel chains to padlock it shut. The discharge alerted some of the undead that were lurking around to their head toward their location. Sensing the fresh blood, they raced towards where they heard the sound and violently attacked the gate. Hands, fists, arms, and legs pushed against the strong iron fence as the undead savagely reached for the survivors. The group of undead quickly became twenty strong as more arrived and tried to force their way into the compound. Visibly fatal wounds marred the undead as the survivors witnessed a horrific scene of mutilated bodies covered in blood. Each of the undead's eyes were completely blood shot and covered erratically with black dots. The two in front were reaching through the gates with such force that they broke their own shoulders and were able to contort their bodies in a way to allow them to squeeze their upper torso through the iron bars. They wiggled their bodies in such a frantic way that Jonathan could see them somehow forcing their way onto the Embassy grounds. He grabbed his shotgun and took aim at the two before a firm hand grasped the end of the barrel and pointed it down.

"Don't!" another soldier said as he stepped up from behind them.

"What do you mean, don't? If those things get through, then we'll all be in danger!" Jonathan screamed.

"The sound will just bring more to our location; let me handle it," the soldier said as he walked over to the two bodies of the undead that had begun to grab at the ground in an attempt to pull themselves free. The soldier pulled out his sidearm and attached a silencer to the top. He walked over to the first one, put the muzzle of the silencer on its head, and pulled the trigger. The bullet shattered the skull, sending pieces of scalp and skull high into the air. The undead stopped moving permanently as blood and grey brain matter slowly began to trickle out of the hole. The soldier then walked over to the other undead who violently scratched and clawed at his military boot before earning the same sentence as his predecessor. With the two undead neutralized, the soldier holstered his side arm and walked back in the direction of the survivors and the other soldier.

"Name's Major Powers, I'm the acting officer in charge here," the soldier said as he came up to the survivors.

"A ... A ... I'm Jonathan Steambule, a research assistant from the states; I came out here with Doctor Gwen Vierra on a mission trip to help the Huaorani tribe in the Amazon," Jonathan stammered as he tried to catch his breath. Major Powers nodded acceptance in his direction before turning his attention to the other survivors.

"I is Ayung, and this my son Apoyung. We Huaoranian," Ayung spoke up as he introduced himself and his son to the Major.

"Well, it's very nice to meet you, and sorry about the invitation, but that was the only way we could signal you over the constant racket of these slimy dirtbags," Major Powers acknowledged. "This is Private First Class Taylor, he's with my platoon." Major Powers paused as he took a deep breath, "Well, what's left of my platoon," he continued with a sorrowful look.

"Nice to meet you both, and thank you so much for allowing us shelter. We've been footing it for almost two days without any rest. I don't know how much longer we could have made it on the outside," Jonathan replied as he, Ayung, and Apoyung stood up and dusted themselves off before offering their hands in greeting. The two soldiers accepted their greetings with much respect.

"How far out is the Huoranty village?" Major Powers questioned.

"It's pronounced Huaorani, and it's a good couple of hours drive Southeast of here, and a rigorous two day hike if you're bushwhacking the whole way," Jonathan answered as he set his gear down. He stretched his back, trying to loosen the knots from the previous two days.

"Jesus, man! You mean to tell me that you three bushwhacked through the damn jungle to get here?" Major Powers exclaimed, visibly taken back by their explanation.

"Yea, and I would love to sit and chat about it, but my friends and I are beat. We haven't slept in two days, and we've barely had any food and water since we left the village. Do you have any food and water, and a place where we can go to relax?" Jonathan questioned.

"By all means. Let's get inside, and get you boys rested and fed... somewhat fed," Major Powers answered shamefully.

"Somewhat fed?" Jonathan questioned after recognizing the Major's chagrin.

"Well, all we have is vending machine snack food and drinks, and not much of those left. We have scavenged all of the machines on the second, third, and fourth floors, and now all that is left is a few bags of chips and a couple of can sodas,"

"You said the second, third, and fourth floors, what about the first?" Jonathan questioned.

"Let's get you guys inside and rested before we start talking about the first floor," Major Powers answered as he ended the conversation. Jonathan could see in the Major's eyes that the first floor was a lost cause. He thought back to the afternoon that the village was attacked, and he realized that what the Major was feeling; he had felt once before. No wanting to press the issue, Jonathan picked up his gear and looked to the Major for direction.

"Private Taylor!" Major Powers addressed.

"Yes sir!" Taylor responded with a quick salute.

"Get Janine away from that gate, and let's all get back inside. These things smell like shit, and they're really beginning to piss me off," Major Powers barked.

"Yes, sir!" Taylor responded, excited about getting back into the building.

"We'll wait here until they get back, we always go in together… strength in numbers," Major Powers said as he looked back in the survivor's direction.

"Agreed," Jonathan replied as Ayung simply nodded his head.

The major removed his helmet, allowing his bald head some breathing room. Steam slowly rose off of his head as it glistened with sweat in the artificial light. Major Powers was an older soldier with a worn face and deep sunk brown eyes. He had a tattoo on the left side of his neck of the grim reaper with its scythe which dripped red blood onto a saying that read: *Say hello to my li'l friend.* He had a dark goatee that was unkempt which also supported a few strands of grey, most likely earned within the past few days. His slim body barely supported his fatigues, showing signs of serious weight loss and malnourishment from fatty foods. His fatigues represented his rank of major as they showed a gold star sewn in above the left breast. His boots were typical military grade but completely covered in a mixture of mud and dark crimson blood that was caked on, and when dried, fell off in clumps. His unorthodox methods of leadership had won his men's respect, and any one of them would lay their lives on the line for him, a kind of respect that he cherished.

The four of them waited patiently with a watchful eye on the surrounding gate as Private Taylor and Janine came walking up.

"Major, there's more of them than yesterday, and their numbers keep growing," Janine spoke as she approached the group.

"I figured," Major Powers said with a heavy sigh. "Janine, let me introduce you to the survivors that you saved," Major Powers said with a small smile as he stretched his arm out to the three behind him. "This is Ayung, and his son, Apoyung, they are from the Who … Whuaorani tribe, and this Jonathan—"

"Steambule," she said, cutting him off as she stared at Jonathan.

"You're the Janine that I talked to the other night?" Jonathan questioned as he stood and stared at the woman in front of him. Her clothes were covered with dirt and filth, yet in his eyes her beauty shone through.

"That's me. I'm glad you made it, I mean I'm glad all of you made it," she replied, never breaking her gaze.

"We are, too, but unfortunately your boss, Klinefelter," he hesitated "didn't make it. I'm sorry, I didn't know if you two were close,"

"I'm sorry he didn't make it, but he was an asshole," Janine replied with a quick shrug of her shoulders. "How about Russo, Carlos, and Gwen?" Janine asked fearfully as she began to think the worse, as she realized that perhaps all who survived from the Huaorani village were standing in front of her.

"Russo and Gwen, where fine last time we talked to them, Carlos on the other hand was in rough shape after he'd been attacked by the jaguar," Jonathan offered. Janine simply shook her head in understanding as she turned to the major.

"It seems we all have some talking to do, but let's get inside first and get you fellas some food and drink," Major Powers said as he walked over to the right side of the building. As he approached the right side of the embassy a twelve-foot ladder came into view. The ladder was hooked onto a window on the second floor leading into a room that gave off artificial light from within. The ladder was angled away from the lower part of the building, and was about three feet away from a lower window on the first floor. The window to the first floor was shattered, and the room was pitch black. A repulsive odor escaped from the window as the group slowly began to ascend the ladder. The smell reminded Jonathan of the basement morgue where cadavers were kept for med students to practice on. The only saving grace the basement had were several high velocity exhaust fans that would pull the abhorrent stench from the room minutes before a class entered. *Those fans would be a great idea now,* Jonathan silently thought to himself as he continued climbing into the second floor room.

"All clear up here, Major! Everyone's in and secure; you can come up now!" Private Taylor hollered back down to the patiently waiting Major. Ever since the breakdown of society in Quito, Major Powers had made it his mission to protect anyone and everyone he could against this indescribable evil. Whenever anyone was on the Embassy grounds they were never alone, and he always accompanied them, no matter what the errand or trip was. He always made sure that he was the first one to set foot onto the grounds, and the last one to leave the grounds. To the Major, there could be no other way.

As he began his ascent, he looked around at the growing crowds of undead that rattled the fence and gates with an untamed aggression. Their moans and growls filled the nighttime air as their piercing bloodshot eyes affixed to the Major as he was climbing up the ladder.

"Yea, what do you fuckers want from me?" Major Powers taunted as he stopped across from the first floor window and looked around.

"Bunch of dead fucks, can't even reason anymore, they just want blood. Well you're not getting mine TONIGHT!" He yelled again, letting his frustration go. As he turned to continue to climb he heard a shuffling noise coming from the first floor window. The horrible stench became stronger as the shuffling noise grew closer. Steadily he grasped the ladder with his left hand and slowly reached for his sidearm. As he pulled his sidearm up and took aim into the window, he strained his eyes and ears for any sound or sight that might shed light to what was going on. The metallic click arising from his now cocked weapon cast an eerie quietness in the room, as whatever was moving earlier suddenly stopped. Sweat beads slowly cascaded down the sides of his face as he closed one eye and took aim at the center of the window. Two minutes passed and nothing moved from within the window. Realizing that whatever the threat was he was ill-equipped to handle it, he slowly holstered his side arm and began to quietly reach for the next rung of the ladder. As he raised his boot to the next rung, the caked up muck on the boot lost its grip, causing him to slip down the ladder. He yelled out as he lost his grip, sliding back down a few rungs. He quickly recovered with a vice like grip on one of the rungs and steadied himself. Realizing that his current predicament could occur again, he banged his boots upon the outside of the ladder, knocking all of the muck off of the bottom.

"Hey, Major? Everything alright?" Private Taylor yelled down, as he stuck his head out of the window at the sound of the yell.

"Yea, just slipped! I'll be up in a second. I'm fine!" Major Powers hollered back up as he watched Taylor duck back into the window.

As he finished knocking the filth off his boots off, he looked back down, and then looked immediately in front of him at two blood red eyes with speckled black dots as an undead had maneuvered itself to the window and simply stared at the Major who was now three feet away. The undead slightly tilted its head, revealing a cavernous hole on its left side where the lower jaw had been dislocated and simply hung by a string composed of flesh and muscle. The dislocated jaw swayed back and forth as the undead was unable to maintain its balance. Sensing the fresh meat, the undead jerked its hands outward in an aggressive attempt to grab the Major. In a flash Major Powers had pulled his sidearm and fired off a shot before the horrid creature could even make a sound. A small yet pristine bullet hole lanced through the right eye socket of the monster as it fell face first out of the window, tumbling down into the shrubbery below.

The discharge of the weapon sent a chill up Private Taylor's spine as he rushed back to the room, only to see the Major pulling himself over the windowsill before holstering his sidearm.

"What happened?" Private Taylor inquired.

"One of the councilmen didn't make it," Major answered with no emotion. He shrugged his head towards the window, indicating to Private Taylor that he should have a look. The upended body of the former councilmen was sprawled out against the shrubbery below, his tattered suit stained with dried crimson blood simply waved back and forth as a cool breeze whipped across the base of the Embassy.

"Sucks for him," Taylor commented.

"Let's get to our meeting room, and get our guests taken care of; they've been through hell and back," Major suggested as he started out of the room.

"Yes sir!" Taylor replied as he followed the Major out of the room.

The second floor of the Embassy had quickly been converted into a dormitory as offices now housed small Marine Corps cots with small tables sporting office lamps being used as bedside lights to illuminate each of the rooms. Lavish intricately designed desks which use to hold fancy computer equipment and organizational folders, now supported piles of clothes, mainly clean military fatigues. Camouflage ponchos crudely hung from doorways in an attempt to give some semblance of privacy to the occupant of the former office. On the walls outside of the room, names had been carved into the wall representing whose room the office now belonged too. Many of the offices throughout the floor were simply unoccupied and now served as storage rooms for furniture that was cumbersome and usually in the way. The once waxed and polished tile floor that decorated the floors of the embassy now carried the scars of steel toe boot scuff marks, and a mixture of dirt, mud, and dried blood stains.

Small glowing lights faintly led the way around the second floor. Some office rooms had small lamps on to help shed some light throughout the dark hallways, while every fifty feet or so small electric lanterns gave off light bluish ambient light, barely illuminating the walkways in between offices leading into the main opening of the second floor which contained the recently renamed central meeting room. The overhead lights were prohibited for two specific reasons. Firstly, they were a massive drain on the generators that still powered the embassy, and secondly, more light always ran the risk of discovery, and in the current condition of the city, discovery was the last thing anyone in the Embassy wanted.

The central meeting room, a grand room with three walls consisting of glass and a back wall with a massive flat screen, was now the central operations room for what was left of Major Powers platoon. All of the office chairs from the surrounding offices had been piled into the corners of the meeting room to provide space for the new occupants of the now abandoned offices. Two large tables which supported the dwindling food and water supply had been assembled in the back of the room directly under the flat screen. On the right side table about four dozen bags of chips and various candy bars were laid out in organized piles with thick black writing in front of each pile indicating the appropriate ration amount. The piles became increasingly small towards the end of the table as the numbered days increased. The left side table was organized similarly, with rationed amounts of sodas and bottles of water in neat piles with appropriate numbering under them as well. At the rate the rations were going, especially with the new added survivors, the group would run out of food and water within five days. In the center of the room, the original solid mahogany table that normally ran north and south, was slid back and turned east to west. On top of the table rested various computer models with a military radio communication box. Two of the three monitors were off while the third one showed some type of interactive chat log. The last message showing received was over twelve hours ago, and it read: "Multiple casualties, please assist!" by Recon Bravo. Multiple heavy duty wiring and cable bundled together snaked around the legs of the table and exited the central meeting room through the removable ceiling tiles where it continued to wind its way down the hall, ultimately ending at the communications closet where the various cables were connected.

In front of the meeting table some of the office chairs had been organized together forming a semi-circle in front of the main table with a central chair in the middle. As Major Powers and Taylor walked into the central room, three soldiers also dressed in military fatigues stood up from their chairs in attention.

"At ease, ladies and gents," Major Powers acknowledged before he and Taylor took their seats seat. Major Powers sat in the center chair, and surrounding him was what was left of his platoon. Starting from the left side was his First Lieutenant Hagers, then his Second Lieutenant Wallace, followed by Private First Class Taylor and Harris, before ending with Janine. Three new chairs had been added to the semi-circle for the new survivors who were not currently present.

Once they had gotten the survivors in, Janine had set up the father and son in one of the larger offices which could accommodate two of the military grade cots. Jonathan was put up in the office directly across from the father and son, and all three were currently eating their rations for the night and getting some well-deserved rest. Janine instinctively put them up close to her office so she would be close by in case anything went wrong, her motherly intuition shining through. Each survivor had been given a clean pile of military fatigues in sizes that closely fit. Apoyung, being the smallest, was given a female small, and even though it was still two sizes too big, he was able to make do.

"Well, before we turn in, I want a status update on everything. Go ahead Hagers," Major Powers instructed.

"Well, basically our defenses are still somewhat good. The fence seems to be currently holding, and the padlocks can't be broken by brute force, so for the most part the facility is somewhat secure," Hagers began as he took his helmet off and wiped the grime and sweat from his forehead.

First Lieutenant Hagers was in his early thirties with a dark complexion and a lean build. He had a prominent chin and jaw line that slowly blended into his young face; he had dark almond eyes and roughly shaven head. His ears each supported one small gold stud, while the back of his neck embraced a Marine Corp anchor tattoo. He stood approximately five feet six inches tall, and his body was also beginning to show signs of malnutrition.

"Well, I'll tell you that when we got those new survivors in, two of those slimy bastards basically broke their shoulder bones in an attempt to crawl through the gate. They began to worm their way in with very little effort, so with that being said, I recommend that we increase our watches from one every two hours to one every hour," Major Powers explained.

"Agreed, but user your silencers, the less noise and attention that we bring to ourselves the better; these things seem to be attracted to sound, so the quieter the better," Hagers said.

"Good point, Hagers!" Major Powers complemented.

"Thank you, sir. Continuing, I recommend that after each patrol we pull the ladders back up onto the second floor. I know it'll be a hassle, but I don't want to risk letting anyone up here that shouldn't be."

"Agreed, Hagers!" Major Powers piped up.

"And finally, on the last check of the diesel container for the generators, it seems to be still about three fourths of the way full, so our measures to cut back have paid off in the long run. The way we're going right now, I think we have a little over three weeks before we lose all power," Hagers concluded.

"That's good, but our food supplies won't last that long. Thanks for your update Hagers; after this meeting I will help you schedule patrol duty for everyone. Go ahead, Second Lieutenant Wallace," Major Powers said.

"Right, sir," Second Lieutenant Wallace answered before he had a violent coughing fit.

"Wallace? You alright?" Major Powers asked concerned.

"Yes, sir, just a bug." Wallace cleared his throat before he started with his update. "Our food situation is rather bleak. I have rationed out the appropriate amounts for everyone to include our new guests, but at this rate any new comers will cut us completely out of a day of food,"

"I understand Wallace, but I'm not going to turn anyone away who has survived this nightmare," Major Powers said with a heavy sigh.

"No sir, I agree whole heartedly, but I just want everyone to know where we stand. I have organized rations behind us on the tables, and you will get your food on the right side and your water on the left side. I also took the liberty of going around and double checking our fortifications. As everyone knows, the elevators are down based on the fact that we don't know what's in them, so we won't be using them period. I moved a couple of extra desks and tables to the North and South stair access halls and arranged them on top of what we already had," Wallace explained.

"Any reason soldier?" Major Powers questioned.

"On my last trip around the floor, I heard some more banging coming from the North side stairwell, and I figured it would be better to be safe than sorry," Wallace answered before coughing loudly again.

"I can't argue with that. Anything going on above us?" Major Powers asked as he kept a watchful eye on Wallace's body language.

"I walked them again today, and with the exception of basic office furniture, they are practically useless to us. We have already ransacked all of the vending machines on these three floors, and I checked every desk to see if anyone had stashed anything edible in their desks and came up empty," Wallace continued.

"In case of emergency, can the upper floors hold us all?" Major Powers inquired.

"Yes, but the COMM closet's on this floor, so we would be without any means of communication to the outside world, but if worse comes to worse, then yes, we could escape upstairs," Wallace answered as he continued to clear his throat.

"Alright, very good. Wallace, one of the survivors we rescued today has got a background in medicine; I want you to get him to check you out as soon as he is rested. The last thing I need is for you to get sick with a damn cold or something," Major Powers instructed Wallace.

"Yes sir, first thing in the morning when he gets up," Wallace agreed.

"Thank you, Lieutenant; that will be all. Good report!" Major Powers again complemented.

Wallace simply nodded his head in gratitude and took his seat beside Hagers and Taylor. Wallace was an aged soldier who had been with the Major since the beginning. He was nearly half a century old, but up until recently he still felt like a kid at heart, and his charismatic attitude always revealed his inner child. Wallace was about six feet tall, with a wiry build that gave him the nickname "Scrappy." His once healthy façade now resembled a rundown body fighting a losing battle with an unknown foe. Out of all of the soldiers, Wallace looked the worse. His face had shrunken inward, and his charming blue eyes were slowly becoming completely bloodshot. He hadn't shaved in over a week, and his beard had grown out grey and silky as opposed to the normal grizzled stubble that he usually had. Like most of the others, his clothes basically hung off of him, yet the skin on his body looked like worn leather that had to be stretched to cover his bones. His forehead showed signs of a fever while his constant cough began to contain small spots of blood, letting him know that he was very ill.

When the Major had ordered the Embassy gates closed Wallace had joined him in this task. As they pulled the gates closed, one of the crazed people grabbed the Major by the collar and violently wrenched him up against the gate. The crazed person had opened its mouth in an attempt to bite the Major's neck, and Wallace had reached out and buffered the bite with his bare forearm before plugging the gaping mouth with his Glock. The teeth had barely cut the skin, yet the wound was now infected and seemed to be spreading outward in small black spider-webbed designs under the skin.

As Wallace took his seat, he again began to cough and hack loudly as he tried to steady himself in his chair. He pulled out a handkerchief and dabbed his lips as he regained his control, he then wiped his forehead dry from sweat, leaving an ever-present streak of fresh blood that he had coughed up. Major Powers noticed the streak and was alarmed that his longtime friend was struggling so mightily.

"Wallace, you can be excused if you need a break, your report was fine; if anyone has any questions they can come to me," Major Powers offered.

" 'Preciate it Major, I just need to get one good night's rest, and I'll be back to my usually good-looking old self," Wallace accepted with a quick wink at Janine, who replied with a sultry wink herself, and a warm smile.

"Well, I don't know about good looking, but you sure could use the rest. You're excused," Major Powers spoke before turning his attention to Private Taylor. Wallace gingerly got up and took his leave, the old soldier's incessant coughing echoed down the halls as he slowly walked to his room. The others in the room eagerly and nervously looked around as they all realized what was happening, but no one wanted to say anything.

Sensing the horrible silence in the room, Major Powers again turned his attention to the group.

"Private Taylor and I, along with the guidance of Janine, helped rescue three survivors tonight. Taylor, if you don't mind, I'll do your update," Major Powers asked earnestly.

"Floor's all yours, Major," Taylor responded, with a congenial smile.

"Thanks, Taylor. As you all are aware, we rescued three survivors tonight. One has a background in medicine, and the other two are natives from the Amazon, some crazy named village that I can't pronounce. I haven't yet debriefed them on our situation, nor have they explained there's to me, but I want to give them a chance to get some rest before we bombard them with questions. Their names are Jonathan Steambule, Ayung, and his son, Apoyung. Please treat them with total respect and hospitality, and don't volley so many questions at once at them. These three people just bushwacked through the jungle for two days straight. Needless to say they are tired, but resilient," Major Powers explained. As he finished with his update he could hear the quite gasp amongst the group as each of them suddenly realized exactly how hard it would be to get through the jungle, especially considering the circumstances.

"You sure they aren't SEALS Major?" Taylor jokingly said, trying to cut the tension hanging in the room.

"HA, if only we were that lucky!" Major Powers said with serious smile. "Alright, that's my update. Any questions? If not, Private Harris, we're all eager to hear your update on our communication situation," The Major looked around the room for any questions before turning his attention to Private Harris who had patiently waited until it was her turn to explain her updates.

Private First Class Harris had just turned nineteen before the shit hit the fan in Ecuador. She was a short stocky girl in high school with low self-esteem and very few friends. Her IQ was off the charts, and her teachers constantly urged her to apply herself more and more, but in high school if you are constantly ostracized because you don't fit the stereotypical model figure that society wants, it is sometimes hard to be an extrovert. After she graduated she decided that she would make a stand in her life and change it forever for the good. She realized that in order for her to enjoy her life she needed to be confident about herself, and she realized that she could learn confidence in the military. Much to her parents dismay she declined a full academic ride to Brown University and joined the Corps. The first couple of months were brutal, and each night she fought internally with herself about quitting, but she always stuck it out because she knew that in order to obtain something you have always wanted, you have to do something you've never done. She went into boot camp an overweight timid girl, and came out a healthy confident woman both inside and out. Early on in her military career she was passed over for promotions based on her gender, until she met Major Powers. She quickly showed Major Powers that she had more to offer than a blonde soldier with deep blue eyes. He offered to take her under his guidance and help her see the world and sharpen her skills. She jumped at the chance, and even now she didn't regret her decision.

"Well, so far the only feed-back that I have been able to get from HQ is minimal. The dense jungle around us is causing all kinds of disruption and cut-offs. HQ's last transmission is still advising us to stay put as they are putting together some resources to get us out—although I get the sense that we aren't high on their priority list right now," Harris explained.

"What makes you think that?" Major Powers questioned, although he had grown to respect her clairvoyance.

"They just seem to be pacifying me right now. They keep telling me to sit tight, and they will be here to get us, but I don't get any definitive date or time, and when I ask for confirmation all I get is that they're working on it. To be honest Major, I think whatever is going on here has spread, and they have got their hands full. That's my guess, but each day I try to gain more ground. Although it's very frustrating that I have to explain every day to someone new what has happened and what we are experiencing. I mean, how many times does it take to tell someone that the dead are rising and attacking people?" Harris said, frustrated, before collecting herself to continue with her report.

"Easy Private Harris, I know it's frustrating, but we have to try and stay the course," Major Powers spoke softly trying to figure out why some many different people wanted to hear her explanation.

"Yes sir, please excuse my frustration. We are going on over thirteen hours since we last received correspondence from Recon Bravo. Their last known coordinates were on the outskirts of the city to the North of us, and they ran into heavy opposition. I haven't been able to make contact with any of them as of yet, but I keep trying. As for the Mexican Embassy, they are still receiving and broadcasting with me, but are under strict orders of lock down. No one goes in, and no one goes out. That's all that I have sir, and I am sorry that I don't have any other good news," Harris finished as she gently shook her head in defeat.

"Nonsense, Harris! Every piece of information we can get is at least some sort of information, and at least HQ knows that we're still here," Major Powers said as his voice rose. "Good work Private Harris, stay on it, and let me know the moment anything changes ... especially if you make contact with Bravo,"

"Yes sir, Major!" Harris replied.

"Well, last but certainly not least, Ms. Janine. What's new in your neck of the woods?" Major Powers asked as he turned his attention to Janine.

"Unfortunately, nothing new. I've set up the survivors in the two new rooms that we just cleaned out. The father and son are in one room, and Jonathan is in the other one. Their rooms are close to mine so if anything goes on, or if they need any help, I can be right there. When Jonathan gets fully rested I definitely think he should be the one that you speak with first. I am pretty sure that he has had firsthand experience with this type of situation," Janine spoke softly.

"You mean with our... infestation situation?" Major Powers questioned.

"Yes. His call that came in from the Amazon jungle requesting help might give us some more of an understanding as to what happened, or more importantly, what is happening. He was working with one hell of a good doctor named Gwen Vierra, and what I know about Gwen is that she only takes the best with her on her mission trips. I'll be willing to bet that he can possibly shed some light for us," Janine explained.

"Well, I'll be sure to talk with him first, but I still want to give those fellas some rest. Janine, I was sorry to hear that your former boss didn't make it. I don't know if you two were close, but I wanted to offer my condolences," Major Powers said respectfully.

"Major, I appreciate your sympathy, but don't waste another moment on it; that womanizing, arrogant, over-weight, snobby, bastard didn't deserve to live another day on this earth," Janine replied venomously.

"Tell us how you really feel, Janine!" Major Powers said with hearty laugh that instantly became infectious amongst the group. "Well, that concludes this meeting. Hagers, be sure to pull the ladders up. Taylor and Harris, you two have the first watch, and Hagers and I will trade up with you around three am. If anything happens, remember the signal," Major Powers instructed as the group exited the central room.

"Yep, got it, three shot burst," Taylor quickly answered as he began to check his gear before he joined the rest of the platoon and exited the building.

Major Powers leaned back in his chair and closed his eyes while gently rubbing his temples. His headache was getting worse, and combined with the frustration that for the first time in his military career, he didn't know the correct path to take. Leaving the security of the Embassy was a bad idea as he had already discovered with Bravo group, yet slowly withering away into nothingness was just as bad. With their current food situation it wouldn't be long before everyone began to lose hope, and the only thing that comes after hope is insanity. In all of his years in service, all of the crazy missions he had been on, all of the times that the odds were stacked against him and his men, he never lost hope, but against the current insurmountable odds, he didn't know how long his perfect record would stand.

"Major?" Janine softly asked as she watched with growing concern.

"Yes!" Major Powers answered, startled, and completely unaware that he wasn't alone.

"You okay?" Janine quietly asked.

"Yea, just a headache, nothing more," Major Powers answered, guarding his inner feelings.

"I'll let that one slide this time, but next time I don't accept white lies," Janine responded warmly as she stood up and walked towards the exit. "We'll be alright, Major, you've done an exceptional job!"

"Thanks, Janine," Major Powers said, half believing in what she stated. As she left the room, he stood up and stretched his legs and arms before heading to his room for a couple hours of rest.

As Janine walked down the shadowy hall to her room, she heard scratching sounds coming from the direction of her room. Cautiously she backed up against the wall and strained her eyes down the poorly lit hallway for any sign of movement. She carefully and deliberately inched her way down the hall, stopping after every sound she heard. As she approached her office, she heard the sound again, but it wasn't coming from her room, it was coming from Jonathan's room. Quietly she reached into her room and grabbed a makeshift club that had been created out of broken pipe with glass shards attached to the end. She clutched the weapon in her hand and inched down the wall until she was right outside of Jonathan's room. She quickly glanced down and could see no light escaping underneath the poncho. A shuffling resonated within the room as she could make out the distinct sound of someone slowly walking around in the room. Her grip on the weapon was so strong now her ghostly white knuckles shone through the darkness, and she reached up and yanked the poncho off the door in a violent fear driven rage.

"YIEEEEEE!" Janine screamed as she yanked the poncho down and went into the room swinging.

"Holy Shit! Don't KILL ME!" Jonathan screamed out in fear, as he dove to the ground and covered his head with his hands.

Hearing the audible response, she stopped swinging long enough to try and let her eyes adjust to the thick darkness in the room. Hagers blasted into the room behind her with his flashlight on and his weapon drawn.

"WHERE IS IT, WHERE?" Hagers shouted as he erratically whipped his light around in the room, searching for a target.

"HAGERS, HAGERS, HAGERSSSS!" Janine shouted trying to get the marine's attention.

"What?" Hagers yelled back as he continued to wildly swing his flashlight around tossing shadows on the wall.

"It's okay, no problems! We're good, I ... I ... I thought one of those things had gotten in, but it was just Jonathan!" Janine shouted in explanation, as she reached over and turned on the small lamp on the table beside the cot. Jonathan was lying face first on the floor, his body shuddering with fear.

"Alright, good! Whew!" Hagers replied as he quickly regained his breath. "The hell are you doing on the floor man?" he questioned Jonathan as he holstered his weapon.

"Trying to live?" Jonathan squeaked from the ground. "I woke up and didn't know where I was, and I couldn't find the light switch. While I was looking for it, she came in swinging, and I hit the deck," Jonathan explained with a trembling voice as he slowly rolled over to face them.

"For future reference, the lamp is on your right side," Hagers said now in a normal voice.

"I'll be sure to remember that next time ... Shit!" Jonathan replied before accepted the marine's help in getting off of the floor. As Jonathan stood up and dusted himself off, Hagers shoulder attached radio barked to life with the voice of the Major booming throughout the room.

"Hagers, sitrep!"

"Situation clear, Major, just an accident. We're good here. Over," Hagers answered.

"Good to hear, now keep it down! Major out!"

"Yes sir!" Hagers replied back, before turning back to the two civilians.

"I think we're good here Hagers, sorry for the scare," Janine said visibly embarrassed.

"Yes, ma'am, better to be safe than sorry. Hope you don't need new shorts sir!" Hagers chided Jonathan as he turned and walked out.

"I think I'm good," Jonathan replied as he sat back down on his cot, clutching his hands together to stop from shaking.

"Sorry about that, I just didn't know, and with everything that's gone on around here as of late, you can never be too sure," Janine softly apologized as she sat down beside Jonathan on his cot. Her normal defensive barriers suddenly non-existent as she calmly placed her hand on his shoulder.

"No need to apologize, anyone would have done what you did, if they were in your shoes. I just can't believe I almost got my ass beat by a girl!" Jonathan said with a smirk as he turned to face her. In the dark glow of the room Jonathan was mesmerized by her beauty. Her long brown hair was greasy and matted, while muddy smudge stains appeared on her face, yet he could tell that she truly was a beautiful woman.

Fearing that she could see right through him, he stood up abruptly and began to fidget around in his room, explaining to her what they had been through. Recognizing that she had intimidated him, she stood up with a genuine smile and offered him an escape.

"Jonathan, I really do want to hear what you guys experienced, but I don't think that I am the first one that you should tell," she quickly explained as she headed for the doorway.

"Yea, I guess I should talk to Major Powers first," Jonathan agreed.

"Come on, I'll show you the way to his office," Janine said as she stole a quick glance at him bending over the desk in his office to grab a candy bar.

Jonathan followed Janine down the dark hallway until they came to another room with a camouflage poncho hanging in the doorway, ambient light glowed through, and the smell of cigar smoke wafted out of the room. Janine lightly rapped on the wall beside the poncho.

"Yea, who's there?" Major Powers answered from within.

"Major. It's Janine—" Janine started before he cut her off.

"By all means come in," Major Powers called back, as he quickly jumped to his fight and put his cigar behind his back. Janine pulled the poncho back and walked in with Jonathan in tow.

"Major, Jonathan wanted to talk if you had the time," Janine offered.

"Of course, of course! You sure you up to it soldier? You've gotten what, two or three hours of rest?" Major Powers questioned as he pulled up two chairs.

"Yes sir, I think I'm good; besides maybe what I know can help," Jonathan answered humbly.

"Well, I'm going to leave you two gentlemen to it. I'm worn out, and I almost beat Jonathan to death with my new modified talking stick. Therefore, I need some rest. I will talk to you fellas in the morning, and Major, tomorrow I'm going on patrol duty as well, it's completely nonsense that you won't let me help your men. I am living like royalty here, and I need to be able to pull my own weight. Besides, you saw tonight that I can handle myself," Janine demanded as she stood in the doorway.

"No way, Janine! No offense, but you're a civilian, and those things are nasty fucks out there—pardon my language—but it's out of the question," Major Powers protested confidently.

"Major, the way I see it, is that either you can schedule me like everyone else, or I will just start making my own schedule and patrol when I want to. It's really up to you, but I'm not going to freeload anymore. Your choice," Janine replied defiantly as she turned and began to walk out of the room.

"I'll see what I can do," Major Powers retorted, disgusted, "but you're with me the first couple of times; I won't have it any other way."

"I knew you'd see it my way," Janine called out from down the hall, "and one more thing Major ... use the ashtray that I gave you instead of the nasty plastic bottle,"

"Is there anything else your majesty?" Major Powers jokingly called out as he turned his attention back to Jonathan.

"Not now," Janine called back as her footsteps echoed quieter down the hall. Jonathan snickered at the Major's comment before quickly erasing his smile as the Major turned and looked at him with stern conviction.

"She always has to get the last word in ... always," Major Powers said as he shook his head, realizing that he would always be fighting a losing battle with Janine. "So tell me soldier, how'd you fellas do it?"

"Major Powers, it's a long story," Jonathan replied as he leaned back in his chair, trying to steady his already frayed nerves. He watched the Major's facial expression change from stoic to a more concerned expression. The Major then stood up and walked over to the back corner of the office, where he opened up a cabinet and pulled a glass bottle out with two small ornate rocks glasses. He returned to his cot and placed the glass bottle on the floor, and then looked back into Jonathan's eyes.

"I don't really care for stories unless I have a drink in my hand and a cigar at my beck and call. Seeing now that I have both, how about I offer you a drink, and you tell me just exactly how you fellas made it through hell," Major Powers offered cordially.

"I'll accept, but before we get started, on behalf of me and my friends, I wanted to tell you thank you for the shelter," Jonathan replied as he stretched his arm out to receive the glass.

"No thanks needed soldier, you'd a done the same thing had you been in my shoes, I can see it in your eyes."

For the next couple of hours Jonathan explained everything he could remember, going all the way back to the moment that Apoyung told him and Gwen about Gabo and the hole in the ground. The Major never said a word, he just soaked in all of the information.

CHAPTER 17
WHERE THERE'S A WILL, THERE'S A STAIRWELL...

The hot summer air flowed through the windows of the Embassy, stifling its occupants as they tried to get some rest. The nighttime sky sporadically blazed white as a powerful thunderclap formed in the West and slowly made its way toward the survivors holed up in the Embassy. A distant echo of thunder rumbled every so often, drowning out the mumbled moans and growls of the undead as they continued their mindless assault on the sturdy iron fence. Privates Taylor and Harris kept a watchful eye over the Embassy's grounds while continuing to monitor the progression of the approaching storm.

Jonathan had been going at it strong for a good couple of hours before the Major had stopped him in order to take a break and get a quick breath of fresh air. The Major's main goal of the break was to check in on Taylor and Harris to ensure that all was well. The Major excused himself for about fifteen minutes while he got to the roof for a quick update. He returned to the room to find Jonathan genuinely more relaxed after telling someone what he had seen. When Jonathan first sat down to talk with the Major, the Major noticed that the poor boy was a bundle of nerves and would probably crack at any loud noise, yet after realizing that his story wasn't crazy, a strange sense of peace had overtaken the young man. The Major summed it up to one of two things, either exhaustion had finally won, or they young man was able to gain some part of normalcy back to his life when the Major informed him that he wasn't crazy. Either way, the young man seemed more confident and sure of himself than when he had first met him and witnessed the wildness in his eyes.

"So let me get this straight, you and Ayung witnessed one of these rare white spiders attack a jaguar in the jungle?" Major Powers questioned as he refilled his glass and took his seat.

"I know it sounds crazy, trust me, I didn't want to believe it myself, but unfortunately, we did. These same spiders are the ones that tried to attack me and my friends when we went to investigate the cave where we found Gabo," Jonathan answered quietly, his thoughts going back to Gwen, Russo, and Carlos.

"Well son, on any regular day you'd be right in supposing that I think you're crazy, but based on what I have seen over the past couple of days, I would not categorize these past days as normal. Hell, I wouldn't even categorize them as abnormal; I'd just say that they're fucking weird," Major Powers calmly reassured Jonathan.

"I just don't understand what would possess a spider of all creatures to attack, especially two apex predators. That makes absolutely no sense, but then again a person with three bullet holes center mass getting back up and walking doesn't make that much sense either," Major Powers said as he began to talk to himself.

"Tell me about it," Jonathan commented.

"Alright, so let's think this through. An earthquake happens in the middle of the jungle, and it opens up a cave that is home to a new species of spider that is highly aggressive and has possibly spread this disease to other animals, including humans. This disease makes the host became crazed and attack anyone or anything within its reach, and the host can now transfer the disease to another host. Does that about sum it all up, or am I missing anything?"

"That's pretty much it, only you left out the only effective way to stop the infected person,"

"Yea, you're right. The only way to stop the person is to shut down the brain. A simple shot to the head seems pretty effective down here.

"Have I got it all?" Major Powers questions earnestly.

"Yep that about sums it up, alright," Jonathan answered, hoping that his information was helpful to the Major.

"Thank you, Jonathan, you have given me a chance to re-evaluate our situation with your expertise. I have just a couple more questions,"

"Go ahead, Major Powers, the more information that I can get you, perhaps it will help you more than it help me.

"You believe that this disease is transferred from person to person, or animal to person, or animal to animal by just simple bits; or is there a secondary way?"

"As far as I can tell, that seems to be the only way it is transferred; it seems to have to get into the blood stream in order to spread,"

"Ok, next questions," Major Powers turned to face him, his face looking more worn right then than during any part of the day. "Is there a cure, or a vaccination, or something to give to person who has become infected?"

"Unfortunately, no, Major Powers; I don't know if the rest of the world knows what has happened here … yet."

"That's what scares me," Major Powers replied quietly.

"Major, based on the way you asked that question, and now the fact that you can't look me in the eyes, you're telling me that you have someone here that you think is infected with this disease. Do you?" Jonathan asked calmly, sensing the intensity of this situation. The Major leaned back into his chair and stretched his arms, back, and legs while never looking Jonathan in the eyes. He just continued to stare at the floor before he reached down, picked the glass bottle off of the ground, and gave himself a refill. Jonathan waited patiently as he realized what the man's body language was telling him. Jonathan knew at that point that someone in the Embassy had been attacked and most likely infected. He shifted uncomfortably in his chair and began to open his mouth. Before he could ask again the Major quietly answered him.

"My second Lieutenant is infected. He saved my life by putting his in between me and certain death. I can see it now in the fact that he's extremely sick. This infection that he has, it was meant for me," Major Powers said quietly as a clear tear slowly trickled down the left side of his face.

Jonathan saw the tear, and chose to give him a break to regain his composure; he could see the implications of the tear and the emotional weight that it carried for the Major.

After a couple of moments of silence, Jonathan offered the Major some possible time, but the inevitable would still happen, and there was nothing he could do.

"What can you do? By saving my life he has given his a death sentence,"

"Major, that best thing I can do right now is possibly slow the infection down, but I won't be able to stop it, it will eventually kill him, and that is a dangerous thing because we all know what happens next," Jonathan offered cautiously.

"How can you slow it down?"

"Gwen was able to slow the infection in Gabo down by the use of morphine. The problem with Gabo was that he was too far along by the time she got to him. If Second Lieutenant Wallace is still coherent and walking about, then I might be able to give him another day or two—maybe. One things for sure, I can make it so he doesn't feel that much pain during the next couple of days," Jonathan explained.

"We have some vials of synthetic morphine in the first aid kit, I can get that for you."

"That'll be great Major."

"Well, before we do anything, I want to tell him first. It's the very least that I can do for the man. Shit! If it wasn't for him, I'd be the one getting the morphine to keep me alive for more than just a couple of hours. The first aid kit is behind you in one of the cabinets. Do what you have to do; I need to talk to him … alone," Major Powers whispered as he stood up and slowly exited his room. As he walked down the long dark hallway, the gravity of the situation hit him hard as he realized that he was going to have to not only tell his best friend that he was infected with the same thing that infected the masses outside, but that he would eventually have to put him down. The military had trained the Major on every tactic known to man, and he had excelled in not only learning these tactics, but also being able to teach these tactics to his fellow soldiers. Sadly enough, though, there was no training for what he had to do; it had to come from within, a character building block that the Major would just as soon disassemble if it meant saving the life of his best friend.

The lights in Wallace's office were off, but the repugnant smell coming from Wallace's from there struck Major Power's nose long before he stood in front of Wallace's room. The stagnant muggy air combined with the stench of body odor, sweat, and fresh bile forced Major Powers to gag as he reached up and tentatively knocked on the outside wall of the office. He received no reply at first, so he knocked again, louder this time, with his right hand on his sidearm. From within he heard a ghastly cough followed by the expulsion of phlegm before Wallace feebly answered the knocking.

"Who's there?" Wallace's frail voice completely alien to himself and to Major Powers.

"Wallace, it's me," Major Powers said calmly.

"Major, is that you?" Wallace questioned weakly.

"Yea, it's me. Can I...er... come in?"

"Sure Major, just let me get the light for you. Please excuse the mess, I'm still pretty sick," Wallace answered back before convulsing in another coughing fit.

Hearing the fit, the Major waited a few seconds, allowing Wallace to collect himself and not humiliate himself by letting the Major see how messy his office was. The small lamp clicked on followed by Wallace's voice, letting the Major know that the he could come on in. As Major Powers pulled the camouflage poncho back the horrid smell coming from Wallace's room was almost too much for him to take as his eyes began to water and he gagged again. He leaned out of the room and took another deep breath before entering.

"Sorry about the smell Major, I was meaning to throw out some of that waste, but I'm just too weak right now," Wallace offered as he saw the vivid discomfort the Major was in.

"Nonsense, Wallace, you know my old stomach can't take much anyway. Hell, I can't even walk into a Mexican restaurant without my stomach doing flips," Major Powers said as he tried to play it off. "Mind if I have a seat?"

"By all means, Major," Wallace said as he tried to stand up and pull a chair out for him.

"Let me Wallace; just rest and save your strength," Major Powers quietly said as he pulled a chair around and sat in it backwards, resting his elbows on the top of the chair. Wallace gradually sat back down on his cot and the two men sat and stared at each other for a couple of minutes. Both men could see the pain that the other was experiencing, and somewhere deep in the back of Wallace's mind he knew what the Major was going to tell him.

"Major, I've known you for a long time, and I've never known you to be at a loss for words, but right now you are, which is telling me that you haven't come to give me good news," Wallace offered, breaking the eerie silence.

"No, Wallace, I'm afraid I'm not."

"I'm a dead man, ain't I?" Wallace asked, already knowing the answer.

"Wallace, you're infected with whatever is killing everyone, and…" Major Powers paused before collecting himself, "and there is no way we can stop the infection from spreading."

Wallace made no response as he simply tilted his head forward and stared at the floor, silently accepting his predicament. He slowly closed his eyes, whispering a silent prayer before straightening himself back upright and facing the Major. As he looked up he noticed a small glimmer of light reflecting off the Major's face, directly below his eye.

"How long do I have?" He questioned.

"One of the new guy's that we rescued tonight thinks he can possibly give you a day or two with morphine in your system. He explained to me that he has experienced this before, and the only way to slow it down is with a heavy dose of painkillers. Evidently there was a child that contracted the infection in the mission hospital that he was at, and the morphine was the only way they could slow the infection down."

"Major, can I still be useful to you for a couple of days?"

"Of course you can be, but it's not up to me, this is your decision Wallace; unfortunately I can't make it for you,"

"Major. Promise me one thing."

"You got it, whatever it is!"

"You be the one to put me down. Don't let me ramble and moan down the streets like these rat fucks. I don't deserve that, nobody does!" Wallace instructed as he began to violently cough again.

"I will, I promise, but you're right, you don't deserve it. It should be me sitting where you are, not you. That bite was meant for me, not you," Major Powers said, aggressively allowing his emotions to take over.

"Don't take that away from me, Major. I did what I did, and you would've done the same thing for me had the roles been reversed. Let me have that glory moment," Wallace said, choking back tears.

"You got it soldier. When you're ready I'll take you over to my office where Jonathan will get you feeling comfortable, at least." With that,

Major Powers stood up and stepped outside of Wallace's office, allowing him some time to get ready.

The two men walked slowly back towards the Major's office. Wallace was able to keep his balance by using the wall and the support of the Major's shoulder. As they walked in, Jonathan had already put together two leather office chairs, creating a cradle in the middle. Major Powers and Jonathan assisted Wallace into one of the chairs while propping his feet up in the other one.

"Alright Wallace, here's the deal. I'm going to give you enough tonight to put you out for a couple of hours. The sleep should do you some good," Jonathan explained as he pulled the small vial out of his bag.

"That's fine, I could use some sleep," Wallace said back as his breathing became shallower.

"Wallace, Jonathan's going to check on you throughout the night, but I'm going to join Hagers on watch duty. If you need anything, just let Jonathan know. Alright?" Major Powers instructed as Jonathan rolled up Wallace's sleeve and injected him with the clear liquid filled syringe.

"Thanks Major, I should be good ..." Wallace said as he could feel the cool liquid invading his body. Within minutes he seemed more relaxed, and a general warm feeling wrapped itself around his body. He slowly closed his eyes as the full effect of the medicine set in, finally giving him some peace.

"He should be good for a little while. Major, I'll keep an eye on him," Jonathan said quietly.

"Keep me posted on how he's doing throughout the remainder of the night. If anything changes, let me know first," Major Powers said as he handed Jonathan a radio resembling the one that he carried on his belt strap. Jonathan nodded his head in understanding while clipping the radio to his waist.

"Major there is something else that I wanted to talk with you about," Jonathan said.

"What is it?"

"Look, I know you and your team have done a great job in rescuing us and keeping us alive, but none us are going to make it very long on greasy chips and candy bars. We need some actual food and some more water. Are there any places around here close that we could attempt to get to?"

"Around here, no," Major Powers answered in disgust. "Trust me, I've been thinking about this dilemma for a while, and we are kinda out of options. We have one possible solution, but it's very dangerous,"

"What is it?"

"The Embassy had a small cafeteria built here in the building to primarily feed their staff, but it was also frequented by the guests of the embassy," Major Powers explained.

"Ok, great, where is the cafeteria!" Jonathan asked enthusiastically

"It's on the first floor," Major Powers mumbled under his breath, loud enough for Jonathan to hear, yet quiet enough for Jonathan to realize that the Major was ashamed of the information that he had just given Jonathan.

"Shit, you mean the floor that has no flowing electricity?" Jonathan questioned.

"No, it has electricity, at least to the cafeteria, but we have cut all of the other power to it, because ..." The Major trailed off, as he took a long slow deep breath.

"It's filled with them," Jonathan said, finishing the Major's sentence.

"Exactly."

"What happened? How did it happen?" Jonathan questioned in disbelief.

"The same way it's going to happen everywhere else until people start realizing how deadly this infection can be. Let me ask you a question. Could you turn away a friend, a co-worker ... a loved one, if they've been injured and are begging for you to help them? Could you? That's exactly what happened here. People who had worked together for many years can't just turn away when their friends are in danger and not offer help. It only took one person being let in to turn the whole Embassy into a walking graveyard," Major Powers explained apathetically.

Jonathan said nothing, he just leaned up against the desk in the Major's office, his eyes clouded with the revelation of what the Major had just explained to him, and he quickly began to understood exactly what the Major was talking about. It would be damn near impossible for mankind to turn away their own friends, families, and loved ones, even if they understood the ramifications of what could happen. A sense of learned helplessness washed over Jonathan as the room began to spin wildly out of control. He reached back and grasped the desk firmly with both hands, trying to steady himself as a flood of emotions and thoughts ravaged his brain, and he was suddenly unable to maintain at least one clear cohesive thought. He slowly closed his eyes while his breath quickened, and his hands began to shake uncontrollably. An overwhelming feeling of nausea overcame him, forcing him to turn and run around the back of the desk where he quickly located a small aluminum trashcan. He stayed on his knees long after he had gotten sick, as the room wasn't spinning as badly from his prone position as it was when he was upright. As he sluggishly regained his composure, and he felt a firm yet caring grip on his shoulder as the Major was gently pulling him to his feet.

"Come on, soldier. You can do it; remember, slow deep breaths, and don't get up too fast," Major Powers said coaxingly as he gingerly helped Jonathan to his feet. The Major assisted him back to a chair in his room, grabbed one of the candy bars on the desk, and gave it to him.

"I don't want anything else to eat right now, Major," Jonathan objected.

"It'll help. You need your strength and energy, and I need you awake and coherent to keep an eye on Wallace so we don't run into the same fate as the first floor," Major Powers said as Jonathan finally accepted the food and slowly began to eat it. The chocolate and the sugar instantly began to shock his system back as the spinning room stood still once again.

"Thanks, Major, you were right. I just can't believe that his is happening… I mean, I never would have imagined something like this … I just … I …" He trailed off as he could no longer find the words to express what he was feeling.

"What you're feeling, I've been feeling for a couple of days now. It'll pass and you'll learn to accept the situation as is. Our goal now should be to protect everyone we can, and let people know what is going on, and our first order of business tomorrow morning is going to be to protect ourselves. We need the first floor cleared and fortified because we can't continue to live on Snickers and Lays Chips," Major Powers explained.

"I agree, and now that Ayung and I are here, you now have two more bodies to help clear out. We may not be soldiers, but we know how to fight and to survive," Jonathan explained as his strength gradually returned.

"I don't know about that, I don't want to risk any more lives; besides, you're the resident doctor now," Major Powers disagreed, fearing that adding two more civilians into the mix could only increase the casualty numbers, but he unfortunately had no other choice. Sweeping the first floor was going to be extremely difficult; two more weapons could alleviate some of those difficulties.

"Alright, you two are in, but you're in the back. No questions!"

"Understood, Major," Jonathan said, grateful for being allowed to help.

"Major, I'm going to my office to get some things and then I will stay here with Wallace and monitor how he's doing. You go ahead and do what you need to do, I'll take care of him,"

"Good, thanks! Hagers and I got patrol duty until the morning, so we'll be walking around the complex. If you need anything just give me a holler on the radio. I want to do a quick meeting in the morning so we can plan how we're going to take the first floor back. Seeya then, soldier," Major Powers said as he picked up a rifle that was propped up against the wall before exiting his office.

Jonathan did a quick check of Wallace's vitals before he exited the office. After a few wrong turns he found his way back to his office. As he walked up he heard murmuring coming from Ayung's room which was across from his. As he got closer, he could hear the father and son quietly talking between themselves.

"Papa, why people mean, try to hurt us?" Apoyung questioned.

"I not know son, but they not get you!" Ayung said assuredly.

"You stop them Papa?"

"Yes, I protect you,"

"You protect Jonathan too?"

"Yes, I try to protect Jonathan too, but he big strong man, he not need much protection. He protect you also," Ayung said with a hearty laugh. "Now come, go back sleep, you must rest," Ayung spoke softly as he urged his son back over to his cot. Apoyung groggily climbed into the cot while Ayung pulled the sheet over his body, gently tucking his son in.

"Papa?" Apoyung questioned, fighting sleep.

"Yes, son."

"You tell me Mama will always be with me. She here now?"

Ayung hesitated before answering his son's question as guilty pangs stabbed at his heart. He knew in the back of his mind that he had done what was right, because the Nateachy that he knew wasn't the same monster that tried to attack him and Jonathan, but the fresh emotion scar still bled. He looked down at his son's almond eyes which were barely open, and he did his best not to reveal the pain and sorrow he was feeling when he answered his son.

"Yes. She always with you. Right here. Always" Ayung said with a quivering lip as he pointed to the center of Apoyung's chest. Apoyung smiled before placing his hand over his chest and whispering goodnight to his mother.

Jonathan leaned up against the doorframe watching Ayung lean down and kiss his son's forehead as a tear trickled down his face. Ayung looked up and recognized Jonathan with a smile as he quietly stood up and walked in his direction. Jonathan tilted his head back towards his office before exiting the room and walking into his. Ayung followed very quietly as to not disturb his sleeping son.

The two men entered Jonathan's room, and Ayung grabbed a chair as Jonathan sat down on his cot, pulling out some of his gear from his pack.

"What's new, Jonathan?" Ayung questioned as he studied his friend's face.

"Nothing good, to be quite honest, Ayung. One of the soldiers is infected, and the only thing I can do is slow the infection down. I can't stop it," Jonathan answered as he frustratingly slammed his bag back down on the floor.

"What can do to help?" Ayung offered, watching the frustration battle his friend.

"Unfortunately, there's nothing that any of us can do, until we find a cure to this infection, and as it's looking right now, that ain't happening. Not to change the subject for some more bad news, but we're also pretty low on food and water. Tomorrow morning the Major is going to plan a way for us to possibly clean the first floor to get some more food, but it's going to be dangerous because the first floor is crawling with those things," Jonathan explained.

"Evil people?"

"I guess you could call them that, but whatever they are, the first floor is full of them. I volunteered us to help out, I hope you don't mind. I guess I should have talked with you first, but they need the extra hands,"

"My spear is yours!" Ayung replied proudly.

"Good, I'm glad you're here, buddy! It's nice having a friend along for this nightmarish journey," Jonathan said as he stood up and patted Ayung on the back. "I have to go back to the Major's office to keep an eye on Wallace. You should get some rest, tomorrow morning is going to be rough."

"Jonathan, before you go, I tell you story, ok?" Ayung said over his shoulder before Jonathan had left the room.

"Okay," Jonathan agreed, not really wanting to hear a story, but something about the way that Ayung looked at him told him that he needed to hear this story.

"Jonathan, I not smart like you and Gwen, but I thought this early," Ayung started as Jonathan sat back down.

"First off, you're very smart and just as smart as Gwen and me, but in your own way. We work with medicine because we chose too, and that is where we have gained experience, something you don't have. You have experience hunting and knowing what animals are poisonous or deadly, and I don't, so technically you're smarter than me with regards to that aspect. Don't discredit yourself just because you haven't experienced something," Jonathan corrected as the last thing he wanted was for Ayung to lose his confidence.

"I think I understand, but back to story. I remember long time ago when I was Apoyung age, hearing stories from my papa's papa," Ayung started.

"Stories about what?" Jonathan asked intrigued.

"Tagaeri," Ayung said solemnly.

"Tagaeri, like the cannibals that you talked about earlier. The statues from the cave that Apoyung and Gabo found. That Tagaeri?" Jonathan questioned, shocked at what Ayung was talking about.

"Yes, my papa's papa told stories of the Tagaeri, and how they evil, and what they did. Stories about evil and how evil the Tagaeri act," Ayung explained.

"Okay, but I don't follow you, what does Tagaeri have to do with what is going on right now?"

"Evil people outside act like Tagaeri from papa's papa story," Ayung said as he gazed into Jonathan's eyes.

"Wait a sec, so the stories that you heard are exactly like what is going on outside. Is that what you're trying tell me?" Jonathan questioned, astounded. Ayung made no response as he simply nodded his head.

"Thanks for telling me this, Ayung, and we'll definitely talk more about this later, but right now I need to go back to the Major's office and check on Wallace. I'll see you in the morning; now get some rest," Jonathan said before heading out. As he walked back down the dark hallway heading towards the Major's office, his thoughts revolved around what Ayung had just explained to him. Could it be possible that this type of virus has had a run in with humanity prior to the previous couple of days? Either way, this information needed to be relayed to the Major and to Gwen.

***

The night came and went without incident while ushering in a rather large storm front that colored the atmosphere in a dark gray hue. Rain began to steadily fall late into the night and increased in intensity as a damp morning welcomed the survivors holed up in what was left of the Embassy in Quito.

Major Powers wanted to give everyone a quick debriefing before they got the day under way, and had requested everyone to meet in the central meeting room at eight sharp. As he walked into the room, he noticed that everyone was already present with the exception of Wallace, and the thought of what Wallace was going through made the Major quickly wince in pain. As he looked around the room, all of the soldiers had risen to salute him when he walked in. He could see the apparent restlessness in their eyes as he realized that no one was sleeping well, and he chalked it up to the current situation and the lake of healthy food. All three of the new survivors were also standing when the Major walked in, showing their respect and gratitude for saving their lives.

"At ease, ladies and gentlemen. I trust that everyone got at least some sleep last night," Major Powers said rhetorically.

"Well, Major I got to shut my eyes, but I don't know exactly how much sleep I was able to get," Private Taylor commented.

"We have a few things to discuss this morning and one thing to take a vote on before we get going with today. First things first, I want to let you all know that..." Major Powers started, but was unable to finish as he couldn't find the words to express the fact that his good buddy, and one of their brothers in arms, wasn't going to make it. Wallace was not only his good friend, but he represented the morale of the platoon, and right now morale was a luxury they couldn't afford to lose.

"As you are all aware Wallace has been extremely sick as of late, and I wanted to explain to you the gravity of his condition. Wallace has been infected by some type of virus, mostly like the same kind of virus that is currently affecting our visitors that are outside of our gates," Major Powers stopped letting what he had just explained sink in to the group. As he looked around he could see a mixture of emotions decorating the faces of the group: anger, despair, sympathy were just a few that he recognized. He waited for a couple of minutes to see if anyone wanted to say anything, and after no one volunteered, he decided to continue.

"Wallace got bitten by one of those fu ... freaks outside of the gate." Major Powers tried to correct his language as he noticed Apoyung staring at him, listening intently. "Jonathan Steambule is currently treating him as best as he can. From what we know there is no cure, but heavy-duty painkillers can at least slow the infection down. Jonathan has been administering morphine to Wallace throughout the night, giving him some more precious time and rest," Major Powers took a deep breath and steadied his nerves before continuing.

"As it looks right now, the virus will fully take him by tomorrow, if not earlier," Major Powers spoke quietly as the group listened intently. "If you want to go and talk to Wallace, I recommend you do it early because as it gets worse it's going to be harder for him to talk to you or even recognize you."

"Major, what's going to happen when he ... goes? Is he going to turn into one of those things?" Hagers asked concerned.

"Most likely... yes, unless we ..." Major Powers trailed off, unable to finish what he was going to say. Even though he didn't get a chance to finish his statement, the group understood what he was trying to convey, and they all agreed that they wouldn't let it come to that, Wallace was one of them, and he would get the honor of dying like one of them.

"We'll make sure he doesn't become one of those," Private Harris said as she spoke up.

"Agreed," Major Powers calmly replied, as he then realized that Wallace wasn't going to have to worry about roaming the compound as a mindless freak looking for his next meal.

The group sat in silence for a couple of minutes, as they all began to come to terms with Wallace's situation, and what they would have to do. After a couple of minutes of silence, the Major lifted his eyes from the floor as his steel resolve returned to his already haggard face.

"Alright now, let's get a quick update on communications. Harris, have we heard anything else? Any new information? Anything?" Major Powers asked.

"Actually, yes, Major, but I don't know if it's good information or bad. Basically HQ is requesting us to assist two other Embassies. They want us to go and assist the Embassy in Bogota, Columbia and the Embassy in Panama, Panama City. They informed me that both Embassies are under attack, and it is our duty to go and assist," Harris explained.

"Have they had any word from the other Embassies, like Brazil, Argentina, or Chile?" Major Powers questioned.

"No, sir, these were the only two current objectives. I did ask about the other Embassies, but the response that I got was, *You're a Private, let the big decisions be made by the people who know how to make them.*"

"What the hell is that supposed to mean ... by the people who know how to make them. Bunch of bullshit artists,] who don't want to get any dirt on their hands," Major Powers exclaimed, visibly frustrated by the lack of support that he had been getting from HQ, and now upset at the derogatory comments that were made to one of his platoon members. He looked around the room and noticed the whole second floor seemed to get darker as another approaching storm made its way towards the Embassy.

"Well, you tell them that we need help as well, and that we're getting attacked on all fronts. Sheesh, I mean we could use some help too. Figures with the Brass, living in a penthouse suite looking down on the world. I bet if we brought them here they would demand food and to be brought in. Once they were in they'd never help in obtaining any type of supplies, just order us around. What a bunch of good for nothing idiots!" Major Powers said as he stood up and paced across the floor. The room fell disconcertingly quiet as no one knew what to say after the Major's outburst. Nobody had ever seen the Major act this way towards orders, let alone the brass, but it was apparent that he was more concerned with everyone's wellbeing then orders given from thousands of miles away.

"Major, I tried to tell them that, but they informed me that this is an order, and they told me that WE WOULD complete the objective," Harris finished explaining.

"Orders! Now they're giving us orders; when did they send *us* help? When did they tell *us* that help was on the way?" Major Powers shouted wildly as his pace quickened.

"Alright, alright," Major Powers said as he calmed down and returned to his chair, realizing that the more he lost his control everyone else would begin to loose theirs, and he didn't want that to happen.

"Well, for right now, we need to take care of ourselves first. I don't care what orders HQ is sending us. If we don't find some more food and water, we're done for. Therefore, I propose that we take back the first floor," Major Powers stated calmly as he watched the faces of everyone in the room. All of their faces drained white as they suddenly grasped what the Major was saying. The first floor was completely full of the undead, and retaking it would mean that they would have to put their own lives in danger. Seeing the despair in their faces, the major understood the gravity of the situation and what he was asking of them, but he also recognized the simple fact that they couldn't live any longer without food and water.

"The way I see it, is that we can stay here, ration what we have, and slowly die away, or we can give it a shot, and get more food, ammo, and supplies so we can possibly break out of this prison. I know what I'm asking you is tough, and I won't fault you if you don't want to help, but I don't want to sit up here and waste away. We already know that HQ isn't sending any help our way, so basically we're on our own. If we can retake the first floor, we can get plenty of food and water supplies from the kitchen and more ammo and weapons from the armory. Plus, it will allow us access to the underground basement where we have our vehicles, and maybe, just maybe, we might be able to get out of this hell hole," Major Powers explained.

"Major, I'm not against you, but I just don't want to get my ass eaten... er ... butt eaten," Private Taylor said with a quick glance in Apoyung's direction.

"Taylor, I don't want to get eaten either, but I also don't want to wither away up here," Major Powers retorted. Taylor made no comment, he simply nodded his head as he stared down at the floor. A silence filled the room as everyone stared at the ground, not wanting to make eye contact with anyone else. Major Powers took a heavy sigh as he began to think that his plan of saving everyone was too risky. He was getting ready to scratch the idea altogether when Ayung stood up.

"Major, I not want to die here, and I want my son to grow up strong and good man like you. I join you downstairs to clean out evil spirits," Ayung said proudly as he glared at the Major with admiration.

"Count me in too!" Jonathan said as he walked into the room.

A grin slowly creased across the Major's face as an overwhelming feeling of gratitude permeated within his body.

"Major, you're crazier than bat...er ... wings ... but we've been with you from the beginning, and I know that when I speak, I speak for all of us when I say that where you go... we go!" Hagers said as the rest of the Marines nodded their heads with sly grins plastered on their faces.

"Thank you all!" Major Powers said.

"I hate to be the killjoy of the group, but I sure hope you have a plan, because going in their half-cocked like a girl scout SWAT team is going to earn us all an early lunch, and I don't think we're going to like the menu," Taylor commented as he checked the clip in his handgun.

"Why, Taylor, I heard that human's taste like chicken?!" Janine jabbed with a smile.

"Well, I ain't going to find out if that myth is true or not..." Taylor said as he sniffed his arm and violently shook his head while sticking his tongue out.

"Alright, cut the chatter, we need to get serious people, because this surely isn't going to be a walk in the park," Major Powers said as he stood up and walked over to the large dry erase board easel and slid it over to the center of the room. He grabbed one of the markers and crudely drew a layout of the first floor. The layout looked like a large box with an inlay cut out in at the bottom, with various rooms, offices, and cubes littering the inside of the box. In the center above the cutout was a crescent shaped box labeled "front desk." To the right of that was a larger box, labeled "kitchen." with smaller three-sided boxes on the outer wall labeled "cubes." Above the kitchen box, lining the back wall were three larger boxes labeled "offices," and one smaller one close to the top left corner labeled "supply office." Below the supply office were more "cubes," and on the very bottom was another large box, labeled "military office / armory." The diagram, though crudely drawn and hastily put together, was good enough for the marine's to understand what the first floor roughly looked like. In the bottom right hand side and the top left hand side were half-circles around the corners with arrows describing them as stairwells.

"Alright folks, here's the first floor based on the blueprints I found in my office. This is a rough guesstimate of what I think it looks like; excuse the crudeness of the drawing. Based on this we have two points of entry, one here and one here," Major Powers said as he pointed to the two diagrams marked as stairwells.

"Major, you want to split our forces?" Harris questioned, concerned.

"Yes, Harris, that way we don't get into a bottleneck situation. We'll have two teams, Alpha and Bravo. Alpha will consist of myself, Harris, and Ayung; while Bravo will consist of Hagers, Taylor, and Jonathan. Sorry, Janine, but you're on babysitting watch with the child," Major Powers explained as he turned his attention to Janine, expecting the protest.

"Got it Major, I'll take care of Apoyung," Janine agreed as she reached over and softly massaged the boy's shoulders.

"Thank you, Ms. Janine," Ayung said quietly as he looked in her direction.

"Alright, good. Now that the teams are divided, here's our plan. Hagers, I want you to redirect the power from the third and fourth floor to the first floor, and get those lights on. I don't want to fight this enemy in the dark," Major Powers instructed.

"Got it, Major!" Hagers complied.

"Next, Hagers I want your team to go in first, and use your silencers if you can at first to get into the doorway. Once you have cleared the doorway, take the silencers off, and clear the northern and western hallways from your positions. The sounds should pull any of these freaks in your direction, allowing us the come through our doorway. We'll clear the six cubes to the south and make our way into the military office where we will set up a fall back point if we get overrun. Hagers, move your team down the west hallway, and clear out the three cubes, and we'll meet you in the front lobby. From there, Harris and I will head to the northern wall and clear out the supply office and the three offices on the back wall while you all setup on the outside of the kitchen. The way that I see it is that the majority of them will be in the kitchen, as that was the original place where they took the wounded. Once we have cleared the northern wall, we will meet you back at the cafeteria entrance. I would like to position two of us on both sides of the cafeteria entrance, and then we basically pick them off from the doorway. Based on the information Janine was able to recollect from earlier, we're looking at twenty-one councilmen and twenty employees. I've already taken care of one of the councilmen, so that leaves us roughly forty undead freaks to take care of. Try your best to keep count so we know where we stand. Once we have cleared the cafeteria and the kitchen, Taylor, you, Ayung, and Harris have got window duty, so use whatever you can to board up the windows, and do it as fast as you can; it's only a matter of time before they start squirming their way through the gates. That's it, any questions before we head out?" Major Powers asked as he looked out in his audience expecting to see uneasy faces, yet all he saw was steel reserve determination written across the faces of his group.

"Well, alright then. Hagers, get topside and reroute that power. Once the first floor is cooking, get back down here,"

"Major one more thing," Jonathan spoke up after studying the diagram.

"Go ahead, Jonathan."

"Guys, aim for the head. The only way to take these things down is to destroy the brain, body shots don't amount to anything," Jonathan explained as a small taste of fear quickly spread through his body as he remembered vividly the assault from Gabo and Ga.

"Good point. Men, kill shots are the only way we're going to survive this. Alright, if any of you have any questions or want to back out, now's the time," Major Powers said stoically.

No one raised their hands as the Major finished his debriefing. Slowly they gathered their things, and each exited the room, headed towards their own quarters to get ready for what lay ahead. Jonathan waited until everyone had left before he walked up to the Major.

"What is it soldier?" Major Powers questioned as he could see the concern on Jonathan's face.

"Well, Major, I really don't know, but it could be something. After we get done with this, you and I need to talk about something Ayung explained to me," Jonathan explained.

"You got it. Is it anything that I need to know before we take back the first floor?"

"No, sir, it's just something that I think we need to discuss at a later time. Right now, it has nothing to do with what we're about to do,"

"Alright, good. How's Wallace?" Major Powers asked as his whole demeanor changed.

"He's resting right now, but the infection is spreading quickly. I will keep you posted on his progress."

"Do you think he'll make it through the night?"

"I don't know, but I'm hoping."

"That'll have to be good enough for me. Thank you for taking care of him. I just wish there was something else we could do."

Major Powers looked as if he was getting ready to say something else, when his shoulder harnessed radio came to life with Hagers voice.

"Major, I've re-routed the juice, so the first floor should be lit. This is going to be a major strain on the generator, so we need to hurry," Hagers shouted over the hum of the generator.

"Got it, Hagers. Everyone, now it's time. Alpha and Bravo, take up your positions on the stairwell. Clear out the doorways so you have a wide berth, and … good luck!" Major Powers said into his radio as he and Jonathan exited the central meeting room.

Jonathan walked swiftly down the semi-lit hallway heading towards the stairwell to join up with Bravo group. As he walked by one of the vacant offices he stole a quick look outside at the building grey clouds off in the distance. A sudden flash streaked across the sky, causing him to blink as a rolling clap of thunder echoed in the distance. The storm would be upon them within the next couple of hours. He pulled himself away from the office and joined Hagers and Taylor in removing the blockade from the doorway to the stairwell.

It took the men nearly fifteen minutes to clear the path of debris from the doorway, allowing them wide angles to protect themselves. As they finished moving the heavy furniture away, the doorway to the stairwell violently crashed against the thick steel chains that held it together as a forceful impact bowed the door outward. The sudden noise startled the men as they froze in fear as each one of them slowly turned and watched the door strain against its bonds. Growling and moaning could be heard from the other side of the door as the unseen force continued to push against the heavily chained door. Hagers reached for his radio to inform the Major of their situation.

"Major, we have a slight problem," Hagers voice came shakily across the radio waves.

"What is it Hagers?" Major Powers quickly questioned.

"They already know we're here. We have multiple ones pushing on our stairwell door; there's no way we're going to be able to go in quietly. Any ideas?" Hagers explained calmly, even though sweat was beading up all over his body.

"Dammit," Major Powers cursed under his breath as he angrily thought of a solution to the problem.

"Maybe I can help ..." Wallace said as he staggered up to team Bravo. "I just gave myself another one of your wonder shots, Doc, and I have enough strength to at least get you boys through the door. Hagers, let me talk to the Major," Wallace instructed as he stretched out his hand.

"Major, it's Wallace. I'll get your boys in over here, no worries," Wallace spoke into the radio.

"Wallace! What are you doing up? You're in no condition to participate in this. I order you to go back to your room!" Major Powers frantically said into the radio.

"Sorry, Major, but I'm not following your orders. Look, I'm already dead so a couple more bites won't hurt me, and besides, you're stuck and can't get into the first floor without me," Wallace said into the radio as a grin slowly creased his face, and he realized that what he was going to do would save the lives of his friends.

"You listen to me ole buddy, I can figure out another way; don't do this. It's a mistake, and you know it," Major Powers frustratingly said into his radio.

"No, you can't, so just wait until you don't hear any more scratching or moaning from your direction. We'll meet you in the middle. Wallace out," Wallace said as he handed the radio back to Hagers.

"Good Luck ,ole buddy," Major Powers quietly replied as he put his radio back while lowering his head, closing his eyes, and saying a prayer for his old friend. "Alright crew, when I give the signal, take the chains off of the door, and let's clear this fucking floor,"

"Alright, you boys get behind the blockade, and let me undo these chains. No matter what happens, don't try to save me. I'm already dead; just clear out these infected, pus filled maggots," Wallace instructed as he pulled out his Glock and checked the clip before jamming it back into the butt of the gun.

Hagers tossed him the key, from behind the blockade before instructed the rest of Bravo to check their weapons. Hagers and Taylor pulled out their service Berettas and attached silencers to the tops while Jonathan loaded his shotgun, while putting the remaining shells into his pocket.

Wallace unlocked the padlock on the chains as the pressure against the door suddenly subsided at the sound of the metal clanging of the chains. Wallace yanked the chains off of the door and jumped back as the doors became free. Spine tingling seconds seemed like hours as the four stared at the door cautiously waiting for them to explode outward. The sound of Wallace cocking his gun sliced through the silence like a foghorn alerting the enemies of their presence. The wooden doors burst open as seven undead councilmen dressed in tattered and bloodstained business suits funneled into the hallway. Wallace unloaded on the first two, creating cavernous holes above their eye sockets, before the rest gang tackled him in a feral rage. Their savage saliva laden mouths found their way to his already taut skin as their jaws clamped down, tearing the already infected flesh from his body. Wallace screamed in pain as he wildly kicked and swung his arms in erratic motions. Adrenaline coursed through his body as he suddenly had the strength of ten. He reached up and grabbed the closest undead, and with a quick twist he snapped its already fragile neck, instantly stopping its onslaught. Two quiet reverberations barely audible in the massive fight on the floor joined the cacophony as two bullets found their way through two more skulls, instantly dropping two undead while scattering skull fragments about the floor. Smoke slowly wafted from the end of Hager's silencer as he opened his eye from behind the barrel of his Beretta.

The last two undead were completely unfazed by their dwindling numbers as they continued to violently pull and bite at Wallace's exposed flesh. He continue to swing at them before one finally caught his flailing arm and sunk its ragged teeth deep into his forearm causing dark red blood to drain down his arm before splattering on the floor. Wallace screamed out again in pain as Taylor hopped the barricade with his KA-BAR knife in hand. He ran to Wallace's aid and thrust his blade into the temple of the undead. The knife penetrated the grayish skin with ease, forcing the undead's eyes into the back of its skull. The body fell limp to the floor with its teeth still lodged in Wallace's arm. Seeing the second attacker, the final undead quickly jumped to its feet and let loose a horrible growl before charging Taylor. Sensing the danger, Taylor quickly tried to pull his knife free, but the undead was too quick. He looked up with his eyes wide as his pursuer dove through the air aimed at his head. He quickly tried to shield his face with his arm while slamming his eyes shut and gritting his teeth. He felt the impact of the body, but strangely enough, the body deflected off of his, landing on the floor with a loud thud. Silence enveloped the room as the four survivors quickly regained control of their breaths.

Taylor slowly opened his eyes and looked around in bewilderment at the scene, trying to figure out why he wasn't attacked. He saw what was left of the undead that had tried to attack him, an older, overweight councilmen with gray matted hair in a hideously bloodstained plaid suit, with a small opening under his chin about the size of a quarter. He quickly scanned upward, and he found another hole in the head, this time twice the size of the first, shattering the cheek bone and the eye socket before the bullet exited the undead's head. Taylor heard Wallace gurgle as blood coated his lips before dribbling out both sides of his mouth and slowly draining down towards his neck. As he looked at the old vet, he noticed his Beretta in his right hand resting on his heaving chest, a small trail of smoke lingering above the end of the barrel. Wallace looked up at Taylor with a strained grin on his face as his eyes rolled into the back of his head.

"He ... He ... saved my life," Taylor stammered as the shock of the whole situation was finally getting to him.

"Then save his soul by not allowing him to walk this earth as a mindless idiot, only craving the living," Jonathan said quietly before he climbed over the barricade, his weapon steadily aimed at Wallace's head.

Taylor said nothing, just simply nodded his head and pointed his Beretta at his old friend. He took a deep breath, and with a single tear rolling down his cheek, he pulled the trigger. The bullet careened through Wallace's skull, giving him the peace that he requested before he died.

"Hagers!" Major Powers's voice screamed through the radio, "What's going on, what happened?"

"Doorway's clear Major; we took down seven of them, but ..." Hagers trailed off searching for the words.

"That's good Hagers, I understand, no need to say it ... Continue with your mission, we've still got to clear this floor," Major Powers replied, not allowing Hagers to explain what everyone already knew.

"Ten-four, Major. Listen to your door, they should be heading our way soon. Hagers out,"

"Roger that, maintain radio silence until we meet up, no point in broadcasting our locations,"

Hagers and Taylor nodded to each other as they quickly shut off their radios and prepared to head down the hallway. The north hallway was cluttered with broken glass and destroyed office supplies. Three of the five ceiling lights were working while the other two had been busted out, leaving a checkered lighting path down the north hallway. The hallway leading to the center of the first floor supported three cubes consisting of six feet tall metal dividers covered with gray felt, displaying the occupants various awards and pictures of their families. All of the ceiling lights down this hallway were still intact, illuminating their path to the front entrance. This path held just as many obstacles as the northern path, as metal file cabinets rested on their sides, the contents of the drawers strewn about on the floor. Two computer monitors lay face down in the hallway, dried blood stains present on the corners of the monitors.

A large clap of thunder rattled the building as the three of them slowly began to walk down the hallway leading to the center of the floor. Hagers fisted his hand to stop those behind him and leaned up against the wall, angling himself to the opening of the first cube. He signaled to Taylor with a hand motion that represented something coming from his throat. Taylor looked at him with a perplexed look for a second before he realized what Hagers was trying to get him to do.

"Oh, yoo-hoo, undead freakazoids. Over here, I'm ringing your dinner bell," Taylor hollered loudly while aiming his Beretta at the opening of the first cube. A shuffling sound echoed down the hall as something rustled around in the cube. The three looked on as the undead tried walking through the downed file cabinet, only to trip and fall face first onto the metal cabinet. The undead fell awkwardly, instantly breaking its right arm, the snapping of the bone causing the men's stomach to roll. The serrated end of the bone pierced the gray skin spilling dark blood onto the floor. The undead seemed completely unfazed as it turned its head towards the men. It pushed itself up off of the ground and let loose a horrendous moan before it jumped down and started to rush towards Taylor. As its head crossed Hagers path a soupy spray of brain matter, skull fragments, and blood misted the other wall as the undead fell face first, completely immobilized. As the first one hit the floor, another moan sounded further down the hallway. The men waited patiently as a sliding sound filled the hallway. Taylor crept forward with his gun raised, trying to get a better view of what was causing the noise. As he got to the metal filing cabinet, he could see on the other side another undead viciously dragging itself across the floor with bloody fingers. He looked behind the body and noticed that it was dragging two mangled legs that looked as if they had been crushed by something. The ankles and the feet were completely parallel as the undead reached the side of the filing cabinet. It started to climb over and reach for Taylor who put his barrel on its head and pulled the trigger.

Taylor cautiously peered into the first and second cubes, and after determining there was no threat, he gave the all clear signal and the group continued to move down the hallway. As Jonathan started walking, he heard more moaning coming from the northern hallway, and he let out a quick whistle to alert Hagers and Taylor. Both men froze and turned back as Jonathan quickly spun around and peered around the corner, down the northern hall. Two more undead were drawn to the noise as they slowly shuffled down the hallway. Jonathan looked back and motioned to Taylor and Hagers that he had it, before he stepped into the middle of the hallway. Seeing the fresh food, the undead's eyes grew wide as horrific howls escaped their mouths before they made a mad dash towards Jonathan. One of them was completely missing his stomach while the other one's arms and legs had massive bite wounds on them. Jonathan steadied his nerves and raised his shotgun, as he realized that he'd only get one good shot off before they were on top of him. He decided to wait until the very last second before he squeezed the trigger, hoping to get two with one shot. At the very last second the shotgun barrel erupted as shrapnel peppered the distance between him and the undead, effectively taking both of their upper torsos clean off. Blood and body tissue splashed upon the wall as the two sets of the legs fell forward twitching for about two seconds.

Hagers and Taylor ran around the corner with their guns drawn but quickly lowered them as they realized the threat had been neutralized.

"You sure you're not some mercenary soldier for hire?" Taylor questioned in a whisper, while putting his hand on Jonathan's back. Jonathan simply smiled as he quickly shook his head, before rubbing his hands on his pants to dry the perspiration forming on his palms. The trio waited for a couple of minutes to ensure that no other undead were making their way down the northern hall to flank them. After a couple of minutes, nothing shambled down the hallway and the trio turned to follow the Major's plans. They could hear moaning and scratching coming from the other side of the wall as the undead trapped in the cafeteria had heard the commotion and were trying to come through the wall. As they came around the corner they could see another corpse at the end of the hallway directly in front of the third cube. The undead corpse only had one arm as the other one seemed to have been ripped off at the shoulder. Mangled flesh, muscle, and bone covered in dark blood hung haphazardly from the shoulder as the undead corpse aimlessly walked in circles trying to determine where the noise was coming from. It turned its body towards the trio and froze when it saw them. Its bloodshot eyes grew wider as it began to open its mouth before its head violently jerked backwards as a bullet exited the back of its skull, spraying blood against the white backdrop of the back wall. Hagers reloaded his Beretta as he slowly crept forward.

The report of the shotgun reverberated throughout the hallways of the first floor, penetrating the ears of the undead as they turned their heads sharply in the direction of the noise. The shuffling of their feet slowly guided them in the direction of the sound as the overwhelming hunger potential drove their mindless bodies in search of potential food. Hearing the shotgun blast, Major Powers quietly unlocked the padlock as he gently slipped the chains from the door. With Harris covering him, he gradually pulled the two doors back and quickly jumped out of the way. Harris cleared the doorway as none of the undead were standing in wait. The Major's crew exited the stairwell cautiously as they entered the first floor. One of the lights in this hallway worked, while the other three erratically blinked with an electric hum. The group turned south towards the row of six cubes where all four of the ceiling lights were working properly. The offensive smell of death assaulted their nostrils, forcing all of them to pull the front of their shirts over their mouths and noses as they struggled to breath. Major Powers surveyed the hallway and immediately noticed a pair of panty-hosed legs stretching outward from the first cube on the left. He held up his fist as the others froze behind him. The legs weren't moving, as they lay in a pool of blood, but the Major had long since learned that looks are definitely deceiving. He carefully crouch walked up to the first cube and slid his back up against the felt divider as he cleared the cube across from the legs. The cube was clear, as he observed a paper cutter missing the blade. *At least someone put up a fight,* he thought to himself before he pivoted across the opening with is pistol now aimed into the cube with the legs. He couldn't see any movement, just more destruction. The body of a female employee lay face down on the floor, blood pooling around the body. He pulled his KA-BAR knife from its sheath and gently poked at the legs which didn't move. He began to realize that her body was already dead, as a sudden blast of rotten smell filled his nostrils. He quickly looked around and couldn't find the source of the smell. He heard a low growl, followed by the sound of wet drops hitting his helmet. In a flash he jerked up and saw an undead glaring down at him with its mouth open and bloody flesh clinging to its teeth. The Major froze in fear as the corpse's eyes zeroed in on him with an animalistic rage. Just as soon as the Major realized that this was it, a whistle carved the air around him as a chunk of flesh and skull exploded outward as the undead corpse toppled off of the divider onto the floor beside the Major. He frantically kicked the corpse away as he looked back to see Harris reload her Beretta with a quick wink in his direction. He slowly nodded his head as he realized that he might have to change his pants before the day was over.

Harris checked the northern hallway leading to the first of the three large offices, and couldn't see any movement before she and Ayung joined the Major at the entrance to the cubes, completely unaware of the former employee exiting the supply office, slowly walking in their direction. One by one they cleared each of the six cubes, and only found more of a mess in each of the cube, where papers, pens, pencils, and cd's were strewn about.

Major Powers and Harris exited the row of cubes and approached the military office door, which was oddly shut. They positioned themselves on both sides of the door as Ayung stayed in the middle of the last two cubes, his modified axe clutched in his hands. As Major Powers reached for the door handle, a low growl filtered down the hallway, forcing the three of them to stop in their tracks. Harris jerked her head around to see an undead standing directly behind Ayung, its bloody fingers stretched out about two feet from Ayung's neck. The once councilmen now a mutilated mass of flesh lurched toward the father before slipping on the office paper covering the floor. The corpse crashed onto the floor with a thud as Ayung jumped away, spinning to face his foe. Without hesitation he brought his axe down on the corpse, splitting its skull directly down the center. Ayung jerked his axe out of the skull before quickly wiping it off against the felt divider.

With their attention focused on Ayung's attacker, none of them noticed the military office door open as a former employee with a deep neck wound exited the room and latched onto Harris's back. She shrieked in fear as she struggled against the massive strength of the undead. It wrapped its arms around her neck, effectively cutting off her air supply as she struggled against its weight. In a fluid motion, the undead corpse bit down on her shoulder as she screamed out in fear. She continued to struggle against her foe as Major Powers grabbed it by the hair, yanking its head backward before impaling the head with his KA-BAR knife. The moment the blade punctured the skull, its grip slackened as it slumped to the ground. Harris fell to her knees sobbing uncontrollably as she frantically pulled her gear off to see if the teeth had penetrated her skin. As she pulled off her jacket she could feel moisture under her shirt, but no stain appeared on the outside. She wrenched her shirt off and hysterically checked her shoulder where it had bitten her. Major Powers quickly wiped the dirt and sweat away from her shoulder while pouring water from his canteen onto her shoulder. Neither one could find any puncture wounds, just purple and black bruising under the skin, but no fresh blood. As they continued to expect her shoulder, Ayung tapped them both on the shoulder while holding the undead's hair in his hand. They jerked around, startled, as they saw Ayung pry its mouth open with is axe blade. A black plastic box trickled out of its mouth as her shoulder mounted radio fell to the floor. Ayung smiled as he looked back up and met the two of their eyes. A wave of relief rushed over Harris as she simply broke down sobbing into the Major's shoulder. He calmly patted her head and soothed her before he whispered, "We have to keep going, we still gotta clear this floor."

Harris nodded her head slowly before wiping the tears from her eyes and pulling her clothes back on. They cleared the military office and armory, and they found another dead corpse in the back corner of the office, its head completely blown away, a Beretta still clutched in its right hand.

"Change of plans. You two stay here, I'll get Bravo over here, we need to re-group and set up our fall back plan, and I can't think of a better place to hole up in than in here," Major Powers instructed in a whisper. Harris and Ayung nodded their heads as the Major quietly slipped out of the room, headed for the front entrance.

All of the lights in the military office were working properly as Ayung and Harris began to explore the supplies in the room. The back wall of the room was a chained closet armory that held all of the weapons, ammunition, and supplies for the Embassy. Harris walked over to the desk, searched under it for the keys, and found them taped to the bottom of the desk. She pulled them out and walked to the closet door to unlock it while Ayung picked up a small desk and moved it over to the doorway, effectively blocking the lower part. Harris unlocked the closet and pulled the door open, smiling as she suddenly felt safer in the presence of all of the weapons. In the back left corner of the closet stacked all the way to the ceiling were three separate towers of steel ammunition crates, three wide, fifteen tall. The first stack contained the ammunition for the standard military issued handgun the Beretta the second stack contained the ammunition for a military rifle, the M4 Carbine, while the third stack contained the slugs for the M4 Super 90 military shotgun. On the back wall, the polished shine of the black metal glimmered in Harris' eyes as she counted the weapons, finally feeling somewhat secure since the onset of this horrible virus, infection, disease, or whatever the hell it was.

Normally a military armory, especially in an Embassy, was a skeleton supply, but since Homeland Security had raised the terrorist threat recently in South America, all Embassies were ordered to increase their stock in case an attack occurred. For once, Harris was glad of the resulting increase in the military stock. She counted twenty-five Berettas, fifteen carbines and shotguns, and five "big daddy" grenade launchers accompanied by ten special ammo crates. She didn't understand why the military would have insisted on stocking grenade launchers, but based on her current situation she decided that it would be stupid to question. She and Ayung commenced to separating the weapons on the desk while pulling the ammo crates out for easy access. Ayung had pulled another desk close to the doorway which would serve as a strong blockade if needed, but he wasn't going to put it up until everyone was in the room and accounted for.

Meanwhile, Major Powers slinked his way down the hall, heading for the front entrance to meet up with Bravo group. As he approached the front lobby, he could see two of the undead trapped behind the front desk lobby, constantly bumping into one another as they tried to get towards something in the opposite direction. Major Powers cleared the hallway leading to the northern wall before he cautiously approached the front desk. The two trapped undead looked to be former receptionists as their clothing resembled that of professional secretaries. One of their tops had been ripped exposing her breasts, and two savage bite marks around the rib cage, while the other one walked awkwardly as the Major noticed that the foot was broken and pointing in the wrong direction. Three gouging bite wounds peppered the leg, and dried blood crusted over around her mouth. Both of their arms were outstretched in the direction of where Bravo team would be coming as they continued to moan and run into the desk. Major Powers shook his head in disbelief at the mindless actions they were exhibiting. He couldn't understand, nor did he want to understand, what was happening. He needed to keep his focus on getting his team to safety. As he pulled his Beretta up, both of the heads of the undead suddenly jerked backwards as two bullets exited the skulls, embedding themselves into the computer monitors behind the desk. The two undead fell into each other before landing on the ground, ceasing all movements. Startled, Major Powers lowered his weapon as he looked around and found Hagers stepping out of a dark corner, lowering his weapon. Taylor and Jonathan followed as they met in the middle of the front lobby. The outer doors of the lobby were shattered, while the inner doors seemed to be shatter proof as deep scratches were present, yet the glass was still intact. Major Powers quickly shook hands with the three men before motioning them to follow him towards the military office where Harris and Ayung had set up a fall back point. All four of the men entered this military office before Ayung and Taylor piled the desks up to block the entrance to the office, allowing the group a brief break in the action.

"How did you guys fair?" Major Powers questioned Hagers in a quiet tone.

"Good. Well, except for Wallace, but he saved our asses; there was no way we'd have been able to enter this floor without him," Hagers explained as he rested up against a desk, while taking a swig of his water.

"Did you take care of Wallace?" Major Powers questioned.

"Yes, sir, we couldn't allow him to be a part of these freaks. We put him down," Taylor said quietly as he stared at the floor.

"Good work soldier, that's what Wallace wanted, keep your head up," Major Powers said calmly as he reached out and patted Taylor on the back.

"Major, from my last count, we took down seven at the door, three in the western hall near the office cubes, and two coming down the northern hall from the back of the building. That makes twelve that we got. How many did you guys take out?" Hagers asked.

"I counted five before I got to the front desk with the twin secretaries. You add those two up and I've got a total of seven, and combined with your twelve, that makes nineteen," Major Powers counted.

"That leaves us twenty one left, provided we don't have any person unaccounted for," Harris spoke up, quickly doing the math in her head.

"Alright, good work men, now all we got to do is clear the rest of this floor out, and we'll be in business. Harris, what do the supplies look like in here?" Major Powers questioned before he had a chance to look at what Harris had already laid out on the table.

"We're locked and loaded Major, plus I found a surprise or two for you in the back," Harris said with a grin as she pointed to the end of the table where the grenade launcher sat.

"Hot damn, sweet Betsy!" Major Powers exclaimed as he walked over and picked up the massive weapon, "Now that's what I'm talking about."

"Well, it's time to finish what we started before it's too late," Major Powers said as he pointed towards the window. Everyone turned and looked, and immediately realized what he meant as the normally brightly lit sky was hideously gray as lightning streaked across the clouds.

"Agreed!" Jonathan exclaimed, as he picked up a new shotgun, and loaded a few rounds.

"Harris and I will travel back towards the northern wall and sweep the office rooms clean before joining up with you at the doors of the cafeteria. Don't waste your time in investigating the floor for supplies just yet. I need a head count of the cafeteria the moment I get back so we knew exactly how many we're dealing with. Hagers, take Taylor, Ayung, and Jonathan with you. Post up outside the room, and try your best to get a headcount without being detected. If you are, use the shotgun, and we'll come a running. Any questions?" Major Powers asked. No one raised their hands.

"Very well. Harris, you're with me," Major Powers instructed as he reloaded his Beretta before grabbing his new favorite toy. The group quickly moved the desks away from the door before Major Powers and Harris exited the room, crouched and running down the hallway towards the northern wall.

Hagers and Taylor reloaded their weapons before grabbing a couple of the carbine rifles for added support.

"The way that I see it is that hallway is going to be very clustered with all four of us in there trying to pop off some of these freaks. I think that two will suffice, and any more could be a death trap, especially if we're charged. Any volunteers?" Hagers asked, looking around.

"Ayung and I will hold back. Where do you want us?" Jonathan volunteered as he pocketed a few more shotgun shells and with a slight nod in Ayung's direction.

"Good, you guys post up in the front lobby. That way if we need to fall back that is an open area we can retreat to, giving all of us a clearer line of sight," Hager explained, content with the plan.

"Agreed," Jonathan said quietly as he walked over and stood with Ayung.

"Well, what are waiting for, let's go kill some undead fucks," Taylor said loudly as his cowboy spirit shone through.

"Shhhh! While I don't express his enthusiasm, I agree we need to get moving," Hagers said as a loud clap of thunder shook the building, causing everyone to tense up.

Jonathan and Ayung moved into the front lobby and backed themselves into the corner wall adjacent to the hallway where the cafeteria was, as Hagers and Taylor slowly crouched walked towards the opening of the cafeteria. Inside the cafeteria they could hear multiple people shuffling their feet across the floor as the undead purposelessly paced around the cafeteria with no direction. They posted up against the wall and waited patiently for the Major and Harris to join them across the opening into the cafeteria. They heard three shrill whistles followed by quiet thuds before they saw the Major and Harris move into position on the opposite side of the door leading into the cafeteria. Major Powers signaled a four with his hand, followed by a face down hand with a thumb pointed at his neck, before sliding his hand across his throat. He was symbolizing that they had taken care of four more undead before they arrived there. Major Powers and Harris posted up on the outside of the wall leading into the cafeteria. He stole a quick glance into the cafeteria and realized that taking back the cafeteria was going to be a lot harder than he had first imagined. Major Powers looked to Hagers to see if he had a plan, and judging by the eye contact, he realized that he did.

Hagers held up one finger, then quickly pulled his hand across his neck indicating a cease motion. He then repeated the motion a couple of times before the Major caught on to what he meant. One of them would lean in and shoot one of the undead, hopefully killing it clean, and as the undead fell, they would duck back around the doorway as the corpse crashed to the ground. Major Powers nodded in agreement as Hagers affixed a silencer to his Beretta. He leaned around the doorway, aimed, and fired a quick shot entering the neck of an undead and exiting his through his ear. Blood sprayed into the air, getting more of the undead's blood over its counterparts. The body fell like a sack of potatoes, knocking over a stack of chairs. The cacophony of the chairs clattering to the ground caused everyone to tense up and strain their ears, listening and praying that they weren't discovered. After a few tense minutes, the Major nodded at Hagers and slowly leaned around the alcove of the doorway, taking aim at another undead. As the Major looked in, he noticed three of the undead huddled in the back corner on all fours cowering over what looked like the remains of an employee. His business suit pants were completely covered in blood as his feet supported only one business shoe; the other leg was missing a foot as the jagged flesh and bone ended at the ankle. Forcing back a build- up of bile from the horrid stench in the room, the Major steadied himself and took aim at the first of the three undead. He calmly pulled the trigger, sending a silver tipped bullet into the upper back of an undead. The bullet sliced through its grey skin, entering the body at the apex of the spine while exiting out at a forty-five degree angle from where it entered. The spine splintered, sending bone shards outward while redirecting the trajectory of the bullet. The corpse fell face first into the body, splattering blood onto its partners who paid no attention as they continue to rip and tear at the flesh of their victim. The Major fired two more rounds, effectively stopping the relentless assault of the already deceased victim. Two more wet smacks filled the room as their bodies hit the floor.

As the Major opened his other eye to refocus, he realized too late that he had leaned too far into the doorway, making his position visible. A cold boney hand jerked out from the room, grabbing his wrist with a violent tug.

"SHIT!" Hagers exclaimed as he watched the Major struggle with the vice like grip of the undead. In a flash the undead let out a blood curdling howl as it reached with its other hand in an attempt to pull the Major into the room. The rest of the undead, immediately affixed their eyes to the doorway, seeing the struggle between the undead and the Major. The Major jerked his arm back, pulling the undead to the ground as he reached with his free hand for his KABAR knife strapped above his boot. He flipped the buckle off and unsheathed the knife before jamming it upwards under the undead's chin, instantly covering his arms with dark crimson blood as it twitched before falling motionless to the floor.

With their cover now blown, the survivors scrambled away from the doorway as the group of ten undead charged towards the door in an animalistic rage, their howls filling the hallways of the first floor while echoing throughout the building.

"GET DOWN!" Harris screamed as she pulled the grenade launcher up and knelt in front of the doorway taking aim at the center of the mass quickly approaching.

Hagers and Taylor scrambled back into the lobby while the Major dove into the front desk office area. Harris pulled the trigger twice, sending two grenades into the chest of the first undead as it charged her. Both projectiles embedded themselves into the already rotten flesh, one in the chest, and the other below the waist. The undead continued its charge, seemingly unfazed by the ticking bombs now residing within. Two seconds passed before the undead's chest and lower body exploded in a bloody splash. Shrapnel radiated from within, turning the carrier into a red soup as blood, flesh, and bone splashed outward as the body imploded. The concussion from the grenades knocked the surrounding undead to the ground, giving the survivors time to escape. The blast from the grenades shaved off the arms and legs of the two closest undead as they were blown into the various tables and chairs. Landing face down, they continued to moan and squirm on the ground as they could still sense that the survivors were still close.

Major Powers pulled Harris away from the doorway as Hagers and Taylor set up a firing line in the lobby, eagerly waiting the rest of the undead. Another howl escaped the room as the rest of the undead poured into the hallway searching savagely for the survivors. Seeing Hagers and Taylor in the lobby, the first one let out a deep growl before charging the two marines. As it ran around the front of the desk, and Ayung, who was crouched behind the desk, swung his axe at its knees, taking the undead's feet out from under it. It crashed onto the tile floor with a sickening crunch as pieces of its teeth scattered across the floor. Still unfazed by the loss of its legs, it struggled to stand up and desperately reached towards Hagers before its skull exploded as Hagers' bullet ripped through.

Two more rushed into the lobby, leaping over the corpse on the floor before landing into Hagers, taking him down with their momentum. Instinctively he put his hands up in defense while he struggled with his attackers. He could hear their jaws snapping shut mere inches away from his face as he let out a scream of help while trying to deflect their teeth with his carbine.

Ayung grabbed the feet of the closest one, and yanked back with all of his might, pulling it off of Hagers before jumping to his feet and splitting the skull in half with a massive swing of his axe. Taylor ran up and kicked the other one in the head so forcefully that he broke its neck; its head fell motionless onto Hagers shoulder, its neckline now running parallel to its shoulder line. Jonathan reached down and pulled Hagers back by the straps on his shoulders while Ayung and Taylor quickly kicked the other bodies out of the way, as the rest of the undead mobbed out of the room and ran directly towards them.

Seven more undead crowded the hallway as they looked on at the survivors with rage filled eyes. They clambered down the hallway as Hagers scrambled to his feet, his rifle raised and ready. The survivors opened fire on the undead mob. Bullets whizzed through the air, penetrating gray flesh, and spewing blood in all directions. The staccato of the fight echoed throughout the building as the survivors continued to pull the trigger until their weapons clicked empty. As Hagers feverishly slammed another clip into his rifle he looked up, expecting to see a ghastly face, when he realized that they had neutralized the mob. He held his hand up while shouting for everyone to cease-fire as he looked at the carnage that was displayed in the front lobby. A gruesome scene lay before his eyes as the bodies of the seven undead lay in pools of their own blood, and their mangled flesh looked like it had been put through a grater. Gaping holes covered their skulls while bone fragments were scattered amongst the pools of dark blood. All four of the men quietly stood up, never taking their aim away from the group of corpses as the Major and Harris peeked over the desk of the front lobby. Hagers quickly looked up in the Major's direction.

"Well, Major, I think that does it for the rest of our friends on this floor," he said as he then glanced back over the bloody carnage that lay before him.

"Do we have any injuries, Hagers? Specifically, did anyone get bit?" Major Powers inquired earnestly.

Hagers looked around at Ayung, Jonathan, and Taylor, each man quickly shaking their heads before he checked himself. His fatigues had been ripped where he was attacked, yet he had no visible breaks or tears in his flesh. He took a deep sigh of relief as he slowly shook his head in the Major's direction.

Seeing Hagers response, the Major let out a slow breath while slightly nodding his head in approval. They all stared at each other before another loud clap of thunder boomed outside, startling them out of their daze.

"We got work to do men, and the sooner we get it done the better. Hagers, I count forty in total, including the one still in the cafeteria the others were feasting one. Is that what you got?" Major Powers questioned.

Hagers took a moment, running the numbers in his head before he nodded in the direction of the Major, "That's what I got, unless we got one running around here that we didn't know about."

"Unlikely, because if we did this commotion would have brought them out, and judging by the fact that we haven't seen one, I think we're in the clear. Just to be safe, though, I want you and Harris to do a full sweep of this floor while Taylor, Jonathan, Ayung, and myself will deposit these bodies outside while fortifying this floor," Major Powers said, as he looked outside to the approaching storm.

"Sounds good, Major," Hagers said before walking in Harris' direction.

Over the next couple of hours the whole team of survivors worked tirelessly as they cleaned up the first floor, carefully throwing the bodies of the undead out the windows before shielding the windows with broken desks, inner doors, and filing cabinets. Each of the first floor windows looked like a patchwork work quilt consisting of jagged desk wood, broken oak doors, supported by empty filing cabinets. Their intentions were not to make it look fashionable, just to make sure that nothing could get in. With all of the windows completely covered, the group then focused on the front lobby. The windowed corridor was too large to board up with desk furniture and doors; besides they had nothing to anchor them to. As the Major stood and stared into the corridor, he heard Taylor call for help behind him. As he turned around Taylor was struggling to move the solid oak receptionist desk towards the lobby. By eyeing it up, it looked like the desk could be wedged in completely, and they could then anchor other stuff to it to completely cover it up. It took four men to slide the oak desk into the opening, but it did the job. Next they fastened two doors to its back, completely blocking the front entrance, before attaching two more doors one on each side, covering up the windows, while connecting the doors to each other. For more support Taylor found a couple of iron pipes that were stored in the maintenance office, and he put them in between the outer doors, giving the blockade support so the small nails wouldn't carry the brunt of the force. Somewhat satisfied with the job, Major Powers sent for Janine and Apoyung, and the group had a quick de-briefing in the cafeteria while finally being able to eat something other than candy bars and sodas. The refrigerated items had long since spoiled, but the non-perishable cans of vegetables, soup, and beef were a welcome change, even if they had to eat them at room temperature.

As the group sat and ate, a small feeling of satisfaction came over them; they knew the world outside was rapidly changing, and it would probably never be the same again, but a small victory like the one that they had accomplished today was reason to celebrate.

Major Powers stood up and started divvying out duties to everyone while they continued to eat. He wanted everyone to remain upstairs for the majority of the day, with the stairwells locked off at night. They would go down to the first floor together for breakfast, lunch, and dinner, and no one was allowed access to the first floor without company. It wasn't that the Major didn't trust his people, he didn't trust what was on the outside of the compound as opposed to the inside. All of the weapons and ammunition were to be stored upstairs in one of the empty office rooms. Taylor was in charge of cataloging all the munitions and keeping the Major informed on their numbers. Harris was to continue to work with HQ and explain their situation, and hopefully HQ would take pity on them and send for an immediate evac. Jonathan, Ayung, and Janine were all given rotating guard duty with the rest of the soldiers, while Apoyung was given the duty of being a lookout on the roof of the building. Major Powers had given him a pair of high -powered binoculars to use and explicit directions that if any new groups approached, he was instructed to find Major Powers. The group would hole up in the Embassy for now until another better solution presented itself.

Jonathan, tired from day's adventure, went to bed early that night so he could be rested up and ready for his guard duty in the morning. As he lay in his cot his thoughts drifted to Gwen and Russo and he wondered how they were doing, when he realized that he still had the SAT phone, and he should try to contact them. The phone's battery meter read one bar, and he figured he had just about three minutes to talk to her—if she answered. As he dialed the number, the automated voice message box kicked on before a ring, indicating to him that she had turned off the phone—or worse. Forcing those thoughts out of his head, he left a hasty message for her.

"Gwen. It's Jonathan. I'm alive, so is Ayung and Apoyung. We've made it to Quito, and as of right now we are stuck in the American Embassy in Quito with a Marine Unit. Gwen, this virus spread faster than anything I've ever read or heard about. All I know is that it seems the dead or recently deceased are coming back to life, I know that sounds crazy, but I've seen it. Listen to me. The only way to put these things down is a head shot; I know it's not the prettiest picture, but it works. I pray that you, Russo, and Carlos made it; I pray you're still alive, and I pray that I get to see your faces again soon. Please be alive out there ... Please ..." Jonathan said before the SAT phone battery died on him. He reached over and plugged it into the wall, before falling into a deep sleep as the thunderstorm outside raged on.

CHAPTER 18
THE WORST IS YET TO COME.

Darkness was all Carol saw as she slowly rocked her body back and forth. Her arms shook as they corralled her knees close to her chest, while she rested her forehead on her knees. She silently said a prayer as she continued to rock, tears streaming down her face, as her rapid breathing only allowed a small amount of oxygen into her body. After she had hung up the phone with Russo, a group of the crazed attackers had run down the hall towards her desk, and she instinctively hid under her desk. The compartment that housed her computer tower and printer was emptied hastily as she threw the tower and printer on floor before she climbed into the small cubbyhole, pulling the door shut, eliminating all light. As she cowered in her hiding spot she could hear the shuffling footsteps of the group of undead she had spotted as they vigorously searched her desk looking for her. She kept very still while trying to hold her breath. She could hear them searching combined with smelling the horrible stench of rotten flesh. She fearfully watched the silhouette lighting lining the opening of the cabinet as shadows began to erratically move around it. She was able to ascertain that there were three of them, as she saw three distinct shadows randomly moving in and out of the light. Two of the shadows soon disappeared while the third one stayed. She could hear the rummaging of papers, followed by a crunching sound as hard plastic containers were smashed under the footfalls of the dead as they aimlessly searched the front office.

Slowly she leaned forward towards the small key hole in the cabinet door, trying her best to peer through the hole to see what they were doing. As she struggled and squinted through the hole, what she saw horrified her, forcing her own hand to quickly cover her mouth stifling her scream. The body of a patient, an elderly male, half covered by his bloodstained gown, stood in front of the cabinet doors, his back to the doors. His old and shriveled legs were caked over in dried blood. His exposed right hip had been injured by an attacker as chunks of flesh were completely missing, and the exposed bone, began to glisten from the light. Further up the front of his body bite marks and scratches increased leading up to his head. From his right arm hung IV connector tubes, as some of the tubes looked like they had been pulled away angrily. The normal tape that hospitals used when securing these tubes was barely hanging on to the tube as the tube still clung underneath the flesh. Carol noticed black vein like lines originating from each of the bite and scratch wounds. These vein like lines spiraled outward, like intricate spider webs, completely covering his upper body. She strained her body awkwardly trying to see his face before shuddering as he turned his head overlooking the desk. The left side of his face had been mauled as his eye was missing, and what was left of his lower jaw hung below the chin, still tethered by a thin strand of muscle tissue. His other eye was completely red and sported small black dots surrounding his pupil.

He lowered his head and suddenly affixed his only eye at the keyhole below where he stood. Carol froze as her eye locked with his, sending a spine tingling sensation down her spine. She didn't move, mainly out of fear, but also because she wondered if he had actually seen her or if it just seemed like he had seen her. Her thoughts were answered as he dove down on all fours and started to attack the cabinet door ferociously with unbridled anger. Carol screamed in a panic as she quickly spun around, pushing her back up against the back of the cabinet and her feet against the door, hoping to block him from getting in. She screamed for help, but only attracted more undead as her attacker was suddenly joined by three more. Sweat poured down her face and body as she frantically thought of any idea that could get her out of the trap that she was in. Sadly, nothing came to mind as the pounding continued. Within minutes the first attacker had broken a piece of the wood from the door, splintering it inwards as light suddenly breached her dark confines. The pounding stopped long enough for the undead attacker to quickly look into the hole to see its frightened prey. Seeing its rage-filled eye, Carol did the only thing she could think of, and she grabbed her pin from her breast pocket. She clicked the pin on and jammed it into the hole, puncturing the red eye with a vicious thrust. The attacker fell back and howled in pain before yanking the pin out of its eye as a gelatinous ooze seeped out from the wound. Completely blinded from the wound but with a more determined rage, it continued its assault on the cabinet door. The sturdy wood from her desk creaked and cracked as chunks of wood began to splinter off.

Realizing that she was trapped and the end was near, Carol gave up hope and released the pressure on the inside of the door, succumbing to her fate. One of the hinges gave way before a powerful explosion coming from outside rocked the building. Carol slammed her eyes shut and covered her ears as the ringing was quickly giving her a headache. When she opened them, she realized that the pounding on the cabinet door had ceased, and she could hear screams coming from outside of the office. Morbidly appreciating the simple fact that she wasn't the only one who could hear the screams, she slowly began to catch her breath as she stared through the hole looking for her attackers who were nowhere near the front desk. She slowly regained her composure while she strained her ears for any sound.

She waited a heart-pounding fifteen minutes before she decided to get out of her tomb and find shelter elsewhere. She slowly and quietly climbed out of the cabinet, brushing away debris from the floor as she didn't want to cut her hands on any broken glass. She looked all around the front desk area, and besides the tornado that had been through it, she saw no attackers. She quickly glanced over her right shoulder and could see no attackers leaning up against the "U" shaped desk that she use to call her office. Very carefully she got up while dusting herself off. As she began to look around at the destruction of the office, a powerful putrid smell filled her nostrils followed by what sounded like an animal scratching at a door. Fear crept back into her mind as she slowly turned around and came face to face with Nurse Ratchet—or what was left of Nurse Ratchet. The woman standing before her was hardly recognizable as the Nurse Ratchet she once knew. This woman was covered in blood while rotten flesh hung from her teeth as her mouth continued its chewing motion. As their eyes met, Nurse Ratchet stopped chewing, allowing her red eyes to glow wildly. Carol stared back as another life-threatening situation presented itself to her. At this point she had grown tired of the defenseless feeling she was experiencing, and she decided it was time to fight back. She remembered what Russo had told her concerning where they're the weakest at as she walked over to her desk and yanked a small flat screen monitor out of its socket, sending sparks flying.

Nurse Ratchet's corpse watched in awe at the fiery red sparks as they flew through the air, disappearing as fast as they originated. She turned her gaze back to Carol and let loose a menacing howl, spraying bloody spittle across the floor and onto the desk. The howl pierced Carol's ears, but her determination wouldn't be broken.

"Bring it on you bitch!" Carol said coldly as she approached the desk with the monitor raised above her head. As she approached, Nurse Ratchet reached out quickly with a couple of broken fingers, grasping the front of Carol's scrub top and violently pulling her towards her mouth. Carol reacted quickly, slamming the monitor down on the arm, listening to the sound of broken bones as the bones in Nurse Ratchet's arms snapped like a twig. She released her grip, and stumbled backwards from the blow, but quickly recovered as she leapt up against the front of the desk, this time her whole upper body came over the top of the desk as she reached with both hands. In a rage filled fury, Carol slammed the monitor down again, this time connecting with the Nurse's head. The glass from the monitor screen shattered, raining shards on the desktop and into Nurse Johnson's skull. She slowly lifted the monitor back up before hearing another horrible growl escape the nurse's mouth as it writhed around, inching closer to her as the nurse continued to claw its way over the desk.

Carol, determined to kill the nurse, repeatedly slammed the monitor onto her head dozens of times before she finally jammed it so hard on her head that her bloody skull came through the back of the monitor. Blood poured down the nurse's neck onto the floor as the nurse lay motionless, sprawled over the desk. Carol slowly walked backwards until she was back up against the wall. She slowly slid down the wall, the muscles in her arms and shoulders screaming in pain as her circulation slowed along with her breathing; she was utterly exhausted.

She sat and stared at the now dead woman, cautiously shaking her head back and forth. Minutes slowly ticked by as the sun outside began to set while dark black clouds of smoke rose into the atmosphere from Cedar Mill across the highway. Seeing the smoke, Carol became nauseated as she began to realize that these creatures had not only terrorized the hospital, but now the terror was spreading, and spreading fast. After a few more minutes, she decided that she needed to find shelter, and God willing, other survivors. As she stood back up the body of Nurse Johnson twitched violently, as the nurse raised its mangled head upwards staring back at Carol. Her nose and both jaws were smashed inward, and the majority of her teeth were missing as dark blood drained out of her mouth. Her blood-matted hair pulled against the monitor frame as large glass shards broke off in her skull as she squirmed against the desk. She tried to push herself up, before her arms slipped in the massive amounts of blood, sending her head and upper body crashing back into the desk. Again and again she tried, only to receive the same results each time, but as her body continued to slam against the desk, the wood, began to crack and bow in the center, unable to support the weight.

"What do I have to do to kill you?" Carol screamed as she lifted her exhausted body from the floor. She quickly looked around her desk for anything she could use as a weapon before her eyes landed on a long handled screwdriver that maintenance had accidentally left on her desk. She ran over and grabbed the handle before slowly walking over to Nurse Johnson's corpse. She raised the screwdriver above her head with both hands as Nurse Johnson continued to struggle, her mouth persistently opening and closing with no comprehension of what Carol was about to do. Carol took a deep breath before she brought the screwdriver down with as much force as she could muster. The tip of the screwdriver penetrated the center part of the nurse's skull with a sickening slurp as she rammed it through up to the hilt. Nurse Johnson's head twitched for about a second more as blood flowed out of her mouth and her head fell down; this time she didn't move any more.

"I never liked you anyway, bitch!" Carol said as she stepped back away from the blood and the corpse. She surveyed the front desk area to see if there were any more menacing creatures roaming around, and satisfied that she couldn't see anymore, she quickly walked over to the security cameras and started checking the cameras for any survivors. As she scanned through the cameras, each room seemed to be worse than the previous as blood splatters decorated the walls and people who should already be dead slowly ambled around, walking into walls and doors. Tears began to slowly cascade down her face as the images of death became too numerous for her to handle. Friends, co-workers, even patients she had grown close too, were all dead, yet they were still walking. How could this be? A flood of emotions washed over her as her head began to swim while bile slowly climbed its way up her throat. The room spun wildly around her as fell to her knees, vomiting profusely onto the already disgusting floor. After a couple of minutes she regained her composure, steeled her nerves, and continued to scan through the cameras, praying to finds someone alive. When she tried to access the higher floors, all of the security cameras had been blocked, leading her to believe that at least someone was alive in the building. In order to block the camera access, someone has to manually over-ride the system. A small feeling of hope filled her spirits slightly as she realized that she wasn't the only one trapped in the hospital. She continued to scan the cameras until she came across a room that was completely dark except for the light slowly creeping in from the window. She continued to stare at the screen until she realized that the people moving in this room had direction, and they were survivors. Two men and two women were huddled together in the back corner of the room where the hospital bed normally was. As she continued to stare at it one of the men stood up and walked over to the window, and as the light caught his face she realized it was Malone and knew that she had to try to get to him. They were in one of the patient rooms on the first floor just around the corner from the front desk.

She quickly grabbed the phone and tried the room number but got no signal. Realizing that she would have to walk down the hall to that room, her hands began to shake, but she also realized that staying out in the open wasn't any safer. She also realized that she needed some type of weapon just in case she wasn't alone in her search down the halls. As she looked around, she couldn't find anything more than a broomstick she kept under her desk for when she needed to sweep the front entrance. An idea popped into her head as she walked over to a drawer and pulled out a roll of duck-tape and the broomstick. Within a couple of minutes she had a modified spear, from the blood stained screwdriver, the duck-tape, and the broomstick. Pulling the screwdriver out of Nurse Ratchet's head wasn't the happiest thing she'd ever done in her life, but it was her only option at that time.

Armed with her spear, she slowly crept down the hallway towards the room where her friends were trapped. The abominable smell of rotten flesh filled the hallway as bloody streaks occupied the normally white walls, and mangled corpses lay lifeless in pools of their own blood. As she came up on each corpse, she carefully poked their bodies from a distance, making sure that they were truly dead. As she came up to the corpse of another dead nurse, she suspiciously rolled the body over with her broomstick, wanting to know who it was for some unknown reason. As the body slid on the floor its right arm suddenly jerked backwards and grabbed a hold of the broomstick. The female corpse arched its back while turning its neck to face Carol. Eyes completely red and with a gaping maw, it furiously flipped over onto its back, grasping the end of the broomstick with both hands, trying to pull herself up. Carol, frozen with fear, stared at her, realizing that the corpse wouldn't be able to walk as she had been attacked in the midsection and leaving only her naked spine which barely connected her upper and lower body by small slimy strands of muscle and nerve tissue. Another wound that would normally be fatal, yet this woman was still alive and now trying to attack her.

A forceful yank on her broomstick from the undead nurse shocked Carol out of her reverie, allowing her to regain control of the situation. She yanked her weapon upward as hard as she could, freeing it from the grip of the corpse before spinning it around and jamming the sharp end into the nurses eye socket. Blood spewed from the eye socket as the corpse twitched before falling dead onto the tiled floor. Carol yanked her weapon out of the skull and continued to slink down the hallway towards the room.

As she got to the room she lightly tapped on the door after checking both sides of the hallway to make sure that she didn't have any unwanted attention. No answer came, as she tried again this time loud, but still no answer.

"Malone? Are you in there?" Carol quietly said as she rapped on the door with more force this time. She heard footsteps coming from the room, followed by whispering that she couldn't make out.

"Malone. It's Carol, are you in there?"

Malone turned and looked to Dr. Hampstead who jumped off of the floor and ran over to the blocked doorway.

"Carol, its Dr. Hampstead!" She said excitingly.

"Oh, Dr. Hampstead, it's good to hear someone's voice. Who else is in there with you?"

"Malone, Russo, and Gwen are here. We're safe, but the doorway is blocked. Are the hallways clear from those … things?"

"For the time being, but I don't feel safe out in the open for long. Is there another way into your room?" Carol questioned as she nervously looked around.

"Carol, it's Malone. Being holed up in here is just another death trap; we need to get out of the hospital and get help. Have you been able to contact the authorities?" Malone questioned eagerly.

"Mr. Malone, I don't know if they can help right now… It's bad, real bad out here," she said, her voice trailing off as she remembered the black smoke rising from Cedar Mill mall.

"Damn!" Malone said as he turned and started pacing around the room.

"Malone, how many floors does this hospital have?" Russo questioned as he grabbed a pillow off of the floor and carefully positioned Gwen's head on it after slowly removing it from his shoulder. Utter exhaustion had taken over, and she had fallen into a fitful sleep.

"Fourteen if you include the rooftop, but to access the floors nine and up you have to have a director or hire badge access, and I don't have one, and neither does Dr. Hampstead. Only Materson, Sarah, board members, and luxury guests have 'em," Malone said quietly, trying to not wake Gwen.

"Well, I think for the time being we should try to get as high as we can so we can at least survey what is going on outside, unless you have a better idea," Russo offered.

"I don't like the idea of being treated like an animal," Malone retorted.

"Yea, and I don't like being hunted like one either," Russo came back at him.

"I don't like either idea, but I think if we can get to some of the suites we can at least lock down the stairwells and elevators for the time being until we figure out what our next move is," Dr. Hampstead offered as she calmly placed her hand on Malone's tense shoulder.

"Well, I don't like it, but anything is better than waiting in here to die," Malone said begrudgingly.

"I agree, but how do we get out of here?" Dr. Hampstead questioned as she pulled the curtain back on the window. The three of them stood there and stared in disbelief at what they saw. The normally luscious green landscape of Miami Med was horribly replaced by a carnage that none of them could comprehend. Body parts littered the campus as pools of dark blood seeped into the ground, blotting the green grass. Dark clouds of black smoke rose on the horizon from the Cedar Mill while the distant echo of sirens rang in their ears. A group of half-clothed patients was crouched on the ground feverishly tearing at the flesh of a person long since dead. They jammed handfuls of blood soaked flesh into their mouths while continuing to reach with their free hands for more. Numerous bodies clumsily paced the grounds; some were missing limbs while others had sheets of flash barely hanging on to their bodies, simply swaying in the wind. Their mouths were covered in dark blood while their teeth sported ragged chunks of rotten flesh.

As the group stood and stared in disbelief, a corpse dressed in a police officer's uniform stumbled out of the hedgerow in front of the window before slightly turning his head in the direction of the window. He was missing his left ear as harsh bite wounds were carved into his skin, starting at his scalp, and randomly trickling down his neck. As he turned towards the window, he stopped and stared at his observers on the other side of the window. He cocked his head back, releasing a barbaric roar before slamming his body into the window. Hearing the roar, other corpses stampeded towards his location with a visceral glare in their red eyes.

Russo jerked the curtains back as he looked at Dr. Hampstead and Malone's faces. They had turned stark white in disbelief.

"I think we need to get out of this room—" Russo started before he was cut off with the dull thud of the former cop's fists banging onto the glass.

"Now!" Russo urged, shocking the others out of their stupor. "Malone, how strong are these windows?" Russo quickly questioned.

"They're reinforced, but not bullet proof!" Malone exclaimed before the banging on the window multiplied as the other corpses began to join in.

"Guys, I don't like being out here by myself, can you let me in?" Carol cried out from the hallway.

"Carol, in here isn't safe anymore. We're going to need to get out of here and in a hurry. Can you check the room next to you, to see if it's clear?" Malone questioned.

"I... I... I'll try to," Carol replied, edgy as she crept up to the room to the right of where they were. She noticed that the door was slightly ajar. She gripped her weapon tightly as she realized the only way to go in to this room was to go in swinging. She took a deep breath and kicked the door open. She came into the room swinging wildly at anyone or anything in the room. The room was empty, the sheets on the bed indicated that someone had been there, but they were no longer there. She quickly checked under the bed, in the freestanding closets, and in the bathroom. Once she had determined that the room was clear, she shut the door and locked it.

"This room's clear!" She called out close to the wall while hitting it with her fist.

"Alright good, we need to move. Malone, get into the bathroom and remove the ceiling tile above the toilet, were going to have to go through the ceiling," Russo instructed.

Malone nodded his head in agreement as he and Dr. Hampstead rushed to the bathroom while Russo leaned down and gently shook Gwen awake.

"What's going on?" Gwen asked, startled, as her eyes hadn't adjusted to the darkness of the room.

"We're going now!" Russo said as he heard the window glass splinter.

"Oh, shit, where are we going?" Gwen said, suddenly aware of the situation.

"The next room; come on let's go!" Russo said as he picked her up off of the floor. They ran into the bathroom, just as Malone had handed the tile down to Dr. Hampstead who quickly discarded it into the tub.

"Russo, I need a boost," Malone said as he pulled out a small flashlight from his pants. He turned it on and placed the end of it into his mouth while he leaned up against the wall as Russo came over and gave him a boost. Malone climbed into the ceiling, carefully positioning himself over the frames so he didn't fall through the ceiling. He punched a hole into a tile over the other room, and he could see where Carol had tried to pad the floor with sheets and pillows. He pulled the tile up and moved it aside before dropping feet first into the other bathroom. The landing sent shockwaves of pain up his legs, but he didn't hear the sickening sound of bones snapping, and he realized that he was just getting older.

"I'm through, come on! Support yourself on the frames so you don't fall through," Malone hollered back up into the hole.

"Alright, you're next," Russo said to Dr. Hampstead as she slowly stepped onto the top of the toilet and into his palm. With a hefty heave Russo launched her into the ceiling where she sprawled out like a crab across the frames. With adrenaline coursing through her body, she staggered across the frames until she saw the opening.

"I got you Doc! Don't worry, I'll catch you," Malone coaxingly spoke as he could see the fear written across her face. She started to climb over the hole, but lost her grip, and fell shoulder first into the arms of Malone. She crashed into him, and the two tumbled across the tiled floor.

"Are you hurt?" Malone asked, panicking at the way she landed.

"Just bruised, I'll heal, but thanks for the ride Malone," Dr. Hampstead said with a wink as she rolled off of him.

"Any time."

"Hey, you two ready? We're running out of time over here!" Russo yelled into the hole as he heard shards of glass shatter on the room floor.

"Yea, send Gwen over!" Malone hollered back.

"You're next," Russo said to Gwen as she began to climb on top of the toilet.

"What about you, how are you going to get up here?" Gwen questioned fearfully.

"Don't worry about me, just get up there; I'll be right behind you, I promise."

Gwen hesitantly placed her foot into his palms, and as she began to open her mouth, he heaved her up into the ceiling. She climbed over the framework with little difficulty before dropping down the hole into Malone and Dr. Hampstead's arms.

"She's clear now; get your ass over here," Malone shouted.

About the time he heard Malone, Russo turned and heard a window come crashing down as dead moans filled the air. The first two corpses fell into the room through the shattered window, followed by three more. Their mangled bodies thudded onto the tiled floor as they clawed their way back up to their feet, eyes growing wider as they saw Russo standing in the bathroom. The first corpse to regain its balance howled at the top of its lungs before it charged towards Russo in the bathroom. Russo grabbed the door and slammed it into the charging corpse. A dull thud echoed into the bathroom as the corpse' head slammed into the hollow door, leaving a large impact in the middle of the door. The corpse hit the ground, but was back on its feet in a second; two others joined in as they began to pound on the door unrestrained.

Russo pushed his shoulder into the door, trying to hold it in place as he quickly locked the door, knowing in the back of his mind that the flimsy lock wouldn't hold long. The concussions from the door vibrated against his shoulder as he looked up and could see the screws holding the hinges in place being violently jarred loose. He knew he only had a couple of minutes until the door gave way and he would be overrun.

"Russo, what the hell's going on over there? Where are you?" Malone hollered into the open hole in the ceiling.

"Ahhh, having a little bit of difficulty right now..." Russo yelled back as he continued to brace the door with his shoulder. Before Malone could stop her Gwen jumped back onto the opposite toilet and jumped up to the ceiling, bending one of the frames while dangling in the air.

"Gwen, NO!" Malone said, but it was too late as she was hauling herself up back.

"Wait, Malone! Help her, don't pull her back!" Dr. Hampstead shouted from behind him as he ran to her feet.

"Oh, hell, he we go again," Malone grumbled to himself as he got under Gwen's feet and supported her as she scrambled back across the ceiling.

"Russo! Grab my hands!" Gwen hollered as leaned back into the bathroom, her midsection being coarsely supported by the dry walled divider.

"Gwen! I'll just pull you back down here with me, get back!" Russo yelled back at her as the door slammed into his shoulder this time harder than before as more corpses joined in.

"Don't argue with me, just grab my hands, Malone's got my feet; just do it now!" Gwen screamed at him. Russo looked up at her as another pound came against the door, and this time the force knocked him to the ground as the hinges pulled loose. He hopped up and ran to the toilet, using it as a step he jumped up and locked hands with Gwen. The sudden strain on her hands pulled her harder against the divider as the metal frame, punctured her stomach. She cried out in pain before she pulled up with all of her might. Hearing her cry and feeling the sudden added weight, Malone pulled hard on her legs as the pulled Russo higher into the air. Russo planted his feet against the wall and pushed outward, letting go of her hands while sprawling out and locking his hands on the frame as he began to pull himself upward. With the sudden weight gone, Malone easily yanked Gwen back down into his arms, blood from her stomach smeared across his chest, as she squirmed out of his arms and fell to the ground. She rolled over onto her back, clutching her stomach in pain, as Dr. Hampstead and Carol fell to their knees surrounding her.

"I'll be fine... just help Russo!" Gwen said as a tear slowly cascaded down her cheek.

"We've got you Gwen," Dr. Hampstead said smoothly as she waved Malone off.

As Russo was pulling himself up into the ceiling, the bathroom door finally gave way with a wood splitting crash as the door fell against the tub, before snapping inward from the weight of the corpses. Russo looked down in horror as the room was suddenly filled with the undead. As he was pulling his feet up a bloody hand missing two fingers reached up and grasped his ankle before yanking downward on it. Russo lost his grip and slipped back down into the room, barely hanging on by his arms as his free leg flailed wildly. He looked down just in time to see the mouth of the dead police officer opening as his bloody teeth extended towards Russo's ankle. Russo took a quick and calculated aim with his other foot and kicked out as hard as he could, connecting with the forehead of the cop, instantly snapping his neck backwards. The cop released his grip on Russo's ankle as the force from the kick sent him spiraling into the other corpses as they all tumbled onto the floor.

With what little energy he had, Russo let out a scream before pulling his body back up into the ceiling before the corpses could rise again. Russo climbed over the divider and dropped into the other bathroom as Malone guided him to the tile floor.

"A little too close this time, hero!" Malone said as he patted Russo on the back. Russo never made a comment as he looked on the ground.

Seeing Gwen on the floor with a large bloodstain on her stomach brought him to his knees as he quickly slid behind her and tried to support her head.

"What happened?" he asked frantically.

"I'll be fine," Gwen said painfully, as she tried to clutch her stomach, "I cut myself on the divider when you and Malone had me as your personal seesaw," Gwen said with a struggling laugh.

"Dammit, I'm sorry Gwen!" Russo apologized, while shaking his head.

"The only thing you should be apologizing about is not listening to me when I told you reach for my hands. That was too close, and it better not happen again," Gwen said with conviction-laced eyes.

"Alright superwoman! I've got you patched up, but we going to need to get you some antibiotics soon to stop any infection from occurring," Dr. Hampstead said as she and Carol helped Gwen to sit up.

"Can you walk, or do we need to help carry you?" Russo asked urgently.

"I'll be fine; what's our next move?" Gwen asked as they could all hear the howling and moaning coming from the other bathroom as their previous shelter was now overrun by the undead.

"Well, based on what just happened, I think it'll be suicide if we try to go outside; besides, I wouldn't know where to go," Malone offered as he quickly checked to make sure the door to that room was secured.

"I agree with Malone. I have a family out there, but I know that they're smart enough to realize that staying in the house would be smarter than coming out in this mess. Besides, one of those things that tried to attack us was a cop, and if the cops are having problems then …" Dr. Hampstead said while trailing off as she suddenly began to understand the magnitude of what she was saying.

"I vote for up, then; maybe we can get back to our suite and lock down the floor if it hasn't already been overrun," Russo offered.

"Somebody has already beat you to the punch on that one, Mr. Russo," Carol explained, "Before I left the front desk I checked the security cameras to see if anyone was trapped in the elevators. The elevators leading to those floors have already been locked down, and they can only be overridden by Mr. Materson or a board member,"

"That bastard, I'm gonna kill him," Russo said.

"No worries, ol' buddy," Malone said calmly, attracting everyone's attention as he leaned up against the wall with a sly grin written across his face.

"Malone, do you know something we don't?" Dr. Hampstead questioned eagerly.

"Yep, that stuffed turkey upstairs doesn't know his building as well as he likes to brag to everyone that he does," Malone said as the grin erupted into a hearty laugh.

"Do explain, but in a hurry, because our friends on the other side aren't going to take too lightly to the fact that they can't reach us," Russo said.

"Right, well, here's what I know. When this monstrosity was built, the engineers weren't able to create an elevator shaft in the middle of the building, something about not enough support, so the elevator shaft leading to the upper floors, the luxury suites, has to start from the ground like the other elevator shafts. There is a maintenance access room on this floor, and in the back is a small hatch that leads to the shaft; no one knows about it except me and the engineers. They had a hard time explaining to jackass upstairs, so they just told me. Only when it needs servicing is the hatch used. It's a tight squeeze, but we can make it through," Malone finished explaining.

"Marvelous, absolutely marvelous. Materson's arrogance is going to be our ticket to some shelter," Dr. Hampstead said with a hearty laugh.

"How far is the maintenance room from where we are?' Russo quickly questioned.

"Just around the corner, opposite the front lobby. Carol, do you remember if any more of those... things were walking around in the halls?" Malone questioned.

"There was a group that I slid by around the corner that were eating somebody. I can't remember how many," Carol answered with a shudder as the visual image slammed into her brain.

"Alright, then we does this quickly and quietly. Gwen are you ready?" Malone questioned.

"Yea, I'll be good," Gwen said, struggling to her feet.

"Before we go—here," Malone said before tossing Russo a new clip for his Glock, while slamming a fresh one into his sidearm. "I'll lead, followed by the Doc, then Carol with her spear looking thing, then Gwen and Russo bring up the rear. Everyone needs to be as quiet as they can be, this ain't gonna be a walk in the park," Malone said before releasing the safety on his Glock.

No one responded, they simply nodded their heads as they got in line while Malone carefully unlocked the door leading to the hallway. Malone peeked his head out of the doorway, looking down both ends of the hallway before he opened the door fully. He slinked out of the room followed by the others as they quickly jogged down the hallway towards the front lobby. The hallway was cluttered with debris as bloody hospital gowns lay strewn about combined with numerous medical charts and random pieces of paper laying around. The putrid rotten smell of decaying flesh stifled the air, forcing the groups to cover their noses as they ran behind Malone.

As they turned the corner, the same group that Carol had mentioned were still on all fours ripping bloody chunks of flesh and stomach intestines out of a body while shoveling handfuls into their mouths. Malone quickly jerked up a hand, halting the others as he stood watching the corpses from the other side of the hallway. He checked down the opposite end of the hallway where they were headed to make sure it was clear before he motioned for Dr. Hampstead to join him. With a quick point towards a door at the end of the hall with large white lettered writing on it, he advised Dr. Hampstead where the room was. She gave a quick nod before quietly running down the hallway followed by Carol, Gwen, and Russo. Once they had gotten past the corner, Malone slowly walked backwards down the hall, his eyes never leaving the four corpses which seemed completely unaware of their presence.

"Malone, we need a key," Dr. Hampstead whispered.

"Got it," Malone whispered back while digging into his pocket and pulling out a set of keys. As he pulled out his key ring, he tried to thumb through the keys while keeping his gun trained on the undead, when he accidently dropped the keys. They landed on the tiled floor resonating like metal chimes down the hallway, alerting the undead to their presence. All at once, the undead stopped what they were doing, and the four sets of blood stained eyes suddenly stared down the hall at Malone.

"Ahhh shit!" Malone said as he watched each of them stand awkwardly before howling at the tops of their lungs. Their howls attracted five more who were ambling around the front lobby in search of food. In a split second the hallway suddenly sounded like a stampede as nine of the undead came running down the hallway.

"Russo, COVER ME WHILE I FIND THE DAMN KEY!" Malone shouted as he fell to the ground grasping for the keys.

Russo stepped in front of him and took aim at the first corpse running down the hallway, its boney knees and shins were completely bare as Russo noticed that only the bones remained, as the flesh and muscle tissue had been ripped away. He took a deep breath before pulling the trigger. The bullet separated the distance between him and the corpse in a split second as the back of its skull was suddenly blown apart as the bullet cracked through. The corpse's head jerked back involuntary before its feet went out from under it, sending it crashing to the tile floor, splaying dark red blood across the tile.

As he took aim on another one, he heard the sweet sound of a key unlocking a door, and he quickly turned around to see Malone ushering everyone into the maintenance room. Russo turned to join before he heard Malone shout his name. Sensing the imminent danger in Malone's shout, he whipped his head back around and pulled the trigger just in time, as a corpse had covered this distance faster than he had expected. The bullet careened into the rotten corpse's throat, blasting a bloody chunk of flesh outward, spinning the corpse around, and slowing his progression, but not stopping it.

The shot bought Russo enough time for him and Malone to jump into the maintenance room. As Malone tried to slam the door shut, the rest of the undead had made it to the door and were ferociously clawing and pulling at the door. Russo and Malone jammed their shoulders into the door as hard as they could, but a battle of attrition waged on as the strength of the undead was slowly overpowering Malone and Russo's strength. Malone's gun clattered onto the ground as he struggled with the door; hideously bite ridden arms and hands gouged at the door while bloodcurdling howls rebounded into the room.

Dr. Hampstead saw Malone's gun hit the floor and she picked it up, slowly pulling the hammer back before sliding in front of the opening slit of the doorway. She calmly took aim at the first corpse head she could see. Another female nurse, her hair brown hair pulled back in a ponytail, as a massive bite covered the right side of her cheek, exposing the back of her throat and the jagged edges of her front skull was attempting to get to them. Dr. Hampstead closed her eyes, aimed the gun at the undead's mouth, and pulled the trigger. The bullet ricocheted off of the corpse's teeth sending enamel shrapnel into her throat, slicing through her skin. Her eyes rolled into the back of her head, and her body slumped backwards against the others before falling to the ground. The disruption from her body gave Russo and Malone enough of a break to slam the door home while severing several fingers in the process. Malone locked the door while Russo desperately looked around for something to wedge the door. He found a small steel pipe leaning up against the wall in the back of the room, and quickly tossed it to Malone. Malone slid the pipe into the door handle and braced it up against the doorframe. It was a crude locking mechanism, but it would work for the meantime.

The maintenance closet was a typical off-limits closet; one that senior management only wanted employees to see due to its archaic setting. Rows of steel grate shelving lined the walls as various spray bottles filled with marked chemicals cluttered the lower shelves. The middle shelves housed other types of cleaning supplies from latex gloves to cardboard boxes of paper towels. A single naked light bulb hanging from the ceiling with a pull cord attached was the only source of light in this drab closet. Stacked in the four corners of the walls were several boxes labeled as previous years employee files that had not been properly disposed of, creating a claustrophobic feeling in the room as the boxes occupied what little open space the room had. A small molded drain was drilled into the center of the room allowing for any chemicals to be poured out. Surrounding the drain was a raised tile wall preventing the chemicals from splashing onto the floor. The distinct smell of bleach filled the room, slightly stinging the groups eyes, as an exhaust fan was non-existent.

The group, exhausted from the altercation, fell quietly on the dirty, dust stained floor of the maintenance room while each of them tried to catch their breath. Their break was short-lived as the door was pounded mercifully from the outside. Malone looked at the door incredulously as he watched in awe as the steel pipe began to bow as the pounding continued.

"We don't have much time," Malone said to the group as he quickly shoved some boxes out of the way, revealing a small hatch that was screwed in tight.

Carol pulled the light switch in the room, giving Malone some more light to work with as his small flashlight was beginning to fade.

"I need a flat-head, there should be one hanging up on the wall!" Malone hollered from the ground.

Everyone quickly searched the wall that was closest to them before Gwen hollered that she had found it and tossed it to Malone's open hands. He grasped the screwdriver and went to work on the screws as the incessant pounding on the door rang loudly in their ears. Seconds seeming like hours ticked away as the rest of the group watch Malone frantically unscrew the grate. As he got to the last screw, the doorframe itself began to tear away from the molding as the barrage continued with added strength as more of the undead heard the ruckus and came running.

"Russo, grab some of those boxes, and get them ready to stack behind us, because once we go through this shaft, we won't be able to put the grate back up to block their path," Malone instructed as he quickly took his duty belt off and threw it down the shaft, making it easier for him to squeeze through.

"Gotcha!" Russo answered back as he and Carol pulled some of the heavier boxes down and angled them in front of the small opening.

"Alright, here's how were going to do this," Malone started as another jarring blow landed against the outside door, bending the pipe even more. "Carol, you're first; once you crawl through you won't have enough space to wait for the rest us, so you'll need to start scaling the elevator shaft. There is a small ladder attached to one of the walls cut out in an alcove on the opposite side of the shaft. Take that ladder all the way to the top where you run into the elevator itself," Malone quickly instructed.

"What if the elevator's moving?" Carol questioned fearfully.

"It won't be. These elevators were designed to be dead once the shutdown code has been entered. The only way to get them going again is to reboot the whole power grid to the hospital, and I don't think that is currently on anyone's mind," Malone explained.

"O ... O ... Okay!? Then what do I do once I get to the elevator itself?"

"This is where it gets tricky, but I can walk you through it. There are multiple harness hooks, kinda like iron rings that hang from the bottom. They connect to this apparatus," Malone explained as he grabbed the climbing harness with a black coiled rope from one of the shelves.

"Basically it's an adult diaper. You slip your legs into it and then tighten by pulling these two straps. Once you get to the hooks, take one of these ends with a carabiner on it, and hook yourself under the elevator. Once you're hooked on, the hook will support your weight, and you will need to unscrew the grate leading into the elevator," Malone calmly explained as the racket outside droned on.

Malone got closer to Carol before gently placing both of his hands on her shoulders. As he gripped her shoulders she lifted her eyes and met his before slightly nodding her head, signaling that she understood what she had to do.

"Carol. Are you sure you can do this?" Malone asked.

"Yea, I'm su ...sure!" She said, in a non-convincing tone. Malone paused for a brief moment before he turned back to the rest of the group.

"After Carol, Doc you're next, followed by myself, then Gwen, and finally Russo. Russo and I can assist you ladies, IF you need it. This ladder isn't exactly the largest nor the easiest to scale. Carol, once you hook in, drop the rope down the shaft. We might need it as a guide. Any questions, folks? I know this was a crash course in scaling an elevator shaft, but based on our circumstances it'll have to do," Malone finished explaining.

"Sounded good to me, Joe!" Dr. Hampstead said hurriedly with a pat on his back.

"Alright, let's get going. Carol, you're up!" Malone encouraged as two decisively large thuds impacted the door, denting the heavy door inward. Malone shot Russo a glance of uncertainty that was reciprocated. Either the corpses had combined their efforts, or they were using something to try and bust the door down.

On the outside of the door, a six-foot nine firefighter missing half of his stomachs and with long gauge marks present on his face, was effortlessly using the bottom of a fire extinguisher to viciously slam against the door. The dull metal on metal ringing going unfazed to the now nine corpse strong swarm outside of the maintenance closet. The firefighter continued the relentless pounding on the heavy door as the collective moans of the swarm grew louder and louder.

With each jarring hit, the group jumped as they soon realized that time was not on their side. Carol's hands were shaking uncontrollably as Malone continued to coil the black rope up before he gave it to her with a look of concern in his eyes as he saw the vibration in her hands.

"I'm good, I'm just tired of hearing that pounding. It's driving me batty!" Carol tried to explain as she steeled her nerves once again.

"Alright, up you go!" Malone said as Carol crouched down and crawled through the small access hatch leading to the shaft. The small hatch was no bigger than a ventilation shaft, and the aluminum sided walls echoed as she crawled through. The access tunnel was just about ten yards long before it opened up to the elevator shaft. As Carol entered the elevator shaft she shone her flashlight upward, and at the very end of her light she could see the bottom of the elevator nine floors up. The shaft was completely dark with the exception of small track lights illuminating each floor and the powerful light that Carol had in her hands. A mechanical smell of grease and oil combined with stagnant air soaked the shaft, forcing Carol to cough as it assaulted her body. She located the small ladder leading up the shaft in an alcove that provided the climber very little protection from the elevator itself as the alcove was only about three feet deep. If the elevator were to be coming down while a person was climbing, that person would have to flatten their bodies up against the small ladder so they wouldn't be smashed by the elevator.

"I found it, and I'm heading up; go ahead and send in Dr. Hampstead," Carol knelt and shouted back down the access tunnel before beginning her ascent.

"Good job, Carol!" Malone hollered back before turning to Dr. Hampstead. "Well, Doc, you're up. Remember, slow and steady, no need to rush. I'll be right behind you."

"I'll be fine, you just focus on taking care of yourself, don't worry about me," Dr. Hampstead answered before she ducked into the access tunnel and scurried down towards the shaft. Malone turned to face Russo and Gwen as another concussive blow landed on the door.

"You two right behind me, no hero stuff this time!" Malone said loudly over the cacophony coming from the other side of the door.

Both Russo and Gwen nodded as they had no intentions of hanging back this time. Malone ducked into the tunnel and followed Dr. Hampstead, followed shortly and very quickly by Gwen and finally by Russo who tried his best to cover their tracks by sliding a box close to the hole before crawling through. The persistent pounding on the door, invariably weakened not only the door, but the doorframe, and before long the whole doorframe began to cave inward. Little by little light crept into the room as the frame pulled away from the sheetrock in chunks. With each slam against the door, another rotten hand reached up and tore plaster and sheetrock from the frame until a hole the size of a basketball was opened on the side, allowing for sight into the maintenance closet. The corpse that was once a firefighter leaned to its right and studied the hole, peering in with one of his blood red eyes, watching Russo duck into the access tunnel. Seeing him, the corpse let out a barbaric howl before slamming the fire extinguisher into the door once more, this time with renewed force and intensity. This final blow was all that was needed as the door and the metal frame caved into the room haphazardly, allowing the corpses to climb over the door into the room.

The swarm filled the room within seconds, and began to savagely tear the room apart. The shelves were ripped off of the walls, while chemical bottles were punctured and spilled onto the floor, immediately clogging the central drain. The pitiful cardboard box blockade that Russo had set up was swiftly knocked aside as a former patient of Miami Med clambered into the access tunnel, immediately howling as he saw Russo's feet sliding out at the end of the tunnel. His howl reverberated down the tunnel, sending a chill up everyone's spine as the ghastly howl was followed by others, then by the heart stopping sound of the corpse dragging its body down the tunnel.

Hearing the howls forced Carol to climb faster as she eagerly counted the numbers in the shaft corresponding with the floors she was climbing above. Dr. Hampstead and Malone had already begun their ascent when the howl erupted from the tunnel forcing Malone to jerk his head back down with a concerned glare plastered across his face.

"Gwen!!! Russo!!! You two better double time it, you ain't got much time," Malone hollered as he toyed around with the idea of going back down to help before Gwen latched onto the third rung and began climbing. As she got to the sixth rung, she still didn't feel the added weight of Russo and she looked back down, shocked to see him still standing on the shaft floor. He was leaned up against the other side of the shaft, with his pistol aimed directly at the opening.

"What the hell are you doing, you can't make a stand down there!" Gwen shouted, as the others turned and looked down in awe. As soon as Gwen finished her statement the head of the corpse popped out of the tunnel, turned its head upward towards Gwen, and growled as bloody saliva drained out of its mouth. It started to slide its body out of the tunnel while reaching with up towards Gwen, before its head jerked back and bounced onto the floor as dark blood escaped under its chin. The report of Russo's pistol echoed loudly in the small shaft, but the calculated measure had bought them some time. The now truly dead corpse lay half in and half out of the tunnel, temporarily blocking the others access.

Gwen looked back in fear, but was happily surprised by a flood of satisfaction as Russo grasped the rungs and began his ascent. She looked back down at the corpse and realized why Russo waited. The undead's ruthless attack wouldn't be stopped, but it was now going to be delayed by Russo's actions.

The howls from the other corpses continued echoing down the tunnel and into the shaft, but the temporary blockage was slowing them down considerably as the group put distance between them. Carol reached the top of the eighth floor, and she could see the bottom of the elevator about three feet above her. Just as Malone had described, the bottom had multiple circular rings attached to the bottom in a spiraling design originating from the center of the elevator. Carol locked her legs around the rungs of the ladder, before she connected herself to the bottom of the elevator. As she locked the carabineer down, she waited before letting her weight be fully supported by the harness. As she hung there she tried to collect herself before she heard Malone below her,

"Carol, I promise you it'll hold,"

Carol looked down at him and the others before gently nodding her head and slowly releasing her grip. As her hand gave way, she held her breath as the strap slipped a little before tightening, allowing her to hang freely underneath the elevator. A wave of relief rushed over her as she took another deep breath. The sense of relief was short lived as the moaning from below suddenly became stronger, forcing the group to turn and look down.

The undead had managed to push the dead corpse out of the way and they were rapidly filling the bottom of the shaft. Outstretched arms raised high above their heads combined with completely bloodshot eyes was a picture that none of the survivors cared to look at long as they all turned their attention to Carol who was already unscrewing the grate to the elevator floor.

As she finished with the final screw, she leaned back and let the grate fall, nine stories down, crashing into the heads of the undead. Unfazed, they continued their moans and growls as they stood and stared unblinkingly at the group. Carol felt vibrations above her on the elevator floor, and she began to panic as she realized that the undead were on the ninth floor as well. The hatch leading to the elevator floor was suddenly pulled back, revealing the opening. Carol tried her best to swing out of the line of sight, but in her attempt she lost her grip on the rings and simply swayed back and forth under the opening. She flinched as she swung back under the opening before looking up and seeing the smiling face of Materson.

"Oh, thank God, it's you, and you're not dead. You're not one of them," Carol said, elated as she tied off the black rope and let the coil go down, the bottom of it hanging just above the outstretched hands of the rotting corpses below.

"What's going on, Carol? Who is it?" Dr. Hampstead asked, after she heard Carol's statement.

"It's Mr. Materson, he's alive," Carol exclaimed.

"Mr. Materson, it's Dr. Hampstead, Malone, Gwen, and Russo. We're trapped, and we need some shelter, please help us!" Dr. Hampstead cried out.

Materson made no reply, he simply stared down at Carol with cold uncaring eyes as he folded his arms across his chest. After a couple of seconds Materson decided it would be a good time to break the unbearable silence and break the bad news to the group.

"I am sorry that you all are trapped, and it seems like you have persevered so well, but unfortunately, you're going to have to find other means of shelter, because this area is off limits to you," Materson said coldly, with a sinister sneer.

"What! WHAT THE HELL ARE YOU TALKING ABOUT?!" Carol screamed as she stared in shock.

"What's going ON up there?" Malone hollered as he craned his neck trying to see what the commotion was about.

"Oh, is that you Malone. Tsk, tsk, you should've taken the garbage out last night, and you wouldn't be in the situation that you're in right now, so I guess you only have yourself to blame for this problem," Materson continued as he walked around the open hatch. "Oh, and Ms. Gwen and Mr. Loudmouth tough guy himself. Not so tough now are you?" Materson antagonized.

"Materson, you son of a bitch. This is murder!" Malone cried out as his face became flushed with anger.

"Actually, this is just an operational decision for the better of the company; no hard feelings, it's just business, that's all," Materson said coyly.

"I tell you what," Materson started again as he crossed his arms and slightly tapped his fingers on his bicep. "I'll let two of you come up here if little Miss Gwen promises me that... well, you know what I mean," Materson offered with a sleazy wink at Gwen.

"No fucking way. I'm going to rip your heart out, you bastard!" Russo yelled from below.

"Have it your way. Ta Ta!" Materson said with a smirk before he began to close the hatch, laughing out loud. Carol saw her chance and took it as she jammed her weapon into the opening preventing the hatch from completely sealing, and stabbing Materson in the ankle in the process. Materson screamed out in agony as he fell to the elevator floor writhing in pain. Carol unlatched her harness which was still attached to the ladder, giving her free range of motion. She climbed across the bottom of the elevator using the rings for support before grabbing the inside of the hatch. As she dangled above the elevator shaft she slowly began climbing up into the elevator itself. She paused for a couple of seconds to regain her breath when she suddenly realized that Materson was screaming like a baby anymore. She looked up in fear as he stared down at her with hatred-filled eyes.

"You scrawny little brat! This is my fucking hospital, and I'll do what I want, when I want, and however many times that I want to, and I'm going to start by getting rid of all of you!" Materson screamed before he stomped on Carol's fingers instantly breaking them, forcing her to let go. She cried out in pain as she clutched her hand while flying head first down the elevator shaft. Time seemed to slow to a crawl as Malone watched in horror as Carol's body torpedoed by him, her screams piercing his soul.

"RUSSO!" Was all Gwen could say as the events quickly unfolded.

Russo stretched his body as much as he could, effectively grabbing her by her pants leg as her body rushed by. Russo was unable to stop her momentum as her weight slammed against his body pulling every muscle in his arm. He was able to keep his grip on the ladder, but couldn't control her body as she swung into the side of the shaft with a sickening crunch. The blow to her head knocked her unconscious as her body hung downward, her arms pointed towards the floor. Fresh blood drained out of her head where it had slammed against the wall. Visible edges of jagged grayish skull shone through in the dimly lit shaft as Russo tried unsuccessfully to pull her up. Her fingers dangled about two feet above the outstretched arms of the undead who violently waved and strained their arms, trying their best to grab her.

"Hold on, Russo, I'm coming to help you out!" Malone hollered as he started to climb down.

"I don't know how much longer I can hold her!" Russo struggled to say. He took a few deep breaths, and with all of his might he tried once again to pull her up, but the dead weight was just too much as he slumped back down. A searing pain streamed through his arms as he struggled to support his own weight as his other hand began to loosen on the ladder rung. He looked around the shaft in a panic, trying to figure out what to do before his eyes fell onto a former firefighter whose massive body shoved the other corpses away. The corpse reached up, grasped her arms with both of his, and viciously yanked on them, almost pulling Russo off of the rung in the process. Russo screamed as the torture on his arms became too much. The inverted seesaw affect brought Carol back as she stared up at Russo's contorted face with a puzzled look. She suddenly felt the rotten balmy hands on her arms and the constant tugging motion, then realized what was going on. She screamed in fear as tears erupted up her face as she struggled against the vice like grip of the corpse.

"RUSSO! Don't let me go, please don't let me go!" Carol screamed as Russo continued to strain against the swarm.

"Russo, your other hand!" Gwen shouted as she watched his grip on the rung begin to slide.

"I can't... keep... a..." Russo began, but never finished as the corpse reared back and yanked harder this time, breaking Russo's grip, pulling Carol to the floor. Her screams filled the shaft as the swarm closed in around her, tearing her body into pieces. Her screams only lasted for seconds before they became muffled and gargled with blood, before all that could be heard were the ghastly wet sounds of flesh being torn apart.